THE BEST of ENEMIES

THE BEST of ENEMIES

WILLIAM W. JOHNSTONE

AND J.A. JOHNSTONE

PINNACLE BOOKS
Kensington Publishing Corp.
kensingtonbooks.com

PINNACLE BOOKS are published by

Kensington Publishing Corp.
900 Third Avenue
New York, NY 10022

All Kensington titles, imprints, and distributed lines are available at special quantity discounts for bulk purchases for sales promotion, premiums, fundraising, and educational or institutional use.

Special book excerpts or customized printings can also be created to fit specific needs. For details, write or phone the office of the Kensington Sales Manager: Kensington Publishing Corp., 900 Third Avenue, New York, NY 10022. Attn. Sales Department. Phone: 1-800-221-2647.

PINNACLE BOOKS, the Pinnacle logo, and the WWJ steer head logo Reg. U.S. Pat. & TM Off.

First Printing: September 2025
ISBN-13: 978-0-7860-5165-6
ISBN-13: 978-0-7860-5166-3 (eBook)

10 9 8 7 6 5 4 3 2 1

Printed in the United States of America

The authorized representative in the EU for product safety and compliance
Is eucomply OU, Parnu mnt 139b-14, Apt 123
Tallinn, Berlin 11317, hello@eucompliancepartner.com.

CHAPTER 1

The first thing the man felt was heat, heat from the unforgiving sun baking down. By the time he came around, it had already reddened his upturned face and blistered his lips.

The next thing he noticed was yet more heat, but this time it came from within himself, from below himself, as if from the earth on which he lay.

He forced his eyes open, just a crack at first; all he could see were stinging pinpricks of light through a gauze of pink that edged out to redness. Jagged, brittle snatches of memory drizzled back to him at the same time. And not a bit of it impressed him.

All this told him was that he had to be dead, given what he was recalling. He almost wished he had lost his ability to recall anything, so awful were the bits of memory of what he had seen and lived through. Or had he?

Then sound flooded in and became more pronounced. But at first, all he could hear was a whooshing and thudding.

With more effort than he'd bet he'd expended on

anything in ages, the man lifted his head. It wobbled on its feeble stalk of a neck. He cracked his right eye wider than its slit and saw bright, warm light and little else. How on earth did he get here? And where was *here*?

All he could recall was fighting. Seemed that was all he'd done since he was born. What did that mean?

Notions, facts—or perhaps they were fabrications, he could not yet tell—flitted in and out of his mind. He gritted his teeth and fought to keep his eyes open. There, he looked down along the length of his body and saw himself, stretched out on his back in the sun. His clothes looked sodden—*must be sweat*, he thought.

And then, as if someone had clapped their hands to awaken him fully, he remembered who he was. And from that revelation, it was a short jump to how he got here. Wherever *here* was. He figured that in time, that, too, would come.

And then he remembered—the war. The war and the cursed Yankees who started it. And there he was, all laid out, baking in the sun, not certain how alive he was, or if he was on his way out. The latter possibility seemed the most likely, given the pain he felt, the light burning away at him, and the rush of memories flooding into his mind.

But right then, he figured he knew who he was, and that was pretty good. He was Chaw Dagworth, private in the army of the Confederate States of America.

He glanced down at himself again as he struggled to raise himself up onto an elbow. And if he was in the

Confederate Army, then that meant his uniform would be gray. And if that was the case, why was it so sodden-looking? Ah yes, the fighting. The cursed, fool big War Twixt the States, a protracted fracas, as his old colonel used to say, caused by Yankee bellicosity.

Chaw grunted and felt a stinging in various parts of his body that quickly gave way to lancing pains, as if someone were sliding knives in and out of his arms, his sides, his legs. What was happening? And then he knew that he wasn't seeing a sweaty uniform, he was seeing a blood-soaked uniform. And as soon as that dawned on him, the rest of his situation became as clear to him as a cool mountain stream.

As he shoved himself up, despite the constant throbbing all over his body, more memories came gushing on in. Uninvited, but there they were anyway. . . .

His company had been taking a ridge, below which was a hollow—what was it called? Deadeye Gap, that's it. And then he'd seen a bluebelly and had taken off after him. That's right, that bluebelly and Chaw got into it pretty good. For a Yankee, the man was brute enough. Must have had Rebel bark somewhere in the woodpile.

In fact, Chaw recalled shouting that at the man as they tore into each other, each giving as good as they got. That comment sure got the bluebelly riled. That foul Yankee had called Chaw a slave trader and a child killer and all manner of raw names, none of which was true. Chaw found this humorous, considering the Yank was a foul traitor and a child killer and a secret slaver himself!

Of course, Chaw had no way of verifying such, but

he didn't doubt the bluebelly was guilty of that and a whole lot more. He was a foul Yankee, after all, wasn't he? That alone was reason enough to pin the entire mess on him.

As he lay there, Chaw pulled in as much of a breath as he could—it wasn't a deep one nor was it clear. Sounded to him as if he was breathing through a ragged pig's bladder. That reminded him of pig killin' time, when the menfolk back home used to inflate and tie off the bladders for the kiddies to bat around.

None of that mattered much now. He was likely dying, and would as likely never see his poor old family ever again. Not Ma, nor Pa, nor Jube, nor dear old Daisy the hound.

Chaw grunted and slowly swung his gaze over to his left. What he saw somehow did not surprise him, although it should have. But he reckoned some part of him knew what he would see before he looked there. And what he saw did not fill him with satisfaction, as he had expected it should. Nope, seeing that dead Yank not but a few yards to his left only made Chaw Dagworth feel almighty awful.

Even if the man was a foul Yankee, that carcass left Chaw hollowed out inside, even more than before. Because it only meant that, as bad as he felt, that Yank was worse off. For he was already dead.

And so that meant that Chaw had given away his own life, and for a cause that had become so muddied and confused for him and most of his fellow Rebs, most had, at one time or another, considered running off in the night. Even though it meant risking getting shot in the back. And now, here he was, surely about to die himself, and that was a raw, hard thing to take.

The Yank, in Chaw's brief glimpse of the man, and then on repeated forced looks, appeared to be in particularly rough condition. The bluebelly, too, was sprawled out on his back, and he, too, was covered with what looked to be a whole lot of dried blood from gashes and rents in his once-blue uniform. He knew this because there were a few spots of blue wool still visible through the darkened blood.

Was this it, then? Nothing more than kill or be killed? How on earth, he wondered, would his death, or the death of that foul Yank beside him, be helpful to the cause of the South, or for the cursed North for that matter?

Chaw closed his eyes for a moment and worked to breathe a bit more. And he came to the conclusion that there wasn't a single scrap of usefulness in his sacrificing himself for the dang cause. No sir.

And then he heard a sound. From his left.

Chaw grunted and worked to angle his gaze back over in that direction. He blinked hard and opened his eyes again, forcing them wide. Couldn't be. He could swear he saw that foul Yank move!

Long before he opened his eyes, Private Fullcup Trace, of the Union Army, lay awake. Keeping his eyes closed on waking each morning was a lifelong habit, and something that, even in the much-abused state he knew his body to be in, he nonetheless maintained.

He found it beneficial to slowly, over the course of several minutes, allow himself to come around to full consciousness. In this way he could take account of who he was, what had happened to him, and where he was at that moment.

All of this came to him as he lay there, sipping air between parted lips. He knew who he was—Trace, he was called—for he became aware of such as if someone had whispered it to his mind.

But it also soon became obvious to him that his normal method of waking was not going to work this day. For memory reminded him in the harshest way just what it was that had landed him where he was, and in the state he suspected his body of being in.

First, he felt a thudding building within him. It started down low, deep in his guts, and rose as if it were marching right into his chest and on up his gullet. By the time it wormed its way into his mouth and nose, he had begun to ache all over.

And then the memory of the events leading up to all of this flooded into his mind. The lashing agonies that came with what surely were a thousand cuts, stabs, cracked ribs, broken fingers, and more thrummed with a sudden and searing pain all over his body. As bad as was that pain, it bowed down before the thudding of the cannonade playing out betwixt his ears.

With more effort than he felt capable of, Trace cracked open his eyes. The sunlight that had been there, awaiting this moment with supreme impatience, drove forward and inward. As Trace squeezed his eyes shut once more, although too late to avoid this fresh, raw wash of pain, it felt as if forge-fired daggers were jamming themselves like steel vipers into his skull.

An unbidden moan, low and fragile, was accompanied with a deluge of memories that flooded over him. And he knew without doubt where he was. The battle atop that cursed ridge above Deadeye Gap, it was called. They'd found that wily Reb company they'd been chasing for weeks.

Those foolish graybacks fought like cornered lions, with claws out and fangs slashing and with a hard pistoning of their gunfire that seemed not to let up. Trace recalled wondering out loud, with some of the other Union men, if maybe the Rebel soldiers truly didn't know that the war was all but over for them.

No, there hadn't been any surrender as such, at least not yet. But it was bound to happen soon. That was what they had all thought going into the latest fracas with the elusive, dastardly Rebs. The enemy numbers were raggedy and slowly dwindling, but they nonetheless fought at every turn as if they were freshly minted men.

Trace groaned again as the rest of the preceding events came back to him. He recalled how he had made his way down past the far side of the battle, chasing after a pair of Reb snipers. He knew from experience that they'd been looking to sneak up around to where the Northern Army was encamped. That would not stand.

Trace had gotten the drop on them, sure, but instead of letting him take them as his prisoners, they'd put up a fight. He'd expected that, anyway. He didn't recommend it to anyone, even a foul Rebel, but he could hardly blame them, now, could he?

As he fought, trading shots with the two snipers, Trace realized from the sounds of the battle above and behind him, atop that ridge, that the melee was not about to end in favor of these maddening Rebels and the rest of their Southern ilk.

He was all but through with these two, having pinned them pretty well, despite being a lone soldier against two men. He had the landscape to thank in part for that, too. He had been able to position himself behind a boulder the size of a wagon, while the two Rebs he'd been pursuing had found themselves at the bottom of a gully with nothing but knee-high rocks and crusty pines no thicker around than a man's arm.

Then he had touched finger to trigger and been about ready to send those two Rebel curs barking to the netherworld. Despite how he felt about them and their cause, there was that flicker of a moment when he regretted ever being involved in this foul mess to begin with.

It had less, far less, to do with the individual soldiers, no matter the side, than it had to do with the cause each side fought for. And for all that, he knew that all these deaths could be laid at the feet of the leaders on both sides for their failure to keep talking, keep shouting at one another across the back-room negotiation tables.

Trace didn't care how angry they got or how many days or weeks or months or years it would take. All of it would have been breath and time well spent if it had saved a single life of one of the soldiers on either side. Instead, they had ended up fighting, either by choice or, as had proved the case, by force, to fight and die for their respective so-called causes.

And Trace knew he wasn't the only man in the Union Army who felt that way. And he had it on good authority that most Rebs felt the same darned way, too. Much good it had done any of them.

All of that flooded into and out of his mind in that whisper of a moment before he squeezed the trigger to take yet another Rebel man's life. And at that moment, a shot whipped by his head from behind him. It spun Trace's gaze hard over his right shoulder. At the same time, instinct drove him down to one knee.

There he spied yet another grayback. This one, however, wasn't oblivious like his fellow soldiers. Trace had, after all, gotten the upper hand on those two Rebs down in their gully, looking this way and that.

In recalling that day, however many days before, Trace now realized that moment could well have ended it all, and in eyeblink speed. But for some reason, that crazed Rebel he'd seen over his shoulder, with his rifle aimed right at Trace's head, had decided not to shoot him.

What he did instead genuinely surprised Trace. The man had delivered that shot at him. And when he faced him, Trace saw that the Reb hadn't been far enough away to have missed him. *Why hadn't I heard the rascal sneaking on up behind me?* thought Trace.

As if in answer to the question echoing in Trace's skull, the Reb who'd shot at him from behind, and who held a revolver aimed right at him—he must have used his rifle to deliver that first, too-close-to-have-missed shot—shouted from about sixty feet away.

The Reb eyed him down the short barrel and barked, "I am a son of the South and as such I am too proud to shoot a man in the back, even if he is a foul, yellow, blue-bellied Yankee!"

By then, of course, Trace had his own gun aimed right at that Rebel's gut. He rose once more to a standing position. Behind and below the big boulder, he heard a voice shout to another, "Let's git gone back to the fight! That Yank's done for!"

That told Trace he didn't have much to worry about from those two. He could concentrate on dealing with this crazy Rebel. A man who had him dead to rights, but who made him turn to face him before he would shoot him was a crazy man. Or a man with a conscience.

Make that a Rebel with a conscience. He knew there were a good many of them because he'd learned a whole lot since he started in on this war, with all its marches and lousy, maggoty food, and surly officers and lack of leadership with brains.

He'd learned that most Rebs were just about the same as most Yanks. That was to say, they were all just men. Men with wives and children and parents and cousins and friends and homes and farms, all of it.

And now here was one who wanted to fight him, face-to-face, fair and square. *All right, then*, thought Trace. *Let's get to it.*

He rose back to standing height, keeping his rifle

aimed at that man's chest, and said, "What's it going to be, Reb? We have each other square on!"

"Shut up and approach. We'll see how far you make it, you stinking Yank!"

And so they had advanced on each other, slow step by slow step, their respective barrels not faltering, their boot steps sure and well placed, their eyes never leaving the other's, their trigger fingers ready to dole out the last sound the other man would ever hear.

But neither man pulled a trigger. Neither man dared to be the first, apparently, for they each advanced and strode with caution and unwavering concentration right toward the other.

And then they were close enough to see the grime caked in the lines on their faces, to see that they each could use a real shave, a haircut, a month's worth of sleep, and the same of food.

"Enough!" growled Fullcup Trace, flinging away his rifle. He didn't care any longer.

They'd been staring each other down for long, long minutes, slowly circling, and the situation had grown more than tiresome. A vital need had grown in him that they fight like men, men who were unafraid to cower behind the false cowardice of a gun.

As Trace regarded the other man, the grayback sneered, and he, too, sent his own gun spinning to the dirt. That was when things really began to head off into an interesting direction.

Again, as if by mutual unspoken agreement, the two men both sneered, their lips pulled back over tight-set teeth. Their eyes narrowed and growls crawled up out of their throats.

Arms drew up fast and their hands sought each other with clawlike fingers, fingers that closed on the other, on arms and chests. They balled wool tunics and at the same time jerked the other man this way and that, hoping to gain the upper hand.

They each gave voice to a deep rage that, while directed at the other man, really represented the anguish and frustration and fear and confusion they had each felt for the past couple of years at being forced to kill or be killed.

Propelled by a clot of such feelings fueling their rage, the two men grabbed onto each other hard and fast, neither uttering any sounds that could be recognized as words. Instead, they were growls and barks and the utterances of seething anger.

They circled, breaking their holds, only to collide again, one arm grasping clothing or hair, it mattered not. The other was curled into a thick fist that drew back, then drove forward, like a sledge wielded by a railway man.

Their blows staggered each other, sent blasts of starlight even during the day before the receiver's sweat-riddled eyes. The punches and cudgel-like shots staggered each other, and yet neither man relented. Once they had agreed to brawl it out, neither man gave the other a moment's peace. Legs kicked, circled around other legs, seeking to trip.

Once, the Reb was able to use his momentum to drive the Yank backward. One of the man's blue-clad legs lay pinned beneath him, and the Reb knew something had happened to that bent knee. It had not broken, for the man would have yipped like a kicked dog, but nonetheless he knew something very painful had overtaken the man.

He grinned, his gritted teeth stained yellow and gray, as if to match his uniform, and he used the moment's pain to his advantage, jamming his own knee into the Yank's middle.

But his hubris at finding himself atop the other was short-lived, for he had lost, for a moment, his accounting of the Yank's left arm. And as the Reb bent low to deliver a pulled-back punch, he left his own right side exposed.

The desperate Yank's left fist slammed into the right side of the Reb's ribs with the force of a hickory log being jammed, butt end first, into the man's torso, with deadly, unexpected momentum.

The blow shoved any air the Reb had in his chest up and out in a rush that ended in a wheeze. The worst of it for the Reb was feeling the sickening, sharp, lancing pain deep inside. He'd been down that painful road before and knew he'd just received a broken rib or three from that foul Yank.

The Reb collapsed to his left, falling off the pinned Yank long enough that the man in blue could also roll to his left. Again, as if by mutual consent, the two men rose to their knees, facing each other, panting their rasping breaths. Hatred, directed at each other, glowed through their narrowed eyes, their chests working like bellows.

The Yank put little weight on his bum knee, for it

pained him already and he knew it was swelling. He bet that something inside, the stringy bits in a man's body that hold flesh to bone, had torn or separated somehow.

The Reb raised his left hand to rest it against the right side of his ribs. He knew it showed a weakness, a wound dealt by the Yank, but he had to do it. Trace probed gingerly and again could not help the sharp-drawn breath of limping forward. With the Reb sipping shallow breaths, they each drove at the other. Now each was intent at furthering the damage he had already inflicted on the other man.

How long they fought, neither man knew. Not that either of them cared. The brawl had become far more than two enemies having it out to some sort of end. It was the long-pent result of years of hardship shoved on them every day by their superiors, by the weather, by other soldiers, by bad food and worse water, by unforgiving terrain, and by the long-forgotten reasons behind why each was told they must kill other men.

And so it went, for hours or days or weeks, neither man knew nor cared. At some point, one of them— neither could recall later which—tugged free his knife barely an eyeblink's worth of time before the other did.

Thus the fight went on, continuing with each man guessing the move of the other, growl for growl, punch for punch, kick for kick, driving knee for driving knee, butting head for butting head, lunging, snapping teeth for the same. And now was the deadly promise of honed steel.

The appearance of blades in their scar-knuckled, brawl-reddened hands kindled in each man a renewed fire, a burning rage to kill and to not be killed. It was no surprise to either man that his opponent wore a sheath knife on his belt. Most soldiers did, and frequently these tools were brought from home, cherished items that a man regarded with as much or more fondness than his gun.

A hip knife was perhaps a man's most-relied-upon possession. It was a tool he used many times a day. Men shaved with them, used them to cut hair and trim beards, to skin, gut, and slice fresh-killed critters for the fry pan or pot, from turtles to swamp rats to rabbits and more.

A big-bladed knife also could be used to split lengths of branch wood for kindling, for sharpening sticks, for cooking and hewing stakes for tents. And as long as a man had a whetstone in his possibles sack, it could also be used to dig a cat hole in the steel-dulling earth, should a man care that much about covering his leavings with more than forest duff.

Occasionally, although the men agreed it was happening more and more as the war dragged on, these knives had begun to be used to defend one's life, and to attack a foe as well.

As each man, Trace and Chaw, lifted free his knife, a sneer rose unbidden on their faces. Without warning, they rushed at each other, snarls of rage ripping from their mouths.

They fought with bedraggled bodies sporting blood-shot eyes, bruised and bloodied mouths from split lips and smacked noses, and sweat-plastered hair. They wore the grime of repeated slamming and rolling in the dust and churned soil of the small, scree-riddled plateau they each had been stomping and trampling and kicking and furrowing for hours.

They fought as beasts, coming together amidst howls and clouds of dust, slashing and driving, peeling apart and wielding keen blades afresh with each parry and thrust. Over and over they attacked, not seeming to lose the renewed, whetted appetite for blood they shared.

Their thirst for killing clouded their usual individual sensibilities and they fought hard and viciously. They rarely fell apart without leaving hacked slices in the arms of woolen tunics, on through into the sweat-soaked, longhandle underwear beneath, finally drawing blood in scarred skin befouled by war and hard living.

Cuts more than gashes, although there were plenty of those as well, covered each man's head, face, torso, arms, hips, backsides, and calves. It seemed to each man as if they were covered with the denizens of a huge hive of deadly hornets, for with every move they made, their bodies screamed from the constant, stinging pain of a thousand lacerations.

Over time—neither man knew how much—the welter of agony each found himself mired within began to take its due toll.

Each man, the Reb and the Yank, after hours of cutting and slashing, howling and colliding, clubbing and flailing at the other, hammer and tongs, staggered backward.

Trace, the Yank, had no idea how he had managed to stay upright for so very long as his knee had somehow endured far beyond ordinary pain.

When he had been able to steal a quick glance at himself, he had been shocked to see, through the slashed fabric of his trousers, that they were no longer showing any trace of blue. They were matted with a reddened black, and were sodden with sweat and blood. His own and that of the foul, determined Reb.

What had shocked him most was the size of his knee. It had swelled to what seemed the size of a man's head. The ragged trouser leg about it, although slashed, had also brought with it a cold dose of luck. The knee had been able to swell and not be constricted by the fabric itself, for good or ill.

The Reb, leaning against the boulder before which the Yank had begun the fight, felt his breath wheezing in and out of his damaged breadbasket and rib cage. He hated to admit it, but that Yank had delivered into his side one mighty wallop, a pummeling such that the Reb was certain he might never again breathe as a normal man.

That thought had been from who knew how long before. Before the brutality their knives had inflicted. Now the Reb was a gasping, wheezing mess.

It was all he could do, now that they had fallen back apart from each other once again, to maintain his tender hold on his knife. He glanced down at himself and saw nothing he recognized.

Not his right hand, nor the knife in its grasp. He knew there was a knife there somewhere, hidden under a thick, syrupy coating of red-black gore that streamed and sluiced in steady rivulets down his drooped arm. The hand and fingers were covered with their own slick gore, beneath which dozens of cuts screamed at once. As did his entire body.

Chaw glanced up once more, as he held his left hand to his right-side rib cage, the tenderest spot on his entire savaged form. "If I . . . look . . ."

He swallowed and licked his lips, his voice a cracked, croaking thing. My, how he longed for a long sip of cool, clear water. "If I looked as bad . . . as you . . . Yank . . . I'd up and die already."

The Yank regarded the Reb while he leaned against the trunk of a much-scuffed pine. What he wanted to say was, *Of course you would! You're a weak-kneed Rebel!* But what came out, between huffing gasps was, "Could say the same . . . to you, Reb. . . ."

In all the time of that fight, neither man had not uttered much more than grunts and shouts, sounds that were not words. Though they did not much care. But now, hearing their voices, after hearing nothing but raw animal sounds from themselves, they surprised each of them.

It also seemed to trigger something within each of them once more, yet another animalistic lunge to satisfy the unreasoning rage each felt at nearly being killed by the other.

They bolted forward, once more as if they had nodded in agreement with each other, and yet they hadn't. This did not slow them down, but the wearing, atrophying pain of the protracted battle had shown its strain as each man shoved up and away from the only things that were really keeping them upright—the boulder and the tree.

They lurched forward, staggering and eyeing each other through blood-flecked eyelashes, blinking and wheezing, their knives held halfway up in weak grasps. Each man with his eyes fixed on the other advanced. Paltry, feeble step by lurching, halting step, they drew closer, slowly, grunting and wheezing, bleeding and groaning.

And, as had happened since they began their attempt at mutual destruction, they each faltered within ten feet of each other, and the last thing each man saw was the other, his sworn mortal foe, sagging and collapsing. Eyes rolled back in heads, knees buckled, heads slopped backward on their weak stalks as their bodies slowly sank to the churned, bloodied earth.

Each man slopped to the side, then flopped sprawled flat on his back, but a couple of yards apart. Each still held his dagger in a death-clench grip, stiffened into place by sticky, drying blood.

When Chaw Dagworth, private of the Confederate Army, came to, and as he gazed on what he assumed was a dead Yank not but a few feet to his right, a Yank he had apparently killed, the entirety of the brutal fight came back to him. And he did not feel one sliver of goodness about it, not one slender thread of pride or satisfaction in having laid low yet another Yankee soldier.

Instead, he thought about how evenly matched they were. Too much so, it seemed, for it had been one heck of a fight. And as much as he had tried to outmaneuver that blue brute, the fellow had done the same to him, as if they were each reading the other man's thoughts.

How long had they fought? Had it been mere minutes? Hours? The way he looked and the way he felt, it surely must have been days, days in which neither man was aware of light or dark passing. When neither one broke away, despite the fact that they yearned for a drink of water from their respective canteens.

But now, with the thought of water, the wetness of it touching his lips, cooling his parched, burning throat, now all Chaw could think of was water, of getting a sweet, sweet drink into himself.

Where was his canteen?

He looked down at himself, but no, it was not strapped about his chest as usual. Nor was the rest of his gear. Where was it all?

And then he remembered—he had shed the canteen, the blanket roll, his pack—in the dried grasses at the base of the tree. That tree that somehow the Yank had ended up closer to than Chaw.

He glanced back that way, beyond the Yank, and Chaw saw he'd been wrong. For the man now looked not to be alive but dead. Deader than dead, as his old Pap used to say. If he could only get on over there, past the Yank, over to the tree, where his gear still lay in a heap. Get to that canteen.

Then he saw what he had assumed was trickery of his eyes, that cursed Yank was moving again. Yes, he was alive! His chest was rising, falling, rising.

Chaw could not understand two things—how the

man could possibly be alive, for Chaw had convinced himself that he alone had survived the awful fight. And the second thing he could not fathom was why he felt relief, immediate and flooding, through his mind as he saw that bluebelly breathe.

Hadn't he fought such men for years now? Hadn't he vowed over and over again that he would kill every Yankee he came across?

Chaw groaned and squeezed his eyes shut, then opened them again, the dried blood cracking slightly about them. *Back to the water*, he thought. *Concentrate on getting water or nobody, not you or the Yank, is going to live for much longer.*

And then Chaw had what at that moment he knew was the very best idea he had ever come upon in his whole life. He turned his head slowly, painfully, to the left and saw the massive boulder where the Yank had been standing when Chaw first popped off that warning shot. And there, at the base, was the Yank's own gear pile. And among it, not but a few yards to Chaw's left, sat a canteen.

He grunted, trying to shove himself over onto his left side, pinioning himself from behind with his bloody right hand. That was when Chaw felt his knife still gripped tight in that hand. He tried to let go of it, but it stayed there, attached somehow to his palm.

He raised it and saw that it was glued to his hand, then he knew: It was the blood, likely his own, thick and mostly dried, holding the knife there. The sight of it made his head and guts churn. He flopped back to the earth with a gasp from his wounded ribs, his wind pinched and painful.

Why hadn't he shot the cursed Yank when he had the chance? What stayed his hand? Surely it wasn't just not wanting to shoot a Yank, even if it was in the back. He'd done it a few times before. Yeah, it left a sour taste in his gut and mouth and mind for days after, but then, he'd seen a new atrocity committed on a Reb by a Yank, and he'd gotten over it right quick.

A few feet away, Private Fullcup Trace of the Union Army managed a good few pulls of breath and worked at trying to open his eyes all the way. Something not unlike a child felt when he awakened with eyes half-crusted shut following a night's sleep.

But this was different, and something he'd not felt before, not in all his adult years. He scrunched his eyes and worked his cheeks until whatever it was freed up a bit, enough for him to force, then pop open, first one eye and then the second.

He tried to raise a hand, but neither wanted to respond. And then, with a bit more concentrated effort, he was able to twitch life into first his left and then his right. But the left felt heavier. He gritted his teeth and forced his eyes open wide. It was a mighty effort, and he didn't want to let his mind trail down the path of finding out why. Not yet. First he had to find out what that new sound was, off to his left.

Instinct told him to keep his movements as quiet as

he could, but for all that, he grunted as he worked to raise himself up onto his left elbow. He looked down at his left side and saw that his hand, a blood-encrusted claw, was curled tight around what looked to be a knife. Yes, it was a knife: his hip dagger.

Trace looked at his fingers but somehow could not make them do his bidding. He'd have to use his right hand, which seemed to be working all right. He again heard a sound from his left and, reminded of why he had been roused in the first place, looked over to the left.

The first thing he saw was the big boulder, and he recognized it as the one he'd been hiding behind . . . for some reason. What had it been? And then he saw before the rock a body, but it was moving, faced away from him, doing something. . . .

On seeing it, in a finger snap of time it all came back to him, and Trace recalled everything that had happened. Chasing those two Rebs, pinning them down in the draw, then being jumped and surprised from behind as he hid by the boulder.

He'd spun and seen that Rebel. He was a tall, rugged-looking, scruffy, gray-clad fellow who'd gotten the drop on him. But instead of shooting to kill Trace, he'd missed him, missed him with intention.

It had made no sense to Trace then, and it still didn't. Despite the fact that the Reb had shouted something about how he'd not resort to shooting a man in the back, even if that man was a lousy Yank.

Trace almost grinned at the thought of him being

referred to as *lousy*. He reckoned he'd been called a whole lot of things in his life, but not quite that. And then . . . then they had fought. Oh, how they had fought.

Hammer and tongs, as the old-timers used to say it. Neither man had been willing to give in, let alone give up. It had been the hardest, rawest, most brutal fight of Trace's life.

A hawk's piercing call from high up sounded. Other than that, and the slight sounds the Reb was making—what was that fellow doing?—there were no others. Nothing. Not even battle noise. There should be that, at least. It was . . . Deadeye Gap, that's right.

Something seemed . . . not right. He should hear something, feel something. But all he felt was . . . numb. As if he'd spent a week inside a whiskey bottle and still hadn't reached the bottom of the thing.

He looked around himself, down at his bloodied mess of a body, and saw his right leg, puffed at the knee. So much so, in fact, that it looked as though there were two limbs in that trouser leg. *If I'm that bad off, why can't I feel it?*

He squinted and tried to see what the Reb was up to, but the man was faced away from him, looking at the boulder but doing something over there.

So why, thought Trace, *can't I feel something, anything at all other than this fuzzy, sort of numb sensation?* And then a thought came to him: *I must be dead. This must be what it's like to be gone. Or maybe in that limbo place, because I have not been sorted out yet by whoever was in charge up there. Or . . . no, can't be down there. Can it?*

I'm stuck in this middle layer of whatever this is, neither dead nor alive. He'd read about that, or maybe he was just recalling it from his Gran's growled interpretations of the Bible. *Either way, here I am*, thought Trace. *Dead or dying.*

Had that Rebel bandit killed him? As bad as Trace was beginning to feel, it must be so. He must have been killed in the fight. He sure knew it was a fight for the ages. And yet, when you're dead, or nearly so, what did that matter? You might well have fought for some cause you believed in, sure, but when you're dead, what good is that cause to you?

Heady stuff, he figured, but the upshot of it was that Trace was convinced more and more with each second that passed that he was sitting, or lying down, on Death's doorstep.

And the Rebel?

Trace wagered that if he himself was dead, it stood to some sort of reason that his licks had laid the Reb low, too. But then, why was that rascal here as well? Must be he had killed the Reb at the same time the Reb had done for him. Must be that one of his licks managed to find purchase on the Reb's body, a blow that surely had laid the man low.

As memory trickled, then flooded in, so had his begrudging admiration for the Rebel. As with most of his kind that Trace had come across, he was a scrapper.

"Hey!"

Trace jerked as if slapped. What had that been? Or who?

"Hey, you! Yank!"

Trace had heard that, hadn't he?

"Hey now, Yank!"

The voice had come from his left. He looked over that way once more and saw that the Reb was now facing him and looking his way. And he held a canteen below his lips.

At the thought of that word, Fullcup Trace felt a quick zing of something charge into him. Water. He would kill all over again for a drink of water.

"Yeah, I see you heard me."

Trace looked at the man once more. Was the Rebel smiling? Can a man smile when he's dead? Oh, but this felt all too confusing.

"You best do what I did and crawl on back there behind yourself. My pack's there, not but a few feet behind you, at that tree. Got a canteen there."

The words somehow leached through the gauzy, thick scrim that Trace felt covering himself, and he knew that even if he was dead, he had to try to act on those words. They were important somehow. For they meant there was water at the end of them, and even if he was well and truly dead, which seemed pretty likely to him, he sure could use a drink of water.

"Wake up now, man, and go get that water. We ain't through tussling with each other yet."

Trace glanced once more at the Rebel to his left, then shifted his body such that he looked to his right instead. Sure, there was the tree; it was the tree the Rebel had been standing before when Trace was tipped off by that shot that should, by rights, have killed him.

But it hadn't, and now here he was, and the Reb

was telling him he needed to go get water. If Trace was understanding all this correctly, that meant the Reb was telling him to go get the Reb's water. And that sounded like a trap. A trick. Rebel treachery.

But then it occurred to Trace that the Reb was drinking water, and it was Trace's water. His very own canteen. Why was he doing that? But did that mean that he trusted Trace? No, it only meant that he was thirsty.

All of this thinking amounted to nothing more than confusion for Trace. He glanced at the Reb's dropped gear at the base of that tree, not all that far from him to the right, and he thought he could see the man's canteen. And the sight of it gave him an overwhelming urge for water.

He grunted and worked to flip himself over onto his right side. Even as he did this, he slowly stuck his thick, swollen tongue out of his mouth and touched his lips. He had to get to that canteen.

Ever since Fullcup Trace was a child, he could recall no time when he did not accomplish a thing once he set his sights on it. And that water waiting for him was no exception. He saw it and he wanted it, and that was all there was to it. That and crawling on over there.

In his mind he was nearly there. But when he glanced quickly down at himself, he had only planted one elbow his right, to the dusty earth. He still needed to get himself righted and angled so he could make it over there.

He squeezed his eyes shut and gritted his teeth, and somehow he managed to get the top half of his body angled where it should be, aimed for that water. He made for it somehow, and felt himself actually moving forward, slower, he was certain, than an ant. But then again, he was dead, or nearly there, so why should he complain? He was moving pretty well for a dead man.

He almost laughed at that, but somehow he hadn't the strength. He moved forward with one elbow and then the forearm of his left arm. And there was that knife, still gripped in his locked fingers, and he couldn't figure out how to let go of it.

Maybe it was best he didn't. That Reb might be sneaking on over to ambush him at that very moment!

Trace wondered about this and figured that as bad as that man looked, he wasn't moving any faster than Trace. And besides, he was nearly to that water.

Then he felt something down low that he hadn't felt before. It was on his legs. No, just the one leg; ah yes, he thought. That swollen right leg. It was paining him something awful.

Could that be right? If he was on his way to death, just waiting for someone to tap him on the shoulder, would he be able to feel that pain?

As he crawled, now no more than a few feet from the water, the leg began to throb hard. He groaned again, and let himself do it. It was a sound, after all, and that might lead to him being able to say something. Or to shout, should he need to call for help from one of the boys. They'd take care of that Reb, and right quick, too.

Trace saw it now, just ahead of him, jumbled with a small pile of gear that looked a whole lot like his own. He spied a bedroll and a pack and, leaning against the pack, a canteen, round and carved wood and bound with what looked like rawhide, tight and shrunk to fit.

A strap handle of some sort of grimy cloth, knotted and looking as if it had been through a war.

At that thought, Trace did snort just a bit. His lips split as he did so, and he felt the stinging anew.

He brought his left hand up to grab the canteen, which sat right there before his face, but that blasted knife was still part of his hand. He shifted his weight over to the left elbow and reached with his crusted, filthy right hand.

It was a shaking thing that looked like it should be attached to some old dead man. But it did the job after a couple of grabs, and he felt the canteen jostle, heard the water inside, felt the promising weight of it; it felt more than half full.

He drew it to his face and leaned it against his nose while his fingers fumbled with the wooden bung. It was attached with a strip of string and he grunted and made a slight, squealing sound deep in his throat trying to get it dislodged.

When he finally was able to drizzle that warm, although soothing liquid onto his lips and into his mouth, he nursed on it like a feeding piglet, and he didn't care who heard him. Never, never, never—and he could not be convinced otherwise—had anything in the history of the world tasted as good to anyone. Ever.

He sipped and slurped and guzzled, and although he knew he really should ration that precious stuff, somehow he could not make himself aware, could not make himself do the thing he knew he needed to do.

Which was to ease off on the water and . . .

"Take 'er easy, Yank, or you're liable to get a gut ache and throw it all up again. Then where will you be?"

Trace paused when the man first began to speak. It reminded him of what he had forgotten—namely, that he was not alone. He angled himself to face the man, finding it easier to move and maneuver now that he had been somewhat revived due to the water.

He saw that the Reb was still where he'd last seen him, over by the boulder. But now he was seated and leaning against it.

"Huh?" said Trace, surprised at hearing his own voice. "Huh?" he repeated, more to hear his voice falter. But at least he could still hear and feel.

All his senses appeared to have been rejuvenated by the water. It was a lesson he'd long known, but as he'd experienced throughout life, it often paid to be reminded.

"I said to back off the water. Rest up!"

Trace let those words sink into his mind a moment, then said, "Why?"

"Got to take care of you . . ."

"Why?"

The Reb chuckled. "So I can kill you fair and square, that's why!"

"Don't count on it, Reb."

And so it went, each man resting and occasionally nibbling on the canteen of his enemy. Remembering, in his fatigue, to look across the few yards toward the other, taking stock and planning just how he would, with very little strength and a body sliced and stabbed and broken and bruised and aching, renew his attack. That was about all they had strength for.

This kept up for hours, and the sun began its descent.

"Reb!"

"Yeah?"

"You got food in this pack?"

"Not much. Hardtack. Coffee. You?"

"About the same. No coffee, though."

"Have at it, Yank."

"You too, Reb."

Neither man did much more for long minutes as the shadows grew. Trace had been able to pry the fingers of his left hand from around the handle of his knife. He still couldn't flex them fully, but they were moving bit by bit a little better than they had been.

Then the Reb said, "If we built a fire, we could have ourselves coffee."

"I don't have any coffee," said the Yank.

"I do, like I said. In my pack. But no flint nor steel."

"I have those."

"All right, then," said the Reb. "Where?"

Silence, then Trace, the Yankee, said, "Best by that boulder where you are."

"Yeah. All right. Bring my gear?"

"I will," said Trace, trying to figure out how he was going to do that and get himself on over to the rock where the Reb sat with Trace's own gear. But he did it.

At the same time, the Reb managed to get himself up to his feet, although he leaned heavily on the rock and worked to toe up tinder and duff from the ground.

The entire knobby plateau on which they sat was

sparsely treed, mostly with low stunty growth, but there was enough of that. There were also a few dropped branches, and a long-dead tree, brittle and dry. So finding fuel for the fire did not look to be a problem to two men used to scavenging for such on behalf of their respective outfits.

Trace managed to also get to his feet, although his swollen knee proved a painful hinderance to his being able to move any faster than a snail with no ambition. Still, he pressed on, dragging the Reb's pack and canteen and blankets, as well as the man's rifle, lugged by its sling, along with him so a return trip to the base of the tree would not be necessary.

Although they had spent the past few hours but twenty or so feet apart, the two men approached each other with slow caution and grim looks. Each once more held his knife, and Trace was relieved to see that the Reb looked about as bad as he did.

He'd wondered earlier, since the Reb was so chatty, at least compared with himself, that maybe the man wasn't as bad off as Trace felt.

He knew that wasn't a very charitable way to think, but after all, this was a man who was a member of a group he'd been told to hate, so much so that he must kill him. But at that moment, seeing the haggard Reb before him, a man who, when he'd had the opportunity to shoot Trace, had not done so, gave him a strange sense of calm and relief.

He knew then that, at least for the time being, however long that might be, they had reached a truce of sort and would break bread and share coffee. After that . . .

well, that was a bridge they would cross when they reached it.

Together, they managed to kindle a fire and keep it fed. All the while, from opposite sides of the fire, the two men stole glances at each other, stern faces not slipping a bit.

They exchanged snatches of speech and answered the other's brief questions without much elaboration. Soon, it became apparent to each man that the other was tired.

"Dog tired and bone weary, as my old gramps used to say," said Chaw.

Darkness descended on them, and while they had dragged back to the fire enough snapped wood and half-rotted lengths and sticks and such, they knew they would be unable to keep it fed through the night.

Trace fought to keep his eyelids open. Finally, he sighed. "Am I safe?" There was a brief pause, and he realized he had likely just awakened the Reb from a catnap.

"Safe? From me?" The Reb chuckled. "Yeah, I reckon. As long as I am from you."

"Yeah, okay. Truce for sleep."

"Truce for sleep. . . ."

CHAPTER 2

The next morning, by mutual unspoken agreement, they worked to rebuild and rekindle the fire, on which they might then cook up a meal. Alas, they soon realized it was a meal neither man would be able to contribute much more to than a bit of hardtack and weak coffee.

They each rose and staggered and stumbled off to tend to their respective ablutions, making water and such. Each found, after much stretching, that he felt a whole lot better. It had been a long night of deep sleep for both of them, and although each had awakened nearly at the same time with a jerk of surprise, they soon calmed when they realized the other man wasn't yet set on killing him.

Good news came when Trace, hobbling back around the boulder, said, "I just saw a glint of water from down below. A stream, I'm sure of it."

"That sounds good to me," said the Reb. "If we have the strength, you think we ought to make for it?"

"We should," said Trace. "No chance for coffee otherwise."

"That decides it for me," said Chaw. "Can't do without my coffee."

"Where'd you get all that coffee, anyway?" said the Yank, genuinely curious.

"Traded for it, same as you all do. Give up my tobacco for it. I can always smoke corn silk in my pipe for a spell."

"You smoke a pipe?" said Trace. "Me too."

They had traded packs and gear the previous evening, and each man was relieved to once more have his own gear in hand. They lugged it, with much effort and in a slow-moving fashion, down the long rocky, brush-studded slope.

Eventually, they reached the shaded, forested base of the small vale, where they found the stream to be clear and cool and the shade from the sparse but ample forest welcome.

"I haven't heard anything of the battle, not since yesterday some time," said Trace as they waited for the coffee to boil.

"Maybe they moved on. Can't imagine why my side hasn't sent scouts or such," said Chaw.

"Just how important do you think you are?" said Fullcup Trace.

Chaw Dagworth glared at him from across the small fire. "I reckon I'm vital to the cause, you bet!"

Trace smiled and poured the coffee. "As vital as any other private, sure."

Neither man spoke for long minutes, each sipping

his hot coffee and musing on the whereabouts of their side, their fellows, and what might be next for them.

They were each still too bedraggled and lame to travel far, at least not for a while yet.

Chaw's broken ribs and who-knew-what-else had him pulling shallow breaths and wincing whenever he exerted himself. And Trace's leg was still swollen and paining him something fierce. He'd cut loose his trousers and inspected it, but nothing looked or felt broken.

"Wrenched it bad," said Chaw, nodding at the purpled limb. "I've seen such before. You'll heal, I reckon, but it's going to take a spell."

Each man bathed himself and tended his wounds streamside, and used handfuls of the fine sand along the silt-free bottom of the stream instead of soap as a way to scrub the blood and dried dirt from his skin and clothes.

It was a long process, but by the time each had finished, they felt relief and, for the first time since they had tangled, as if perhaps they might not die from their wounds.

They rested up, each laid out along his side of the fire, their gear, guns, and knives out and within easy reach.

"How long do you reckon this truce will last?"

Trace looked up from the flames toward his enemy camp mate. "Why? You planning on attacking me?"

"Naw, Yank," said Chaw, offering a half grin. "Not yet, anyway. I'm too tuckered for that. I'll let you know, though."

"Good to hear," said Trace. "Reb."

They sat like that for a while, then Chaw said, "Seems

to me you have a name, same as I do, that ain't Yank or Reb."

Trace nodded. "I do, indeed. Of course, if we resort to using our names, it might be trickier later, when it comes time to kill each other."

"Nah," said Chaw. "Not for me. I was raised on a farm. We'd name piglets and play with them, then up and eat them in a year or so."

"I was raised on a farm, too," said Trace. "Up in Vermont."

"Oh, now, that's something. See, I knowed a gal from there. Or maybe it was . . . no, no, it was Vermont all right. She and her family come down to Tennessee when she was a girl to live with relatives. They liked it just fine and stayed. Always was Yankees, of course, but they was all right, despite that character flaw."

Trace smiled at the comment. "My name's Trace. Fullcup Trace." He looked up and was tempted to stick out his hand over the low fire. He could not recall a time in his life when he'd introduced himself to another man and not offered his hand to shake.

The Reb beat him to it. With a stern, narrow-eyed look right into Trace's eyes, he said, "I'm Chaw Dagworth." He thrust out his hand, and with but a moment's hesitation, Trace grasped it, each man offering the other a firm shake, eyes locked.

On meeting another, the first measure of a man, each had been told in his youth, was how bold and forthright his handshake was. In this instance, each gave and received well enough.

Neither gripped too hard, attempting to overpower or choke the fingers off the other. For that is a sign of a man who is not confident in himself, a man who senses weakness in himself, a man who is uncertain of his skills, a man who doubts his own worth.

These two were not such men.

CHAPTER 3

"I'll still likely have to lay you low, just so you know."
Chaw Dagworth grunted as he adjusted in his seated
position across the fire from his new camp mate and
nemesis.

"Not if I do for you first." Fullcup Trace kept right
on massaging his sore knee. He'd been soaking it in the
cooling waters of the stream, and he believed it was
helping.

The two men had been at their makeshift camp
alongside the stream for three days and were far into the
territory of feeling hunger pangs. They had rationed the
hardtack and the coffee, but the coffee was nearly gone,
despite the fact that they had been cautious in using and
reusing the mashed, pulped beans.

It turned out that well into the second day, once they
had established, despite their mutual bluffs and weak
stabs at bravado, each man had hidden something from
the other. Items of use—scant but nonetheless useful—
to them both.

For Chaw, it was a slender packet of tobacco,
jammed way down at the bottom of his pack. "It was to

be for emergencies. And, actually, I hoped I might be able to use it to celebrate good news."

"Such as?" said Trace, interested in this mild revelation.

"Such as somebody running through camp to tell us all that the war was over. And Dixie was top of the heap, naturally."

"Well, part of that sounds all right with me, but I can't imagine . . . oh, never mind."

"No, go on. Go ahead with what you were going to say."

The look on Dagworth's face, defensive but already knowing, already resigned, told Trace to tread with caution on this topic. A whole lot of folks had died so that one side or the other could claim victory.

But really, everyone who put thought into their lives knew that in war, there were no victors, only survivors. Scarred and mutilated, inside and out. In a lowered voice, Trace said, "I was going to mention that your side has been taking some hard knocks lately."

Instead of glowering and sending back a verbal defense, Chaw surprised the Northerner by sighing. "Yeah, I know. We all know it. Doesn't mean we'll go belly up any time soon, though. Into things too far, I reckon."

Trace nodded. "I think the Yanks, at least those of us doing all the work, feel the same way." Then he brightened. "Hey there, I have something to offer, too. I don't want you to think you're the only one to help the cause."

"What?" said Chaw, suppressing a grin. "Don't tell me you're about to go against the bluebelly grain!"

Trace kept his mouth shut and rummaged in the depths of his rucksack with his right hand. His knife hand was still sore, specifically in the finger joints, but it was getting better, the digits more limber. He expected he'd put a brutal amount of strain and stress on that hand while gripping its unforgiving walnut handle.

His fingertips found what they'd been snuffling for and pinched the small parcel, carefully wrapped in several layers of brown paper and tied with twine. He pulled it out and held it up in the air between them.

"What is it?" said Chaw, his eyebrows drawn together like bird wings.

Trace smiled. "This?" He almost said, *my friend*, but skipped over those words. "This is nectar, this is ambrosia, this is . . . oh heck. Here!"

He handed over the package, and Chaw accepted it with reluctance. With an encouraging nod from Trace, Chaw untied the string and peeled back the brittle, much-worn paper to reveal two thumb-size nuggets, one orange and one red.

"Boiled sweets!" said Trace, as if he could not wait a moment longer to share the news.

"Well, now," said Chaw, smiling. "That is a treat. Not the taters and gravy I was hoping you'd find, but a sweet will do nicely. Oh, yes sir." He held out the package to Trace. "You choose first."

"Oh no, you're the guest."

"Guest?" Chaw looked around the campsite.

"Well, you know what I mean."

Chaw closed his eyes and, still grasping the opened paper bundle in his right hand, worked it around until the contents were as mixed as they were going to get. Then he patted them with his left hand and pointed with a finger. "I'll take that one." He opened his eyes and found his fingertip resting on the orange candy.

He plucked it up and handed the bundle, paper, string, and sweet, to Trace. "That's yours."

Each man stared at their sweet for a moment. "Should we save them?" said Trace.

"How long you been lugging them around?"

Trace shrugged. "Pretty near since the start. A couple of years or more now."

"And you've never been tempted?"

"Truth be told, I forgot they were there."

"Lucky for us, then," said Chaw. "I for one don't like waiting." He popped the orange-colored candy in his mouth and closed his eyes. In a few moments, he smiled and said, "Oh, I haven't tasted anything like that since I was a child." He opened his eyes. "Thank you, Yank."

Trace popped his into his mouth and began to suck on the red candy. "You're most welcome. And I thank you, Reb, in advance for the smoke we'll enjoy in our pipes later on. After we eat our steak and potatoes and gravy and pie."

"Now that, Yank, ain't even funny."

Then both men settled back and closed their eyes and enjoyed their boiled sweets.

"All right," said Chaw. "Now I know, I know, I bet money and all, and I am not much of a betting man, and I am sure that you have been asked this before, but—"

"The name," said Trace, nodding.

"Yes, that name of yours. Where on earth . . ."

"I could say the same thing, Chaw Dagworth. Chaw? That's really your name?"

"Sure it is!"

"Chaw is your legitimate name? It's not a nickname friends gave you?"

"Nope." The Reb sat up straighter and rasped a hand across his stubbled jaw. "My dear old Pap, he was a man partial to his baccy, he was. Spit and chew, spit and chew, that's one of the things I recall him doing the most."

"So you were named after tobacco?"

"Nope. Nope, I was not." The Reb shook his head with vigor. "I was named after my father's fondness for something he considered particularly Southern and fine. Just happened to be tobacco he was fond of."

Trace nodded. "Oh, I see." But really, he didn't. It barely made any sense to him, but then again, who was he to speak? "Well, as to my name, my mother, she was an optimist, poor thing. And a Quaker. You put those two things together, you have yourself someone inclined to name their first and only child Fullcup."

"Wow." Chaw shook his head as if in lament. "And your pa? He have anything to say about it?"

"Not really, not where Mother was concerned. She was a force to be reckoned with, was my mother."

"I hear that, mister. Mine was the same."

They were silent for a few moments, each lost in rumination of times long gone. Then Trace said, "You spoke of your father in the past tense."

"He's dead. Yep. Mama too."

"The war?"

"No, thank the Maker. It was cholera. Just awful how it raked through our holler."

"I'm sorry to hear that."

Chaw nodded, acknowledging the comment. "And yours?"

"Same. Oh, not cholera, but age, hard work, life, a little of all of it. I was not only their only child, I was a surprise to them much later in their lives than most folks have children. They were already older when I was a child."

"Oh," said the Reb, not certain how to respond. Then he grinned. "Hey, that makes us the same. At least in one way."

"How do you see that?" said Trace.

"We're both orphans!"

"That we are, that we are. Funny, I never thought of myself that way before. But it's true. I don't have any close living relations that I know of, anyway. You?"

Chaw shrugged. "A handful of cousins. Cholera took care of most of the rest of my kin, though."

And so it went, with each man getting to know the other, yet still bristling at times when they realized they were dealing with a man who they should have killed at first chance.

"How could we go from all-out wanting to kill each other to, well, to whatever this truce deal is now we've arrived at?"

"You kidding me? I aim to gut you the first chance I get. I'm just waiting you out, choosing my moment. . . ."

Chaw was turned away from Trace when he said this, but the Yank bet the Reb was grinning. He knew that neither man intended to kill the other anymore. Just wasn't something they intended to do.

That didn't mean they wouldn't return to their former lives once they got back with their respective armies. But for now, they each knew they were safe from dying a violent death, at least from each other.

"By my reckoning, it's been nearly a week since we tangled, Yank. Do you reckon you can travel a while on that pin of yours? Those rabbits I snared and that fish you noodled ain't nothing but a memory now. We had best find a kindly soul and get ourselves some food."

Trace ambled back from the stream, where he'd been laving water onto his afflicted knee. The swelling had gone down quite a bit and the garish bruising, reminding the bearer of a purpling dawn sky, had calmed itself as well. "Yes, I believe I can do it. And you're right. If we wait much longer, we'll risk not having strength enough to walk on out of here."

With little more agreement than that, and with each man coming to accept the fact that they were usually thinking the same thing at the same time, they gathered their belongings. And with no more thought than an exchanged nod, they set off on foot eastward.

Chaw Dagworth moved slowly, held back not only by his companion's limited ambulatory abilities, but also by the fact that his ribs, although knitting, were still paining him with sharp stings and dull throbs whenever he moved too quickly.

Fullcup Trace had found a stout hickory limb with a bend in it and hewed it roughly into a cane, which he used as a third leg, allowing it to pivot his weight as he walked, taking some pressure off the puffed knee.

CHAPTER 4

"How many years has it been, anyway?"

"Since what?"

The man who asked the first question, Chaw Dagworth, shifted in his chair at the corner table in the cool shade of a back corner of the saloon. He looked at his companion at the table and shook his head. "Ain't nobody never told you it ain't polite to answer a question with a question?"

"What?"

"There you go again!"

His table mate, Fullcup Trace, sighed and closed his book. "You do realize you did it, too, right?"

"Did what?"

"I stand corrected. You did it twice to my once."

"What on earth are you on about? Oh, never mind!" Chaw glowered into his nearly empty glass mug, eyeing remnants of foam that represented the last of the beer he could buy with the last of his all-but-gone cash.

"I take it you mean how long has it been since we nearly killed each other by Deadeye Gap?" said Trace, sipping his barely touched beer. He noted that Chaw's beer was in far worse shape than his, and he grinned.

"Something like that, yeah."

"Well, a good few years, that's for certain. I know I still limp."

"And I still wheeze when I run."

"When was the last time you ran anywhere?" said Trace. "Oh yeah, when that drunk shouted something about free whiskey outside that bar in Deadwood. When was that? Two years back?"

"That wasn't funny! Nearly did myself in, and all for nothing! He was just some crazy old soak having a funny. Should have punched him on that bright red nose of his," Chaw grumbled into his glass.

Trace ignored him and sipped, lost in a reverie for a moment. "Yes, that was some time ago. But we both lived through it. Emerged, you might say, as new men."

"New! Ha. I'm the same ol' Chaw Dagworth who went into that War of Yankee Bellicosity."

"I meant that we embody the notion that whatever does not kill a man will often make him stronger. And for the record, it was an unfortunate, drawn-out mess caused by uppity Rebs, nothing less."

"You . . . " Chaw sat up straight and held a knobby, scarred finger high in the air. The only other folks in the bar at that time of the afternoon, one fellow at the bar, and the barkeep himself, both turned to look at him. He settled back into his chair. "Ah, never mind."

"Still," said Trace, sipping his beer. "It was an interesting time."

"That's one word for it, yep."

Trace ignored him and continued: "To think that we hated each other with as much bile and suspicion as any two men might." He shook his head. "Glad that's behind us."

"You and me both, pard."

Trace snapped a finger. "See? That's what I mean, right there. Who would ever have thought that we would have ended up here."

Chaw looked around at the dim interior of the saloon. "Don't crow too loud, Trace." He leaned forward and lowered his voice. "This place ain't all that much."

"I meant still alive, and what's more, we're friends."

Chaw leaned back and yawned. "You do have a habit of stretching things a bit."

"Nope. You're the one who gets tangled up in his own windies."

"All I meant was despite being sworn enemies we stuck together, even after the War."

"Had to," said Chaw. "Way I figure it, you owe me the use of a lung, and until I can figure out a way to collect on that debt, I ain't about to let you out of my sight."

"I could say the same thing about a knee, don't forget." Trace sipped his beer, regretting that they were hard up enough that a second round wasn't to be.

"How could I?" said Chaw, leaning back with his eyes closed. "You blather on about it every chance you get!"

"Well, as for me and collecting on that debt you owe me—namely a new knee—I finally figured out how to do it."

"Oh? Do tell."

"I'll just shoot you in your sleep."

"How's that going to get you a new knee?"

"It won't, but it'll save me from having to listen to your snoring. Sounds like a steam locomotive crashing into the bottom of a ravine. Over and over and over."

Chaw chuckled. "You're welcome. It's the least I can do. Besides, it's just my way of struggling to breathe with this bum lung you give me."

A few more moments passed, then Trace said, "Whose bright idea was it to head West after the War, anyway?"

"Reckon it was a mutual decision, if I recall correct." Chaw leaned forward, suddenly remembering he might have squirreled away a few coins in his possibles bag. He rummaged in it as he spoke. "Neither of us had much in the way of family nor homeplaces to return to, and the fool War was over with by the time we crawled out of the wilderness, half starved and half healed. . . ."

Trace resumed the well-worn bit of conversation: "So we decided to skip the foolishness of getting mustered out of our respective armies and wasting another few months—"

"And years in a foul Yankee prison camp!" growled Chaw.

"Maybe so," said Trace. "At any rate, here we are, doing our best to slough off the residue of filth that war leaves on a man."

"You do come out with the oddest things to say, you know that?" said Chaw, grinning because he felt a mysterious coin and tweezered it out with a thumb and forefinger. "That, my friend, represents a beer!"

"And this," said Trace, setting down his own coin. "Represents another."

"You was holding out on me!"

"So were you."

The two best friends glared at each other over the small tabletop as they waited for the bartender to bring them another round.

"You know, if it wasn't for you," said Chaw. "I'd still be employed, and that means I'd have me some money. And that means I'd have the ability to buy myself another beer. And even a slug of rye."

"Nah, wasn't for me, you'd be dead."

"How do you figure?"

"If your memory wasn't so awful," said Trace, "you'd recall that you were about set to gut that foul trail boss, McClanahan."

"And he would have earned it, too. A nastier fella ain't never drawn breath."

"I can't disagree there. But he was also handy with a gun, and more to the point, he had men who liked him just fine. And even more to the point, he worked for a man who was close, you might say, with that fellow, oh, what's his name . . . Senator Talbot."

"So?"

"So, they'd have strung you up high for even thinking about spoiling McClanahan's supper, let alone gut him with that blade of yours."

"So?"

"So I'm the one who kept you from killing him and

thus saved your hide. Why? I do not know. Ask myself that every morning."

"*Thus*? Did you say *thus*?" The big man in buckskin garb grinned and shook his head. "My word, three days in a fancy town and you start talking like you own something more than a broke-down old horse, a couple of worn guns, and clothes that are more hole than cloth."

"Oh, I am sorry, were you describing yourself?"

Chaw narrowed his eyes, and a low sighing growl rose up from his throat. "I regret ever chumming up with a Yankee."

Trace returned the look. "And I rue the day a Reb crossed my trail."

An hour later, after they had mooched as much time as they felt they could in the saloon, they emerged back out onto the main street of the latest settlement they'd wandered into.

"What's the name of this town again?" said Chaw, squinting at the spring day's light.

"Hmm." Trace looked up and down the street, then saw a sign over a shop. "Mankley."

"Huh," said Chaw. "Where's that?"

"No idea."

A man passing slowed. "Pardon me, I couldn't help overhearing. You two men sound as if you are newcomers to our quaint town."

"We are, indeed," said Trace, smiling and doing his best to compensate for what he knew would be a scowl on the bearded face of his buckskin-clad compadre.

"Well," said the dapper local, "I am Winston Mc-Cready, and you two men are in Mankley, Territory of

Utah." The fellow smiled at them with thin lips, and his eyes took them and their attire in with an air of primacy, as if they were a dullard and needed his assistance. "I should add that I am an important figure in this town. You won't have to go very far in Mankley to find that out." He nodded, as if agreeing with himself.

"Well, now," said Chaw. "That's something. Ain't it something, pard?" He looked at Trace with raised eyebrows.

"Yes, indeed," said Trace. "How very nice for you to be looked after by all these fine folks." He looked around, then returned the man's indulgent smile.

The man's own brows rose and he reddened, said, "Well, well, then . . ." and turned and bustled on down the boardwalk.

The two pards grinned and shook their heads, then resumed looking up and down the street.

"You know," said Chaw, "you can tug on that vest all you like, but you still look like a dandy who ran out of money before he finished cobbling together a set of togs for himself."

"At least I don't look like I crawled out of a wolf den. Or smell like a bear's backside."

"Hey now, these buckskins are practical garb and not prone to wearing out like fool cloth garments."

"Maybe so," said Trace. "But in the process, they take on the stink of everything foul they happen by. You know, it wouldn't kill you to clean them, oh, every few years or so."

Chaw smiled. "See, that's the thing with buckskins.

You don't need to wash them. You ever see a deer taking a bath? I expect not!"

"No, that's true. But they are usually crawling with ticks and fleas." He looked Chaw up and down theatrically. "Yep, there they are now."

"What?" said Chaw, looking down at his dark-stained tunic. "Where?"

But Trace was already looking away, past Chaw, toward the street. He watched a woman in a fine black dress and impressive feathered hat picking her way with great care across the muddy spring street. She was trying to avoid the runnels of muck and fresh drops of dung. And not making much progress.

Trace pushed past Chaw, who was still eyeing his garments with great scrutiny. It was true he'd been feeling a mite itchy lately. Might be he would need to consider thinking about scraping off . . . one of these days. "Hey, where you making for?"

But his pard was already ambling away, that hitch in his step keeping him from moving too fast. Chaw worked to catch up to him, holding a hand to his right side. "Cursed ribs," he muttered. "Look here, you rascal, what are you—" Then he, too, caught sight of the woman.

Chaw made it to her side two strides quicker than did Trace, but he was so winded he was unable to speak. His puffing presence alarmed her, and she paused in her road-crossing efforts and stiffened, her big doe eyes wide.

That was when Fullcup Trace showed up. He tipped his hat and smiled. He was secretly pleased that he had taken pains to smack the trail dust from his black wool jacket and gray-and-black-striped vest and black trousers after they arrived in town and had left their mounts at the cheapest stable they could find.

He had also trimmed his own peppered hair and beard just the day before. And now he offered the fetching dark-haired woman what he had grown to be certain was a pleasing smile. "Is this ruffian bothering you, ma'am?"

He flashed a menacing look at the now only slightly gasping Chaw Dagworth. "Allow me to escort you across the street."

"I . . . but . . ." said the woman, looking beyond them to the sidewalk but seeing no one else about.

"Don't do it, ma'am!" said Chaw in between breaths. "He's . . . wanted . . . in three states!" He shoved himself between Trace and the woman, knocking Trace back a couple of staggering steps, and held out his own elbow.

Chaw also offered her what he had been told by various dance hall dollies was a devilish grin. "Let me protect you, ma'am. At least until the law catches up with him!"

Just then, Trace's arm flashed out and snagged that elbow and sent Chaw reeling. The two men squared off and prepared to tussle.

The woman stepped back from them both and placed her gloved hands on her slender waist and glared at them both.

They each caught sight of this and stood, side by side, uncertain what to do next. What she did next shocked them both. Slowly, a smile crept onto her perfect features.

"Gentlemen," she said, "I am beginning to suspect you know each other, and what's more, I do believe you each have it in mind to help me cross this filthy street."

"Yes, ma'am," they each said, already falling in love with her fiery ways and with the Irish lilt in her voice.

"Fine, then." She stuck out her elbows and lifted her dress slightly with those gloved hands. "It is true, I prefer to not sully my boots. But I shall risk it in an effort not to sully my dress. If you two boys can stop your bickering long enough to get me there," she nodded toward the far side of the street, "I shall be much obliged to you and shall endeavor to make it up to you."

Chaw and Trace had to let her words sink in for a brief moment. "Yes, ma'am," said Trace, hustling to her left side.

"You bet!" said Chaw, at her right.

They nodded to each other, then hefted her a good six inches from the rank street and stomped on across, where they deposited her safely and muck-free on the raised boardwalk. They stayed in the street and gazed up at her, soppy grins on their faces.

"I am grateful to you both, so I am. And to thank you, I shall be pleased if you would allow me the honor of buying you each a cup of coffee and a slice of pie at the café, just there." She nodded upstreet, to her right. "It belongs to my good friend, Ruby. She is the best cook I have ever known. And I am confident in saying she is the best cook I shall ever have the honor of knowing."

"Wow," said Chaw.

"In that case, ma'am," said Trace. "Lead the way and we shall endeavor to follow. But we have to clean off our boots first."

She giggled and walked on up the sidewalk, toward the sign that read "Ruby's."

"Endeavor?" said Chaw. "Just where'd you hear that word?"

"From her," said Trace, hustling to get his boots clean before Chaw. He'd shove that smelly Reb into the street if he had to in order to get in that café quick enough to pull out a chair for the lovely woman to seat herself.

"So, gentlemen, how did you come to find yourselves in Mankley, in the foothills of the Wasatch Range?"

The two men could only look upon her fair face with admiration. Finally, she smiled and said, "Shall I assume you've gone dumb on me? Eh?"

"Oh, oh no, ma'am," said Trace. "At least I haven't. As for him," he jerked a finger at his friend and rolled his eyes. She laughed, and he liked hearing that sound. He would have to think of more subtle ways of making her laugh. He could think of a few already.

"Pay him no heed, miss. He's addled." Chaw spun a finger beside his temple. "Kicked in the bean by a mule when he was a youth."

Again, she appeared as if she was uncertain how to take these two men.

Finally, in this lull, Trace spoke. "We have been drift-ing from one job to another, ma'am," he said, playing with the thick pottery mug before him. It was still half filled with coffee.

Chaw rubbed his chin and leaned back in his chair. "As long as there was a dollar in it, I suspect we've tried it, miss. Done an awful lot of punching cattle. Was on two trail drives—that's raw work, let me tell you. Which ain't nothing compared to herding sheep! Oh, but those woolly brutes are smarter than they look."

"Most critters seem that way to you, Chaw."

The Reb shook a big-knuckled fist at Trace. "You just wait, pard. You just wait!"

Trace ignored him and said, "We've worked as loggers, rivermen on a barge. We even rode shotgun on an overland stage run a few times."

This seemed to impress her, for she leaned forward, eyes narrowed, and planted her elbows on the tabletop. She brought her hands together before her pretty chin, drumming her fingertips together. "Can you handle those weapons riding on your hips?" She grinned and looked them each in the eye, first Trace and then Chaw.

Both men looked away, ears and cheeks red. Trace said, "Ma'am, we are handy with six-guns, you bet. Also gut shredders, pardon me, *shotguns*, and sabers—"

"And blades!" said Chaw, nodding.

"And," resumed Trace, "we also like the company of women, we like to drink, we like to mix it up when we drink, and we like having money and dislike not having it."

"So you drink and carouse and gamble," she said, watching their faces for a reaction. They were, as she expected, speechless, and she knew they'd never likely heard a lady say such a word. "Oh come now, gentlemen. It's only a word, one word among many. Let's dispense with propriety over such things." Then she leaned forward. "Gentlemen, I am recently widowed."

Neither man spoke, but it was obvious they were surprised by what she'd revealed. Sure, thought Trace, that would explain the fact that she was dressed head to toe in black. Although she wore no gauzy veil such as he'd seen women who looked this fancy wear while in mourning.

"I'm sorry to hear that, ma'am," said Chaw.

She shook her head and waved her hand, as if dispelling an irksome fly. "I don't mention it because I am looking for sympathy, but thank you just the same. No, I will explain." She sipped her coffee, then said, "My late husband was Count Roscommon, also from Ireland, as you so accurately surmised of me." She looked at Trace and nearly grinned.

A delicious shiver shot up his spine.

"He died . . . unexpectedly three months ago. Since then, I have taken over the day-to-day management of our business."

"What might that business be, ma'am?" said Trace, more in an effort to appear interested than in anything else. In truth, she could recite nonsense and he'd be transfixed.

"Sligo Star Freighting, sir."

"Freighting?" said Chaw. "Huh. Big firm?"

She shrugged. "We had planned on becoming such, yes. And for a time it looked as if we might make good on that intention."

"But . . . " said Trace, prompting her.

She complied, in a roundabout way; they were to learn this was more in keeping with her demeanor than in responding in a direct fashion. "I can only suspect that you are aware of the strikes in the hills hereabouts."

"Strikes?" said Chaw. "Lightning?"

Trace almost chuckled, but he didn't want to hurt his friend's feelings. Nonetheless, he, too, was uncertain of what she meant. But he was intrigued.

"No, not that, but something equally as exciting. Gold strikes."

"Oh, that," said Chaw, reddening, his ears blooming where they stuck through his silver and brown hair.

She nodded. "Yes. And that has opened up all manner of opportunities for new businesses, from cheap whores to hardware sellers."

Neither man spoke, although they could not help but look surprised.

"Oh, don't be so shocked, men. I am a woman, yes, but women can speak every word that a man can. And sometimes with far more emphasis."

Trace nodded. He heartily agreed. Was there nothing this woman could do that would not thrill him? He glanced at Chaw and saw that the brute was gazing at her in much the same manner, and he knew exactly why. She was handsome.

"Excuse me, ma'am," said Trace.

"Yes, Mr., Ah . . . ?"

"Trace, ma'am."

"Yes, Mr. Trace?"

"You mentioned that your husband is, or was, Count Roscommon, yet the business is called Sligo

Star. I don't know a whole lot about the country of Ireland, but I do know that Sligo is not in the same spot as Roscommon."

"You doubt me, sir?" she said, showing the first hint of annoyance with them.

"Yeah," said Chaw. "What's wrong with you, Trace? You doubting the lady?"

"No, not at all," said Trace, horrified that his comment had been construed in that manner. "What I meant was—"

Then she smiled. "Calm down, Mr. Trace. I was only kidding with you. You see, that's a question I have been asked before. The truth is, Sligo and Roscommon are not terribly far apart, but in many ways they differ. Much like my husband and myself as youths. You see, ours was a forbidden love. We almost were unable to marry for Bennet's family—Bennet was my husband— was of royal blood, and they did not approve of him marrying a common girl such as me."

"Common? Why, miss, you are nothing but common!" Chaw nodded in finality.

Trace was about to comment, but she said, "Coming from you, Mr.?"

"Dagworth, ma'am."

"Very well, Mr. Dagworth. I will take that as the compliment I assume was intended."

"Um, you bet. Yep."

"At any rate, we were compelled due to familiar circumstances I just hinted at to emigrate. The idea of striking out on one's own and earning one's way was very important to my husband, gentlemen. He was a talented man filled with energy and life."

Her eyes glistened for a moment as she paused in thought. "Ah, you see, it will take time yet, I fear, to, as they say, get over him."

"You never can get over something like that, ma'am. At least in my experience," said Trace.

"No?"

"No, but you can get through it. Take it into your life and come to peace with it and keep on going. After all, what else is there?"

"There's pie, I can tell you that much," said Chaw, winking at them as a waitress set down three ample wedges of still-steaming spice pie.

For a time, none of them spoke, so intent were they on enjoying their pie. Finally, Chaw said, "I hope you don't mind me saying so, ma'am, but you . . . well, you're not shy about your pie."

"Why should I be? I like pie and I dislike corsets."

"You are a corker, ma'am, and no mistake," said Chaw, red-faced and grinning at the table.

"Thank you, sir. But I tell you all this to fill you in on what's happening now." Even as a widow, the woman seemed somehow difficult to rile.

When the time comes, thought Trace, *I hope I'll be able to find myself a woman as lovely and as surprising as the widow.*

"We ended up here, as most people in Mankley have, because Bennet felt that it was prime gold country. And he was right! He used to say, sniffing the air and smiling, that he could smell the very ore itself!" She laughed again, and something told Trace that no matter the hardships in her life, this was a woman who was going to face them with dignity and with a smile.

Then her smile disappeared and she looked at them. "I'll come right out with it, so I will. I have need of two good men."

Again, they were shocked and did not know what to say, as various thoughts of explanation danced in their minds. Before the obvious truth dawned on them, she continued, "I need two experienced freighters to haul goods to and from the notorious high-mountain mine camp known as Boarwallow Gap. Other goods will need to go all the way to the big, bustling town of Richness, Utah. It is over the mountains that way. Beyond the Gap, as it happens." She looked over her left shoulder at the wall behind, westward, as if she could see right through it.

"Um, ain't there any men hereabouts who'll hire on to work for you, ma'am?" Chaw prodded the crumbs with his fork on the little plate before him.

"Why, gentlemen, I thought you just said you do most anything if there is a dollar in it for you."

"Well, yes, ma'am, we did, but . . ." said Trace.

"But?"

"But the thing is, we haven't ever freighted goods. Not as such." He exchanged a glance with Chaw.

What they each knew and were not about to reveal to her was that they had had a bit of experience with a freighting outfit. It had been early on in their wandering days, and they had not really figured on how much work the job was going to be, nor the long hours, nor the dangerous aspects of it. It had not ended well, in fact.

They had done their best, but they had been held up by masked gunmen and beaten. And then they lost the goods, the wagon, and the team. It had been a humiliating experience, and one they had taken pains over the ensuing years to avoid.

"If it is a case of money, gentlemen, I can assure you, I have ample cash in our illustrious bank, and contracts aplenty. What I don't have are drivers."

"Well, ma'am, as I was wondering about earlier . . . local men . . ." said Chaw.

"Ah yes, well, there are very few available anymore, I'm afraid. They are either engaged in ranching or in businesses in town. But the rest of them are off in the very hills I haul goods in and out of, all looking—"

". . . for gold," said Trace, nodding. "I see."

But what he really did see was the pretty widow's face gazing at him and then at Chaw alternately, the merest hint of disappointment crossing her features. It was a sight he could not bear to look upon. "Ma'am, ah, let me and my partner here discuss the situation, and we can let you know. Where can we find you?"

Her face brightened. "Very good, that sounds very good indeed." She stood, fetching her small satchel. "I have two errands I must attend to, and then you will find me at the far western end of town in the depot there. You can't miss it. It's the only two-story building in that direction. And the sign out front says 'Sligo Star Freighting.'"

"Oh," said Trace. "Ma'am, it's a bit embarrassing, but we, ah, the pie and coffee, see . . ."

She looked confused for a brief moment, then laid a gloved hand on his arm. "Not to worry; this was my treat, after all, to thank you for saving me from the treacherous crossing of that foul lane out front. I run a tab with Ruby. This is where I take my morning pie each day."

"You eat pie every day, ma'am?"

"Why not? Life, as I have learned, gentlemen, can be a short thing. Shouldn't we enjoy it while we can?"

The comely Widow Roscommon left them standing at the table, watching her as she walked on out of the café.

"Oh, what's she going to do if she needs to cross that filthy street again?" said Chaw, as if speaking a private thought aloud.

"Something tells me she didn't need us to do a thing for her back there in the street, Chaw. She knew what she was doing all along."

"Does that mean what I think it means, pard?"

Trace nodded. "I do believe we are now in the freighting business, pard."

"Heaven help us."

A short while later, back outside and rubbing their bellies, the two men looked up and down the street. There were a few more folks about, a couple of women in calico and gingham dresses, carrying laden shopping baskets, and walking side by side, chatting.

They also saw one child, a bedraggled boy, shoeless and smudged of face and hands. His knee pants and coat were well-patched and looked to be too small for his bony frame.

"You think everything she told you is level and true?" said Chaw.

"You doubt her?" said Trace.

"No, no, not in the least. But I do wonder."

"Well, now," said Trace. "If there's one thing I have learned to be wary of in life, it's a good thing."

"Oh, here we go. Next you'll be telling me you don't want to drink beer or play cards, huh?"

Trace's eyes rolled. "I didn't mean that and you know it. A fellow can use all the help he can get in life, eh? And the cash will cover our various, um, requirements for a whole long time to come, pard."

"Yeah, sure, I get that. But you and me both know that we don't really have much freighting experience, and it looks like she needs men who do."

Trace nodded. "I don't disagree on any point there, but there are two things that tell me we need to take the work."

"And they are?" said Chaw, beginning to walk toward the west end of the street.

"They are, as I said, that the job will pay for whatever it is we would like to do with money for many months to come. And I think she really can use the help."

Chaw scratched his bearded chin. "She really is something, ain't she?"

"Yes, that she is," said Trace, thinking that getting to know the sparky Widow Roscommon would be yet another benefit of taking on the work. "Besides," he resumed. "It's not like we have to do it forever, right?"

"Hey," said Chaw, grinning at him. "That's right. We do the work, we move on. It's how we do things, anyway. And another thing that just come to me is, how difficult can driving a wagon from one place to another be? The horses or oxen or mules or whatever critters she has, they'll do most of the work, anyway!"

"True, true. That all makes sense, pard," said Trace. "So, how do you want to play this out?"

"What do you mean?"

"I mean, should we go there now and tell her, or wait a while?"

"Hmm," said Chaw. "We ought to check on the horses, see what they know. Maybe then we pay her a visit."

"Sounds good, but remember, we haven't given the stable fellow any money yet. And we don't want to let on we don't have any because he'll likely boot us and our horses out."

"What's it matter?" said Chaw, grinning even wider. "Say, I got me an idea."

"Oh? I bet it's very similar to the one I just got, myself. Seeing as how we all but have honest employment again. And at a depot, it stands to reason that there will be stable space for our own horses there, no?"

"That's right, pard," said Chaw, nodding and smiling and liking where this was going.

"So I am guessing that you are thinking something about getting our horses and gear on out of that expensive stable before the man in charge can see us at it?"

"Something like that, yep."

"Only thing is, this town's not that big. He's liable to see us kicking around and want his money."

Chaw shrugged. "Horses ain't been there that long, but a few hours."

"But his placard said something about a minimum charge of half a day per animal."

"What? Why, that's robbery!" Chaw looked around. "Where's the lawdog in this town? I'll have that stable thief locked up!"

"Easy now, Chaw. Don't put your wagon before your horse, if you know what I mean. One thing at a time. We go there and try to weasel our mounts on out of there. If he sees us, we'll say we're coming back, just paying a visit to an ailing old aunt."

"That's good. What's her name?"

"Who?" said Trace.

"The ailing old aunt? Got to have a name."

"I don't know and I don't care! Now listen—"

"Ethel. That's for sure an old aunt's name. I knowed a girl once—"

"Chaw?"

"Yeah?"

"Shut your Reb mouth and listen for once."

The man from the South narrowed his eyes at his pard and rasped a hand across his jaw, but he kept quiet.

"Good. Now, skip the aunt story. We'll just tell him the truth and pay the money."

"But we don't have any."

"But we'll tell him we're going to work for the Widow Roscommon and her Sligo Star Freighting outfit and that'll be that."

"But then we'll have to pay a full day for the horses."

"No, only a half a day."

Chaw shook his head. "Half a day for each. You just said."

"Well, that's only fair, Chaw. I—oh, never mind. Come on. By the time we get this mess all sorted out, she'll be moved back to Ireland or some such."

As it turned out, the two men were able to mince their way through the gathering and loading up of their mounts with their gear. They led them out a side door and up a side street that brought them to within one hundred feet of the Sligo Star depot.

"Got away with it, pard," said Chaw, grinning.

"Sure we did, but not in the way you mean."

"What do you mean, not in the way I mean?"

"We still have to pay for the time they were in his care."

"Like heck we do!"

"Well, I'm paying, then."

"You pay your half. I'm sticking to my plan."

"Well, then, when they haul you off to prison, don't expect me to come visiting." By Chaw's silence as they walked their horses toward the depot, Trace knew he'd gotten through to the man's weak spot. Chaw Dagworth was petrified of going to prison. Even a night in jail turned him into a hard case of trembles and shivers and shakes.

They halted before the depot's front loading dock, then glanced around.

"Might be wiser to make for the alley yonder," said Chaw. "See if it leads to the Sligo stable."

They did, and found a handy hitching rail running along one end of the rear loading dock. Off to their right sat an open-door stable with several big horse faces staring out at them. In a paddock farther out back, four oxen grazed in their own fenced pasture, while four more big horses did the same in their own pasture.

As they lashed their reins about the rail, a door at the far end of the loading dock slid open on oiled tracks. They looked up to see the comely widow emerge from the darkened interior.

"You are right on time," she said. "Come on in, gentlemen." She turned and walked back inside. They exchanged a quick look, a shrug, and then climbed the stairs and crossed the worn puncheons of the loading dock.

Each man was mired in thought that was part trepidation over the unknown, part excitement, and part dread. They had each seen but had not commented on the impressive sight of the several heavy work wagons lining the side yard. They all looked in solid condition, with greased hubs gleaming and paint jobs not flaking nor too worn by the weather.

And they also saw, through wide-open doors at one end of the stable, in addition to the big horses that all looked well-tended and well-fed, racks of tack, polished, oiled, and hanging, ready for use.

And then there was the size of the depot itself, and the fact that they knew precisely what the interior of depot storerooms looked like—stacks and stacks of barrels and crates and sacks of feed and lumber and everything else in between. They also knew that each of those items had to be brought in and unloaded and stored when they arrived.

And then it all had to be unstacked and loaded into the big work wagons and driven to the high-mountain camps and unloaded. Then, once they were at those camps, they had to load up those wagons once more with ore and such, and then drive it on to that big town she'd mentioned—Richness, was it? *Oh boy*, they each thought as they approached the open door through which she'd walked.

Oh boy.

"After you," said Chaw, stepping aside so Trace could enter first.

"Nope, you go on ahead. You were before me anyway."

"No, I insist," said Chaw.

From inside, they heard an old man's voice say, "Oh for Pete's sake, did you really hire two men who can't figure out how to walk through a doorway? I think, Widow, that we might have been better off as we were. I ain't too old to drive, you know."

"Hush now, Hector," said the woman's voice. "Gentlemen, come in, please. We have much to discuss, I am certain. And then you can settle into your room in the stable."

"Yeah," said the old man's voice. "If they can figure out how to get in and out of it again!" He cackled and ignored her second directive for him to hush.

The men entered and let their eyes adjust to the interior light, not as dark as they had surmised. To their right they saw two large windows overlooking the rear yard, stable, and loading area. And beneath this, but angled such that she could look out the window as she worked, sat a large, tidy desk with two wooden chairs across from it.

"Please, take a seat and we can discuss business."

There she was, behind a big desk piled with ledgers and papers and all manner of official-looking gear atop it. Trace and Chaw felt, as they turned their respective hats round and round in their thick fingers, that perhaps they had been a pinch hasty in thinking this career choice through.

The other thing that made their guts tighten was the way she looked. Sure, the Widow Roscommon was still as handsome as they come, and sure, she was still smiling, but there was something about her now that scared them a little. She was a woman. She was a boss. And she was soon to be their boss . . .

"Aw," said a man's wheezy voice from a shadowy corner to their left. "Set yourselves down, she don't bite."

They looked toward the voice and saw an old man leaning against the wall. He looked to be no taller than five feet and to weigh no more than one leg on either of the men.

"Hector, please . . ."

Before they knew what had happened, she had introduced them to the small old man, the Hector to whom she'd spoken. Then she extracted from them that they indeed did want to work for her.

Then, with a smile and a nod, she dismissed them from the room, what they now knew to be her office.

They followed the old man named Hector out the door, across the loading dock, and down the steps that led to the vast back alley and acreage beyond. In daylight, Hector was even smaller and more wizened than he had appeared indoors. But as with the woman, there was something about him that told them he was a whole lot more than what he appeared to be.

He walked with a hitch in his gait, his left leg looking a little stiff. Halfway to the stable, he turned and, with fingertips resting about his trim waist, he squinted at Trace and Chaw. "You two look big enough to do the job, but I don't mind saying you both look as though you could use new parts and pieces."

He nodded at Trace. "You walk about as odd as I do. And you!" He fixed his fiery gaze on Chaw. "For a mountainy-looking man, you sure wheeze. I expect you been gored by a bull or some such."

"Something like that," said Trace, smiling at the unintended compliment. At least that was how he was going to regard the rib-cracking blow he'd dealt Chaw all those years before.

"Now you just look here, old-timer," said Chaw, pointing a meaty finger at the old man.

Hector didn't flinch. He looked at the finger, and then at Chaw. "Last man who did that drew back a bloody stump."

"That a threat?" said Chaw.

"Nope." Hector turned and proceeded on toward the stable. Over his shoulder, he said, "Just a fact."

Chaw and Trace exchanged looks and followed the old gent. He thumbed the latch on a door and swung it wide. "Come on in, fellows. See what you got yourself into." He cackled and disappeared inside.

They followed and found themselves in a dim space lit only by the daylight coming in through the open door. "This here is where you'll stay. Bunk there." Hector nodded toward the back corner tucked against the wall separating the room from the stable. "And another one there." He nodded once more.

The bunks he indicated were narrow, about the width of a coffin. Thin, hickory-stripe mattresses stuffed with a flimsy amount of straw rested atop a weaving of rough hempen rope.

"You can stash your gear and whatnot in here, but your horses should have their own paddock for a while. Just in case they rub the other horses the wrong way, if you understand my meaning."

"No," said Chaw, puffed. "I guess I don't. You saying that my horse ain't good enough for your stable?"

"Nope. Said nothing of the sort. It's for their protection as well as my own beasts. You see, a single sliver of that sickness can bring harm to my horses, and even to those two old oxen out back." He raised an arm in the general direction of the still-grazing beasts. "And I won't stand for it. So we will do as I say and separate them for a spell."

"If you don't mind me saying so," said Trace. "Those two oxen look, well, a little old to be doing the job of hauling freight."

"Old! Old?"

It was as if they had set fire to Hector's trousers. He

rounded on them and poked a bony old finger up at Trace's face. The Yankee couldn't help but recall what Hector had said about Chaw's finger. He wasn't inclined to smirk, though, because Hector seemed genuinely frightening.

"Them two old oxen, as you think they are, could pull the hide off any of these here horses. And these horses are the best you'll find anywhere. That's how bold those old brutes still are!"

Again, Hector turned and waved a hand at the wall, indicating hooks and shelves and a low bench beneath. As if nothing had happened, he said, "You can hang your gear here. There's a dogtrot kitchen yonder outside; I'll show you. Follow me." He walked back out through the door.

"He's a mite touchy, ain't he?" said Chaw in a whisper to Trace just before they stepped back out through the door into the sunlight.

Hector was staring at them. "I'm old, but I ain't deaf. And yeah, I'm a mite touchy. These horses and those two old oxen are my charges. I take extra care of them. Like them better than most any person I've ever met. And I'll treat your horses the same, so rest easy on that score."

Chaw surprised Hector and Trace by apologizing and offering the old man his hand. Hector was startled, but he shook.

Trace stepped forward and offered his hand as well. "Me too," he said. "I never should have said that about the oxen. And as for horses and such, I reckon we both feel much the same about them. World's full of hard and odd folks, but any horses that are that way were made so because of folks, no fault of their own."

"Well, now," said Hector, offering the beginnings of a wry smile. "That's what I always say!"

Chaw and Trace were relieved to see that the old fellow appeared to have come around to cordiality with them. At least for the moment.

"Same with dogs, I've found. Used to have one, an old hound name of Pip. He'd been beat on something fierce every day of his life by an old drunk. Finally, the drunk died and Pip, he was half starved, as he had always been, when I come across him, he lifted a lip and tried to bite me when I offered him some meat, but he didn't have the heart to do it.

"Took a while, but I showed him plenty of kindness and he come around. Lived a good long while, too. Wasn't half as old as I thought he was when I first come on him. Just tired. About like I was when I started working for the widow and her husband, the count. But kinder folks you'd be hard-pressed to find. It's why I stayed."

Trace and Chaw both stood and listened to the man as he shared all this unexpected chatter with them. Finally, Trace broke the moment of silence. "You don't mind me asking, Hector, how did the count die?"

The old man glanced toward the depot, then turned and walked beyond, toward the stable. They followed. He stroked the long nose of a big workhorse, and the horse in the near stall stretched its head over for a scratch. Hector worked on them both and, without looking up, in a low, steady voice, he began speaking.

"If you two are going to stick around for any bit of time, there's something you ought to know. You're stepping into a boiling pot of soup, men." He looked at them, and they saw the hard, serious look on his face. It was alarming and sobering. But they moved in a little closer, as if his pause had beckoned them to do just that.

"The widow, she didn't tell you this, but not because she's shifty or some such, no, no! I'll take on any man who dares to say that in front of me. No, she didn't say anything about any of this because she's too kind. Always a hopeful sort, you see. It's the Irish peasant in her. Always wants to believe the best in folks. Much as I admire that trait, sometimes it don't get you to the meat of the matter."

"And that would be?" said Trace.

"I'm getting there, sonny. Don't crowd me!"

Trace nodded but said nothing. Chaw gave him a perturbed glance, as if he were fully on Hector's side now and could not believe that Trace could utter such a fool question. Trace was used to this from his pard, ignored him, and waited for the riled old rooster, Hector, to continue.

"Now, the other reason she didn't tell you what else is happening hereabouts is because she knows I will. I ain't big on secrets nor shadows. I like things out in the open."

He took a deep breath and licked his lips, then he tugged out a battered silver flask from the back pocket of his trousers and nibbled back a hit. Then he looked at them. "For my rheumatics. You two fellows ain't looking none too spry neither. Here." He handed over the flask and each man knocked back a swallow.

Once Hector had tucked his flask back in his pocket, he licked his lips again and said, "Sligo Star is being filched blind. Being bled dry, slow, to be sure, but it's happening. Having its pins gnawed away by what they call a consortium."

"What's that?" said Chaw, nearly breathless. He imagined some sort of terrible wasting disease afflicting the beautiful woman back up in the depot.

"It's a group of mine owners. But not the small operators, the men who own one or two claims, working them for all they're worth. No, it's a passel of big-time money folk from back East." He nodded in a rueful way.

"Oh, they don't want to kill Sligo Star, no, no! They want to take it over. Along with the mines, all of the little ones. See, they have men who work for them. Men who know all about the rocks and samples they've been collecting at the various test diggings. And they think the hills hereabouts," Hector nodded westward, toward the looming mountains, "are filled to brimming with gold. And what's more, they are right. So they've been trying to buy up the small claims and force out the men who own them. When those men don't move on, the big boys, they come in and work them over.

"Used to be they'd threaten them—steal a few things to make life hard for them. Then they brought in big brutes from cities to whomp on them. And that worked on a good many of them. Those miners who got worked over, they'd up and sell and scamper off in the night. But the ones who didn't give in, well, they'd get the next line of treatment."

"Let me guess," said Chaw. He dragged a finger across his throat.

Hector nodded. "Sure, you bet. A good many of them who held out woke up dead!"

"Are they all gone? The small miners, I mean," said Trace.

"No, that's the funny thing. Oh, a good many of them died in odd circumstances—cave-ins, rockslides, beatings, all unexplained, of course, and not traceable back to the consortium, not so you'd be able to pin on any one person, anyway. They been mighty careful about that. But yep, there's still a passel of miners who stuck to their guns, holed up at their places, a whole nest of them. Formed a consortium of their own, they did!"

Hector's eyes glowed with admiration for what was obvious to Chaw and Trace to be a bold effort on the part of the small-time miners.

"I reckon they figure they ain't got nothing left to lose, so they might as well give it their all, eh?" said Chaw, who was also nodding and rasping his hand across his bearded jaw, a sure sign to Trace that his pard, too, was mighty impressed with the holdouts.

"But all that was a while ago. Since then, it seems the consortium has backed off a bit. At least for a few months. The bullies and threats dwindled first. Then the beatings and such all but stopped. Despite that, or maybe because of it, the freighting trade hereabouts, which would be us, has skinnied down to a trickle."

"So, do you think the consortium has given up on the hills?" said Trace.

Hector snorted a laugh and shook his head. "I'll forgive you for being so green about the matter. Truth is, they are just regrouping. Of late, word's come down from the hills that a new bully, a killing sort and a serious one at that, has ridden on into the hills and is raising havoc up there."

"Who is he?" said Chaw.

"That's just the thing," said Hector. "Nobody's quite seen him. At least nobody who's still alive, that is."

"My word." Chaw rubbed his jaw even harder.

"That doesn't explain why there's nobody around to work for you and the widow."

"Well now, it just might. See, I think it's a combination of things. I think most men hereabouts are off digging for their own fortunes, sure, but they're also afraid to hire on."

"But we, on the other hand, are strangers," said Trace, shaking his head.

"Nope, not just strangers," said Chaw. "Dumb strangers."

Hector laughed again. "I prefer to think of you two gents as being in the right place at the right time."

"For you or for us?" said Trace with a grin.

"Too soon to tell!" Hector cackled again.

"How do you know all this, anyway?" said Chaw.

"Aw, see, the small miners don't dare leave their claims for long. Certainly not long enough to come to town for supplies. But they cover for one another, and a single man will trek on down, make quick runs, but on foot he can't lug much back for him and his fellows, in the way of vittles and such."

"Anybody else up there with them?" said Chaw.

Hector nodded. "Yep, and you asking that proves to me that you know something about mine camps. There's a few women and tots who come up with their menfolk to seek their fortunes."

"I bet they never thought they'd end up hunted and holing up like rabbits," said Trace.

"No, I'm sure not. But now look here, they got more spirit than that. They're fighting back, I tell you," said Hector. "They just need supplies!"

"And you think Sligo Star is the outfit for the job," said Chaw.

"I do. Sligo Star and you two men. Truth is, and I don't like to admit this, I am too old and gimpy to make runs into the hills." He leaned close and spoke. "Sometimes it's all I can do to get around here and tend to the beasts and such."

Chaw and Trace let all that information sink in for a spell. Then Trace said, "I assume that means that the consortium is responsible for the death of the Count Roscommon?"

Hector nodded and tapped the side of his old bony nose with an equally long bony finger. "Yeah, man. You guessed right. It happened, oh, some months ago. He was on his way back to Mankley from a run on his own. That wasn't unusual. He often helped out when our drivers was spread thin. And they was mighty thin at that point. But . . . oh, this ain't my story to tell just now!" The old man grew red in the face and he looked lost in thought for a few long moments.

Chaw scratched his beard. "I know what you said before, Hector, but it sure does sound like you are telling us that this here consortium wants to kill Sligo Star."

Hector grunted and shook his head, and from the doorway behind the men, the widow said, "Not necessarily, gentlemen. But then, Hector would have said the same."

Trace and Chaw spun, hands on the butts of their guns.

"I am pleased to see that you men are more than able to defend our property should you be ambushed."

They settled back, relaxing and wondering how she could have cat-footed up on them like that.

Hector said, "Not should they be, but when they are."

"It's getting that bad again, eh?" said Trace.

She walked in, carrying a small silver tray with four glasses of what looked to be whiskey on it. She held them up and each man took a glass. "I'm afraid so," she said.

"As for your previous question," she continued, "it ties into this one. The consortium doesn't want to kill Sligo Star, it wants to take it over. We control, or controlled, most of the freighting in and out of the mine camps in the hills hereabouts. Just now, as I'm sure Hector has explained, it seems we are in a bit of a lull. As if we're all awaiting the consortium's next move."

"And from what I've heard from my friends in the

hills, it ain't going to be pretty, nor legal, nor too long from now."

The widow nodded. "I will say, should business somehow pick up again—that is, if everyone can somehow come to terms with the money men from back East—there's room for another firm, certainly. And I wouldn't complain. We are, or were, far too busy most of the time."

"That sounds like a good problem to have for just about any business," said Trace.

She smiled but did not respond. Instead, she raised her glass and said, "Gentlemen, as Hector knows, I am a believer in signs, in portents—"

Chaw's brows drew together and Trace, too, had to think for a moment; then he leaned to his pard and whispered, "Signs."

"I know it! I know it!"

She smiled again at the interruption, then resumed: "It is good for business, yes, but it isn't good for all the people along the way and in the mine camps, who rely on us for supplies. But back to my toast—" She eyed the two new men, as if to say without saying it that she wanted no more interruptions. And they gave her none.

"I believe you two men were delivered to us here in Mankley as a response to my prayers for help during this trying time."

"Should have prayed harder . . ." muttered Hector, then giggled.

"Hector!" she said, directing a hard look at him. "Now, between the four of us, let us see if we can't get Sligo Star Freighting rolling hard once again!"

She and Hector slugged down their whiskey, and Trace and Chaw exchanged looks of concern. Just what did she mean by that? And just what was it they were getting themselves into?

They knocked back their drinks, and when everyone's breath had come back, Trace said, "Pardon me, ma'am, but, um, you said, 'rolling again.' Does that mean you aren't currently in operation at all?"

"Well, yes, technically that does mean that, yet. You see . . ." She looked toward the door, as if there might be someone out there listening.

This was the first time since meeting the dynamic Irishwoman, that she had seemed less sure of herself.

Hector cleared his throat. "My fault, you see, men. I nearly lost a load and . . ."

"No, Hector. I appreciate what you're trying to do, but that's not the truth. The truth is, gentlemen, that since my husband died—"

"Was killed!" growled Hector.

She went a bit white in the face, then said, "Very well, then. Since we're putting all our chips on the table, yes, we believe my dear husband, the Count Roscommon, died in a most unexpected and strange way."

"Ambushed, he was! We all know it, and the local law is useless, too! We all know it!" Hector's old, work-knobbed hands clenched tight in fists and his face was a shaking, raw thing.

"It's only right, really, that you know this," said the widow, rubbing a hand on Hector's arm. "After all, you may well be risking your own necks out there in the hills, and I don't want you to feel as though you weren't sufficiently warned.

"You see," she continued, "some years ago, this town was little more than a passing-through point; then someone inevitably ventured into the hills with a pick and a shovel. Before long, they found gold. It was the first of many such strikes, and now Mankley is as you see it."

"Bigger than we expected to find way out here, that's for certain," said Chaw, wishing she had brought her bottle with her. It was tasty whiskey, and he considered himself a bit of an expert in such matters.

She nodded and continued. "We turned up here because, as I mentioned earlier, my husband felt it to be a promising place to start a business. We were endowed with a modest amount of saved money and little else. And all this despite his family's misgivings about our marriage. They could neither revoke his title nor dissolve our marriage. To make those saved funds into something worthwhile and long-lasting, we—or rather he, as I knew little of such things—decided that a freighting outfit was just the business this growing area would need."

"And he was right!" yipped Hector.

"Indeed, he was. We began small and modestly, and within two years we had grown to a fleet of six wagons and twelve full-time teamsters, plus Hector, who kept the entire affair, along with my husband, rolling back here at the depot."

"I was too old and gimpy to drive a team for long,

but I still can if I need to!" Hector thumped his chest with a thumb and nodded.

"I worked as the office staff," said the widow. "And for a time it all came out as we had hoped. Business was good, and more and more miners flooded into the hills. We were able to arrange a contract with the train depot in Richness, Utah, over the mountains to the west, to receive and ship in goods. And we had intended to open an office in that town, too, in an effort to sort of have a start and finish to the routes, you see, but then the consortium moved in. Within a matter of weeks, and certainly months, everything seemed to change.

"My husband spent more time attending meetings with the representatives of these new claim owners. Really, they were and are just men with huge amounts of money from back East who come into regions like this and buy up as much land as they can. Then they set up massive mining operations and make all the small miners sell up to them. Then they enslave them and make them work for them for pennies. All the while, these unfortunate miners accrue so much debt in the company stores that they never are able to pay it back.

"They can't afford to leave the work, because they'll be arrested for nonpayment of debt, so they stay, stuck in jobs that slowly kill them, grind them into paste. And all for gold. What a sad waste."

"Is there no one who can stand up to them? The consortium folks, I mean," said Trace. "Hector mentioned there are still holdouts, miners who refused to sell and who have formed their own little consortium of sorts."

"It's true." She nodded. "They seem to be the only hope in this mad game. The consortium folks can afford to wait them out, though. And they're waiting us out, too. Meanwhile, the miners—even the ones with determined families—are beginning to starve, because every time we've tried a run, the consortium folks have crippled us. It's a mess, gentlemen."

She looked at her glass almost wistfully, as if she, too, were thinking the same thing Chaw had.

"What can we do about it, then, ma'am?" said Chaw. "I mean, we're happy to try, sure, but if things are as you say, won't the consortium folks try to put a stop to any goods we drag on up there?"

"They will try. But we have to as well. There are men up there fighting the good fight, gentlemen. And there are families up there, too, in Boarwallow Gap and beyond, with children and women who followed their men up there and now they're all stuck. The ironic part is that many of them are sitting on and still working claims that might well make them rich, but they have no way of letting the world know."

Trace rubbed his jaw and then made an odd sort of noise with his nose. Chaw knew what that meant—his pard was thinking deep thoughts and was fixing to speechify. And that nearly always meant trouble for them both. Chaw groaned and steeled himself for the inevitable.

"Ma'am," said Trace. "I have a question, well, two. They're, no doubt, the first of what I am certain will be a whole lot more. But let's start at the beginning. What makes you think the two of us can make any difference at all in what sounds like an awfully rough situation? And . . . you're sure there are no other drivers around?"

Hector jumped in. "The answer to the second question is as I told you earlier; those men all got scared off! Run like children, they did, out of town, up into the hills, working for the consortium, and a few of them have disappeared." He nodded gravely. "Along with two of our wagons and teams. And gear and goods, too!"

"Disappeared?" said Chaw, swallowing. "I reckon by that you mean they've been killed?"

"That is our assumption, yes," the widow said.

"My word, ma'am," said Chaw.

A long, quiet pause followed, and then Trace said, "Well, that is honest. I'll give you that."

"The ironic thing," she continued, "is that we have a warehouse full of goods, most of it paid for, that have been brought here at great expense by us and by others. The consortium does not seem aware of the fact that we are as well-stocked as we are, and I've tried to keep it that way. There are many folks who are waiting for those goods, but we have no way of getting them to them back in the hills."

"Again, ma'am, I guess what my pard asked is what I'm about to ask . . ." said Chaw. "All due respect, ma'am." He blushed and looked down.

She smiled. "You're right. I'm avoiding the question. I believe that the two of you gentlemen are the ones to help Hector and me save the business because, well, there is no one else. It truly is as simple as that, to be honest. We have no one else to whom we can turn."

"Tell 'em about the information we got! Tell them about the timetable!"

The widow nodded. "I was getting to that, Hector."

Trace and Chaw waited, eyebrows raised, to hear this information.

"He will not tell you this himself, but four days ago, and at great risk to himself, Hector returned from a scouting foray into the hills. He has set up a series of relay men to get messages up to and out of Boarwallow Gap. From here, the news we send them gets out into the smaller camps and single mines that are spread out all over up there. On this night, Hector returned and was waylaid by someone, isn't that right, Hector?"

The widow turned her pretty face on her hired man and friend. He scratched at his ear and pulled a pained face and looked up and down and cleared his throat and, eventually, red-faced, he nodded. "Like I said before, I am old and gimpy."

"Nonsense!" she said, directing a stern look at him. She shook her head and then looked once more at Chaw and Trace. "He is modest and silly. He was able to make it back here in one piece, and with the team and wagon and, most importantly, with his life."

"Who attacked you, then?" said Trace.

"That's just the thing!" said Hector, riled and warming to the topic. "It got late. Couldn't see much, but the team, they know their way. Besides, just a brace and a light work wagon. Managed to get some goods to them anyhow."

"Man alive," said Chaw, shaking his head. "Ain't there no justice in this town? I saw Mankley has a lawdog's office."

Hector made a spitting sound and turned away.

The widow leaned forward and lowered her voice. "What my friend is trying to say is that Mankley's lawdog, as you called him, Marshal Quimby, is . . . how to put this delicately? Well, he is, shall we say, more concerned with the affairs of the consortium than he should be."

"More concerned? Bah!" growled Hector. "He's a crook is what he is! As crooked as a dog's back leg!"

"How about sending for law from elsewhere? How about from back East?" said Trace.

Again, she and Hector shook their heads. "Oh, we tried that. My husband did, we have tried, others have tried, but nothing comes of it. You see, the consortium is backed by politicians and several of the wealthiest men in the country. They have a death grip on the law everywhere, it seems. I have sent several more wires out, but . . ." She shrugged and let her hands drop.

"Hmm," said Trace. Then he looked up and smiled and smacked his own hands together.

"Oh boy," said Chaw. "I know what that means."

"Well," said Hector, "I don't. And if it means this Trace fella thinks he's musical, he best think again."

"No," said Trace. "I can't carry a tune in a satchel. But I do say we had best get to work. If me and Chaw are the answer to your prayers, Widow Roscommon, then we had best live up to that lofty task. Eh, Chaw?"

"Sure thing, pard," said the buckskin-clad Southerner. But inside, his guts were rumbling. He sorely wished she'd break out the whiskey for one more round. Anything to distract him from what they were now facing.

CHAPTER 5

"You had best listen to me now, listen better than you have been. You got that? You should have gone when you had the chance. Now you don't have no more chances."

The man who spoke did so through the right side of his mouth, the left corner being filled with a thick, stubby cigar, unlit.

Here was a hard man, hard as the stone his current victim was used to pounding day after day with his hammer and rod, pick and shovel.

The man being held down looked up into his tormentor's face and saw narrowed eyes and that hard mouth pulled into a froglike grin. And that cigar jutting from the side of it.

"You . . . you're Cigar Tim!"

The thin lips parted, with the cigar staying put, and said, "That's what they tell me. Only way you'd know that is if I was fool enough to let one of you squatting beasts live. I reckon I won't make that mistake again."

The man on his back on the gravel of his claim was George Minty, a member of the Holdouts, as they called themselves. They were a group of men who had taken on that name because they were among the dwindling number of hard-rock diggers who were left, largely alone and scattered throughout the hills and ravines betwixt those hills.

They had persisted, despite the threats, and then the beatings, and now the killings. And still they held out against the consortium, the big-money men from back East, who by now were owners of the majority of the claims thereabouts.

The consortium also owned most of the rest of the mountains the small-time miners were familiar with thereabouts. Heck, the consortium even laid claim to tracts that nobody ever thought would be useful, much of it land that nobody was certain was even for sale. Then again, most whites figured that nobody really owned the land in the first place.

The closest you could come to naming owners of it all would be the Indian tribes, but they didn't really count because they didn't seem to place any dollar value on anything. Even the small-time miners agreed that the savage tribes could be vexing to deal with at times. So noted the earliest rock rats who scurried on out there as soon as the rich, sweet tang of gold had wafted into the air.

For all those little miners, it had been a long few years, but busy ones, too, and good ones. There were few rivalries in the early days, as each man staked his claim and worked like a gopher to pierce the sometimes brutal, knobby terrain.

Each was convinced of the fact that somewhere, sitting

like a glowing gift that had awaited him and only him for all those years of the earth's life, sat a vein—perhaps a chamber!—filled with the warm, honey-colored glow of ripe gold.

If one had the patience, pure gold was rumored to be everywhere thereabouts, thicker and sweeter than the less handsome but equally valuable ore, the bits and clots and veins locked in the rock that hosted it.

Yes, those early days had been brutally difficult ones but good ones. Days when they had each found just enough of a taste of gold on their individual claims to keep them excited and hopeful from day to day.

They had had whiskey at night to fuel their share of rampant dreams and strong coffee in the mornings to wash away the fuzziness of the prior evening's revelries before hoisting high their picks once more and sinking the tip into what each hoped would be a promising bonanza of a strike.

It mostly never worked out that way for any of them. Though it usually did happen that, at the moment when a man swore he was giving up and giving in, he would unearth just enough to keep him teased and dreaming. He would dig on, attacking the hard-won rock chunks of his latest pile for something, anything that might pay his way for a few more days, weeks, months. . . .

Those were the lifers, the true rock rats. And it would eventually occur to each of them long after it did to others of their acquaintance, peering in at them from the outside, shaking their heads at the oddness of it all, that they were doing this, living like this, for one reason—they liked it.

The true revelation that many of these tough miners came to was that yes, you bet, it would sure be nice to strike it big. But then what?

Would they really enjoy living in a fancy suite of rooms in the poshest hotel in Denver City? How long would the favors of the ladies and the finest wines and the tastiest meals and the fanciest togs feed their souls?

Each of these rock grubbers had come to know eventually that finery would be, well, fine for a spell. But then they would want to put a mighty distance between themselves and all that money, that filthy, life-thieving money. And then what?

Why, then they would return to the very thing that brought forth all that money. They would return to their claims to do it all over again. And they would not have it any other way.

Somehow, even though most of them never even got to the point where they were wealthy and living like sultans, each man knew that they would do that very thing.

And it was that feeling, that they were born to dig, born to tunnel, born to sluice and sift and sort, that offered them the only true solace they each had known. This knowledge was a balm unlike any other.

And it was that abiding belief that had carried them through, for good or ill. But it was these past couple of years that had been most decidedly ill. For that was when the consortium bloomed, right in their midst.

First it was the realization that claims were being bought up all about them by strangers, men who, as it turned out, didn't stick around to work them. Sure, some of it was good land with visual promise of color in the rocks. But much of it was useless, not good for anything except walking across to get to better, more promising land.

And then they noticed that their weaker friends had agreed to sell their claims to those same men who had come in in the night, men with clean duds and pink hands. Within months, the ones who had held out, who had refused to sell their claims, had begun to receive notes with no signatures. The notes were terse, warnings that hinted at dire consequences should they not take with all seriousness the offers to buy their claims.

Most of the men smirked and went back to digging. But then the notes began to be hand delivered by men, strangers who did not wear the nicest, fanciest duds anymore but the clothes of men who earned their money doing other things, such as molesting the lives of innocents.

And that was what these strange men had done. Oh, at first there were no fists thrown, no backhands, no shoves, nothing of the sort. But there were hard looks and harder words.

And then one day, Paco Stibane, a German-Mexican man who everybody on the first ridge past Boarwallow Gap knew well and liked, was found by his pal and nearest claim neighbor, George Minty, dead at his diggings.

It's not as if there hadn't been deaths here and there throughout the hills. Men who worked their hard days, day in and out, and often expired from exhaustion. Or from the heartsickness that makes folks lonely and a little crazy. All manner of natural reasons caused death in the diggings, but Paco's death was no natural occurrence. It was also no accident.

And so had begun the third wave of the nightmare that the consortium's presence in the hills had become. For them all. They had complained about these nefarious doings to the law, going so far as to send special notices signed by them all, in Mankley and in Richness, the two towns that flanked the mountain pass that led in and out of the diggings.

It had done no good. All the miners strongly suspected that the lawdogs in both towns were already wedged deep in the pockets of the consortium, paid for with promises of coming prosperity to each of their towns.

The man who had delivered the rounds of pummeling to Paco Stibane was that rascal with the cigar. He'd been seen afterward, bold as polished brass, lurking around the hills and casting hard glances at anyone daring enough to stick around once a man was beaten to death.

There were several of these strangers, but the one most of the Holdouts would recall was the cigar-chewing fellow. He was rarely seen smoking that cigar, but he surely did chew it. And he never seemed to be seen without it protruding from his hard mouth.

Of course, it wasn't the man's smoking habits that anyone found fault with. It was the deadly beatings he doled out that caused the trouble. The second of his bludgeoning victims happened to survive, at least long enough to tell his friend, a man who'd wandered over from a nearby claim that morning to beg a cup of coffee.

He'd revealed that his attacker was a cigar-chewing brute who called himself Cigar Tim.

The victim, a miner by the name of Kinsey, was dealt with harshly, and shared some of the same injuries as other of the cigar man's victims. His fingers were bashed with a rock hammer until the bones inside were pulped, the hands little more than swollen flesh bags covered in bruising and cuts and dripping with blood.

Each of the cigar man's victims were bound and gagged about the face, presumably before any of the wince-inducing beatings had taken place. That way none of the men on nearby claims would hear.

Sometimes a man's eye would be missing, having been plucked out by a probing, grubby finger. And two of the men had sacrificed tongues. The ragged stumps that remained inside their puckered mouths would never again taste food or water or whiskey, nor would they usher words of glee or anger or frustration or screams of agony.

Yes sir, they agreed: This cigar-chewing brute had much to answer for.

It was the day of his third victim's death, one Duff Crawford, a short, slight fellow everyone liked a whole lot, that the Holdouts was officially formed.

The remaining miners, a couple of dozen in all, had gathered at a central claim, that of George Minty, neighbor of the first victim, Paco. There they had in haste agreed to join forces and weapons to track the brute.

But then, that very night, the cigar-chewing man was joined by others, and since then the Holdouts had played a game of cat and mouse with this death squad. It was all too obvious that they were in the employ of the consortium, and that if they gave up now, they would perhaps save their lives, but they would lose their claims, which for many of them had long since proved to be their very reason to live.

Most of all, it was the thought of giving in to such unpleasant men that drove the Holdouts to form their group, to take to bunking in with one another, to stay armed while they worked, to patrol in small groups at nights. And still, once a week, it seemed, one of them would be missing or worse when they awoke.

They came to learn that the man's name, the worst of these newcomers, was called Cigar Tim. He was no-nonsense, a burly man with arms like lengths of stove wood and a plug of a body that seemed all muscle.

And now here he was, at long last, expected and thus his presence was not a particular surprise, though an unwelcome one at that, in the shanty that George Minty had built four years earlier on arriving at his claim.

Unlike a lot of his friends on the mountains rising above Boarwallow Gap, George had nobody back home, East or South or anywhere else. His family was long gone, and he had never married. George had just seen one of the other men, Rock Le Clerc, back to his own diggings and had made his way through the promising rays of the early morning back to his own claim.

He knew he should not feel that sense of false hopefulness solely because daylight had come once more to shine down on their claims. But somehow its warmth and brightness was comforting nonetheless.

He had even indulged in a quick, trilling whistle, hoping to entice the camp bird—maybe a jay—that he sometimes heard these past weeks in the trees below his claim. While he whistled, George poked at the dead embers of his cook fire and thought about what he was going to do that day.

It was to be a special day for him, nothing by way of earth moving. He'd done that the day before. Now he was set to explore a vein about a dozen feet into the hillside that he had noticed late in the afternoon of the day before, after he'd brought in his little tin oil lamp with the reflector shield.

It was a mighty little lamp that he used sparingly, as the oil was costly and had to be lugged in, as did everything, and supplies were getting mighty hard to come by since the consortium had entered their lives.

Mostly George used the lamp at night to read from the one book he owned, a collection of verse by someone named Whittier.

He had been reading and rereading that book for years, and in truth could only understand some of it. And yet the words, and how they were put together, gave him such pleasure that sometimes he spoke snatches of them aloud.

He had done just that the night before, feeling particularly gleeful, because the vein he'd seen from the light of the little lamp looked promising, as much as any had looked to him on this claim. He had nibbled a little of his precious store of whiskey and to the stars had recited some favored lines from the poem, "Snow-Bound: A Winter Idyl":

> *"The wind blew east; we heard the roar/*
> *Of Ocean on his wintry shore,/*
> *And felt the strong pulse throbbing there/*
> *Beat with low rhythm our inland air."*

George topped off the performance with another nip of whiskey, a bow, and then jammed the cork tight in the bottle and went to bed.

The next morning, as he bustled about camp, he gathered the scant items he'd need to cook up a spot of breakfast. He lifted free the small cast-iron fry pan and peeled back the scrap of old shirt he used to cover it. At certain times of the year, he had to set a scrap of planking over it, but only when the mice were sniffing their way back indoors after a long summer roving out and about, raising broods of young and whatnot.

George always did his best to keep critters from sullying and soiling his goods and gear and food without resorting to killing them, if he could help it. He had long ago figured that he was just another critter in the world, same as all the rest, no better and no worse. Why should he think he had the right to kill some other beast just because it annoyed or inconvenienced him?

He measured out just enough coffee to satisfy his taste for it. Usually, he would get a second or third pot out of the wet grounds from the day before, but he felt as though he should honor the special feeling the day had already taken on.

He sliced off three decent-sized slabs of smoked bacon from the dwindling lump of meat that, because of the cooler night air, was still keeping all right. Lastly, he popped open the tin in which he kept his oats and dumped a measure into the small pot he used to boil them.

With laden hands, he kneed open the shack door and made his way to his cook-fire pit.

It took him another few minutes to work his way through the well-practiced ritual of building and then setting flame to a fire. It began small, as always; then, as he added sticks and fluffy duff and larger sticks, the young, hot beast grew. Under his practiced hand, George soon had a usable fire ready to do his bidding.

He smiled as he adjusted the wood. And then he felt a tap on his right shoulder.

Even as he spun, he knew, in that eyeblink of time, George Minty knew who it was who had tapped him and what it meant. Still, he turned—what else could he do?—and looked up into the scowling, half-smiling face of Cigar Tim, and his guts jellied.

"That's right, fella. Your turn." Cigar Tim's right hand lashed out like a striking viper and struck George's cheek, whipping the miner's face to the side and knocking the crouched man on his back.

"You . . . Cigar Tim!"

His lips parted, though the cigar held firm. "That's what they tell me."

The brute said more things then, but George did

not seem to hear them. He was too frightened to do much of anything other than chase after the rabbit his mind had become. Around and around it ran inside his addled head.

George tried to stand, but he was on his back with his legs out in front of him, far too tricky to spring up. He jerked to his left, and his left forearm knocked against the handle of the fry pan. He kept going, working to regain his feet, all the while keeping an eye on the terror of a man who had descended on him without his hearing.

He cursed himself for humming and giving in to what had been a jovial feeling, the first time he'd felt that way in months, if he had to be honest about it. And now here he was, staring at Cigar Tim, the man he and all the other members of the Holdouts knew to be Paco's killer. And Kinsey's and Duff's.

The beating began in earnest then, one pummeling shot after another. George tried to fight back, tried to defend himself, but it was no good, no good. . . .

Then, after what felt like the better part of a hundred years of beatings, Cigar Tim was about to dole out what George, in his haggard, dazed fog knew would be the final shot, a death blow.

It might come in the form of a knife-gutting, might be a rock to the head, who knew? But George was incapacitated enough to know it would be delivered on him in mere moments. *And here I am*, he thought, *unable to do a cursed thing about it because he's about beaten out of me any ability I might have had to keep defending myself.*

George almost chuckled at that thought. *No kidding,*

he chided himself. *Isn't that the way all fights end up? With the loser too weak to defend himself and the winner standing over him, set to do the final, worst thing a man could do to another. And now here I am, the loser.*

And as George Minty looked up, through a wet, hazy scrim of blood and sweat, he saw Cigar Tim's face clearly. And that stocky, angry-eyed face leered down at him, that same parted-lip look, not quite a smile, not quite rage, with that nub of thick cigar jutting, albeit now saggy and raggedy-looking, from the side of his mouth.

The stocky brute raised something in his right hand, back, back, then George saw it for what it was— a three-foot-long cudgel, with a worn grip at the end. He held it in a meaty fist, and it widened, thickened at the far end, the darker end, stained with something—*blood*, he thought.

Oh no, the blood of all my friends, and now mine, too, will stain that wood. And who will be next?

As if summoned by that very thought, a whistling sound from the west edge of George's little clearing rang out. And it was drawing nearer with each hammering thud of George's heart.

It was Rufus, George just knew it. One of the miners from across the treed ravine. If the wind was right, sometimes George could hear the man singing, whistling, humming. He was a great one for always seeming chipper and cheerful. And he was a stalwart member of the Holdouts, always patrolling either alone or with another man.

For a moment, it seemed to George that Cigar Tim was not going to heed Rufus's presence, so intent did his gaze still seem on George's face. That odd look about the brute's mouth pulled wide into a leer, and George saw that the man was hesitating, his killing blow stayed by Rufus's shouts and crunching gravel footsteps and maybe even whistling.

Rufus was a great one for whistling. Had to be him. Who else whistled that he knew? Most men, in fact, but not like Rufus. Not so melodious, as if the man had swallowed a songbird each morning on waking.

Yes, Cigar Tim should already have delivered the crushing death blow with his brute, bloodstained cudgel by then. But something had stopped him. And it had to be Rufus's sounds.

Then George saw the man's other hand working at his waist. He was lifting that revolver free of his holster.

With all the strength George could muster, as if pulling the last of the juice that gave worth and muscle to a man, even as Cigar Tim yanked on that revolver, George yanked up on that deep-down strength within him. He yanked it all the way on upward, all the way from the toes at the ends of his legs, from his brutalized fingertips, from his pummeled guts, and even from the tips of the sweaty, bloodied hairs of his unkempt beard.

And George shouted, "Look out, Rufus!"

At the same time, two other things happened: the whistling and gravel-crunching stopped, and with whatever smidgin of strength was left to him, George rolled to his left. He knew it was not enough to get him away from the moment when the club connected with his hair and skin and, within, bones brittle under such a whistling, thundering, driving impact.

But he also knew he had to try.

"What's happening here? Hold, I say! Hold!" growled Rufus.

George, awed to find he was still alive, did his level best to continue shoving himself to the side, up onto his left shoulder and then over, and still he did not feel the cruel thudding of the cudgel hammering down at him from on high.

A shot cranked out, and tight with the sound came the snapping ping as the bullet ricocheted off rock.

George did not look up, did not question the new-found strength that had somehow, from somewhere, seeped into his limbs. He just kept squirming and clawing with his busted body, trying to get away from the killer, the man who had come to his little home in the rocks to do one thing, to kill him.

And the wreck of George's body would be left, mutilated and terrorized, to warn his fellow Holdouts to back off, pack up, and go away, before they, too, felt the sneaking wrath of Cigar Tim. Of the consortium.

But Rufus's glorious whistling had changed all that. The hope was slim that Cigar Tim might ignore him and take off after Rufus, who could sustain such a run, after all, reasoned George's frantic, confused, and frenzied thoughts.

His whistling neighbor still had two good legs and no bloody, broken bits to his body. Nothing wrong with him save for the usual aching muscles and shovel and pickax blisters and sore toes from rolling rocks and stinging dirt sweat in the eyes, all part of the work of a day for a miner.

No, Rufus had those mild, common ailments, to be sure, but he did not have smashed fingers and a bloodied head with wounds leaking into his eyes, and pummeled ribs and arms from kicks. And he might also have his rifle with him.

This thought heartened George as he scrambled, uncertain now if he was rolling or crawling, uncertain if he was moving away from the menacing presence of Cigar Tim or inching in his bewilderment ever closer to the devil's boots. But with Rufus distracting the demon, George felt a tiny flicker of the very thing he thought he had lost long minutes before. He had a slender thread of hope.

And he clung to it as if it were a robust rope lowered to him from on high and he had been swinging from the thinnest of ledges by fewer and fewer trembling, quivering fingertips, fewer of them with each passing moment.

But now he had hope. And it bloomed a pinch brighter as he heard that voice. Yes, it was unmistakably that of his neighbor and friend, Rufus, shouting, "You are not only a murderous pig, you are a lousy shot to boot!" Then Rufus followed this with a cackle.

George wondered if perhaps antagonizing Cigar Tim was the best thing that Rufus could be doing in that moment. And then he got his answer, for the killer shouted, "You won't be so bold when I plug you twixt the eyes, vermin!"

And Cigar Tim loosed another shot.

The sound of the gunshots or, more importantly, the absence of them before now, was another thing that George and his fellow Holdouts had thought to be to their advantage. They had thought that Cigar Tim had not fired a gun because he did not want to attract attention to his sneaking, slinking killings. And they were probably right.

But now George realized that Cigar Tim had broken his own rule. And then he felt a rock before him— a large one, he thought.

George dragged a throbbing hand across the matte of blood oozing down over his eyes. Yes, it was the flat-topped rock he often sat on when he cooked. In that moment, George made it his life's mission to get behind that rock. He felt at that freakish moment that if he could only put that big rock between himself and Cigar Tim, he might somehow survive, if only for a few minutes more.

Then he heard boots grinding on gravel, quick steps . . . drawing closer? George found himself pausing in his crawling, dragging efforts and cursed himself. *No, must keep moving.*

But the steps he heard were moving away. That must mean that Rufus was succeeding in drawing Cigar Tim away from George. Had to be that; a wonderful gift, the very best thing George could ever be given by a friend.

He teared up as he slumped slowly forward, guessing he looked like a beached fish who knew that all this air was not what it needed. That the thing it needed was but a foot away, down the mudbank. If only it could flop closer, closer, back to the water, before a killing hand snatched it up and smacked it against a rock.

George vowed in that moment to never kill a fish again. He swore one hundred other things, too, few of them he knew would make any sense to a man not knocking on that big, bolted door sealing Death in. He did not want to open that door. No, no, not yet, not yet.

George leaned against something. Yes, he thought it might be the rock, his settin' rock, as he called it, but he could not be certain. Nothing was certain anymore.

That was George Minty's last thought before his grip slipped from whatever scrim of wakefulness he'd been clinging to.

But Rufus was wide, wide awake and feeling particularly fine. He even giggled as he realized he had succeeded in what he'd tried to do—lead that vicious brute Cigar Tim on a merry lark of a run through the stunty, sparse trees and rocks of the ravine between his and George's claims.

And he knew where he would lead the man, if he could keep him interested. And he thought he knew how—by insulting the plug of a beast. Keep him riled and angry and he'd follow Rufus anywhere. At least that was his hope.

So far, it was working.

"Where are you, you cigar-eating fool? Why are you so slow, man?" Rufus paused, keeping low, his trusty rifle on half cock, held crosswise before his chest, ready to swing. The weapon was a well-used thing with a repaired stock. He'd broken it himself, in a tumble down a slope in these very hills. A sloppy overhang had given way when he'd foolishly stepped too close to an edge to spy on a small clot of mule deer milling below.

At the bottom, he'd found himself with a shirt and trousers filled with gravel, eyes caked with sand and dust, a rifle with a split stock, and no sign of deer.

That had been during his first week in the hills, when he'd thought he might not be there more than a month anyway, so confident had he been in his claim's unexploited riches.

Then he'd tumbled, and by then the claim had not yet yielded anything more than curious black rocks with purple crystals, things he set aside for consideration later. Just then he had been far more concerned with finding ore laced with precious gold.

But he needed game for the fry pan. And so the rifle was a necessity. He had the one, and no other gun. As Rufus had looked down on his wrecked rifle, he had wondered how on earth he was going to fix it to make it useful once more. For he realized that it was a tool for making meat as the other men called shooting game, nothing more.

But he had prevailed. All that was in the long past, and now here he was, on a fine morning, paying his nearest neighbor, George Minty, a visit. George was a funny fellow who always seemed a pinch skittish. But he was all right, a backwoods gent, true and true.

Rufus paused, listening for that cigar-eating beast, but heard nothing. But that meant little. He was no longer a greenhorn to the wilderness. He also knew enough to know he did not know much. And he tried to apply that logic to his current situation. What would he do if he were a murderous gent? He would wait out Rufus, that's what.

And so that's what Rufus did—holding low there, with his rifle held ready and scarcely breathing. He hoped that Cigar Tim hadn't seen where he'd ducked down. Any second now one of them had to make a move. He held there a while, but Rufus just knew he did not have the patience to wait out the man.

He crabwalked forward, embracing a jut of sandstone with his knees to help keep him from toppling over from this awkward pose. With all the caution he could muster, Rufus moved his head forward, closer, closer to the rounded edge of the boulder. Another inch, another one, and he knew he was tickling into the territory when he'd be seen by the waiting Cigar Tim.

Then the man shouted, "Where you at, filth?"

The sound of Tim's voice, closer than he expected to hear it, told Rufus that Cigar Tim had not turned, but he might be making his way back down to George's camp. But probably not, thought Rufus, until he figured he had finished with Rufus.

Now is my chance, thought Rufus. The man all but told him he didn't know where Rufus was. He could spring up, assured he knew the rough location of Cigar Tim.

But what if Cigar Tim, too, was hidden behind a rock? No man was dumb enough to leave himself wide open.

"Tell me this, you cigar-eating fool, are you too poor to afford decent cigars? Yours always seem to be falling apart. Maybe it's because you are a drooling fellow!"

That's what it took, for in that moment, the killer sent over another bullet. It whistled and smacked rock but did not sound off with that tense-as-wire sound that ricocheting bullets left behind.

Rufus didn't know what that meant, nor did he care. He knew now where that verminous creature was. And Rufus was intent on crabwalking farther, thinking he would soon, within moments, see Tim's bulk. He began to creep, craning his neck forward, when he heard a shout from above, up the hill.

"What's the shooting down there?"

The voice sounded to Rufus as if yet another of the Holdouts was closing in. Then he heard two, perhaps three voices, taking small pains to keep their chatter low, conversing.

It was a welcome sound to him, and he pulled back, tense, wondering if Cigar Tim was at that moment sneaking up behind him. He jerked his gaze quickly around to check—nothing there but more rock.

Stop it, Rufus, he told himself, jerking his head back to watchfulness. *You're a fool and a half.* But what if he was there? He might well be anywhere, in fact. After all, he had been able to sneak into and out of camps, kill, and then disappear as if he was a ghost, all without being seen. Most of the time.

Rufus knew Cigar Tim was no ghost, but he didn't want to risk anything by being hasty in his judgments. He heard the voices from above again.

It was some of the other Holdouts, had to be. Which ones, he didn't much care. He held tight there a few more moments, then decided that, since the voices were unlikely to be friends of Cigar Tim, he'd best let them know he was down here.

"It's me, Rufus!"

The response was quick: "You hurt, Ruf?"

It was Slattery, a moody fellow but no fan of the consortium, and a good man to have on your side when your chips were all but cashed. "I'm okay! Cigar Tim is close by! Somebody get to George, nearly killed him!"

Rufus heard nothing for a breathing moment, then boot steps stomping on gravel, over rock, and away, eastward, covering, he bet, the short distance to George's claim.

"You to my right of the rock, Ruf? Wave your hat, but keep low, if yes."

Rufus nodded to himself, then did as Slattery bade. He made certain he kept any such visual commotion he might make with his hat low and tight and quick. He waved his battered felt topper quickly, as if he were shooing horseflies close by his head.

"Got it, Ruf!" And with no more warning than that, Slattery delivered one, then two shots to the other side of the big boulder behind which Rufus crouched.

Rufus winced as the shots spanged off rock, whizzing and whining away. He heard no yelps of pain, so he guessed that Cigar Tim was likely good and gone. The man didn't get to be known as a ghost of a character by sticking around when the fire was hotting up.

Soon, Slattery, with his usual devil-may-care attitude, emerged from behind the array of scrub pines and rabbitbrush upslope and clambered down the rocky, scree-addled slide.

"You okay then, Rufus?"

"Yes," said Rufus, still not convinced standing up and exposing himself was the wisest choice he might make at that moment. But there was Slattery and, just behind him, like a puppy, was Howell.

Rufus stood, trying to eye everywhere all at once.

"You look like a scairt owl!" barked Slattery with a grin.

Rufus ignored him. He knew that the bombastic fellow didn't like that, so it pleased him to be able to do so.

"I expect we run him off," said Howell, also looking about himself with wide eyes.

"Sure," said Rufus. "Have to get back to George." He made for his chum's shack, leaving Slattery and Howell to fall in line behind him.

"I sent Jones thataway!" said Slattery from behind.

"Good!" Rufus answered but didn't slow his pace. He'd heard no further shots from ahead, at George's, so he stood that as a good sign.

When he drew within sight of George's small clearing, he slowed up, looking all about him once again. It would not do to be sitting birds in the bowl of a clearing, just ripe for Cigar Tim to pick off once they all waddled on in.

He turned to Slattery and Howell. "Might be better if you two patrol the outer edge of the camp. We still don't know where that rascal got to."

"Nor will we," said Slattery. "Waste of time at this point."

"No, it's not," said Rufus, annoyed that the fool was so belligerent. "We might yet be able to find trace of him."

Slattery shoved past him. "You go right ahead. I'm going to tend to my friend."

"Friend?" said Rufus in a low voice, looking at Howell. "Since when did Slattery give a care about George or anybody other than himself?"

"Oh, he ain't all that bad," said Howell, shrugging as he always did when deep in deference to the gruff Slattery.

Rufus kept his peace and sighed. "Might as well see if I can find some trace, some clue as to where Cigar Tim comes and goes from. Or at least where he did so today. You want to help? Take that left side, up and over the back side of George's cabin, and I'll cover the downhill and side slopes."

But Howell didn't move, although he kept looking past Rufus toward the camp proper beyond the fringe of brush between them and George's home place.

Rufus knew that Slattery was most likely correct and that sniffing around would like as not turn up no Cigar Tim. But what would it hurt to try?

Halfway down the trail that skirted the campsite, Rufus heard a crack and a groan. He seized in place, uncertain for the moment where the sound came from.

Were they holding Cigar Tim or was he still on the loose, darting from cover to cover, intent on shooting them all?

Rufus ducked and swayed left to right, eyeing the terrain. He didn't have much to hide behind, but that didn't mean he had to stand there like a fool and get shot.

A moment later, Rufus heard from ahead, southeastward and downslope, a clatter and then the quick thundering away of a man on horseback, no doubt fleeing the little valley. Had to be the killer.

Rufus gulped, inched his way up, and scouted, eyeing the terrain once more. And still, he saw no one. He sighed and resumed his task, continuing to poke along the trail he intended, looking for sign of the man.

"What are you doing, man?"

It was Slattery, shouting down at him from George's site, up above. "How's George?" said Rufus, once more ignoring the annoying man's fool question.

"He'll live, but he's beat up sore and bad," said Howell, striding downslope, his shotgun cradled in his left arm.

"What was that shot?" said Rufus.

Howell walked over, shoving a path through a thick clot of rabbitbrush that he could have just as easily walked around. Rufus had known the man for a year and a half and he'd not seen him do one thing that wasn't either condoned by Slattery beforehand or that wasn't just plain odd and usually resulted in making more work for himself.

"That was me," said the blushing man, coming up close and still not looking around himself.

How on earth did this prize turkey make it this far in life? "Well, why did you shoot, Howell?"

"That was a warning shot. Slattery said it'd be a good idea. Him and Jones, they was tending to George, and I didn't see how I could be helpful to them—"

"I asked you to help me and patrol that top rim above George's clearing, in case there was any sign left by Cigar Tim."

Howell looked at Rufus. "You ain't my boss, Ruf."

Rufus sighed. "I know that, Howell. And I don't want to be. I am just trying to keep us all safe and not congested in one spot, paying attention and not acting like sitting ducks."

"Yeah, well," Howell turned. "I expect Slattery knows what he's doing."

Rufus watched him walk back upslope to George's camp and mumbled to himself, "I expect he thinks he knows what he's doing. Not the same thing at all."

As Rufus walked, he wondered how long before the Sligo Star folks would be able to make it back up this way, if they were able to at all. And that fleeting thought led to another that he and every other Holdout had hovering in his mind all day and all night, in one form or another, there with every task they undertook, over and over without cease.

Rufus wondered if holding out against such a mighty group was even worth the effort. He wondered how long before he and the rest of them, all the other Holdouts sprinkled throughout these hills, were forced to kill.

And would that killing, even if it happened to be in defense of their property, or more to the point their very lives, be viewed as unjustified by the bought-and-paid-for law in these parts. And, for all he knew, all over the country. He didn't doubt that the law did or soon would regard the Holdouts as outlaws. Should be the other way around, he mused. But it wasn't, and wouldn't be.

Rufus sighed once more and resumed his search for clues. After this, he'd head downslope and investigate where that rascal had his horse hidden, see what he could find down thataway.

He'd check on George soon enough. At least the man was alive and, as annoying as Slattery was, he did have knowledge of medicinals and such. But Rufus knew that, as George's nearest neighbor, he'd have the lion's share of the task of taking care of George while he mended.

If the man's injuries were beyond their abilities to tend, it might be that poor George would have to make his way down out of the hills—only if he was able to travel. But where to go? Mankley? Surely not, especially with that lawman Quimby. And DeFontaine was no better in Richness. What a mess.

Rufus roved on through the rest of his investigation, ending downslope where Cigar Tim had obviously had his mount tied in a stand of scruffy aspen. Marking the spot was a mound of fresh dung, and boot prints were mixed in with the hoofprints in the gravel and dust about the base of the scraggly trees he'd tied the horse in.

Rufus legged it back upslope to George's camp and, as he guessed, was greeted with Slattery's scowl and a hard remark. "Took you long enough."

"Hush your mouth, Slattery. I take that sort of tongue from no man." It was the first time Rufus had spoken words to the annoying fellow that he truly meant. And he was surprised at the reaction.

"All right, all right, take her easy. I didn't mean anything by it."

Slattery didn't look at him, though. In fact, Rufus noted that the man's ears had reddened. He glanced at

Jones and Howell and they both looked at him with wide eyes. Howell wasn't impressed and looked as if he were trying to be hurt for Slattery.

Jones, however, was smirking.

With reluctance, Rufus leaned his rifle against a rock within reach of himself and began tidying up the mess of a cooking area. As he did so he mused on Jones.

Normally a quiet fellow, when Jones did speak, he offered something of value to a conversation. He was also the only one among them who had had any decent luck in turning up ample bits of ore of worth on his claim.

They all had found color, to be sure, enough to let them know that gold was likely just waiting to be found in the rock all about them. But it was Jones who'd had the biggest success unearthing the vexing, tempting stuff in any quantity. So far.

Instead of growing frustrated and splashing out for a second and third claim and doing a poor and superficial job at all of them, Jones had stuck to the one and, it seemed to Rufus, through dedication to his task, and raw, hard work, the quiet fellow had made it pay for him.

Rufus wasn't certain to what extent it had paid, but it had leaked out to them all now and again that Jones had been adding to a bank account somewhere, and at a steady if slow rate.

Jones lived on work and determination, it seemed, whereas most of the rest of them pinned their hopes on luck and a stream of what-if scenarios in their heads.

Rufus genuinely liked Jones and regretted that their claims weren't closer, enough so that he might visit with him now and again. Although he did not know if Jones would be amenable to evening chats.

George, as an amiable and quick-to-chuckle fellow, was a good replacement for such visits, however, and Rufus counted himself lucky to have him. *Could have been worse*, he thought. *I could have ended up with Slattery across the way*. He suppressed a wry grin and continued tidying up George's cooking area.

The man's bacon had been trod upon, and what looked to be mush was stomped into a sandy, gravelly paste. *Curse that Cigar Tim*, thought Rufus. He knew just what he was doing, though. With each day that passed, they were all harder for food than they were the day before. It was only going to get worse in the coming weeks if they continued to hold out against the big boys.

But Rufus, as with the other Holdouts, felt as if something big was about to happen. Something that would change everything. But what? And when? And when it happened, whatever it was, what on earth were they all going to do?

CHAPTER 6

"Who's that?" The man nodded ahead, and the remaining men turned their heads in the same direction.

All shifted their gazes back, but the new man and another new fellow, who'd showed up with the bold speaker, all looked back at the two newcomers.

"You kidding me?" said one of those looking at them. "That there's your new boss. Heck, if you don't know that, I am surprised you are still drawing breath on your own."

"What's that supposed to mean?"

"Means you have to have been funning, because I don't believe I ever met a soul in this world who don't know who Dade Wilks is."

"That's Dade Wilks?" said the newcomer.

"Sure enough is."

"Huh. He don't look like much."

This time his pard, the other newcomer, said, "Nelson, will you leave it?" He spoke in a quiet voice, nearly a whisper.

"Your pard here has the right idea, Nelson. Dade

Wilks is the kind of fellow you'd do best to get on the good side of and keep there."

Nelson snorted. "Why should I? Me and Petey here, we're pretty good at what we do, too. Seems like there's a whole lot of bowing and scraping for no reason."

Nelson was a thin little whip-quick man with a smile that was equally quick to appear and vanish but not connected to anything. His eyes were flat black, soulless, and narrowed much of the time in a squint of mistrust.

Petey, standing beside Nelson, closed his eyes and offered to anyone looking at him a slight shake of his head. He might well be Nelson's trail partner, but he was not in agreement with the man. Several of the other men noted this.

By then, the object of their attention, one Dade Wilks, walked on up. He was a medium-height man, oiled hair the shade of worn leather was visible beneath the curved, fawn-colored brim of a spotless tall-crown hat. His face was clean—shaven and his gray eyes smiled along with his mouth. His suit was of a dark blue cloth, neatly pressed with thin black lines running up and down and a black string tie jostled as he walked.

His boots were black, pointed toe, and shined as if they had just been brought in from a cleansing rain. He carried used but well-oiled brown leather saddlebags draped over his left arm, and his right hand gripped a carpetbag that looked to have a solid heft.

"Hello, boys!" he said. "How you been keeping?" He nodded to each, saying the names of the six familiar to him as he looked each square in the eye.

His gaze then roved over to the two who were

strangers. He settled on them, and while the smile remained on his mouth, his eyes took on an undecided coolness. He nodded and without taking his eyes from them addressed one of the others. "Chauncey, you going to introduce me to your new friends?"

The man to whom he spoke, the same who had told Nelson who Wilks was, nodded and began to speak but was cut off by Nelson, who stepped forward, arms crossed over his chest as if he were hugging himself.

"Mr. Wilks," he said, "I'm Nelson. And this here," he moved his head slightly to the left but did not shift his gaze from Wilks, "is my pard, Petey."

"Well, nice to meet you, Nelson. And Petey." Wilks nodded to them both.

"Now, I got some questions for you, Wilks," said Nelson.

Dade Wilks's smile remained in place. "Fair enough, but before I answer them," he held up a silencing hand between them because Nelson was about to interrupt him. "As I was saying, before I answer your questions, I have a rule that if pards looking for work show up together, I talk with them separately. You understand, it's just the way I do things." He smiled and nodded and glanced beyond the man to Chauncey.

"Chaunce, what say you lead Mr. Nelson here next door. Buy him a beer while I talk with his chum."

"You bet, boss," said a smiling Chauncey. He was a tall man, taller than Nelson by a head and a half. He draped an arm around the newcomer's shoulders. "Come on. Let's make for the bar and enjoy a glass of cool beer while we wait. Won't take long."

"Well, all right, then," said Nelson, puffing a bit and leading the way, even though he wasn't certain of the direction.

"Well," said Wilks after they'd gone. "Now that that foolishness is done with, let's get down to business." He paused and looked at Petey. "Can I assume you want to be included in these proceedings going forward? If not, well, I am happy to have one of the boys escort you on back to the alley of your choice."

Dade looked for a long, quiet moment at Petey, whose return stare was nothing but wide-eyed and close to trembling.

Finally, Petey began to speak. His voice cracked and he swallowed, then said, "No sir. I mean, yes sir. I'm in. I . . . me and Nelson, we wasn't what you'd call chums."

Wilks nodded and his gaze softened. "I get you. All right, then, Petey. Just one thing and one thing only that you have to keep in mind. You choose to ride with us, then that's it and all about it. Got me?"

"Yes sir, Mr. Wilks."

Wilks smiled. "Dade's good enough, Petey. Now," he turned back to the others, "where was I? Oh yes, getting down to business. I will start at the start. I met with the man from the consortium, back in Ohio. It was interesting, I tell you. Every time I meet one of these back East, citified folk, I thank my stars I spend my time out here where a man can breathe and claim his own, then work for it.

"Which is ironic." He winked at them. "Considering we have been hired to run a passel of men off of their claims on behalf of the consortium. And just in case any of you are curious, I have been told that the consortium has tried everything they know how to get these men to leave, including offering to pay them, in some cases, four, five, six times what they paid for their claims in the first place."

Wilks waited for the men to respond with the expected nods, then said, "That's right. A fine and generous deal. And a good many of them took it. But the ones they really needed to take are holdouts. In fact, that's what they are calling themselves, these scattered rogues. The Holdouts. Imagine that? But they think they know what they're doing, because it's their claims that are the key to the entire thing working out for the consortium.

"I bet I know what you all are wondering. Because I was, too. Why, with all the big money these consortium men have—and we're talking some of the biggest money men you'll read about in the newspapers—why are they so concerned with some paltry claims out there on some mountains in the West?"

Wilks nodded and continued his slow pacing back and forth before them. "Because a year and more ago, they sent a handful of scientists out there to investigate and retrieve ore samples. What they found, apparently, told the consortium folks that there was the potential for the biggest gold haul ever found, right there in that spur of the Wasatch Range.

"Their representative told me that the consortium already owns most of the land around it, including all the hills and two nearby mountains. *Just in case*, he said. Imagine that? Just in case. But out of all that, it's that handful of Holdouts who are causing everything to grind to a stop."

"Why's that, Dade?" said a stick-thin man with a drawn brow.

"Well, I'll tell you. Near as I can make out, it's pretty simple, really. Apparently, those claims sit smack on the only true way in or out of those hills. The only way they can move freight in and out, the whole thing, without blasting away half a range to get in there. Which the consortium is willing to do, but first they want to exhaust, as the man told me, every possible way of ousting those Holdouts."

Wilks sighed. "So it's going to be a battle between us and these half-starved miners. But make no mistake, they're mangy and desperate and hard as the rock they dig.

"Now, as you know, I don't normally agree to take on work such as this, but I figure we can use plenty of tactics that they haven't been able to try. And we'll be acting on behalf of our employers, the consortium. Yes sir, I reckon there's a lot we can do and still stay on the good side of the law." Wilks looked at them and winked.

The expected reply was a chorus of knowing chuckles.

"And as you know, the good side means whatever side Dade Wilks and his boys choose to set on." Wilks let his eyes rest a moment longer on the new man, Petey, who offered a weak smile and chuckle when he saw the boss eyeing him.

Wilks nodded and resumed pacing. "So our task, then, is to drive out the Holdouts by first pinching off the supply line, which is, I have been told, already in a weakened state. It's a gambit that's been tried already and has been somewhat effective. But a local freighting outfit is making noises about starting up again. It operates from Mankley, a town right to the east side of the range. It's a freighting firm called Sligo Star. And hear this—it's run by a woman."

This was met by his men with subtle noises of surprise.

Wilks nodded. "Apparently, she's a comely thing, but hard as an anvil. Well, this dove hasn't met Dade Wilks." His quiet tone told them this wasn't a moment for chuckles.

"Her husband died in a most mysterious way, so says the consortium fellow. Curious, too, that this happened while the consortium had in their employ a fellow you all are familiar with: Cigar Tim."

At that, the six original members of Wilks's mercenary band all reacted as he knew they would. Cigar Tim was a former member of their gang, one of the few to ever leave their tight group while still breathing. They had all assumed he'd been killed while they were on a job out in Wyoming Territory, his body unrecovered.

But it had vexed Dade Wilks to learn, some months after the job, that not only was Cigar Tim alive, but he was in the same line of work as Wilks and the boys. He'd been hiring himself out to various folks: ranchers, timber and railroad barons, and such. And worst of all insults, he'd been undercutting Wilks and his fees, yet using his past association with the gang as his selling trait.

Wilks did not like this one bit, as he had always considered himself a more than fair employer. This was backed up by the fact that he rarely heard complaints from the boys. And when he did, he addressed them, one way or another.

"And recently, it seems that Cigar Tim has returned to working for them and has been doling out a hard time to the very folks we are hired to do that to. Thing is, the consortium fellow swears he fired ol' Cigar Tim. So that leaves us with a double task, I expect. We have to deal with the Holdouts and we have to deal with Cigar Tim. I'll fill you all in on the particulars once we're on the trail and making our way out there. Should be a three-, four-day ride."

Wilks turned that squinty, half-smiling look on the lot of them, letting his gaze rove over them, left to right. "Any questions, boys?"

Nobody peeped, so Wilks reached into his trouser pocket, lifted out a thick wad of cash, and peeled off a few notes for each man, handing them out. "A last night before we set to work. You know what to do." He paused as he handed money to Petey. "By that I mean you have yourself a good time, Petey. But not too good—we ride in the morning, after a big breakfast. All right?"

"Yes, yes sir. Mr. Wi—ah, Dade."

"Good. Now have at it."

As the men filed out, smiling and pocketing their cash, Wilks held one back with a hand to the man's chest. He waited for the rest to leave, then said, "Chauncey, keep a close eye on that new fellow, Petey.

He's . . ." Wilks looked at his second-in-command. "Well, how would you describe him, Chaunce?"

The man to whom he spoke, taller and lean, with a close, neat beard and dark, glinting eyes, looked at the open door through which the boys had walked, as if he could still see them. "I'd say he's a rabbit, Dade."

Wilks nodded. "Good. That's just what I was thinking, too. And in my experience, rabbits can be wily and are good runners, traits that could be useful. But rabbits can also be skittish, maybe even too nerved-up for their own good. Liable to run at the wrong time, if you read me."

Chauncey nodded. "I do. And I expect he's worried about his old pard, that Nelson."

"Mmm," said Wilks. "You sent him on his way, though, right?"

"I did indeed. A one-way trip. Where he's traveling there's no return tickets."

"Good deal. Appreciate it, Chauncey."

"My pleasure, Dade. Fellow like that, why, I'll tell you, he kind of reminded me of Cigar Tim."

Wilks's jaw muscle flexed and he nodded. "That's what I was thinking as soon as he started yammering at me." They both stood like that for a few silent moments, then Wilks said, "Well, at least one of them won't be causing us any headaches any time soon. Now we just have to find Cigar Tim and make it a double."

"I hear that," said Chauncey, following his boss out of the room and into the cool night air.

CHAPTER 7

"Sooner we get on the trail, the sooner we get back here." Chaw grinned and nodded, as if he'd uttered something for them all to chew on. When nobody spoke, he said, "It's talk like that that makes folks think you are smarter than you are."

"No," said Trace, grasping the ears of another bulging burlap sack and swinging it up onto his shoulder. "It's talk like that," he grunted as the sack seated itself on his shoulder, "that makes folks think you're an idiot."

"You best take that back, you raw Yank."

"Can't," said Trace, staggering under the load.

"What do you mean, you can't?" said Chaw. "They're words; you can always take them back!"

"Nope. Once they're out and running across the floor, all you can do is wish them well and then work on more."

It took the two men nearly two hours to load the big work wagon while Hector selected the four-horse team that would be doing the work of hauling the load. He finally led out of the paddock two big, brute pulling horses.

"Part Percheron, part tree," said Trace, winking at Hector so the little gimpy old man wouldn't take offense.

On the contrary, Hector looked to have taken it as a compliment. "They are like children to me," he said. "Better than the ungrateful whelps I raised for years after their mama died on me."

"Didn't know you had children," said Chaw.

"Why would you?" said Hector, eyeing which post he was going to hitch the horses to. "We've only known each other for a few days."

"That's true," said Trace, impressed, but a little shocked, too, by the man's abruptness.

"I bet there are a whole lot of things I don't know about you," said Hector, smiling. It was his way, guessed Trace, of emphasizing the obvious. "When will you two be done loading up? Seems to me you'll want to be away as early as possible."

Chaw was the one up on the loading dock, handing down the goods Trace, who was in the wagon, arranged and rearranged, muttering as to how they might ever get all those goods into the wagon.

Early on they'd worked together, lugging sacks and crates and kegs from out of the dark depths of the warehouse. Now they were mounded up, and both men were busy with their respective roles. Each wondered the same thing: Had they hauled out too much from the warehouse? They were all the goods the widow had told them to bring on out there. But there was no way it was all going to fit in the wagon.

"I thought you two had experience with freighting?" said a woman's voice. They both looked up to see the

Widow Roscommon standing, unsmiling, with her arms folded and a pencil stuck in a bun on top of her dark, pulled-back, mounded hair.

"Well . . ." said Chaw, immediately feeling weak-kneed once again before this beautiful woman. She could be wearing sackcloth and have bones stuck in her hair and he'd still think she was a rare and stunning creature.

Trace felt much the same, but he also had enough mental capacity about him to know that Chaw was about to ramble and run on at the mouth and reveal that their combined efforts at freighting were, while not altogether nonexistent, was fairly thin on the ground.

He cleared his throat. "Ma'am." He nodded. "We have experience freighting, yes indeed. It's just that—"

Hector cleared his throat. "I never did show them where I keep the sideboards, Widow. But I will now. Thanks for reminding me."

This seemed to satisfy her because her facial features softened. "Oh, well, all right then. I figured you'd be loaded by now and ready to depart. It's best to get an early jump on hauls. At least to get to Boarwallow with plenty of daylight should you experience any, ah, problems."

She eyed them all a moment longer, then turned and went back to looking at the papers in her hand as she walked back toward the door that led to her office.

When she was well out of sight and hopefully also hearing, Trace said, "Thanks, Hector. Now, are you telling me you add sideboards to this load?"

"Sure we do." He smiled. "Four horses, after all."

"Ah, right. Okay, then. Where are they at? We'll fetch them."

Hector tied off the two big horses to a rail that appeared flimsy enough to fall over if anybody looked at it too long, let alone having two massive pulling horses lashed to it. But the big geldings stayed put, settling into a standing doze pose, hipshot and with eyes half closed, ears flicking at the occasional bluebottle fly.

"Follow me, behind the far end of the stable. Under that overhang. I'm too old to go hauling those things around, but you two brutes can have at them. Should be enough side and endboards for three wagons there. Choose the best. Hopefully we won't have to do any repairs to them."

Trace and Chaw did as the old man bade them and found that all but one sideboard and all the endboards were in perfectly acceptable, usable condition. They hauled out what they needed and cuffed off curls of puckered paint and flakes of rust from the iron-forged hardware.

Hector showed them how to position them along the sides and front and back of the wagons such that the hardware interlocked.

"Ingenious," said Trace, smiling at the simplicity of it. And then he realized they were not even halfway through loading the wagon. "Best get to it, Chaw," he said, nodding toward the mounded goods on the dock.

"Tell you what, since we are about two days ahead of schedule anyway, and since it's going to be well into the afternoon before you get this loaded up and double-tarped and lashed down, I think we ought to hold off and you gents can depart first thing in the morning."

"That's kind of you to think of us," said Trace.

Chaw nodded, relieved, as he had not been excited about the thought that they would be making for parts unknown—steep, hilly parts—and driving a four-horse team, to boot, while exhausted physically and with but a few hours of daylight before them.

"Bah!" said Hector, coaxing the big gentle team of horses back to the stable for the rest of the day. "Wasn't thinking of your comfort, you big fool."

He smacked the near horse gently along the shoulder. "Thinking of my boys. It'll be bad enough to send them out with you two, knowing as I do that you don't have all that much experience driving teams."

Both men tried to protest, but the old man shook his head as he walked away. "I knew it as soon as I saw your eyes when I showed you the horses. You both looked like two nerved-up farm boys who lied to your schoolmaster."

All that night, one or both of the men was awake, staring up at the plank ceiling, between the puckered boards at the layers of other boards atop. Each knew without conferring with his pard that they would be up well before dawn, would not want much in the way of breakfast food, but would prefer to eat later, on the trail as they rolled.

They reckoned they would ask Hector where they might find bread and such in the village in the morning. They also realized they should have considered this the night before. They hadn't put any thought into outfitting themselves with food for the trail.

They had, however, studied a crude but decent map given to them by the Widow Roscommon, of the route that led from Mankley to Boarwallow Gap and then onward, all the way to Richness. Once there, they were expected, in four days' time, to retrieve yet more goods, this time for a few small claims along a more southerly route that would, in time, lead them back to Mankley.

When they could not contain themselves any longer, they arose, as if by mutual consent, from their narrow but decent bunks in the small room by the stable. Within ten minutes of them lighting the lantern there was a knock on the door. It was Hector.

"The widow wants to see you. I'll get started hitching the team while you two go see what she wants from you."

"How about if one of us goes and the other can stay to help you?" said Trace.

"How about you do as I'm telling you, and what the widow told me to tell you?" The old man shook his head. "Sheesh-a-boy, what a pair."

Chastened, Chaw and Trace made for the loading dock and saw that the widow's office light was on. They knocked and heard her voice: "Enter."

They expected to see her from the lamplit office to the right, but instead her voice beckoned from deeper in, to the left. They had suspected that was where her living quarters were. "Come on in," she said through an open door.

They walked in and were surprised to see a well-appointed room, with a cookstove against the far wall and a braided rug on the shiny wood floor. A polished trestle table dominated the center of the room.

She nodded. "Have a seat, men. Coffee is just about ready."

They removed their hats, looked at each other, and then gently sat down on the trestle bench.

She regarded them as she set down before them large stoneware mugs of steaming black coffee. "You don't honestly think I was going to send you on a run without a decent meal in your bellies, now did you? Eggs and bacon and bread will work for you both, I assume?"

"Yes, ma'am," they said together, nodding and sipping.

"What about Hector?" said Trace.

"What about him?" said the widow. "Oh, you mean for coffee and breakfast. Yes, he'll be in momentarily."

"But he's hitching up the team."

"No, he's not. He always says he's going to do that, threatening to behave as if he's twenty and not far older than that. But he knows better, and so do I. He'll give up on it in a moment and come on in, grumbling that something or other was not done to his satisfaction and so he'll need help from you two to make it right. You can tend to it after breakfast."

As if on cue, they heard a stomping and a scuffing and a muttering as the old man approached the door. He walked straight on in, not caring that he might be walking in on a conversation.

"Ornery critters! No sense in their big heads. They are feeling their oats this morning, I'll tell you! Gonna need help from you two goobers to get them hitched good and proper." He plunked down in a chair that looked as if it might be a regular spot for him at meals. "And I don't want to spend all day in here, neither. You drivers are all the same, stuffing your faces while the rest of us work our fingers to the nub!"

Trace exchanged a glance with Chaw and they both shrugged. Then they caught the widow's eye and saw she was smiling and shaking her head. "Every morning, same thing," she said.

Hector mumbled something else and then shut up and, with his eyes all but closed, seemed to stare ahead at nothing atop the table, a look on his face that was halfway between a scowl and a doze.

"Hector is a little bear without his coffee, isn't that right, Hector?"

"Huh? Oh, now look, Widow. I'm a busy man. I . . ." His words trailed off as he watched her bring over a big mug of steaming black coffee. She set it before him and he looked as if he'd been told he was going to live a long, pain-free life filled with riches and happiness.

The old man sipped from the cup and let out a long, low sigh, sounding not unlike a pressure valve on a steam engine releasing, a sound men make the world over.

For the next half hour, the men enjoyed a fine if oddly quiet breakfast. It turned out that the widow, in addition to being a most handsome creature, was also one amazing cook. Trace knew that Chaw would, later on, mention to him how very tasty that breakfast had been. Over and over.

Chaw Dagworth was nothing if not appreciative of food, and especially so of well-prepared food. He could ruminate on it for quite a spell, mused Trace, and frequently it was not something that Trace cared to listen to over and over.

But in this case, he felt sure he could tolerate it, for the woman had prepared a toothsome breakfast complete with thick, sizzling bacon, copious eggs, flapjacks with some sort of sugary syrup for drizzle atop them— tasty, but not maple, mused Trace as he thought of breakfasts with maple syrup of his youth—fried potato slices, thick slabs of crusty bread, baked beans, stewed carrots, and to top it off, more coffee with wedges of sweetened, buttered corn bread.

She kept urging them to eat their fill, so they did, particularly Chaw, and the Widow Roscommon seemed to take great delight in plying him with more food. Finally, even Chaw had to beg off on another round, although Trace knew it pained the Reb to do so.

"Can't, ma'am. Not that I don't want to keep on indulging in your fine vittles. This was a meal for the memory book, it was."

Once they had all pushed back and belched with discretion a time or three, the widow said, "Now I don't want you gentlemen to think that this is a daily occurrence. But I thought with you being new to Sligo Star and all, we would send you off on today's run with full bellies. No, from now on it's just coffee and eggs and bacon and beans and such. Oh, and toasted bread. And sometimes muffins."

"Yes, ma'am," Trace and Chaw each said, both

wondering what sort of lucky puddle they had fallen in to deserve such treatment.

"And don't forget to check in before you leave. I'll have a hamper filled for you so that you won't have to stop during the day to prepare meals on the trail."

Both men knew, however, that they would most certainly stop, if at all possible, for fresh, hot coffee, a treat neither of them would care to give up.

They then made their way back outdoors to the waiting horses. The coming dawn had just begun to purple the sky's far eastern rim as they set down their lanterns along the edge of the loading dock, alongside which sat the loaded and tight-tarped wagon.

It took them another fifteen minutes to harness the teams and rig. By then, the widow had emerged onto the loading dock, lugging a wicker basket that she quickly explained contained a good amount of cooked foodstuff, including slabs of cheese, bread, dried apple rings, and more.

They rolled on out of the back lot with nary a squawk or a squeak as Hector had well-tended the hubs and axles of the wagon.

The most important piece of gear they carried, apart from the needed supplies and goods, were their guns and the maps. There were three maps. The widow brought them out and unrolled them on the edge of the loading dock, lanterns pinning the corners from curling inward.

"This," she tapped the topmost map and dragged her long, slender finger along the obvious route westward from Mankley, "is where we are. And this"—she tapped again, quite some distance along the page—"is where the first and largest shipment goes."

She nodded at the old man. "Hector tells me it was all loaded per my request, layered with the last items at the bottom for the other settlers along the road to Richness. Once you get there, you'll present this receipt for lading at the depot there. I don't need to tell you that there may well be trouble along the way, although, and who knows the reason, the consortium folks have backed away of late. We can only hope they have changed their minds about ruining peoples' lives."

Hector snorted. "Yeah, well, I wouldn't go counting on them laying low for much longer."

"I know," she said. "I was just giving voice to hope. Did you hear from any of the Holdouts, Hector?"

"Yeah, I did. Last night. Tip," Hector looked at Chaw and Trace. "He's a townsman, but he risks his neck going in and out of the hills. Works for booze. Anyway, Tip rode in well after dark to tell me he heard that the consortium folks were planning something big. No idea when nor what else that might mean."

Trace nodded. "Okay," he said.

What he wanted to say was that the information was all but useless, but he figured that might offend them. Still, it would serve to keep them on their toes even more so than they had been planning to be.

Finally, after a few more minutes of such chatter, they rolled on out of town. In an effort to somewhat conceal their movements, they cut wide to the north, before angling southwestward back toward the far western end of Mankley's main street, well past the last dwindling of buildings.

Both men agreed this was a waste of time as it seemed nigh on impossible, given the plodding pace of the team and the big, laden load they were piloting, for them to leave town unnoticed.

At the western edge of town were a couple of homes and, side by side, a smithy and a wheelwright. Which made good sense, given the fact that the wheelwright needed a blacksmith to do some of his work, namely rims and hubs and such.

"Gonna be a long one," said Chaw, breaking the silence.

"Yep." Trace had handled the lines first, setting a decent but not unsustainable pace for the four big beasts.

He was amazed at how nimble the sizable horses were, keeping a decent pace and not giving in to what Trace had assumed he and Chaw would be fighting, in the form of fatigue and boredom of the horses. But, he reminded himself, it was early in the going yet. Very early. That said, the beasts seemed perfectly matched to the task and pulled the work wagon with seeming ease.

Three hours into their journey toward Boarwallow Gap found Chaw commandeering the big team, every now and then offering the four big horses gentle clucks and kissing sounds.

Trace had to admit that although the horses responded to his efforts, there was something about those hands of his pard that put the team at full ease while still working hard up grades or down declines. He reckoned it was that unspoken something that was a vital ingredient in a relationship between men and horses. Some had it, some did not.

They'd been at it for forty minutes since their last stop, and Trace said, "Up ahead, according to this map—oh, another half a fingertip's width—there's a stream. There's a note somebody wrote here that says it's a good place to water the team."

"Might also be a good place for us to—"

"Brew a pot of coffee?" said Trace with a smile. They were cut of the same cloth when it came to enjoying coffee. Frequent cups of it when possible, and the stronger the better.

"You bet."

They rode on in silence, relieved thus far to find that the route had been while not flat at least relatively kind to the horses. The rough terrain, they saw ahead, was coming and would fill their afternoon.

"Think we'll make it to Boarwallow Gap before dark?"

"Nope," said Trace. "But then again, the widow and Hector said we wouldn't. And they've both been on this route."

Chaw looked over at his pard. "The widow has?"

Trace nodded, pleased that he had information Chaw did not. He would tease out the relating of it. "Yep, it's true. She and Hector made a big run themselves not long ago. Before this consortium business heated up, as near as I can figure."

"Huh," said Chaw. "She's game enough, I would say that anyway. But I'll tell you, she just bumped up even higher in my regard."

"Mine too," said Trace. "Say, you didn't happen to talk over wages with her, did you?"

"Naw," said Chaw. "I was curious, but I didn't know quite how to bring it up, particularly since she treated us so well."

"Yeah," said Trace. "And it's not like we are the most seasoned freighters out here."

"Maybe we are," said Chaw.

Trace nodded. "After all, who else do you see?" He waved an arm wide, taking in the rolling country about them.

"Okay, not the most seasoned, but for sure the dumbest." Chaw guffawed and let the lines lightly tickle the big, broad muscled backs of the horses. "That map tell you how much farther along we have to roll to get to the first best place to stop for the night?"

It was information that Chaw could easily have gained for himself once they had stopped at the watering place ahead, but he was feeling jovial and a mite chatty. It was a trait Trace did not always share, and frequently Chaw found himself having to supply both sides of a conversation just to keep himself awake and amused on the trail.

Trace, however, when he was in a rare foul mood, would call this one-man chatter a "needless perfuming of the air," and Chaw had to admit the surly Yank was right.

"Yes," said Trace. "It looks to be . . . if our progress these past few hours is a fair estimation . . . that it will take us another three, four hours to get to the first marked camp spot."

Chaw groaned lightly. The wagon seat, while covered with a thick, straw-ticked pad, had begun to numb his backside. He had begun to squirm and had taken to standing in the boot well now and again. He expected that by day's end he'd be standing full time and rubbing his sore behind with a free hand.

"Could be worse," said Trace, guessing his pard's thoughts. "We could be them," he said, nodding at the horses.

"No, thank you," said Chaw, pulling a grimace and wide eyes.

CHAPTER 8

They made it to the first place on the map that Trace thought might be a good choice to water the horses, at least according to the distance marked on the map. It turned out that the distance they still had to cover took longer than they expected.

By the time they arrived at the watering spot, which turned out to be a rocky creek, the hoped for ample flow, at this time of year, was more of a half-hearted trickle, although robust enough to form pools and pockets.

Still, it was enough to water the team in one of two pools that showed no signs of brackishness. Indeed, Chaw, whose sniffer was a sensitive thing, claimed with finality and conviction enough in his tone that the water was "good enough to not give us the gut flusters." Trace had learned to trust his pard's opinion in these matters, given his experience in traveling with the picky Rebel these long past few years.

The landscape thereabouts, which had risen at a steady clip as they traveled deeper into the bigger foothills, had forced them toward a cleft in the distance, above and beyond where they were now.

"I see why they both told us it would take longer than we think."

"Yeah," said Chaw, fighting with a surly clasp on the chain that held the gear box closed. The box, secured on the right side of the wagon between the front and rear wheels, was a wide affair. It was as deep, front to back, as a man's forearm, and it contained two shelves, on which were securely nested cooking pots and pans, a coffeepot, tinder, implements, and foodstuffs.

The box on the other side of the wagon also held useful items for the drivers, including three tarpaulins of varying sizes, along with rope enough to help set up camps during rain- and snowstorms.

Along with those there were a hatchet and a camp ax nested in the back of the box behind the neatly folded and coiled tarpaulins and ropes. The hatchet and ax were well tended, with the steel oiled to prevent rusting.

What Chaw was after, however, were various campfire tools and gewgaws, as he kept mumbling.

Trace assumed the man meant pots and pans and such. As he walked by with a harness over one shoulder, he said, "You have to move that big thumb of yours, then you can pull the top open. Ingenious devices, those boxes."

"You just run along or I'll give you an ingenious device!" Chaw held up his big fist and wagged it. He knew that Trace, who did indeed saunter off with a smirk on his face, said that sort of thing to get him all worked up. And it worked, every cursed time.

"You're just riled because I drew the long straw. You

have to set up the campfire and get the coffee brewing while I get to dally with the team."

"You know I'd rather do what you're doing and you'd rather do what I'm doing. Always been that way! But no, you got to be a hardhead about it."

"Yep," said Trace, now taking no pains to disguise his grin. It was a fine late afternoon and they had made good progress, at least according to the map and given that they were unfamiliar with the route.

They also hadn't encountered any blockages on the road such as cave-ins, landslides, washouts, or boulders or trees laid across the path. They had made it to a decent campsite with water, the horses weren't lame, and Chaw was surly. It was a good day.

"Don't know why you're so blamed chipper," muttered Chaw, crouched down and wheezing into the poorly built clot of tinder and duff he'd erected to begin the fire.

Trace had wanted to tell him he'd be better off had he not layered a handful of sticks over the top just yet. Feed them in one at a time as the tinder began to catch and small flames began to lick upward. But he'd held his tongue because he'd said it a number of times in the past and the effect on his pard, while amusing, was something that tended to make him sputter and growl for hours, and Trace was feeling too fine just then to endure that.

He resumed his task of tending the horses. He'd picketed them and was leading them down to the water one at a time for a drink. It was a far easier solution than hauling water to them in the two canvas buckets they also carried on the wagon.

He glanced back up the slope at the camp and saw smoke rising in a steady if thin cloud from beyond the wagon, so he knew Chaw had succeeded in getting the tinder to take. That was always the trickiest part for Chaw. After that, Trace knew, they'd have coffee before too long.

He glanced at the wagon, and remembered he wanted to check that the load was secure, that the tarpaulins were snug, and the ropes were tight and the knots weren't developing minds of their own and trying to loosen themselves.

As the horse drank its fill, Trace ruminated on this freighting business they had hooked up with. He glanced up at the wagon again. There was no lettering there, nothing but the well-tended but faded green-painted planking on the sides.

This would not distinguish it from any other such wagon. And that was precisely the point, as he had been told by Hector when he'd asked why the wagon did not wear the Sligo Star Freighting company's name on the side.

"Seems obvious to me, young fella," he'd said. "Why draw attention to ourselves? Not in these foul times in the hills hereabouts. No sir."

Of course, once Hector said this it was all too obvious, Trace had reddened a bit. He liked to think he was a savvy fellow and not one who missed the nose on his face because he was over- or underthinking a thing. But there it was, he mused as the horse raised its muzzle a last time, water drizzling back down into the gentle flow.

That was when he noticed that the horse had canted its ears forward and was swinging its head back toward the trail eastward, from where they'd traveled.

"What's of interest there, boy?" Trace rubbed the neck of the big, gentle, muscled brute and followed its gaze with his own. The trail, just before it widened and eased to their right and into the site where they were now encamped, had dipped down a bit. That was why Trace couldn't see too far in that direction.

Was someone else coming along? It seemed unlikely, and yet a horse had keen hearing, and Trace had learned through long years of spending much time with the animals to trust their innocent curiosity. They also displayed an unerring instinct for recognizing trouble that was about to deliver itself onto them.

He and Chaw had been tipped off more than a few times to impending woes by paying attention to their mounts, particularly in wooded regions where there were "rascals and rogues and ne'er-do-wells," as Chaw swore that his gran used to say.

Trace realized that if the old girl had been responsible for everything Chaw said she'd proclaimed or done that she would never have had time to sleep. But Trace wasn't about to question Chaw on the topic of the Reb's prized granny.

Trace clicked his tongue and led the big, still-curious horse on up the slight slope back to the others. He still had two beasts to water, but they would wait. He wanted to get back to camp and tip off Chaw, should there be somebody approaching.

They'd heard nothing too good about lots of the folks rolling and riding in and out of these hills, so it was a gamble as to whether whoever it was would be good folks or ill-intended.

He tied up the horse and noted quickly that the other three were too tired to have heard much just yet. They stood hipshot and barely acknowledged the fourth horse's return.

Trace strode to the campfire, alongside which Chaw was still crouched, this time sniffing the newly steaming coffeepot. "You're about on time, for once." The buckskin-clad fellow rubbed his horned hands together. "Got a fine pot of mud about to bubble."

"Good to hear. Hey, Chaw . . ." Trace said this and waited.

Chaw looked up. "Huh?"

Trace indicated past the wagon, eastward with his chin, then leaned to his right and laid a hand on the shotgun still leaning in the boot well. "Might be someone coming."

That was all Chaw needed to hear. He stood upright and took in hand the offered shotgun. Each man also wore a sidearm and a big hip knife, their usual gear when in rough country.

"You see 'em?"

Trace shook his head, squinting in that direction. "Not yet, but the horse was mighty curious."

Chaw held up a big hand to silence him, then whispered, "I heard something. Horseshoe on stone. Somebody's coming, and closing in." He cocked his head to the right. "Single rider, I think."

They both knew that although neither really had hearing abilities superior to the other, Chaw liked to claim he was gifted with "hill hearing," an enhanced ability he attributed to having grown up in the hills of his youth, of running behind baying hounds treeing raccoons.

Within seconds, Trace heard the sound of an approaching horse. If the rider was looking to keep quiet, he was doing a poor job of it.

Without turning, in a low voice, Chaw said, "You reckon whoever it might be was following us?"

Trace shrugged, also keeping his gaze on the eastward trail. "No idea. We did pass a few feeder trails coming down from the north."

Chaw nodded. "Well, we'll see. Any minute now."

As the rider drew closer, they heard the telltale signs of hooves stepping hard and a horse breathing—that last stretch was a bit of an incline—and then saddle leather creaking. And then there appeared a horse, a black mount with a wide white blaze on its forehead.

The rider emerged shortly thereafter, and it seemed his gaze was already on them before he even crested the rise. He never slowed nor increased his pace. He let the horse continue on in its own time and fashion, the mark of a seasoned rider. Presently they drew up alongside them, although still on the trail.

The stranger gentled the reins and the horse halted; despite its obvious tiredness from the climb it perked its ears toward their horses' pickets back to Trace's right and off behind the camp.

The man was, they saw, a medium-height fellow but stout, wearing a black, slope-crown hat and dark, well-tended clothes. He wore a double-gun rig and had a rifle in a saddle scabbard. His face was clean-shaven, ruddy, and he held a cigar in his mouth, tucked to the left.

He puffed up a blue cloud; then, without taking the cigar from his lips, he nodded and smiled around it. "Good day to you, men."

Chaw nodded, then, as Trace knew he would do, his pard looked to his right, let loose a stream of chaw juice, ran an index finger across his lips, not that the man ever dribbled—he was the tidiest spitter Trace had ever come across—and all without taking his eyes from the newcomer.

Trace offered a slight smile and a nod. "How do."

All three men sat and stood that way for a few long moments, none of them feeling particularly awkward about it. After all, in each of their experiences, this was what men did on first meetings—they eyed each other up and down.

It came to them as from instinct. Bears did it, wolves did it, cockerels, and on and on. The males of the species, each man understood without knowing nor particularly caring why, behaved thus, and that's all there was to it.

At last, the newcomer shifted in his saddle. "Coffee smells mighty fine."

"Oh, heck!" Chaw spun and ambled back to the fire, all his attention directed to the now sizzling sides of the coffeepot as the bubbling coffee sputtered out the spout and drizzled down the sides of the battered gray enamel pot.

"No worries!" said Chaw, not glancing over as he snatched up the steel bail, shifting the coffeepot with a charred leather scrap from the cook box. It was something used many times by many men and likely a few women—or at least one that they knew of—to keep fingers from blistering.

Trace kept an eye on the man, but they exchanged quick, wry, knowing grins at the suddenness of Chaw's change in demeanor. Trace knew it was because where coffee was concerned, all other concerns halted until the bold brew was safely dealt with. He treated each new potful as if it were a newborn bairn.

"I see your partner thinks as much of his coffee as I do," said the cigar-smoking stranger.

Trace nodded, a tension in the meeting having been overcome. "He does like a cup or three, that's certain."

"Indeed I do," said Chaw, perking up from behind. "And seeing as how you saved that potful from being ruined, I reckon that earns you a cup, stranger."

The man on horseback nodded. "That's kind of you. I will take you up on that offer, even though it could be said my arrival is what caused the coffeepot to be overlooked in the first place."

"True!" said Chaw. "But then again, nobody forced me to ignore it."

"All right," said Trace. "This could go on all day and I need a cup of that coffee, even if you two don't."

The stranger nodded ahead of himself. "That a good spot to water my horse?"

"Yep," said Trace.

"Good. I'll do that first, then walk on up and share coffee with you gents, if that's all right."

"Just right," said Chaw, now well warmed to the man. "Bring a cup if you got one."

"Will do," said the stranger without looking back, already riding toward the watering spot.

As Trace and Chaw waited at the fire—and still armed and glancing—for the man, Trace said, "Chaw."

"Huh?"

"Keep sharp."

"Aww, he seems all right. . . ." Then the big buckskin-clad man saw something in his pard's look. "You getting that gut feeling of yours?"

Trace shrugged, then nodded. "We're already on our guard, not a bad thing. But it doesn't hurt to stay good and tight."

Chaw didn't say anything, but he nodded. He was familiar with Trace's gut feelings he got about folks. As with so many others, often when they met someone new, the shrewd Yankee was able, somehow, to know before knowing, that a newcomer in their midst would turn out to be trouble.

Often it resulted in little more than hot words. But sometimes it went further than that, and they had both been aware and ready, armed and able to fend off any furtherance of festering rage.

Neither man spoke more as Chaw poured out their two cups of coffee and set them on rocks to cool off a moment. They awaited the stranger's return to the campsite, each man continuing to keep a weapon at hand should they need to shift from guarded cordiality to a defensive pose.

The man walked along within minutes, leading his horse back up the slope. Both his hands were visible and neither held a gun. One held the reins and the other held the tag end of the same reins. They saw once more that his parted coat revealed that double-gun rig.

The cigar, now little more than a stub, remained in his mouth, but it appeared to have gone out. "Men," he said, nodding at them and offering a seemingly cordial smile as he tied his reins to the handy near wagon wheel.

He ran a hand along the horse's neck, down the saddle, and then to a saddlebag, where he unbuckled it and lifted the flap.

Trace and Chaw kept their hands free, Chaw's fingers close to his revolver, his shotgun having been leaned against a boulder close by. Trace's rifle remained in the crook of an arm, but positioned such that he could swing it up quickly.

The stranger turned, cup in hand and a smile on his face. "Found it." He blew in it, then ran a thick finger around its innards. Then he plucked the sodden cigar stub from his mouth and flicked it into the fire ring.

Trace and Chaw noticed that the man's lips seemed not to want to close back into a normal shape but remained parted, as if waiting for a fresh cigar. The man did not yet oblige.

When all three men were once more equally spaced

apart and sipping, eyeing one another over the cup rims, a mutual unspoken agreement to ease off a pinch came to them all.

The stranger smacked his lips. "This is a bold cup of coffee, and I thank you for it. I like my coffee hot and strong."

"Coincidence," said Trace, sipping. "That's how he likes his women." He gave a sideways nod toward Chaw.

The stranger grinned. "Can't argue with that, neither. So, from the looks of things," he gestured toward the wagon, "I'd guess you two were freighting goods into the hills?"

"That could be said, yeah," said Chaw, not wanting to commit to an affirmative response.

The stranger nodded. "I get you. None of my concern, anyway." He sipped. "I was to hazard a guess, I'd say you was freighting goods to those vermin holed up in the hills around Boarwallow Gap. I'd also guess you're from Sligo Star Freighters."

Neither Trace nor Chaw said a thing, but they continued to sip and eye the man, who did not seem to want to meet their gaze.

Finally Trace broke the silence. "You called them 'vermin.'"

"I did," said the stranger, nodding.

"Why?"

That seemed to catch the man by surprise. He reached in his vest, and Trace and Chaw tensed, ready. The man smiled slightly and pulled out a fresh, finger-thick black cigar the length of two fingers. "Either of you fellas like one?"

Both declined, but mumbled, "Thanks just the same."

He took his time in setting fire to the thing. Then he coaxed a fresh cloud of blue-black smoke to billow upward about him. Finally, he spoke around the thing, its presence only slightly altering his speech. "I called them vermin because that's what they are. Call a thing by its name and you'll not go far wrong in life. That's my thinking."

"But what makes you regard them as vermin?" said Trace.

"Why, the way they're squatting on land that's not theirs. They're holding up progress. My employers are not impressed. Got big plans for these hills, they have, and they can't do a thing until those vermin are all taken care of."

"I assume your employers are the consortium," said Trace, risking sharing a bit more knowledge.

That Trace knew the name of his employer did not appear to surprise the stranger. "Sure they are. And they are not amused by the vermin, or by folks helping them to keep up their foolish, warring ways."

The sideways reference to the fact that they were freighting in goods to the Holdouts was not lost on Trace and Chaw, but they ignored the comment.

"Sounds like a legal matter to me," said Chaw.

"Oh it is, it is!" The man nodded and sipped his coffee. "Trouble is, those vermin won't listen to reason, legal or otherwise. Seem to think the gold under their feet is theirs."

"Isn't it?" said Chaw. "I mean, we heard that those claims are theirs bought and paid for."

"Oh you did, did you?" said the man. "Well, I don't know who you been talking to, well, actually I can guess, but I can tell you that those vermin don't have a legal right to do a thing up there anymore. If they ever did."

Chaw grunted, and Trace gave him a quick *simmer down* glance.

All three men sipped their coffee in quiet for a few more moments. They finished pretty much at the same time, the cigar-smoking stranger having held his cup high and drained it, as if he were desperate to chase down that last drop.

Chaw offered him a refill, but the man refused. "Got to make it deeper on into the hills."

Neither Chaw nor Trace were about to say anything. The last thing they wanted to hear was that the man intended to camp nearby. Although their site was obviously a spot used by others with some amount of frequency, the fact that they arrived first did not give them the exclusive rights to camp there.

It was, however, common courtesy for latecomers who intended to also camp there to instead camp nearby or move on altogether. All in all, there were no guarantees on the trail that privacy was a sure thing.

The stranger stuffed the cup back into his saddlebag, buckled it up, then untied his horse and led it around to the far trail side of the wagon. Chaw and Trace rounded the other end.

"Well, gents," said the man after he'd mounted up, "I appreciate the coffee. I really do. Sometimes a cup of coffee is just the thing, you know? That and a cigar." He smiled and puffed up a big cloud. "Next time our trails cross, I'll return the favor."

"What makes you think we'll bump into you again?"

"Oh, I reckon you will. My work will keep me roving these hills. And from what I see, so will yours."

With that, he expelled another blue-gray cloud and with a two-fingered salute off the brim of his hat, he turned the horse and guided it back onto the path. They watched him as he departed. He was gone long before the last of the smoke trail he'd left behind also faded away.

"What do you make of that?"

Trace shook his head. "That, my friend, was the enemy."

"Part of 'em, anyways." Chaw turned away and returned to the fire. "You think we got anything to worry about with him?"

Trace kept his gaze on the westward trail for a few silent moments, then said, "Nah, I think we're good. As the man said, we'll cross paths again, but not today. He's still figuring us out."

"Me too. Him, I mean," said Chaw. "Fancy calling those folks *vermin*." Chaw looked up from prodding the coals to life once more. "Hey, you don't think there's anything to his side of things, do you?"

Trace shook his head. "Nope. I trust Hector and the widow a whole lot more than I do that cigar-chewer."

CHAPTER 9

The men rose before dawn the next day, as was their custom when hired out to do the bidding of others. Neither man wished to incur the reputation that they were laggards, even though there was many a morning they wished they could sleep in. These sentiments were usually precipitated by a big night before filled with whiskey and women and song.

Also, as was their custom, and even though Chaw was prone to being a chatty fellow, they went about their morning chores almost out of habit and in near silence.

Each man flopped back his blankets, stretched, groaned, yawned, then tugged on his boots by the dog-ear flaps. Then they stood, scratched, and ambled, braces flapping, off away from camp to make water behind a boulder or half hidden by brush or trees.

Whoever made it back to the campsite first was tasked with coaxing the covered coals back to life. Soon, a fresh pot of coffee was set out to cook up. It always took longer than they liked, but there was plenty to do in the interim that needed doing sooner or later.

The horses received attention next and were led one

at a time down to the water. Being encamped at a source of fresh, clean water was a real luxury, and one they did not take lightly. Nor, it seemed, did the beasts, and since they were used to making such runs into the hills, they no doubt were filling up for a long day on increasingly harsher and steeper trails.

They each were fed a special corn, oat, and molasses blend that Hector had come up with for his beloved charges. Indeed, Chaw and Trace had talked a little about Hector's trembling lower lip and openly tearful reaction to their departure.

Trace and Chaw had promised the old man, and the widow, too, that they would take no unnecessary chances with the load, the wagon, or the horses. Once they had been rolling well away from Mankley, they realized it was the horses and their well-being, their very lives, that most mattered. At least to Hector.

"We had best return these horses in better-than-new condition to Hector," said Trace, eyeing Chaw early that morning of their departure. Chaw understood and replied with a nod.

This was why they took their time and did not force the horses to move any faster than they wanted to all that first day. They would continue to do the same during the days to come as they rolled deeper and higher into the mountains.

But while they were still readying themselves and the horses and gear for the day ahead, which they knew would prove to be another long, difficult one, they each considered their visitor of the day before. This gave them their first taste, up close, of the so-called enemy.

"He didn't seem much," said Chaw, gnawing a corner off a fresh plug of tobacco. He normally only chewed the sticky, leafy, pungent black stuff when they were spending long days on the trail.

Trace preferred what he called the *civility* of his pipe, a corncob affair he could puff for long periods. In these moments, he would consider their plight and any hardships they had driven through, what they might be encountering at present or were likely to come up against.

But on this day, knowing such anger and thus danger awaited in the hills beyond, they kept the long, slow hours of rumination to a minimum and instead vowed to themselves to keep alert.

An hour and more after they had packed up, loaded up, and rolled onward, daylight nibbled away the last of the night sky above. They each admired the coming day through the tall tops of the now bare aspens and the needle-topped heights of the ponderosa pines. Chaw, who had been walking out front, sort of leading the team, held up a big right hand, his left lugging his rifle.

Trace pulled back on the lines, slowing and then halting the two-brace team. "What's happening?" he said in a voice soft enough for Chaw to hear.

In a moment, the big man half looked back to him. "I smell smoke. Campfire, I'd say."

They both knew who it was, had to be—their visitor of the day before. So he hadn't made it all that far, as he had hinted he'd wanted to. Both men knew what this meant: The cigar-smoking stranger would be behind them once more, a development that neither man found to their liking, especially now that they'd met the unsavory fellow.

Soon, Trace smelled the smoke too. And from their perked ears, it looked as if the horses had as well. Trace detected something more to the smell—woodfire smoke, yes, but also a thicker tang to it. Perhaps the man was frying up a breakfast . . . and then Trace remembered the fellow's ever-present cigar and was pleased that, at least to him, his pipe's smoke offered a thinner, pleasant smell.

Another couple of minutes brought the stranger into view, settled in a small, tidy camp along the north side of the road, a hollow in rocks not far off the trail at all, and looking as if it were carved by a big, gouging hand just for this purpose.

The man's horse stood, hipshot and only mildly curious about the passing horses. As for the cigar-smoking fellow himself, he was hunkered on the far side of the campfire, perhaps twenty feet from the roadway.

Even in the dim, early light, they saw that he still wore his longhandle suit, along with boots and hat, and of course that cigar, the thumb-size tip glowing now and again as he sipped on a hot cup of coffee and worked an even hotter fry pan.

Chaw, still walking ahead of the team with his right hand holding the side of the near horse's harness, slowed his pace, and Trace responded with the lines.

"Ho there! Good morning!"

Although they did not want to be rude, neither man really wanted to stop and sip coffee with the stranger. They didn't really even want to stop and chat with the fellow. It became quickly apparent that they would be given their wish.

The man, they knew, was not hard of hearing, and as they were close enough to see and be seen quite easily, the man refused to look up and acknowledge them in any way.

"Hey there!" said Chaw, his voice taking on a bit of an edge that Trace recognized as one of annoyance. Chaw did not go out of his way to be noticed in life, but he sure as heck did not want to be ignored. Especially by someone who Trace knew Chaw held in low regard.

The cigar-smoking stranger's lack of acknowledgment irked Chaw, and it irked Trace, too.

Finally, just when it looked to Trace as if Chaw was going to stoop down and heft a rock and lob it at the man, Trace worked the lines gently over the horses' backs and urged them forward again. He glanced at the man again and wondered if perhaps the fellow was truly oblivious of their presence.

Trace doubted it, for just as he was about to shift his gaze back to the horses and the emerging roadway ahead, he saw the man glance up quickly before looking back to prodding his campfire.

As he expected, it didn't take very long before Trace heard Chaw's mumblings of annoyance. His buckskin-wearing pard gave up his post trudging alongside the team, in part because he was tired, and in part because it was no longer necessary, the sun having risen up high enough to cut through and above the trees to their backs.

They were rolling slowly enough that he crossed

before the team and stood still a moment while the wagon rolled up alongside him.

Trace didn't bother to slow it as Chaw set his rifle in the boot well and then grabbed the steel handhold with his left hand and to the front of the boot well with his right. He brought his left boot up into the step, then swung himself the rest of the way into the seat.

"You ever see such a thing?" he said, barely having settled his backside on the seat.

"Huh?" said Trace, knowing full well what Chaw was talking about and hoping to get him a bit more riled before the hour was out. *Just for fun*, he thought.

"Why, that cigar-gobbling rascal back there!" Chaw flung an arm at the loaded bulk of the wagon behind them. "You weren't much help, neither!"

"What was it you think I should have done?"

"At least you could have slowed down some more and shouted at the man, too! My word, you'd think you was born with no tongue in that overstuffed Yankee head of yours."

Trace kept his peace but could not help in breaking out in a smile. Any day that began with Chaw getting all riled up was bound to be a good one.

"You'd think you liked the man or something!"

"No," said Trace. "Not particularly. In fact, I'd say he's going to annoy us for some time to come."

"How so?"

"He's behind us again and that will keep us on our toes all day."

"Ah, yeah, except he might also cut northward."

"It's certainly possible," said Trace. "But I wouldn't

set much money on that bet. He's likely headed to the one place we know of that his so-called employers are interested in—Boarwallow Gap. Same place we're making for."

Chaw grew sullen and quiet for a while, glowering at the otherwise pretty landscape donning a fine, glowing coat of sunlight.

"How long you reckon it'll take us to get there?"

"Most of the day," said Trace, digging out the map and handing it to his right.

"With our luck, we'll take a wrong road somewhere and end up tumbling off a cursed cliff."

Finally, Trace looked at Chaw. "You know, if you spent on enjoying this day what time and energy you've spent on being sour and worked up about that man you don't even like, there's no telling what wonderful things might happen to you today."

Chaw was silent for a few moments, his face a moody mask as he frowned, arms folded over his chest and eyes half lidded. "Don't much care."

"I know it. And while your resolve is one of the things I find to be a worthy trait in you, just now I will admit it's annoying."

"Don't care."

Trace grinned, thumbed a match alight, and set fire once more to the tobacco in his pipe. Then he began singing "Yankee Doodle."

He'd gotten through nearly half a minute of the tune before Chaw looked at him, and although he tried to maintain his squinting glare of anger, it wasn't long before the big Reb was grinning, too. "Aw, heck. I just don't like that fella. Don't trust him, neither."

"I know. Neither do I. Which is why I think whoever isn't driving today ought to keep an eye on our back trail. He'll be along, and if not, then we'll know he either took to a different trail or he's holding back intentionally. And that's the part I don't want to think about, because it means he might be planning on creeping up on us in the night."

"He does," said Chaw. "And I'll let him have it." He shifted in his seat, angling the rifle around the side of the wagon, and following with his head. But he wasn't able to see much more than the length of the big tarped load. "Bah! I should have stayed afoot."

CHAPTER 10

They knew they were drawing close to the town or village or mining camp of Boarwallow Gap, whatever size designation the residents chose to call it. For the past twenty minutes they'd seen more and more indication of folks having been about the place for some time.

There were the usual obvious signs—piles of empty food tins and jars, smashed booze and medicinal bottles, small fly-blown heaps of the picked-over bones of critters—small, such as rabbits, and on up to the larger, ripped-apart skeletons of deer.

"Wherever you find humans," mused Trace as they rolled closer, "you find trash."

"Aw, come on now," said Chaw. "I know you're not all that fond of your fellow peoples, but we ain't all that bad, are we?"

Chaw was in a surprisingly good mood, given that he had been fuming and sputtering for much of the day's travel. Even though they had traded off on the driving duties, he had still found it vital that he swivel his head around every five seconds or so to see if they were being followed by the cigar fiend. Each time he saw no one, he growled and said something such as, "Matter of time before he gets the drop on us, I tell you that for true!"

And each time Trace would roll his eyes and do his best to suppress the urge welling in him to round on his pard and give him a quick lifter to the jaw. He was tired of hearing it, sure, but he reasoned that there was little he could do about it without starting an argument. And it was far too long and boring a ride to do that.

It was bad enough that he had much the same concerns about the cigar-smoking fellow. It was unnerving to know he was back there somewhere, trailing behind and perhaps even lining up a potshot at their heads. Who was to know? And they knew he was working for who they now considered their enemy, through association with the widow and Hector.

"You reckon we'll meet up with these Holdout fellows?"

"I don't see how we can avoid it," said Trace, squinting as he looked at the lane ahead. "Is that a woman up there?"

Chaw spun his head around at the mention of one of his favorite words. "I do believe you're right."

Both men saw what looked to be a dark-haired woman in a begrimed dress standing half facing them, her hands on her hips and looking off the north side of the road into the sparse trees, as if she were searching for something.

"Well, Hector said there were a few families up here. I expect we'll see more women, and children, too, before we light on out of here."

"Can't be soon enough for me," said Trace.

"I know what you mean. Ain't even to the camp yet and already I feel like leaving."

"Well, it's bound to get better. The outskirts are usually rougher than the mine camps themselves."

"I hope you're right. Hey," said Chaw. "I think she's coming at us."

Sure enough, as they rolled forward slowly up the somewhat steep, rutted roadway, they saw that the woman they'd seen from a distance had turned. She had taken her hands off her hips and was now striding downslope toward them. Trace wasn't about to stop the team on the slope.

They crested the rise, then halted the rig. She was standing in the roadway. Once they'd rolled to a stop, she walked to Chaw's side, but he'd already hopped down.

She stood a couple of yards from him and began speaking in a low, quavering voice. He leaned over to hear her.

"She keeps asking me if I've seen anybody name of Paco." Chaw said this as if he were trying to whisper it up to Trace in the wagon's driver's seat.

The woman moved closer to Chaw, and he kept his hand on his revolver. She was not but three feet from Chaw's left side and said, "That's his name, yes. You seen my Paco?"

Chaw looked back to her. "Oh, ah, no, ma'am. I ain't, that is, not today. Not just yet, no. Say, um, how far to get to Boarwallow Gap, ma'am?"

But the woman didn't seem to have heard him. Indeed, she looked as though she had forgotten they were there, right beside her, with their big, four-horse team and lugging a brutally large, laden wagon.

She folded her arms over her chest and strode back on up the roadway, keeping to the side and looking once again into the woods beyond along that north side.

Trace kept an eye on her just in case she decided to continue acting true to her ways so far and took a notion to walk out in front of them. It wouldn't take these big pulling horses much at all to accidentally knock her down. And if they didn't deal her a mortal wound right away, she might well end up with a broken, mashed foot or worse.

"I think she's . . ." Chaw circled a finger beside his right temple. "You know, around the bend or some such."

Trace nodded and waited to respond until Chaw had climbed back up into the front beside him. "As long as she doesn't step out in front of us, we can manage."

They prepared to pass her, and as soon as they came abreast of her, she continued to ignore them as if she hadn't seen them. Then she angled sharply to her left and cut into the woods, walking along on a slightly even stretch of rubble rock and ripped-up bramble and well-axed tree stumps. It was obviously a poorly managed patch of someone's claim.

"What a mess," said Chaw. "If that's her home," he nodded toward a shanty built against the hillside, "and if that Paco fella is her man, then he ought to be ashamed of keeping so poorly a place."

The home, such as it was, consisted of little more than a half-planked, half-stone front, wedged and piled as if it might collapse at any moment. In the midst of the front sat a gaping low hole with a wispy, grimy rag hanging in tatters in it.

Sure enough, the woman walked slowly but steadily straight for it and ducked, shoving the rag aside and disappearing into the darkness within.

Before long, they saw other such hovels built into other hillsides, with rock and stump debris and mounds of recent raw earthworks about them.

"All for want of gold," said Trace, shaking his head.

"Sure, yeah," said Chaw. "But now look here, way I figure it, see, these poor folks are gnawing away like rats all over these mountains, right? But ain't we doing the same thing?"

"How do you figure that?" said Trace, feeling a little annoyed at being equated with the hard-rock miners.

"Well, these folks are obviously living tight to the hide, ain't they?"

"Yes, I'd say so."

Chaw nodded. "And so do we. See what I'm getting at?"

"I guess so, but just because we don't have much cash to spread around most of the time doesn't mean we live like animals in their dens."

Before Chaw could respond, a voice from their right, close to the wagon, said, "Now I realize, gentlemen, that for you to hear each other you must shout a little to be heard. But don't forget that this also means that your voices carry beyond the range of just the two of you."

The speaker walked forward, with a couple of

hurried steps, for them both to look over to their left, toward him.

What they saw was a middle-aged man, bald and thin, with a scruffy beard and garb that could have been a whole lot cleaner. But his step was lively and he had a keen look in his eye.

And, most important, his face looked about set to smile, as if he were just waiting for their nod of approval to go ahead with the venture. He also wore a holstered sidearm and cradled a shotgun.

"I'm sorry if we said anything that rubbed your fur the wrong way, fella, but . . ."

"Think nothing of it!" There came his smile. "If I was in your place, I'd think and say the same thing, I don't doubt it one bit. And don't slow down on my account! Keep her moving! We've been waiting on you! You are from Sligo Star, ain't you?"

"Why, sure we are. And we're sure glad we could make it," said Chaw, winking at Trace.

"Yep," continued the man. "I was supposed to meet you, but I didn't want to leave my seam. Got a promising look to it, so it does."

"Well, good. Now look," said Chaw. "How much farther is it to your town, Boar—"

"Boarwallow Gap! Yep, well, I'm afraid it isn't all that much to look at. Used to be prettier, before the troubles with the consortium. But we can go into that later."

He sighed. "We try, but you know how it is. So, no, it's not so much a town, really, as a cluster of tents and shanties here and there. Most of the action takes place out on peoples' claims. That's the reason we're all out here anyway."

"Huh, all right then. But how far?"

"Right, it's another few minutes on up the trail. See where this straightens and levels off up there, about a hundred and a half feet ahead?"

"Yeah?"

"Right up there. But you've been rolling through the Gap, or the south ridge of it, anyway, for a while now."

"Okay, then," said Chaw. "Long as we get to where we're headed and can unload these goods in peace, we'll be all right, fella."

"Name's Slattery."

"Okay, Slattery, then. What's all this about the Holdouts? Are you one of them?"

"Ah, you must have been filled in by Hector and the Widow Roscommon."

"You bet we have," said Trace, tired of not contributing to the conversation.

The man's mirthful face lost that happy edge and his brow lowered. "As to the Holdouts, yes, I'm one. There are others; some of them, no doubt, have been eyeing you and your progress for a long while now."

"They have?" said Chaw, habit and instinct bringing his rifle to bear up across his chest.

"Nothing to worry about there, Freighter. If you were from the consortium, you'd likely be dead by now."

"You don't mess about, do you?" said Trace.

"Not hardly." Slattery shook his head. "Can't afford to anymore. Things are bad. Worse than they have ever been since the big boys realized we Holdouts are sitting on what amounts to one of the biggest, most promising ore strikes in the history of the world."

"History of the world?" Trace couldn't help but snort.

Chaw did the same. "That's mighty bold talk, Mr. Slattery."

"Laugh all you want, but I'm telling you, the ore samples we all have been packing on out of here, any way we can, under cover of night, on foot or on donkeys, is some of the most promising and highest-content of gold ever seen anywhere.

"And not just from one little spot, neither! From all over the hills hereabouts. Which proves that this here," Slattery paused in his slow walk beside the wagon to stomp a foot before hustling to make up the lost steps, "should be called Gold Mountain!" He nodded with vigor. "And it won't take long, no sir. It won't take long before the world knows."

"Say, how come the law ain't been notified of all this?" said Chaw.

"Right," said Trace, cutting in. "It seems to me if you men all have proof of ownership of your claims, there is little anyone can do about that. Legally, anyway."

Slattery nodded, sighing and smirking as if he'd been asked that question every day for years and had grown far beyond weary of answering it. "Sure, you're right, of course. But that don't matter to ruthless men who have more money than the gods, and who want even more. It's a sickness, you know. Once you get a taste, you'll pay the devil anything he asks for as long as you can get more!"

"How is that different from what a miner does? I

can't imagine there are too many of you that wouldn't like as much money as you can get from your claim, no?"

If the response angered Slattery, he didn't let on.

"It isn't much different, nope. But see, it boils down to who's got the legal right to be here and who hasn't. We have it and they don't. So we're in the right here. They told us they have the power and the money to drive us off, and we said, *try, just try to drive us off our land*."

"And how is it all working for you?" said Chaw.

Slattery was quiet a moment. Then he nodded. "I guess it's working, though not well. They've bought off a pile of us, which is legal. But if they did it with threats, that's another thing. The problem comes with the ones they've driven off with violence. Those fellows, and sometimes their families, too, it was all they got. Their claim was their home, if you know what I mean. And then they up and disappear. Gone in the night? Who can say? I do know that a pile of them woke up dead."

"Bold words," said Trace. He didn't think that would ignite Slattery's smoldering fire anew, but it did.

"Bold! Bold? You bet your backside they're bold words! And backed up by proof! But then we come back to the law, see?" The miner's wry grin, spreading wide across that lined, tired face, told them he wasn't through.

And in some respects, they knew he was just getting started, for they'd come full circle in the conversation and now he was closing in on the meat of the matter. The true treachery of the consortium.

But before they could ask him about who *woke up dead*, as he put it, Slattery said, "Ho, now. Here we are!"

He nodded forward, and the two freighters looked ahead at a huge boulder around which the roadway cut, angling along its left edge.

"Looks like a big rock to me!" said Chaw, smacking his dusty buckskin leggings.

"No, no. Around that. Can't you see the smoke?" said Slattery, not impressed with the Rebel's stab at humor.

Trace and Chaw had both seen the scrim of woodsmoke that hung like a low, dense, unfortunate cloud in the air beyond the boulder. Slattery drifted behind them, and as Chaw looked back, Trace worked the team around the bend at the boulder. Chaw was able to see behind them without resorting to leaning out to peer past the tarped load's long side.

He saw three armed men walking the roadway, all looking much like Slattery—tired and haggard but hard-faced and determined. Chaw guessed, since Slattery was not alarmed by their presence, that they were some of his fellow Holdouts. They had to be the very men he'd spoken of earlier who had likely been watching them for some time.

Nonetheless, seeing more shanties and cabins emerge, along with a variety of faces. The homes from which they emerged, really little more than hovels, reflected the begrimed quality of the mine camp of Boarwallow Gap.

But it was the people who came drifting out of doors to see what the commotion was all about that convinced Chaw and Trace, as if they needed further proof, that they were on a true mission of mercy.

As soon as the strangers clapped eyes on the big, heavily loaded wagon, those smiles worked wider across their gray faces. And twice they saw the fleeting, darting shapes of young children, excited because their parents were excited, no doubt. And this made Chaw's grin wide.

The sight of them was enough to wash away, at least temporarily, the sting that comes with confronting the unexpected moments in life. And this surely was one of them.

Trace regarded the scene with that same blend of relief and optimism as did his pard, but he also tempered it with caution. They were here to do a job—to deliver goods to a remote mountain mining camp, and then on to a few others. Then they would descend slowly down the far side of the mountains, to get to Richness, Utah.

"Hold up here a minute," said Slattery.

They rolled to a stop where he indicated, in what appeared to be the town proper. It was a wide spot in the roadway before a cabin with a low, broad porch bedecked with benches and stumps of wood most likely used for sitting on.

Before they could hop down, one of the Holdouts who'd emerged from the landscape and followed them into town ambled forward and laid a hand on the side of the wagon, looking up at the tight-tarped load as if he could see beneath it to the goods within. "You got coffee? And are my cigars in there?"

Chaw chuckled, and he and Trace both climbed down out of the wagon.

"Well now," said Chaw. "I reckon if you ordered coffee, that's what you'll find. As for cigars, I got no idea. Say, what is it with you hill folk and ceegars? We bumped into a fella on the trail couldn't seem to keep one out of his maw!" He grinned, but the smiles on the face of the residents of Boarwallow Gap slowly slid away.

Chaw turned to his pard. "What'd I say?"

Trace shrugged. "No idea."

"You say you met a man on the trail smoking a cigar?" said Slattery.

"Yeah. It ain't so odd as you make it sound, though," said Chaw.

"Describe him to me."

"All right, well . . ." Chaw looked at Trace, who picked it up from there.

"Well, he was a burly fellow, about average height. Dark hat, horse and gear looked about average. About the only thing that was different about him was that cigar. Never seemed to have it out of his mouth."

"Except when he drank the coffee we shared with him," said Chaw, nodding.

"Coffee! You gave the man coffee? You should have shot him as soon as you laid eyes on him!"

Most of the other folks gathered there nodded, their faces drawn into hard looks.

"But . . . " said Chaw.

"Why, man, you had yourself a run-in with none other than Cigar Tim! I reckon I already got my answer, but tell me again—for sure you didn't shoot him?"

"Shoot him? No, why would we do that? I admit I didn't care for him, but—"

"Bah! 'Course you didn't shoot him." Slattery shook

his head. "My word, but you two ain't half as smart as I thought you was."

"Careful now, fella," said Trace, standing full height and making no attempt to hide the fact that Slattery had annoyed him. He laid his hand on the butt of his gun.

"We are here delivering goods to mine camps, one of which is Boarwallow Gap. It's a job, the same as yours or anyone else's. No more, no less. Now, the fact that you all have gotten in hot soup because of unforeseen and unfortunate circumstances surrounding gold, your land, and such, is not our primary concern. Do you understand?"

"Oh, sure, sure, we understand," said Slattery, not wavering a bit and not backing down, meeting Trace's hard stare with an equally hard look of his own. "At least I understand. I can't speak for the rest of them." He nodded and looked from Trace to Chaw, who was also standing broad-shouldered and full height, but with arms crossed over his chest.

"I understand that you and him ain't got a card on the table, and that's all fine and dandy for you, but we all have been all but starved to death up here, fighting for what's ours to begin with."

He pulled in a quick breath and dove back in. "This here's the true, good fight, you see? And the likes of you two are just drifting through. Okay, then, get gone. Sure, I'm surprised you didn't just slow down, shove out our goods, and keep a-rolling!"

"Don't you think you're selling us a little short there, Slattery?"

"How do you figure that?"

Chaw shrugged. "If you don't see how what you said was off the mark and insulting, then you're a fool, Slattery."

That stunned the man, who shut his mouth for a moment. Then a grin spread slowly on his face and he nodded. "You'll do. Oh, you'll do, all right. Now see here, it takes not a little bit of effort to get me to shut up. Ask anybody up here and they'll tell you the same. But you did it. Good on ya."

"Look," said Trace, annoyed that the man was content to keep talking in circles. "Tell us where to unload the goods, all right? We are running behind schedule and we need to keep moving."

"Sure, sure, follow me."

CHAPTER 11

The wagon sat before what the Boarwallow Gap folks called their warehouse, a cabin left empty next to the stable. They'd been told it had been built, along with what was now the stable, by a big Swede who had come to the town not to dig for gold but to set up as a blacksmith, his chosen trade.

That was in the early days when there was a whole lot of promise and excitement. And that excitement had continued, building up into the first of the boom times, said Slattery, who was one of several men helping them unload.

"Then what happened?" said Chaw, handing down a sack of cornmeal to Slattery.

"Then, well, then all heck broke loose!"

"How so?" said Trace, looking up from the tally sheet. He wanted to keep a sharp eye on the wagon's inventory,

"Slattery! Slattery!" A small, nervous man ran up, wringing his hands and looking to Chaw and Trace as if he might cry.

"What is it, Howell?"

"Pinky's dead!"

"Dead? Pinky? Oh no, now that's awful. How'd it happen? Rockslide or what? I saw him just two days ago or so, and he looked fit and fine to me."

The little man who bore the message stood breathing heavy from the ambling run he'd used to get there, his chest working like a fire bellows. "Nothing like that. No, it was . . . well . . ."

He dug a couple of gnarled fingers into the side pocket of his floppy, begrimed work vest and pulled out something thumb-sized and black. He held it out on the palm of a shaking hand. "I found this."

"What is it?" said Slattery, leaning forward. "Step out into the sun. I can't see what it is."

They both moved a few paces out into the sunlight. The rest of them all paused in their work. Trace and Chaw saw that the townsfolk were stunned, no doubt by the news of the death of their friend.

"Well, what is it?" said Slattery, peering close at the dark, misshapen thing in the man's hand.

"It's a cigar stub."

Slattery jerked upright. "Cigar?"

The man nodded, his mouth a hard line.

"Where was it?"

"In his left eye. Or where his left eye used to be."

A thickset woman standing off to the side said, "Oh!" She clamped a hand to her red face and went back to tidying the stack of full sacks, shaking her head. Chaw was certain she was crying in silence.

Then Slattery looked at Chaw and Trace. "That's the

work of the fellow you two shared coffee with! That's the work of Cigar Tim! What do you think now, huh?"

Nobody said a thing for a moment, then Trace said, "We're awfully sorry that this has happened, of course we are. But to stand there and act as if we are to blame for this man's death, well, that's just wrongheaded. We didn't know who this Cigar Tim was when we met him on the trail. How could we?"

"All right, all right. We're just hotted up about all this just now. And we're sick and tired of being terrorized by that rascal. And all the others, too!"

"How many others are there?" said Trace.

"Oh, lots. I don't know. It's the ones from before. The ones who came in here with money and then threats. I mean, we don't know who they are, but that consortium, they have big, deep coin purses, right?"

Nobody else said a thing, but it looked as if they all agreed with the man.

"So what you're saying is that you don't have proof that there's more than this one man causing you all such grief. At least not right now."

Slattery raised his work-hardened hands and let them fall to his side. "How else can we explain how many folks have been run off their claims? Some of them I know for a fact were die-hard, no-budging Holdouts. But something happened to them. Too much and too many different episodes to credit to a single man."

"That only proves Cigar Tim ain't a man," said a whip-thin old man who'd been ferrying to the side whatever came his way off the wagon, from nail kegs to sacks of flour and an open-top crate of forged steel shovels, picks, and such.

"What do you mean?" said Chaw, always ready to perk up his ears at the faintest whiff of a mention of something supernatural in the offing.

"Jethro means that—"

"I can talk for myself, Slattery! Don't you go butting into everything and talking all over a man. I got something to say, by gum, I'll say it! Don't need you to do it for me!"

Slattery held up his hands as if he were being braced by a thief.

The speaker, who Slattery had referred to as Jethro, resumed speaking to Chaw and Trace. "I said Cigar Tim ain't a man and I meant it."

"What is he, then?" said Chaw.

Jethro leaned forward. "He's a specter!" He nodded. "Only answer for it, yes sir. Otherwise there ain't no way to explain it, you see?"

"Explain what, exactly?" said Trace, eager to hear what this man had to say.

"He's a devil, plain and simple. Surprised you two, meeting up with him and all, didn't get to feeling that he was not human! And not to be trusted!"

"As I said," continued Slattery before Jethro could jump in. "Maybe we are all just too stubborn, but I tell you—" Slattery looked about him to see if his fellow Holdouts were in agreement.

They looked to Chaw and Trace to only be half listening, as if they had heard far too much from this

man already. It didn't seem to slow down the man in
the least.

"Too many folks have been driven off. Just as I said
before."

"Well, what do you want me to do with Pinky's
body?" said Howell, the little man who'd made the
awful discovery.

Everyone in the warehouse, even Trace and Chaw,
turned their eyes on Slattery. If the two freighters were
in doubt as to Slattery's role as spokesman and leader
of the Holdouts, for good or ill, they were no longer in
the dark.

"Seems to me you two brought about Pinky's death."
Slattery looked right at the two freighters and shook his
head.

A growling noise bubbled up out of Chaw's throat.

Trace edged forward. "Are we going to go down
the blame trail with you again, Slattery? Look, all we
were hired to do is to transport these goods to you and
the other mine camps deeper in. We didn't lure that
killer in here and leave him to it. That was just your
friend's bad luck. That man rode on in here of his own
accord."

"I know, I know. But, well . . ." Slattery raised his
hands, palms up, and let them drop back to his sides.

"But?" said Trace. "Well? That don't sound like much
in the way of a logical defense, Slattery. Look, we are
very sorry to hear about your friend. And we are happy
to help bury him, and even take a scout around with

you other men to see if we can scare up this Cigar Tim fellow."

Trace looked briefly to Chaw, who nodded agreement, even though he kept his eyes squinted into a hard look at Slattery.

Trace continued, "But we need to rest our beasts, so we'll stay with them wherever you think it'd be best for us all to be tonight. We'll deliver our goods where we need to, of course, but it would be a whole lot easier on us if you told us how to get to the other camps. Better yet, if someone happened to be going thataway, at least to the first, we'd be happy to follow and get the lay of the land, so to speak."

"Aw," said old Jethro. "Ain't nothing to it. You just follow this here roadway. Take you right past them, and then right on to that pit of sin, Richness. Only way in or out. Surprised you two so-called freighters didn't know that!" He walked away, shaking his head.

CHAPTER 12

"By the way," said Chaw between mouthfuls of biscuit. "We was on our way into your town earlier, not long before we come across you, Slattery—"

"I came across you gentlemen," said Slattery with a knowing head nod.

Chaw's brow wrinkled. "Oh, stop trying to be top dog in every blamed conversation, will you? It's annoying."

Eyebrows rose all around. Chaw did not seem to notice.

"Now, where was I?" he continued. "Oh yeah, and there was this woman in the roadway, walked right toward us. Oddest thing. Anyway, she—"

Slattery and a couple of the others were nodding their heads.

"I see you already know who I'm talking about."

"I bet I do," said a fellow named Rock. "She ask you if you've seen her husband?"

"I reckon she was asking for her husband, yes," said Trace. "But she called him Paco. Asked us if we'd seen him."

"Well, you can thank your friend, Cigar Tim, for that," said Slattery.

Chaw growled and stood up, nearly upending the table in the midst of them all. "Look, for the last time, we aren't his chums! Am I going to have to take a round out of you, man? If that's the only way to settle this hash, then by all means, let's step on outside and get to it. You pushed me about as far as I'm going to go, Slattery."

"Easy now, pard," said Trace under his breath.

"Don't tell me to go easy. You know as well as I do that this . . . this fool has been riding us hard since we got here. All friendly, and then he wasn't. And all because we showed a stranger a kindness. Well, I'm through putting up with it. Yeah," said Chaw, warming to his topic.

He turned and looked at all of them. "I know you've had a rum run of it. We all have. Heck, me and my pard nearly died in the war, like lots of other folks, but we're still here. Thing is, what are you going to do about it?"

Not a soul said anything, but after a few tense, silent moments, Trace said, "Now, what about this Paco fellow? Might be we can learn something that will help you all. We're here, might as well hear it. It can't hurt for us to listen, right?"

A brief silence fell over the assemblage. A few townsfolk shrugged, a few others looked over at Slattery, who, it seemed to Trace, could not wait to tell the story. So he did.

"Paco," said Slattery, rubbing his hands together and trying to tamp down a smile, as if he were enjoying himself. "He was one of the first men up in these hills.

Mexican, as you could have guessed, and a good man. A harder worker you'd not find anywhere. Well, not too long ago, when all this consortium mess started, we all were getting together at night, forming a group of our own.

"But Paco, he was always a bit of a loner, you see. Plus, he'd just fetched his wife back here, to boot. That'd be Marietta, the woman you two met. Well, they hadn't seen each other for some time, you understand, and so they was right busy for a while.

"Turns out Marietta is as handy with a pick as Paco was. They worked that claim together as hard as any two men you could hope to find. And wouldn't you know it, they had themselves a whole lot of good luck, too. Only we all know it wasn't luck they were having, but the natural development that comes from working hard. It pays off if you keep at a thing, but then again, you two fellas know that as well as I do."

"Sure," said Chaw, grinning. "That's why we're such high rollers."

"As to what made Marietta the way she is," said Slattery, ignoring Chaw. "That's a sad story if ever there was one. It all happened one night when we had a big, thunder-cracking storm. I tell you, when the rest of the world gets a storm, we get a whopper. It can be downright brutal up here in the mountains. Anyway, it was a night in what, March, was it, Howell?"

The little man nodded with vigor. "Yeah, sure was, Slattery."

"March, and a storm come ripping up through here. Wasn't fit for man nor beast, but here we are just the same. And Paco and his wife, Marietta, they were holed up like the rest of us are every night after a long, hard day pounding rocks apart, and digging others out. Then Paco, he ducked out back to water a tree, if you know what I mean. Even in the midst of a storm a man's got to do what a man's got to do."

Chaw nodded. "The call of nature will not be denied."

"That's about it, yeah. Well, Marietta, she didn't think anything of it, had herself a thunder pot, you know, but Paco, he's a man and he draped a scrap of oil-cloth over his head and headed on out.

"He was gone a while, so Marietta went on out and called to him. He never yelled back, like he always did. Paco, he wasn't a tall man, but he was wide of shoulder and gifted with a tremendous chest, good for might work and deep breaths and shouting. Well, as I say, he never did shout back. So she waited and waited some more, figuring that the man needed a little privacy and more time.

"Well, sir, a crack of lightning lit the night just then, and she yelped. As she was looking out to shout to him again, another crack did the same. Out to the side and a bit behind their dugout, Marietta saw Paco. Only he wasn't upright any more, like a man with legs ought to be.

"No sir, he was down on all four, sort of leaning against a big rock. It's one of those that there is no shifting for love nor money. So they worked around it, like most of us.

"If you can't split a thing, you got to come to an agreement with such things in life. Anyway, she saw him down on all fours like a critter, but Paco, he was leaning there, like a bear will do, scratching its side against something.

"Only Paco was naked. And he wasn't naked when he went outside. That was odd, she thought. Mighty odd. A man won't shed his clothes just to tend to his body's obligations. She shouted to him, but even though he was less than twenty feet away, he didn't look over at her.

"Didn't move at all, as a matter of fact. Didn't do much of anything except to lean there on all fours, naked. So Marietta bent low, walked over toward him, sort of saying his name cautious-like, afraid somehow he'd taken a fit and was acting crazy. You know, you hear stories of folks losing their minds just like that." Slattery snapped his fingers.

"She walked on over to him, bent low and looking. *Paco?* she said. *Paco, honey, you okay, my man?* She always called him that, her man. Anyway, she got right up close to him and looked down at him. His skin was all wet and shiny and his black hair was all soaked to the skull and stringy-looking, and still he didn't look at her, nothing. That's when she saw it."

Slattery was silent for a moment.

Chaw and Trace both said, at the same time, "What? Saw what?"

"Well, she saw that he was dead, of course! My word, but you two are thick."

Trace jumped in with a reply, lest Chaw beat him to it—and Chaw was not looking any too pleased to continue taking abuse from this annoying man. "What killed Paco, Slattery?"

"Ah now, I'm glad you asked, because that's interesting, that is. See," he said. "It's not just a what, but a who, you see."

"Let me guess," said Chaw. "Cigar Tim."

Slattery nodded, looking a bit disappointed that Chaw beat him to it. But he plowed on with his story.

"You see, when she looked down at Paco, he was all naked, as I said, and sort of leaning against that boulder. Well, she looked closer, not breathing one little bit, and reached out and touched his near shoulder. He was wet to the bone, of course, but by then so was she. She knelt right down there in the mud and muck and grabbed hold of him and pulled at him, screaming his name over and over.

"Paco pitched toward her and flopped into her and onto her and that's when she saw that there was a knife sticking out of his back. She couldn't see it before then because of the shadows and the irregular flashes of the lightning not quite lighting up the scene.

"Well, you can guess that ol' Marietta screamed and screamed and screamed. She yanked on that knife, and it took some doing because, as it turns out, the blade's edge was lodged deep in bone, likely the poor man's backbone. But the tip of the blade, why, that drove on in deeper and tickled and punctured all manner of the man's vitals deep within him there." Slattery made a weak gesture toward his back.

"Worst part of it was that the knife in his back? Well,

that was Paco's own knife. Always wore it on his belt. Used it for nearly everything, he did."

"How did he come to be naked?" said Chaw in a soft voice, as if he were afraid of asking.

"Oh that, well, Marietta found his clothes the next day, all muddied up and such. But as far as she or anybody can tell, ol' Paco, he must have been ordered to strip down.

"I can't see anyone doing that to a man and then stripping him off. And for what reason? No." Slattery shook his head. "As I say, he must have been ordered to strip off, then the brute killed him . . . well, you know."

Everyone there nodded, not saying anything for a long moment. Then Slattery said, "The man was a mess, I can tell you. Deader than dead can be, but a mess. It turns out that Marietta is still in far worse shape than Paco."

"How can you say that?" said Chaw. "He's dead, ain't he? And she ain't."

"Sure he's dead." Slattery nodded. "But she's lost her senses. Pretty much permanently. I don't see how she can ever come back from such a thing. Seems to me it'd be better for her if she had died that night, too. Her and Paco, they were one of a kind, if you get my meaning.

"Anyhow, that poor woman, it turns out that not one of us could hear her that night. What with all these hills and ridges and boulders and trees and such. And besides, there was the storm. It was a whopper, as I said. Mudslides and boulders crashing on down slopes and such. It was a mess. It took us all the better part of a week just to clean out so we could get back to work."

"What did Marietta do with Paco?" said Trace, in an effort to get Slattery to stick to telling his gruesome story.

"Right, yep, sure, but don't rush me now. . . ."

Trace saw that a couple of the townsfolk rolled their eyes and hid smirks behind their cups. He also decided that Slattery was a whole lot like Chaw, which might account for why his pard seemed so annoyed by the man.

"I don't know how she managed it, but that woman eventually came around to what was beginning to be the last of her senses, and she got poor Paco dragged on into their shanty. Laid him out on the floor and worked and worked for most of the night to revive him. She was convinced he was going to come back to life, that it was something he could get himself over if he just experienced some warmth and whatever her loving could do for him. But no. It was not to be." Slattery shook his head.

Trace saw that the two women in attendance were both moist-eyed, and the three men whose faces he glanced at were also heading that way, but the men were taking pains to make it appear as if they were battling smoke in their eyes.

"Oh," said Slattery. "While I'm on about it, even though I think we've all heard about as much as we really need to hear, it's important that you two fellas hear it. So you know what we're up against here, and so you know what you'll be up against, too, now that you're marked men."

"Marked men?" said Chaw.

Slattery nodded. "Yep, that's what I said. Because you're helping the enemy of the consortium. That makes you their enemy, and that makes you marked men. Now, let me finish telling you what happened to Paco that night. Let's see. Yeah, the thing she found that puzzled us all at first, but then we came to learn was a marker, a signature of sorts, you see, was what was in Paco's mouth."

Again, Slattery paused, as if waiting for them to spur him on. One of the women said, "Oh, for heaven's sake, Slattery! Just tell them and be done with it. Bad enough we all have to go through this sadness all over again."

"Okay, okay. See Marietta, she found a big ol' stump of a cigar crammed in Paco's mouth. It wasn't the thing that killed him—that was the knife that did that—but this, as we came to learn, was what Cigar Tim would leave behind whenever he dealt with folks."

"*Dealt with*?" said the woman. "*Dealt with*, Slattery? Call it what it is! The man murdered Paco, then went on to do the same to the others! And he tried to kill George Minty just a few days ago. Lucky for him you showed up."

"Yeah, I know it was." Slattery saw Howell looking at him, appearing as if he might speak. Slattery narrowed his eyes and Howell looked down at his boots and said nothing.

"How many other of you all has this Cigar Tim killed, then?"

"Well, let's see," said Slattery, but the woman who'd been speaking rode right over his words.

"After Paco there was Kinsey." She counted them off

on her thick, callused fingers. "And then Duff Crawford. And George Minty, but he ain't dead. Oh, and now Pinky. As I said, George would have been added to the list of the dead, but Slattery happened along."

"We've been out patrolling together in a group, trying to get a sight on the man."

Something occurred to Trace. "Have any of you ever seen him? Cigar Tim, I mean?"

"Well, you mean right up close?"

"Yep," said Trace. "And lived to tell about it."

"Well, no, none of us, save for Kinsey. He lived a spell, told us the man's name, I guess because Cigar Tim told him. And then there was George. He was being tortured by the man, and me and Howell, we came along and spooked him, I guess."

"And Rufus," said Howell in a soft voice. "He was there, too."

"Right," said Slattery, giving Howell the hard stare once more.

"But you never saw Cigar Tim."

"No, but George did, and he told us near enough what he saw. His memory of some of it is a little fuzzed around the edges, though. You understand."

"Mine would be," said Chaw, nodding. "He going to be all right, then?"

"Sure. At least I think so, anyway."

"Well?" said Chaw.

"Well, what?" said Slattery, looking to Trace as if his hackles were rising once again.

"Well, what does this rascal Cigar Tim look like, according to your man, George?"

"You two know what he looks like! You gave him coffee, after all."

"I think what my pard is asking for is to compare George's description of the man with the fellow we met. I'm sure they're the same man, but it would be helpful to know if there's more than one such fellow roaming these hills, and who treats men the same way, don't you think?"

"More than one! Oh, no, no no." The woman shook her head. "It doesn't bear thinking about!"

"Easy now, Ethel," said Slattery. "He didn't say there were two of them, just that it was possible. Which I don't think is true."

"We can take you to meet George. He's resting up. Rufus is with him, keeping watch with a couple of guns. I'm due to spell him in a few hours anyway."

"Maybe on our next run," said Trace. "We have to light out early, still have a pile of work to do rearranging our load, stuffing away whatever it is you all are sending with us to Richness."

"Sure thing," said Slattery. "You can meet George when you come back. If any of us are left alive, that is."

This time nobody rolled their eyes. They looked at their feet, their hands, and not a one of them looked as if what the man had said was an uncertainty in the slightest.

The silence lasted for a few moments, then Trace said, "If you don't mind my asking, how do you know all this? About Paco and Marietta, I mean."

Slattery looked over at him as if he'd just awakened

from a reverie. "Oh, well, Marietta, she told me all of it. Before she went away as much as she is now."

"And that there is the same woman we met," said Chaw.

The miner nodded. "Of course. And I know what you're thinking. But there was a spell of time there, after the attack, that she was, well, she wasn't so far away, if you know what I mean.

"It took some time, but with each day that passed following that attack, well, she just sort of drifted farther and farther from us all. We tried and tried to convince her to come in closer to town proper, such as it is here." Slattery looked around at the small but somewhat tidy cluster of buildings that made up the heart of Boarwallow Gap.

Ethel shrugged. "She wouldn't hear of it. Then she started talking stranger and odder, and pretty soon we saw that she looked like she was losing weight. She wasn't washing nor taking care of herself. Me and a couple of the other womenfolk here at the time went out there and tried to help her. We managed to get her cleaned up a little, but that was about it."

"How does she eat?" said Trace, looking over his shoulder, as if he might see the woman alone out there in the dark, back eastward up the road from where they came.

"We take turns making food for her, then we bring it out there. She still has sense enough to eat and make a fire and such. But no matter when we drop in on her, we hope to see if we can't catch her at a time when she's maybe back with us, so to speak. And not, you know, not all," she waved a hand near the side of her head, "all . . ."

"Adrift," said Trace.

Slattery snapped a finger and pointed. "That's it. That's the word Ethel wanted, yep. But nope, never can. I think she's gone for good."

"Pardon me for asking this, but aren't you all worried that Cigar Tim will pay her a visit?"

"Sure we are," said the miner. "But what can we do? Short of tying her down, Marietta's not going to change her ways. So we just have to accept that somewhere in that foggy mind of hers, there's a thinking person who has made a decision to stay right there. I assume it's because she thinks Paco's gone off for a spell and she wants to be there for when he comes home."

"Long wait," said Chaw.

"Right, but we don't tell her that anymore. We're not certain how she'd react to the truth these days."

"Does she have any way of defending herself?" said Trace.

"Not hardly, no. Well, she's got her shovels and picks, but no weapons that we know of. We looked because we knew that Paco had himself a revolver and a scattergun, like most of us, but they all went missing once Paco was killed. It's my belief that that cigar-eating brute took them.

"Now she just wanders around asking anybody she sees if we've seen her Paco. Acts like we don't hardly exist. Certainly doesn't seem to recognize us as her old friends. So what can we do? We just leave her be, and if she turns up dead one of these days, well, it's not like we haven't tried to help her. You see?"

Chaw and Trace nodded, each man amazed at the oddness of the situation.

"Do you think that this Cigar Tim character didn't know she was in the cabin?" said Trace. "It's a raw thing to think, but I wonder why he didn't attack her as well."

"We wondered that, too. We'd come to the same conclusion as you did—likely he just didn't know she was there."

"Or maybe he did," said Chaw.

"Huh?" said Slattery.

"Maybe he was there, watching her the whole time she was out there with her husband."

"That's an awful thought."

"Sure it is. But then again, he's an awful fella."

Trace nodded in agreement. "After some of the things I saw in the war, things folks did to one another, just for the pleasure of seeing someone else suffer, well, it wouldn't surprise me in the least if this Cigar Tim fellow was just that sort of man."

Once more, a silence slipped over the small gathering.

After a while Chaw spoke up. "Now, the way I see it, folks, what you need to do is kill it where it sleeps! Your enemy, I mean." Chaw looked about him with wide eyes. "Look here, back when I was a child in the holler . . . Aw, now I see some of you are gnawing at the bit to get me on out of here, but I got the floor, as they say, ain't that right, Trace?"

His pard shrugged. "Afraid so, yep." He half grinned, knowing only too well where Chaw was headed with his story, and knowing, too, that his Reb pard was not wrong.

Chaw resumed his instructive tale. "See, there was this she-bear who went mad, felt wronged about the fact that something or someone had killed her two spring cubs. Well, sir, nobody could blame her, really, because they all knew what had done it. It was Homer Boyle's rogue hound what done it. Thing was a bad one from the start. Should have been drowned as a pup, not unlike a good many folks I have met in my travels."

If Chaw expected to hear chuckles, he was mistaken. These men were in no mood for stories, much less humorous ones, told by a near stranger to them. Sure, they all seemed to be getting along, but just now it seemed they were tolerating him at best.

He cleared his throat. Too bad for them, but he'd be jiggered if he was going to give up on a perfectly good story just because a few folks were bored.

"At any rate, that she-bear, she got so she was molesting folks' chicken coops, their sheep, goats, and such, and all during the day! But nobody could seem to get a fix on her. Or if they could, they hesitated because of a thing I forgot to mention.

"See, right after that foolish hound killed her babies, that big ol' mama bear was seen by three women from the town who were out looking for the last of the season's berries. They come upon her not far from the big berry patch where we all went, and so did the bears.

"But on that day, she was standing over the bodies of her two babies, and she was swaying and chuffing her

teeth and spraying great gobbets of spittle and foam all
over the place as she looked here and there.

"'It was as if she was protecting them babies,' said
one of the women. The worst part, though, was the
sound that she-bear was making. Come deep from
inside of her, way down lower than her throat. It sounded
to those berry ladies like a big woman sobbing. It was a
sound most folks do not forget once they have heard it.

"And how do I know that? Well, I heard it myself,
and all these years later, I do not forget that mournful,
wailing sound. Just like a woman, it was."

Chaw looked to the close-in rafter of that small structure and everyone else did, too. And then a small man
at the back said, "Nice story, fella, but what on earth has
that got to do with the fact that these rascals are popping
up like field mice in a corn bin around these parts,
trying to lay us low?"

"Yeah!" chimed in the others.

"Oh, well," said Chaw, flustered and red-faced and
forgetting what it was his point was supposed to be.

"Gentlemen," said Trace, from over by the door
where he was keeping an eye on the trail leading up to
the cabin site. "What my pard here is trying to say, I
think, and that I happen to agree with for once, is that
you have to track the thing to its den. You have to go to
the source and wipe out the men who are doing this
to you."

"Yep, that's what I'm saying!" said Chaw, beaming
at having gotten to the point of the story, even if it was
Trace who had done it and not him.

There was silence for a moment, and then the little

fellow said, "Well, our enemy is all the way back East. But now I think I see what else you're saying. We have to do to them what they been doing to us."

"In a manner of speaking, sure," said Trace.

"But that means killing them," said the small man. "And there ain't a one of us who is a killer. Not like them."

"I guess what we're saying, then," said Trace, calming the men with a raised hand, "is that if the law won't help us, then we have to become the law. And the first thing we should do is subdue them. Hopefully that will be enough. Take the raiders as prisoner, somehow, and hold them somewhere until we can haul them all to Richness."

"Why Richness?" said a man with a big, bulbous red nose.

"Because," said Chaw, "that's where we're hoping to find a lawdog who isn't already nested in the pocket of the consortium."

"Good luck with that," said the big-nosed man, shaking his head. "My dealings with anybody there tell me that they're all the same. Interested in money more than the lives and complaints of honest folk. And none more so than that Richness marshal."

A round of muttered agreement rippled through the small gathering.

"Well," said Trace. "Does anyone else have any ideas, then?"

The little fellow said, "None just yet, save for the fact that I agree with your man, there." He nodded at Chaw. "We ought to cut the head off the snake, near as we can, anyway. Might be we don't get right to the neck at first, but we have to try."

A round of nods and grunts of agreement sounded. He continued, "And another thing . . . You said *us* and *we*—seems to me you are counting yourself part of our problem, fella. That so?"

Trace looked confused and glanced at Chaw. "Man has a point, pard," said the buckskin-clad man, grinning.

Trace shrugged. "I'd say yes, given that our jobs are to haul freight for you all and all the others being starved and beaten and killed. So yes, your problem is our problem, too."

"Good!" said the small man. "Now I do believe I can trust you two strangers. Time for a draw on the jug and then we'll figure out our next moves. All right, men?"

For the first time since the meeting opened, they all replied with a hearty cheer and smiles, few louder or offering more of a grin than Chaw.

CHAPTER 13

The next morning, it took Chaw and Trace a bit more than an hour to repack and reshuffle the rest of their load. They did this in part to ease the pulling for the horses, centering the weight on the wheels and making certain that the rest of the goods were stacked accordingly.

They also had to accommodate for six decent-sized sacks of ore to be delivered to the agent in Richness, over the hills. They were all packed away and tied down and hidden beneath spare ropes and tarpaulins and other goods still to be delivered to two other mining camps between there and Richness, but smaller than Boar-wallow Gap.

When they were just about ready to depart, Ethel showed up with a kettle filled with steaming hot coffee and a plate mounded with fresh-baked biscuits and thick hunks of greasy fried meat stuffed in the middle of the biscuits. It all looked most toothsome and smelled even better than that. They soon found out that it tasted excellent, too.

"Ma'am," said Chaw, "if I was in my right mind, I'd

up and marry you. Any woman who can cook like this must have a pile more hidden charms to boot!" He winked at her and worked on another delicious mouthful of biscuit, butter, and meat.

The red-faced, dark-haired, buxom woman giggled and turned even redder. "Don't let Mr. Hughes hear you say that!" she said, giggling louder.

"Oh? Why's that?"

"Because he beat you to it, silly man!"

"Oh!" It was Chaw's turn to redden. "You mean that little fellow is your husband?"

"He sure is, been that way for, well, it seems forever and a day. But long enough for us to have three kids."

"Well, I'll be. He's a lucky fellow and no mistake, ma'am." Chaw nodded with vigor and slurped coffee and did his best to keep his attention on his food and drink. And not on the excited eyes of the woman, or on the raised eyebrows and smirk of his pard, that nosy Yankee.

Ethel departed with a smile and a wave, after filling their cups with the last of the coffee.

"You about ready, there, Romeo?"

Chaw rounded on Trace. "Who you calling names, mister?"

"Take 'er easy, pard. I was kidding. You know, you get any touchier and we're going to have a talk. Or rather, my knuckles are going to talk with your nose, you got me?"

Chaw snorted as he finished checking the knots on his side of the wagon. "You keep it up and you're going to end your days soon . . . and in pain."

They passed each other at the rear of the wagon and checked the opposite sides. As they repeated their last-minute checking of the wagon's opposites sides, Trace just chuckled.

He knew if he made another comment, it would lead to yet another from Chaw, and they already were each offering up comments the other had heard for years on the trail, from ranches to cattle drives and towns. He didn't want to continue it at the moment. But he knew that his initial comment had gotten through to his pard. They were fine.

As for Chaw, he well knew he had always been prone to blabbering too long, deep, and often with women. He'd never figured out how to behave around them. Not like other folks he knew, such as Trace, for instance.

Now Trace, that Yankee rascal, when he wanted to could charm the prickers off a cactus. But most of the time he acted as if he never even heard or noticed the women cooing and fluttering whenever they got near him.

Chaw, he'd always had to work at it, and more often than not his efforts produced dismal results. The big, buckskin-clad man sighed as he checked the traces, his mind half on the task. But he knew Trace was also going to check them.

And so his thoughts wandered back to another fellow he had known well who also had quite a way with the ladies. That had been his Uncle Buck. Difference between Trace and Buck was that Buck was never not aware that women found him to be a toothsome treat to look upon and sample. Likely because of this, the man had been a major vexation to his own mama, that'd be Chaw's dear Granny Jean. And then he was more of the same to his wife, Auntie Melody.

Woman lived up to her name, too. She could whistle like a bird and yodel like a goat. That was a good thing, because Buck left her very little else in life to be chipper about. But back when Chaw was a boy, and then onward as a young man, he admired Buck and wondered why his own Pap wasn't more like his brother.

It never came to Chaw that Buck did not conduct himself and his life in a way that didn't leave a pile of folks weeping or confused or angry, chief among them women. So, after all these years, Chaw reckoned he had finally figured out that he was never much like Buck in the ways he had once longed to be like the man.

He was more like his Pap where ladies were concerned. Sort of. Pap had met his mama and had settled down in the holler and raised up sorghum and chickens and children and woke up every morning in a tight little cabin as a happy man with a happy wife. At least until the cursed war.

But Buck, he'd awakened every morning with a skull-splitting headache, seething husbands looking for him, and a dilapidated home with a hurt, angry wife and sad children.

Chaw was pleased to note that although he had done his own share of earning bad headaches from roisterous evenings, he hadn't knowingly hurt many husbands, and he definitely did not have a wife and sad children somewhere, waiting on him to return. No sir. And yet one day he just might have a fine home and family, and that notion was a secret thrill to him, something to think on in the small hours when he could not sleep.

"You about ready to roll on out of Boarwallow Gap, at least for now, pard?"

"Huh?" Chaw shook his head. "Oh yeah, just lost in my own mind for a second there."

Trace chuckled and climbed up into the right side of the wagon's seat. He was going to ride shotgun and Chaw was going to start the driving. "Now that is one place I don't ever want to find myself."

"Huh? Oh, where's that?" said Chaw.

"Lost in your mind. I expect it's a place with no way out."

"Aw, now, pard, you know," Chaw swung up into the seat and snatched up the lines, neatly smoothing and tailing them off between his fingers. "That you are just talking out of jealousy."

"Jealous? How do you figure that?" said Trace.

Without missing a second, Chaw said, "Because I have a mind that is fertile, as I heard a fellow once say of folks with exceptional speed and thinking power. And you, well, pard, I'm sorry to have to tell you this, but you just don't."

Trace nodded slowly. "Okay, then. I guess that is something I will have to come to some sort of agreement with. But for now, could that clever mind of yours tell your fingers to jostle those lines and get moving? We have a whole lot of ground to cover, and most of it is going to be up and down and sideways and dangerous. And I don't just mean from the land and weather."

They both knew that the danger they faced was largely from the consortium's hired gun. At least that was what Slattery and a few others from the Gap figured would be lurking about somewhere on the trail. Might be Cigar Tim, might not be. The townsfolk suspected there would soon be others hired on by the consortium to assist Cigar Tim in the rough work.

When asked what they were basing those suspicions on, Slattery had shrugged and said to Trace, "Stands to reason. It's what I would do."

But Chaw and Trace knew they were right. There was a good chance the consortium had sent, or would soon send, other folks to foul things and do their best to make life for the Holdouts even worse than it already was. And so it stood to reason that they would also be bent on preventing supplies, now that they had started up again, from running in or out of the hills. And since Chaw and Trace were the ones freighting those goods— if they needed any more convincing—it was their fight now, like it or not.

"We'll just have to be prepared," said Trace. "Or as prepared as we can be, anyway."

"Well," said Chaw, releasing the brake. "We made it this far, eh?" He grinned and clucked and snapped the lines, easing the team into action.

They had half expected, after the seeming camaraderie of the evening before, that there might be more folks to see them on out of town. But no, there was just the one grubby child in the street, naked from the waist down, staring at them with wide brown eyes and holding what looked to be a dolly made of an old sock.

They set off on their trip from Boarwallow Gap toward the two other mining camps, their only stops that lay on the route between the Gap and the bustling burg of Richness, on the other side of the mountains. Trace and Chaw had been assured by Slattery that both camps were far smaller than the Gap.

At first, the road was impressive and looked to be a marked improvement on the trailways they had been traversing for the days leading up to their arrival at the Gap. But after a half mile or so of a straight-ahead, clean and clear trail, the roadway narrowed and began switchbacking downward.

"Tell you what I don't want," said Chaw, holding back on the lines and letting the horses step easy and with their own caution as he guided them downward, hugging the uphill edge. "I don't want to see that cursed Cigar Tim on this or any other stretch."

"Might not have a choice in the matter."

"Never said a thing about choice, just said I don't want to see him. It might well happen. If it does, I reckon now he knows we have an earful all about him from the folks in Boarwallow Gap. That might not set well with him."

"I suspect you're right."

They went on like this, down and up and down and up again, with increasingly frequent pauses to let the horses blow. It took them three and a half hours to reach the next mining camp, a pimple of a place that looked fit to burst any second. As soon as they rolled on in, they wanted to roll on out again.

But there was water at a creek, or so they'd been told,

just beyond the camp, and the team needed it. Yet such was the roadway that they were unable to first water the beasts and then easily turn around to unload their goods and then turn again to continue on their way.

The camp proper consisted of a clot of two shanties and a dugout farther up the scree-riddled slope to their right.

"How do!" shouted Trace to the only person about. "Hello there!"

The man stood regarding them, squinting in the full sun, nothing about him to shield its brutal, beating rays. He wore no hat on his sweaty head. There were no trees left nearby—nothing but stumps and gravel. Worst of all, from what they could see, the place was a snake's paradise.

The scree slope was pocked with juts of gray and rust-colored rock, and on and under each they saw the distinct, thick coils of vipers. Occasionally one moved, just enough to show they were indeed alive.

"I can't stay here for long, you know that," said Trace under his breath, his face white and an urge to keep swallowing back a knot in his throat not leaving him any time soon.

"I know, pard," whispered Chaw. "I feel the same way. I don't wish the snakes of the world any ill will, but man, I don't want to spend any time with them, either. How can folks live here without waking up dead and screaming?"

"Yeah," said the man who'd been sizing them up. He was a tall, thin fellow, wearing overalls that should have been patched some time ago, but had long since passed that stage of their life and now were more hole than cloth.

The same went for his once-white longhandle shirt. It was a begrimed thing with one sleeve still sporting the tatters of a cuff, the other ragged and ending halfway to the elbow.

His wrist and elbow bones jutted in a manner that was almost painful to look on, and his grimy skin bore a sweaty, waxy pallor. His gaunt face, sunken everywhere without bone beneath, seemed to meet in the middle, just beneath his long shard of a nose, where his mouth, under sweaty stubble, had collapsed in on itself. He worked this mouth over and over in a motion that suggested chewing.

"Yeah," he said again. "We all live here. What of it?"

His words were a response to a question that had been unasked, but likely was apparent on their faces.

Chaw did his best to keep a smile on his face. "I reckon we got a few things for you folks. Sligo Star Freighters!" he said.

"I know who you are. And there's just one folk now and that's me. Rest of them are all . . . all done for. Left this place, you might say."

"Okay, then. Just let us check our papers here and we can get you what you need. Got anything to send on? Ore or such? We're making for Richness."

The man eyed them some more, his mouth working nothing but the memory of teeth, and then he made to spit but apparently didn't have the ingredients for it. He shrugged. "No ore. No nothing. Times be hard hereabouts."

Chaw nodded. "I see that. Okay, then." He pivoted on the seat as if to swing down to the ground.

Trace touched his arm. "Check for snakes first."

"Oh, right." Chaw did so and then proceeded to lower his boots to the gritty earth. "Tell you what," he said under his breath. "It'll take a miracle for us to get on out of here without one of the horses getting snakebit."

Trace nodded, his color not coming back. He, too, looked groundward and then stepped down, keeping the shotgun ready.

CHAPTER 14

The lanky, toothless man, who, despite his loss of chewers, looked to Trace to be about thirty-five years old or so, sidled on over toward them. They picked at the knots tying down the load, and at the same time were busy keeping an eye on the horses, and particularly on the ground surrounding the horses, and on the earth nearby themselves.

It was going to be a trick to get the goods unloaded, then truss up everything once more, but tighter and leaner, then roll on out of there. But they had motivation everywhere they looked.

"Pard, hate to ruin your fun, and I don't want to see you scream when you turn around, but not six feet from your back, off by the side of the trail, atop that big boulder, a rather large rattler just eased on up to the top from behind it. He appears to be sunning himself, but where these critters are concerned, I don't want to take anything for granted."

Soon after Chaw had begun speaking, it came to Trace what his mumbling pard in the buckskins was conveying to him. Trace froze. "Behind me?"

"Yeah, 'fraid so."

Along about then, the lanky resident of what was quickly becoming evident to the two freighters was an increasingly freakish place paused his shuffling, drag-footed gait and halted about six feet to Trace's right.

Trace glanced at him. In an effort to overcome the cold, sweaty, clammy feeling creeping up his spine and tingling his scalp and face, he said, "So . . . how do you like living here in the mountains, Mr., ah . . ."

The man squinted, his face pruning even more than it had been, and finally said, "Oh, you're talking to me. I get ya. Been a long time since I seen anybody else. Other than them." He twitched his head to his left, back behind Trace.

Trace felt certain that the fellow was indicating another person who had emerged without him knowing it. He turned and looked to where the odd man had nodded, only to see no person there.

But he did see, atop the rock Chaw had mentioned and which he himself had not yet dared to turn to see, one of if not the largest rattler he'd ever seen. And that was saying a whole lot, because in all their years roving the South and the West, Trace had seen a good many of the vipers.

Most of them had been fair-to-middling size, as his old grandfather had put it. But a few had been on the large-to-grand size. And this one was grander than nearly all he had seen. In fact, as he stared at it, seemingly dozing in the full sun, coiled and thick, dull and yet gleaming, he could not recall having ever seen another so very . . . large.

At its thickest, around what he guessed was its middle, the thing was as thick as his forearm. He could not see its tail, but he guessed that the length of the buttons on its rattle must be six-to-eight inches, maybe more.

The entire beast took up the space and roughly the same shape as a big coil of rope looped lazily along the side of the docks he'd seen several times along the East Coast. During the war, the Union Army had marched southward in its zeal to quell and kill in equal measure.

As impressive as the snake's looped body was, it was the viper's massive head, easily the size and shape of a goodly wedge of café pie, that mesmerized Trace the most. Just when he thought he could look away, the mottle-patterned, brown-gray brute snapped open its eyes and flicked out its tongue.

It appeared to be looking right at Trace, as if it was most interested in something. And for the life of him, he could not figure out how to tear his eyes away from looking at the thing, which seemed to be staring straight back at him.

It raised its head, and the meaty wedge swayed slowly back and forth, its thin red tongue slipping out, waggling as if testing the air, then slipping back in again.

"Chaw," said Trace.

"Right here, pard. I see it. No idea if it'll launch itself at us, but I fetched the other scattergun."

"No, no, no. No, you don't! No sir, no how!"

Trace and Chaw glanced briefly at the skinny man.

He was showing more spark and fire than he had since they arrived.

At first, Chaw had thought the man might well doze off while they had attempted to chat with him. But now he was offering them a hard stare, or what might pass for one on his odd face.

"Don't tell me you got a problem with us taking care of one of these here critters for you, do you?"

"Problem?" said the man, unfolding his arms from where they'd been tucked inside his overalls, riding above where a belly might be on a man who wasn't so thin. "Problem? I guess so, mister. Them're my neighbors. You harm them, you harm me."

"Neigh—but they're rattlers, man! Ain't no way a fellow and a rattlesnake, let alone dozens of the cursed things, can live cheek by jowl and survive! Why, one of them has got to go. And fortunately for you, I know which one!"

Chaw began to raise the single-shot scattergun to his chest, his thumb feathering the hammer. "That thing twitches or flicks one more time and it'll be its last twitch or flick, I tell you true."

Soft, quick, dragging, sliding sounds caused Chaw to jerk his gaze to his left. The weird, thin man had somehow made his way to him and was on him. Although slight in stature and just about the same height as Chaw, he nonetheless was quick—quicker than the big freighter expected the run-down wisp might move.

By the time Chaw comprehended what was happening, the man had hurled himself at him. He snatched at Chaw's near arm—the meaty part above the elbow, and held it tight in the bony, clawlike grip of his right hand—while his left scrabbled at Chaw's forearm.

As Chaw drew back, he shouted, "What in the blue blazes . . ." And even as he said this, he saw that the fellow's left hand was a gnarled, wizened thing, the fingers of which were deformed, curled into blackened, raw, clawlike stumps, flexing and snatching.

He continued jerking away, shoving at the man, whose grip was surprisingly strong with that good right hand. The man held on, staggering as he did so on his one good foot. The other, Chaw saw, since the man was barefoot, his right, looked about as bad off as the man's left hand.

That left foot, too, was a deformed thing, all black and purple and twisted, drawn in on itself in a painful-looking hard clot of sinew and bone and tight-stretched skin, welted and knobby as if it had had a hard reaction to a . . . snakebite.

Yep, thought Chaw as he fought the man off, this fool's been bitten by these vile things. And somehow, he still not only lives with them, but he doesn't want to see any harm come to the menacing critters!

All this Chaw thought within moments as he jerked to get away from the man, grasping his shotgun in his right hand while he tried to swing to his left and jerk himself away from the skinny fool.

But the thin man would not be deterred. He shoved his head forward, his greasy hair falling in strings, slapping over Chaw's buckskin sleeve.

Chaw raised the butt of the shotgun to drive it forward into the man's head, not in a death blow but with enough force to stun him, maybe dizzy him up a bit. But beneath the flopped hair and bent head, it felt to Chaw as if the man was . . . biting him.

But how could he, he wondered as he tried to club the man. What might the fool bite him with? He had looked to be stone toothless.

Somehow his blow did little save for glancing off the left side of the man's canted head and slamming down on his hunched shoulder.

"What are you doing?" Chaw bellowed, trying to knee the man, but the skinny wraith clung and hung on, swaying with Chaw's bulk.

"Nnnnhh! Nnnnoooo!" whined the stranger.

Chaw raised the shotgun once more and held it up, ready to deliver another blow to the man's head. This time he did not mess about with niceties. "Now look here, you—you vicious beast!"

The thin man was keeping Chaw's attention on his paltry, soft attempt at biting, making his pathetic sounds and clawing at him, hanging on like a mill pond leech on a swimmer's back.

"Look out, Chaw!"

It was Trace.

Chaw failed to see that the fellow's enfeebled left claw had dropped down to the man's side and had come up with a pitted, rust-pocked dagger.

Trace whipped up his own shotgun and jammed it forward, taking a lunging step so he wouldn't spray Chaw with the thing at the same time. He shouted, "No! Drop it!" But the skinny man was having none of it and continued his odd attack.

Chaw had just managed to free himself by jamming the butt of the gunstock hard against the man's forehead. It worked enough to get the fool away from him by a foot's distance. That was when he saw the blade come arcing up at him. It had been intended for his gut, but it whistled a smidgin before it.

Trace lunged in, attempting to jam the barrel into the man's side. The lean miner sidestepped and moved with twice the speed and vigor he'd had before. Now his face wore a hooded, menacing look. He brought up that good right hand of his and it, too, was clutching a blade, but this one was a gleaming, keen, pointed thing that moved fast, coming in at Chaw's chest from the right.

Chaw and Trace were both backed up to the wagon and could not retreat. They were trapped. Chaw brought up his shotgun and managed to shove the snout of it hard up into the middle of the man's breadbasket just as the shiny knife's tip pierced his rawhide tunic.

Chaw triggered the gun, and the blast seemed to follow its effect.

There was a half an eyeblink's worth of time with no sound at all but plenty of motion as the skinny freak whipped backward. His snaky eyes were wide now, and his lanky, smelly, unwashed hair flailed. The puckered lips surrounding his toothless, black hole of a mouth parted wide, revealing a pink, spittle-dripping tongue nested within, yet lashing as if it sought something in the air.

Then the blast sounded as the man slammed into the raw, craggy, rocky hillside, punching hard against a boulder emerging from the scree and churned earth, raw remnants of his and others' greedy clawings for a few paltry ounces of unrefined ore.

The only thing their dogged work ever produced was the enmity of the original denizens of the place. As the man gasped his last, his eyes wide and his mouth worked like that of a banked fish. His hands and feet—the blackened, wizened appendages and those not yet afflicted—also flexed and writhed.

From every sliver of shadow and from behind every rock, some no larger than a fist, emerged vipers. They made for the weak, withered, flailing man as he bled his last into the dust and gravel of the place he chose to live and die.

The residents squirmed, flailed, slid, skittered, writhed, and roiled their way in haste to the man. Within a minute his still-twitching, moaning form was covered with dozens and dozens, perhaps hundreds of slithering vipers of all sizes.

They flicked their tongues and fangs at one another and then at the man, eager to join in the freakish orgy of feasting, working their way inward, deeper into the growing, writhing pile, deeper into the dying, twitching man.

Seven feet away, Chaw and Trace stood, side by side, backs tight to the wagon, eyes as wide as they had ever been in their lives, muscles tensed and trembling, witnesses to the raw horror of the gory scene working itself out before them.

Somehow, Trace sensed movement to his right. He managed to peel his gaze from the mess to see what it was. And he almost wished he hadn't.

It was the big snake from atop the boulder. He'd nearly forgotten about the thing, which horrified him as well. But now the massive serpent was no longer atop the boulder. It had slid and wormed down the side of it and was making its way, in no hurry, toward the roiling mass of lesser snakes. And its chosen path brought it less than four feet from the men's boots, right before them. And yet they could do nothing but stare at it, for Chaw had seen it as well.

A slight gasp leaked from Trace's mouth, and at the same time Chaw shifted the fingers of one of his hands on the shotgun. The snake halted, seizing in place.

Slowly, as if it was a person who had just heard a comment it did not care for, the snake swung its thick wedge of a head to its left, toward the two men, and angled is snout upward.

It looked from Trace to Chaw, then back to the middle of them, as if sizing them up, weighing the choices open to it. It slowly turned its head, looking forward once more toward the still-writhing mass of snakes. It gazed on that scene for a few long moments.

Neither man could move. It felt as if they had been pinned to the spot by the behemoth beast. They could scarcely breathe but did not realize this until they had been freed from the snake's spell. It began to move and they began, slowly, by trickles, to breathe again.

It never occurred to either of them to blast the thing when they were given the chance. Somehow it felt wrong. Even though both of them separately were repulsed by what they saw happening to the man's body and by the big snake's slow advance on the pile of snakes before it.

Chaw and Trace got the feeling that this was something they would never again witness. And they were fine with that.

Once the big snake reached the left foot of the dying man, it looked the body and the snakes atop it up and down, side to side, and then proceeded to advance, sliding on up the man's big, floppy trouser leg.

It was too much for the two knock-kneed freighters to bear, and they snapped out of their reverie. Without a word to each other, they whipped their glances downward, looking everywhere at once. They saw no snakes anywhere near their feet, nor near the hooves of the horses of their team, which had been growing increasingly fidgety.

It helped that the horses wore blinders, for if they had seen the near-silent emergence and subsequent descent of snakes on the now-dead man, they would have thrashed and stomped and reared. No doubt this would have enticed snakes to advance on them instead of on the fallen toothless man.

With more speed than they had shown in many a year, the men vaulted up into the wagon seat. Trace was at the lines, and he yanked the set brake handle, freeing it and jamming it into place, resting it in its notch.

Trace barely gave it time to do so when he shouted, "Hee yah! Git gone! Git!" He tickled the rumps of the horses with the buggy switch, and as they rolled on out of that vile camp, neither man could help but look back over their right shoulders to look toward the man.

They were alarmed to see half again as many snakes atop the man, and even more shocked to see that the big snake had emerged from within the man's coverall trousers up at the chest. It kept emerging, until its head and the first foot of its massive, long body poked out from beneath the top of the trousers, up beneath the dead man's chin.

It seemed to look down on the man and the others of its kind from its great height. At the same time, the other snakes looked to be backing away, bowing their heads in deference to what most surely was somehow their master.

"Oh my word . . ." said Trace, shaking his head and resuming the driving, lashing harder than he ought to have at the rumps of the rearmost brace of horses.

The beasts seemed to feel the need for haste, and instead of balking, they doubled their efforts and stomped ahead, just shy of a run. It was not quick enough for Chaw and Trace, and yet it would have to be.

"Oh my stars," Chaw finally said, his breath whooshing out as if he'd held it the entire first mile from the place. "I . . . I . . . Oh no!"

"What?" shouted Trace, turning to face Chaw. "What!" He yanked on the lines.

"No! No! Don't slow down!" shouted Chaw. "No! But . . ."

"But what?" said Trace, chest heaving, eyes wide.

"I just had a thought. . . . What if one of them things got into the wagon somehow? I mean, snakes can climb, right?"

"Yes! Yes, they can! And there were a whole lot of

them . . ." Trace kept looking back over each shoulder, then stood in the boot well and looked down, looked at the seat, then at Chaw. "Next time you get a thought like that, you shut up! Just shut yourself up!"

It was long, long minutes before either man spoke again. But they had spent the entire time since that brief, shouted conversation swiveling their heads all about themselves.

This went on for some time, until finally it subsided into occasional glances behind them at the bundled load.

"Hey," said Chaw. "We never dropped the tailgate nor unloaded back there, did we?"

"Nope," said Trace. "Never got that far, thankfully."

Chaw nodded. "Say, what do you suppose that man meant when he said the others who lived there was all done for, or something such as that?"

"Well, given what we saw, I'd say that meant that if we were to look into those few dwellings that we saw up the hillside, if you can call them houses."

"Not me! I ain't never going back there! In fact, if there's a different route that somehow goes below or above that evil place, and I don't care how far out of the way it is, then that's the route I'll be taking on the next run."

"Me too, of course." Trace nodded. "But I was saying that if we were to look into those awful hovels, I think we'd find bones, bones of the others who had lived there. Picked over by who knows what, snakes or . . ."

"No, no, no!" said Chaw. "You don't mean that man,

do you? You don't think he would eat his own kind, do you?"

Trace just shrugged. "Heck, I don't know, Chaw. I can't even be certain that we saw what we saw, if you understand what I mean."

"I do, and I don't want to think about it."

And that's where they left it for a while. They both sat swaying in the seat, guns all set, knives unthonged and ready to whip free of their sheaths. Each man was half lost in his dark thoughts, thoughts he could not shake himself from as they watched the working backs and rumps of the horses. It was some time before one of them spoke.

"Where we headed next?" said Chaw, slowly becoming comfortable once more in the seat, not entirely but enough so that he could stuff a fresh wad of chaw in his cheek. This emboldened Trace, and he worked fresh tobacco into his pipe and set it alight.

"On to the next mining camp, something called Fortune. I saw it on the map. No idea if it's still around. Hector wasn't even certain."

"How come I didn't hear about it?" said Chaw.

"Because you were busy stuffing flapjacks into your big mouth and trying to impress the widow at the same time with your knowledge about hard cider. You don't recall?"

"I recall all right, but for your information, it was her who asked me about cider. Or was it apples? Or fruit? I don't recall. Might be she was talking of fruit. Or pie. Heck, I can't be expected to dredge up every word of every conversation I've ever had, especially with ladies!"

A slight smile played at Chaw's mouth's corners. "Why, if that was the case, I'd have no room for any other thoughts for the rest of my born days and then some!"

"You are far too full of yourself to let that happen, Chaw."

"I don't know exactly what that means, but I'd say it's a compliment. I'll take it as such anyway."

They were silent a moment more, then Chaw said, "Say, you don't suppose that next place, Fortune or whatever you called it, is a snake pit, too, do you?"

Trace's eyes widened, but he shrugged, trying to seem casual. "It's possible, I guess." He looked at Chaw.

The buckskin-clad fellow said, "I sure do hope not. I don't know how much more of that I can take. If I didn't know you'd seen it all, too, I'd swear I got hold of some bad beef somewhere along the line. Except I ain't had no beef of late."

They rode the team on the edge of hard for many more miles and only slowed when they saw the promising glisten of water ahead. They neared it and saw a thin but ample flowing stream coursing down from the hillside to their right.

Trace halted the team, set the brake, and said, "I'll tend to the horses while you check the load for . . . well, you know."

"Why me?" said Chaw, louder than he intended.

"Because I drove. You've just been sitting there looking scared and spitting all over the side of the wagon, no doubt."

"Did not. I know how to spit. That's something Pap taught us all as kids, me and my brothers and sisters, too. I consider that a mighty insult to the good name of Dagworth."

"Fine," said Trace, carefully eyeballing the ground before he hopped down and stretched his back. He kept his hand on his knife as he walked to the horses. He left the shotgun propped but easily reachable in the boot well.

"Consider it any way you want to. I'm not backing down. And to prove it, just eyeball your side of the wagon if you doubt me. I daresay you'll see traces of spittle there. Something to keep in mind before we roll back to Mankley and present the team and wagon to old Hector. I don't think he'll be as impressed as you might want him to be with your family's proud legacy of precision spitting."

Chaw was about to reply, but he suddenly shut his mouth. Trace glanced over the backs of the horses at his pard and noticed the man was deep in an inspection of the side of the wagon.

The remainder of their journey to the next settlement was as smooth as they could expect, given the raw terrain.

Fortune turned out to be less a camp than a wind-blown cluster of paper and plank shanties. Three and a half of them remained from what looked to have been a peak of perhaps a dozen. The remainder were now caved in, scavenged from, or collapsed.

"Hello!"

Chaw's voice echoed off the rocks and stunty trees. Nothing moved.

"Anybody here?" shouted Trace, receiving the same quiet response. They sat in silence and looked about.

Of current human habitation, there were no indications. One they rolled in and guessed, based on obvious signs, that the place was devoid of human life, they still sat in the wagon's seat and continued to eyeball the place. Their gazes lingered on each sliver of shadow for signs of anything snaky or for a flash of movement.

"I don't see nothing. You?" Chaw continued to squint and peruse as much of the scene around them as possible.

"No, no snakes. Yet." Trace acted the same as his pard, keeping a keen eye on as much of everything as he could. "I'd say we're all right in hopping down."

"If nobody's here, I don't believe we need to linger too long," said Chaw.

And so they spent a long, tense ten minutes, during which they each only ventured as far from the wagon as they dared. They wanted to be able to comfortably tell themselves and the widow and Hector that they looked all about the camp and saw no one.

Once done, they nodded to each other, climbed back aboard the wagon, and gentled the lines over the backs of the team. As Chaw manned the lines, Trace kept an eye on their back trail, making certain there wasn't some out-of-breath latecomer scrambling down an embankment and waving his arms for them to stop, come back.

But of such a phantom desperado, he saw nothing.

As if reading his mind, a trait they had continued to share somehow since they first met long years before when trying to kill each other on the battlefield, Chaw said, "We good? Nobody back there disappointed we didn't leave off flour or some such?"

Trace turned around and faced forward. "No, we're clear. If there's anybody back there waiting for supplies from us, they are living mighty rough. That place was deserted some months ago; I'd bet a whole lot of money I don't have on it."

A while later, when Trace had tugged out the map and was tracing their route with a grimy fingertip, Chaw said, "You been getting a feeling as if there's somebody eyeing us?"

Trace glanced up from the map. "Can't say as I have. But now I will. So thanks for that, pard."

Chaw smiled. "Any time."

A few minutes later, Trace folded the map again and tucked it back into his inner coat pocket. "Why, you?"

"Me what?" said Chaw.

"Getting the feeling as if someone's watching us?"

"Oh that, yeah. Been for some time, too. I wonder if it's that Cigar rascal."

Trace looked left and right but didn't say anything.

"How far are we from Richness?" said Chaw.

"Too far to make it before dark at this rate of speed."

"You complaining?"

"Nope," said Trace. "It's best to save the horses. They've been working mighty hard today. If I read the map right, we should make Richness before midday tomorrow. I vote we camp sooner rather than later."

As they normally did while on the trail, and now particularly because they knew without doubt that they were in a country infested with ne'er-do-wells, snakes, and crazy people, they set up a simple watch, spelling each other every three hours.

They used to last longer than that, but they found that one or the other—or both, if they'd had a long day and a big meal—dozed off while on watch. "Which is not the point," said Trace, criticizing himself but knowing that Chaw would also take it to heart.

There had been a specific incident that had forced them to switch to shorter times on watch, even though they knew they weren't really getting decent jags of sleep. It had happened one night in the northern reaches of the Dakotas. They'd been making their way back down south and then west, where they hoped to find ranch work before the weather proved too cold and froze them to death in their saddles—Chaw's greatest fear.

On this particular night some years before, Chaw was dozing in his blankets and Trace was nibbling away at a hunk of jerky and had poured himself yet another tin cup of sludge-thick, near-cold coffee.

Trace, seated with his legs outstretched by the nearly expired fire, slipped into a light snooze with the cup of coffeelike mud balanced on his demure belly. The last half of the strip of jerky remained in his right hand, which rested atop his saddle.

The fingers clasping it softened their grip as sleep took hold of the tired man. The jerky remained loosely held. This was fine . . . until a small hand, or at least one smaller than that of Fullcup Trace's, grasped it and slid the dried stick of meat from his grasp.

The possessor of the hand nearly got away with the theft, but hunger instigated haste and then the slight but hearable enough sounds of grunting and chewing.

As was his habit born of long years of sleeping in situations that were on occasion brimming with risk and danger, Trace had trained himself to awaken without much movement.

This worked well much of the time, and his eyes would open first, wide, and seemingly alert, taking in whatever they might around them. Some of the time, however, this was not the case.

On this particular occasion, Trace, who had slipped into the gauzy edges of a dream involving a certain war widow he'd become acquainted with some years before. She was a woman he'd been smitten enough with that he considered leaving his partnership with Chaw and settling down to help her operate her dairy farm.

And then he'd found out that she wasn't quite a widow. Because her dead husband made a surprising return visit at a most-unexpected moment.

"Too bad," he'd said to Chaw later, once he'd bought new boots and a shirt, two items he'd left behind due to his hasty departure from her caresses.

"Yeah, she was a comely thing," agreed Chaw, even though he'd been a mite hurt when Trace had mentioned the probable dissolution of their partnership.

But their partnership hadn't come apart, and both men had later agreed Trace had escaped back to a life for the better. That didn't mean that Trace didn't still think on her now and again. And occasionally she would make an appearance in his dreams as well.

And so when the jerky was slipped from his sleep-weakened right hand, he'd not noticed. But then, when the hungry intruder began partaking of the jerky, grunting and chewing with vigor, Trace's eyes snapped open wide and with immediacy.

He also flinched and his left hand jerked sideways. It still held, loosely, the loop handle of the half-filled tepid cup of muddy coffee atop his belly. Most of the thick liquid jostled out and onto his shirt and ran down the side of his gut.

By then Trace's unfocused gaze sharpened and, with benefit of the increasing glow of the new day's purpling light, he saw a bizarre creature crouched not two feet from him. It looked humanlike, and perhaps half grown. Then he squeezed his eyes shut and began to rise at the same time, wincing at the wetness of the spilled coffee and at the sight before him.

As he moved, Trace barked, "Hey!" and whipped his torso forward, reaching with his now-empty left hand.

The creature—more like a person than anything else, now that he and it had exchanged wide-eyed glances—had been transfixed by his sudden wakefulness and movement. But not for long, for it spun and fled, bending low and scampering.

Trace scrambled to get to his feet, shouting, "Hey! Hold there!"

By then, Chaw had also awakened, as usual for him, shouting questioning sounds and thrashing outward with both hands. He righted himself and took off after

Trace, who, unbeknownst to Chaw, was also in pursuit of someone.

Chaw, however, was not wearing his boots and was unable to make more than a dozen feet of his journey before he nearly folded up, wincing as he stepped down with his full weight on nuggets of unyielding gravel.

He ended up sitting down on the spot, holding a foot in his hands and shouting into the darkness: "Where you headed? Trace? Supper got the better of you?"

Chaw continued his comments at intervals while he worked his way back to his boots and tugged them on. As he stood, a commotion in the close-by periphery of somewhat darkness surrounding camp became more prominent and louder. Chaw paused, slowly moving his hand to his revolver's grip.

That was when the shadows parted and Trace emerged into the meager light, now visible to Chaw because of the coming morning. "Pard!" he said, a grin spreading on his face. "Thought fellows such as yourself might not have been bothered that much by the hot supper trots."

His weak joke made no difference to anyone within hearing range. But as Trace advanced into the campsite, what Chaw saw shut his mouth and brought him up short.

"Build up that fire," said Trace while he dragged and shoved the small figure ahead of himself.

It turned out to be a girl, no more than thirteen years of age, and she had been a frantic, mewling, fearful thing, more feral than civilized.

Trace now mused on the memory as he sat up in their

fresh camp, a half a day's drive north of Richness, Utah. He gazed into the new night while Chaw snored and his small fire crackled, eager to gnaw its way through a fresh few sticks.

He had been thinking about needing to stay awake, as he always thought, when he was on watch first, while Chaw snoozed. And whenever he thought about needing to stay awake, his mind clicked back to thinking about that young, food-stealing girl he'd caught up with in the dark beyond their camp in the Dakotas that night years before.

The only reason he'd found her at all was because she had crouched down after a stumble, then held still, hoping he'd rush right on by. And he would have, but she had crouched down too close to where he was making for.

He'd lunged right into her, which sent the poor, small thing sprawling, and sent himself flailing, landing hard on his knees in the darkness. He knew as he righted himself that he'd been lucky not to have rammed those knees straight into unforgiving rock.

He heard her sobbing and gasping as he got back to his feet. It wasn't difficult to catch her, and he had managed to clutch on to her arms, pinning them to her sides as he held her from behind. He'd eventually subdued her, despite the kicks and clawing hands and spitting.

Trace dragged her and shoved her and carried her back to camp. They stood there before Chaw, the big buckskin-clad man and he had looked her up and down. "Can she speak, you think?"

"Of course I can speak, you fool!"

That had been the first of many sharp, quick words from the mouth of one Natalia Watkins that they had heard that day and the next. By late afternoon of that second day, they had fed her an alarming amount of their grub stocks.

Then they reached a trading post where the kindly wife of the post merchant guessed correctly, as it turned out, that she had become separated somehow from her family, which had been traveling westward to Oregon.

They'd left word with the woman that if their daughter turned up, she should hold her there and they would return within two weeks.

A bit more time than that had passed since they departed, but the woman insisted they were keen and seemed earnest in their promise to return, on the off chance that their daughter had turned up.

That and the fact that young Natalia had been amenable to staying on at the trading post to await her family was what had parted Chaw and Trace from her company that next day.

Once fed, she'd turned out to be an intelligent, witty, laughing, sharp-tongued youth, only twelve years of age, as it turned out, and strangely silent about how she ended up separated from her family.

As they were leaving, in a quiet voice, she spoke to Chaw, without looking him in the eye. "Sometimes I walk in my sleep."

"Oh," said the big man, reddening and leaning in. "Well, don't let a little thing like that cause you worry. I sometimes snore."

"Like a bull grizz!" said Trace, winking at her.

"I know," she said, looking at each man. "Both of you do. It's awful. As if you're fighting, but with foul sounds!"

"I do not snore," said Trace.

"Ha!" said Chaw and Natalia in unison. This caused a moment of laughter, and then that was all.

It had taken Chaw and Trace a few minutes, once back on the trail, before they had figured out that she had been telling them the reason she became separated from her traveling family.

"Apparently, she just wandered off while asleep and got turned around enough that when she woke up, she realized she was lost."

"Hmm," said Chaw. "Don't much explain how she come to be all clothed and wearing her boots, too."

"True," said Trace. "Maybe she slept in them? We often do, after all."

They decided by mutual unspoken agreement to let it go. They'd played their part in the odd little drama in the girl's life, and if there was anything fishy about her story, then neither man could ever say.

And now here they were, years later, encamped once again. This time they were without their own gear and mounts, but with a freighting team. As he often did in the dark, quiet hours, Trace mused on life and its various twists and turns.

Chaw burbled and growled and snored in his sleep, and Trace grinned, wondering not for the first time how in the heck he had ended up pards with a big, loud, bold Rebel. Sure, he knew the reasons, though they did not matter.

That's when, from off to his right, Trace heard a crunching sound, as made by a boot stepping on loose gravel. He tensed and shucked his revolver, drawing low and edging to his left as he turned to face the direction the sound had come from.

He glanced to his right and was not surprised to see that Chaw was also awake and rolling to his side, his own revolver already in hand.

Neither of them much slept bootless on the trail anymore. At least not when they each knew they were in potentially dicey environs. They exchanged quick glances.

Chaw thumbed his chest, then jerked a finger to his own right. Then he scribbled a quick arc in the air, indicating he'd take the right flank and circle up and around camp. That meant Trace would do much the same, but to the left.

Each man did just that, with Chaw taking the outer perimeter and Trace keeping an eye on camp, while worming his way around. He worked well outside of the fire's low glow, yet back into the brush and rock. They moved silently, each man calling on hard-earned skills of stealth learned and honed while in the employ of their respective armies during the brutal war.

Within fifteen minutes, they met up back at camp, approaching from opposite sides. They continued to patrol, then each man took facing sides of the campfire, mystified that they hadn't turned up anything.

"I know what I heard," said Trace.

Chaw nodded. "I heard it too, pard. Could have been some critter somehow."

"Could have," said Trace, but he didn't need to finish

his thought, which was that they both knew it had not been a stray creature of the night.

As they settled, somewhat uncomfortably, back into camp, each man was tense and ready to bolt into action. Chaw poked at the fire and nudged at the coals. Then he said, "Trace!" in a quick, low whisper.

"What?" said the Yank in an equally low voice.

Chaw nodded toward the fire. At the edge, still smoking, lay half a cigar.

Neither man slept again that night.

CHAPTER 15

They arrived in Richness just about when they'd expected to, midday, the day after discovering the cigar—worrisome evidence of a ghostly visitor that kept them sleepless. But when they rode on to the depot, they found to their surprise that there were two wagons ahead of them.

"You men looking to unload, I take it."

Chaw and Trace saw a short, fat man holding a small ledger book. He sported a pencil behind each ear and one in his right hand. By the time their eyes had settled on the man, he had returned his own gaze to the open book he held, which rested on the top of his jutting round belly.

"If you're talking to us, then yep," said Chaw. "We've come a fair piece and we would like to unburden the horses before they drop in their tracks."

"I hear you, all right," said the man, licking the tip of his pencil. "And if I was you, and I'm not, then I'd tail on out of here until the morning. You can check back later today, but I do believe these wagons, much of them, anyway, will be gotten through by the end of the day today. But not you." He nodded past them. Chaw and Trace both glanced to the left and saw two more wagons and teams waiting. That meant four wagons were ahead of them.

"Sorry about it, but I'm down a couple of hands. Can't keep men on these days on account of the big doings in the hills back yonder where you come from, I take it."

"What doings might they be?" said Trace.

"You're kidding me, right?"

Then, when he realized they were not, the fat man said, "Why, the gold, man! The gold!"

Trace nodded, although it was still obvious to the fat man that this newcomer either didn't know of the gold or didn't care. Either way, Trace was certain he was regarded as an oddity. He knew what the man meant; he was merely trying to discover information about the consortium.

"Look," said the fat man. "I'm not one for chasing such things, no, no." He shook his head. "Not me. But I don't mind others moving on in and looking to make a profit."

"And as a depot owner and shipping firm," said Chaw, smiling, "I guess you don't mind one little bit if they then send their ore and their orders for goods your way, huh?"

The fat man rocked back on his heels and his wide, red face beamed. "I can't deny that business has never been better! And it promises to keep on in such a vein, if you'll pardon the mining reference. Look, if those big spenders from back East follow through with their plans to tear those hills apart and leave no stone untouched in their search for ore, have at it, I say."

He grew serious again. "Not just gold, mind you. Why, Richness will be a mighty hub for shipping, to and from. It's the only place to do it, you see." He nodded, as if agreeing with himself.

"What about Mankley?"

A slight cloud passed over the man's jovial face. "What about Mankley?"

"Well," continued Trace. "Being on the other side of these mountains, it stands to reason that it might also be set up just right to cater to the trade and needs generated by the big back East investors, and the smaller miners, too."

"Well, yes, technically you are correct, of course."

"It seems as if there might be room enough in the venture for both towns. Might even be necessary," said Chaw.

The fat man sighed. "Yes, yes, you are right, of course. I just let my greed get the best of me there for a moment."

"Well now, it happens to the best of us."

The fat man looked at them again. "I assume you are from Mankley, then. And if that is the case, then you must be from Sligo Star Freighters, am I right?"

Trace nodded. "That's correct."

"Excellent! I'm pleased to see that their, shall we say, setbacks haven't prevented that poor woman, the Widow Roscommon, from continuing with the business. As you say, Mankley is also poised to be a valued resource in this boom time on both sides of the hills hereabouts."

"You sound like you should be mayor," said Trace, trying not to sound patronizing.

"You think so? Well," the fat man jutted his chin and looked skyward, "it's a thought. Yes sir, it's a thought."

"So no chance we can unload and reload today?" said Chaw.

"No, no, I'm sorry. As I said, I am down on experienced workers, but I have newly hired men who are doing their best. Now, the thing for you to do is to head on out of town along that road there." He gestured past them to a winding lane heading eastward, the direction they expected to make for the next day.

"About a quarter mile on, on the left, you'll see a big ol' split boulder, split who knows when, likely by lightning. Just there, behind it, actually, is a grand spot for you and your team and load to camp. It's safe and protected, and there's a creek right there. Good fresh water. I send folks there sometimes to camp. Oh, just so you know, there might be a bit of a blow and rain tonight." He looked skyward for a moment. "An old-timer I know name of Willard said his joints were aching something fierce. That usually means we're in for weather."

Chaw sighed and Trace scratched his chin.

"Come back in the morning, not too early, mind you," said the fat man. "I'll do my best to accommodate you then. Now, I really must get back to the dock. I see those new buffoons are not tending to things as swiftly as I need them to. Oh, never buy a depot, men. It's nothing but headache, morning to night. I'm going broke."

And with that, the little jolly fat man was off, waddling at top speed past the driverless waiting wagons toward the loading dock beyond.

"Broke, huh?" said Chaw. "He just got through telling us how busy he was."

"Folks are never satisfied."

"True words, pard. Okay, then, what's the plan?" said Chaw, scratching his chin and looking with unconcealed annoyance at everything around him.

"Nothing for it but to take that fellow's advice and wait it all out. Might as well make for that camping spot he recommended. First things first, though. I think we should park the team and rig over there."

Trace nodded across the way toward a wide spot in the lane way. "Facing east. Then one of us should stay with the team and one should go find the lawdog."

"What on earth for?" said Chaw, his eyebrows arched high.

"Because somebody has to report about that snake-bit fellow. We did shoot the man, after all. And then there's all the trouble stirred up by this Cigar Tim character."

"Yeah, I reckon." Chaw released the brake and sorted the lines. "Since you're so keen, I think you ought to be the one to chat with the law." Chaw glanced over at Trace. "But you knew I'd say that, didn't you?"

"Yep."

They made it to the chosen spot, and Chaw held up and set the brake. "Good luck. And yell if you get yourself in a scrape, pard." Both men knew Chaw was only half kidding.

In their experience, having much of anything to do with the law, especially in these smaller, out-of-the-way places, was risky. Out here, on what felt like the fringe of the discovered world, revealing too much could be a dicey game, with the attitude of the local lawdog determining how the rest of the day unfolded—in a cell or nodding and leaving with a smile.

"Be back soon." With that, Trace hopped down from the wagon, checked his sidearm, and, as he walked on up the street westward, eyeing the signs to either side, he brushed and patted at his coat front and sleeves, raising small puffs of dust.

It didn't take long before he saw, halfway up the long main street of Richness, on the left-hand side, a sign that read "Town Marshal." He made for it.

As he walked, he could not help but cast glances toward the businesses flanking the wide, not-too-busy lane. There was a sign painter, a joiner, and if he was not mistaken, given the smoke rising up from spots at either end of the street, two blacksmiths, each with its own smoke-billowing fire.

There was also a promising bakery and a store with dry goods stacked, wedged, and jammed into every space that Trace could see from his spot on the board-walk out front.

Chaw would be riled at being kept waiting too long, but only if Trace explored the town on his own and took his time in getting back to the waiting Reb. Trace kept his gawking to a minimum and hustled on to the lawman's office.

He reached it and, as the door was propped open,

angling in, Trace poked his head inside. "Hello? Hello, Marshal?"

A young man, approximately twenty years old, looked up from shuffling papers on a desk to the right inside the anteroom. He did not smile, but he did not look perturbed, either.

"Hi there," said Trace, not intending to give him any sort of information about himself than he absolutely had to. *You never know*, said Chaw's voice in his head.

Trace stepped on in and offered a smile. It was reciprocated. "How do," said the young man.

Trace saw that he wore a silver star up high on the left side of his vest. The freighter wondered if this fellow was the marshal, despite his obvious youth.

Before the young man and Trace could begin to chat, a rear door opened and an older man, not looking up, stepped in, then closed the door behind himself. Then, when he faced the room, he looked up.

"Who are you?" said the man, who Trace saw clearly was also wearing a star, and it clearly bore the word *Marshal*.

"Name's Trace. Just passing through and thought I'd stop in to see you, Marshal."

"Why?"

Inside, Trace sighed. This was not the way he had hoped the conversation might begin. It was antagonistic from the outset, and not by him. "Well, my partner and I, we're doing a bit of freighting—"

"Oh, great. Another one," groaned the older man as he walked to the small woodstove and made a big production out of pouring himself a cup of coffee. "Dilbert, we have any of that sugar left?"

The young man behind the desk snapped to his feet and poked around on the desktop amid a scatter of papers. "I thought so, Marshal. If it's here, I'll find it."

"I doubt it," said the senior lawman, sipping the thick brew and wincing. He looked back at Trace as if to say, *What? You still here?*

"I suppose you have some sort of complaint," said the man, setting down his cup on the desk with a sigh.

"More an observation, Marshal," said Trace. He stayed by the door, happy to leave at a moment's notice. It was quickly becoming apparent to him that Chaw might have been correct. Little good might come of this visit. He decided right then and there to skip telling the lawman about the man who attacked them, who they had then shot, and who then was eaten by snakes. He realized it would not come out well in any light.

If the grumpy lawman was also lazy, which Trace suspected might well be the case, then that might only cause him grief as something he'd be expected to follow up on, provided the smaller mining camps thereabouts fell under his jurisdiction.

Trace thought maybe there was a sheriff roaming these parts, too. In which case that death, and everything unsavory and off-smelling that he and Chaw had experienced since they left Mankley would likely be under the purview of the sheriff and not this town patroller.

Still, he was here, and the man was a representative

of the law. Trace plowed ahead, hoping to make this a brief visit.

"We just came down out of the hills, by way of Mankley."

"Oh? What's the name of that hauling outfit over that way?" The marshal said this to his deputy, although Trace stood right there in front of him.

The younger man pulled a confused look. "Hmm . . ."

"Sligo Star Freighters," said Trace.

"Um," said the marshal, observing the planking of the ceiling. "I recall it was something like Sligo Star." Then he turned and looked at Trace. "Now, what do you want, freighter?" He said the last word as if it were a distasteful mouthful of food that he could not wait to spit out.

"I don't want anything from you. I only stopped in here to tell you that there's a crazy man running around loose up in the hills we just passed through. He has killed a few miners up in and around Boarwallow Gap."

The marshal's reaction to his words surprised Trace. The man walked closer and eyed him up and down, a tight look about his features.

"What do you know about Boarwallow Gap? What are you doing up there, anyway?"

Trace felt his blood bubble up a notch higher. He reminded himself that getting in a fix with the local law wasn't useful to anyone. But man alive, he was about ready to pop this fool in the nose.

"As I said, we're hauling freight. All I'm doing is telling you that somebody has been terrorizing the miners up there. They claim it's somebody from something called the consortium, but I have no way of knowing that, nor do I know much of anything about this consortium."

As if the man had been struck in the face, the marshal's eyes widened, and he held up a pointing finger directed at Trace. "You know what's good for you, mister, you'll leave the consortium out if it! Those fools up in the hills—and I know exactly who you talked to—are trying to make it seem as if they're being tormented and shoved off their claims."

"Well, aren't they?" said Trace. He knew as soon as the words slipped out of his mouth that it was the wrong thing to say. It was far too provocative, especially in this situation, but he could not seem to help himself.

The marshal spun in a circle, his face reddening, and when he turned back to face Trace, barely quelled rage trembled his features. When he spoke, his voice came out in a lowered, thin tone.

"Now you listen, and you listen to me good, freighter. You want to keep your lousy freighting job and keep on my good side, then you had best back off anything you might be tempted to say against the consortium. That outfit is operating in all the legal ways possible, and those fools in the hills—the Holdouts, that's what they're calling themselves, ain't it?"

He didn't wait for an answer. "They're a bunch of lying, squatting moochers and thieves. And they're holding up the works for the entire region. Why, think of how much further along the road to prosperity we'd all be if those filthy miners up there hadn't bound up the works!"

Trace was about to just shrug and walk away, but this man was a biased fool and he knew it. Trace knew deep in his gut that there was no way those Holdouts had sold him a bill of goods.

"You know, Marshal, me and my pard were up there. Those folks—not all of them men, and there are a few children up there, too—they're just trying to hold on to what's legally theirs. But this consortium, it's made up of wealthy men from way back East, and they seem bent on having the entire pie instead of settling for three-fourths of it. Doesn't that strike you as, gosh, I don't know, greedy?"

"Greedy! Greedy? Why, those money men back East, they are set to invest huge amounts of money in this region, from Richness all the way over the mountains to Mankley, and every little town between here and there along the lower eastern road, too! Going to change all our lives, and for the better. There'll be mining jobs and prosperity for all."

He nodded, his demeanor softening ever so slightly as he spewed what sounded like pretty lies offered to him by the consortium's advance people. "That sound greedy to you, Dilbert?"

The young deputy, who'd been sitting upright and watching the conversation with wide eyes, said, "No sir. No, not at all, Marshal."

"Then it must be true," said Trace, breaking the lawman's moment of being mesmerized by his own words.

"What?"

"That it's all going to happen, no matter what. And

with the law on the side of the consortium, well, there doesn't seem to be much anybody can do about a few simple murders."

Trace meant the remark to be sarcastic, something that might rile the marshal. But the lawman merely shrugged and reached for his coffee. "You bake a cake, you got to crack a few eggs."

"That may well be, but we're talking about people, not eggs, Marshal. Not to mention that what the consortium is doing is illegal."

The man eyed Trace hard, then shook his head. "The consortium ain't done a thing yet, sonny, that's illegal. Look here, I got my eye on you, and you, freighter, are a maker of trouble." He walked to the door. "The deputy will listen to your whining, take down any information he thinks is worth listening to. Me, I got work to do. I have wasted enough time listening to the likes of you."

With that he walked out the door. They heard his boots punching the planked boardwalk hard for a while. Then Trace turned to the deputy. "I don't suppose you care to hear anything I have to say."

"Oh, well, on the contrary," said the young man. "I . . . that is to say, we can't abide hearing of killings and not do something about it." He flipped open a half-size ledger book and licked the end of a pencil.

"Good to hear," said Trace. "Well, now, the folks up in Boarwallow Gap, they referred to the man they are confident is doing this killing as Cigar Tim. Few if any of them have seen him, but as it happens, me and my partner had ourselves an encounter with him."

"You did? With Cigar Tim?"

"Why? Do you know who that is?" said Trace.

"Me?" The deputy reddened. "No. No, it's just that you have had a personal encounter with this alleged killer. So naturally it is interesting."

"Uh-huh. I see. Well, sure, yes, he followed us on into the hills before we reached Boarwallow Gap, oh, let's see, that was . . . two, three days back now. Of course, we didn't know at the time who he was. We shared coffee with him, then he went on his way. We passed him later that next day, but he never acknowledged us. And then, when we were in the Gap, we heard stories about him."

"How do you know the man they believe has been committing the crimes is the same man that you met?"

"Well, technically, we don't. He did smoke that cigar, though."

"Lots of folks smoke cigars."

"I know, but this man, he was—well, he barely had the thing out of his mouth."

The deputy shrugged, then leaned forward. "For what it's worth, I suspect you're right. But it's tricky, you know? Me being his deputy and all."

Trace's confusion must have been evident on his face, for the young man said, "Oh, I guess you don't know, and why would you? Marshal DeFontaine is my father."

"Ah, I see. Yes, I understand, then, how it might be awkward for you."

"Yes, it's this consortium business. Pop, I mean the marshal, he's been in on it from the get-go. Keen as mustard, he is, that it goes through. You might have gotten the idea that he won't stand for anybody or anything that'll muss that up. He wants prosperity at any price. At least that's what he always says. Just those words, too."

The deputy smiled, but the words chilled Trace. He glanced toward the door. "So, what do you know about the cigar-smoking man, son?" said Trace in a lowered voice.

The young man said nothing, but his red cheeks and ears and his downcast gaze told Trace a whole lot.

"You know the one I mean, Deputy. The one I mentioned earlier. He's called Cigar Tim."

The young man looked up. "I . . . I might know of him, yes sir."

"How so?"

"Oh, it might be that Pap, I mean the marshal, he . . . that is to say, I believe I have seen the man or some man, anyway, who smokes a cigar like you described, all the time, that is, with the marshal."

"Oh?" said Trace, trying to sound as if he were barely interested instead of the opposite. "What was this?"

"Um, a couple of times. I saw them together. Must have been—" Then the young man stared wide-eyed at Trace.

"Let me guess, you were about to tell me how maybe you wonder if that cigar-smoking fellow and the cigar-smoking fellow I was talking about might indeed be one and the same. The infamous and murderous Cigar Tim. And I'll even rove a few steps further and speculate that your father—excuse me, Marshal DeFontaine—has in his employ a man who looks and sounds like that very man. One Cigar Tim. What do you think of that fantastical tale?"

"You think this Cigar Tim works for my daddy?"

"It's a possibility, sure. At the very least he's working for the consortium."

"Well, which one? Papa or Cigar Tim?"

"Hmm, both?" said Trace.

There was a long silence, then the young man said, "Well, sir, I think there might be a bit of something to that. You'll pardon me if I don't say anything else. As Papa has told me since I was a shaver, I flap my gums too much."

"That's all right, Deputy. I didn't come here to get anybody into trouble. Except for that possible killer, that is."

"As Papa says, 'Time will sort it out.'"

"Perhaps, but only if we help it along." Trace offered the young man a two-finger, off-the-brim salute and then departed.

He walked back along the main street, which was slightly busier now than it had been. Despite the odd welcome he'd received at the lawman's office—or rather, the lousy welcome, which was more to the point—he was impressed with Richness.

Even though he'd barely been here, Trace began to feel as though he could see it—or perhaps a town just like it—being a shire town of sorts to him, should he decide to ever settle down, of course.

He knew this was silly, hasty thinking, as he had no

immediate plans to settle anywhere. But still, at a quick glance, the town did have all the amenities he'd imagined it might be nice to have, at least within a day's ride of one's own modest spread somewhere.

Trace glanced up and saw, far along the roadway, just past the last large building on the right side, which was also the south side of the road, a familiar sight: the Sligo Star Freighting wagon. He was pleased to be reminded that the load was much reduced from what it had been when they had departed the depot back in Mankley, despite the added ore samples from the miners in Boarwallow Gap.

The load was lower at the top and he could see Chaw sitting tall and occasionally glancing to all sides, and once in a while all the way back behind him. The man was doing just what Trace would do were he the one who had been left behind. He was keeping a vigilant watch.

He also would most likely be less than impressed with Trace for taking so long. If Chaw was as tired as Trace was, it was going to be a fiery ride to the campsite.

Trace happened to glance to his left and saw Marshal DeFontaine, striding from east to west along the opposite side of the street. He'd just passed two slow-walking women who were chatting to each other and touched his hat brim and offered a smile as he walked by them when his half-turned face looked across the street and locked eyes with Trace's.

Trace slowed as the marshal did the same. The lawman stopped, turned to fully face Trace, and stood that way. He wore a dark scowl on his face, with his eyes narrowed, his arms held with elbows canted out and his hands slightly raised.

He apparently had no regard for anyone nearby. A couple of people looked at him as if they had seen this pantomime before. Shaking their heads, they walked on by.

It looked to Trace as if the lawman wanted to draw down on him. It was then that Trace noticed that the marshal wore a double-gun rig, something he chided himself on not noticing earlier. The double-gun rig was, in his estimation, a nearly useless thing, usually worn by braggarts and insecure fools.

Although he did not know the marshal in the least, his scant dealings with the man left him feeling as if the man were one, if not both, of those types of men. And perhaps a little more.

Then, as quickly as he had squared off on Trace, the marshal relaxed his stance, softened his gaze and, turning, with a last, angry look at Trace, he continued on his way.

Trace did the same, eyebrows high, wondering what in the heck that little charade foretold. He reached the wagon half a minute later, expecting his pard to be sore and annoyed with him. He was pleased to find Chaw puffing his pipe—something he usually reserved for after evening meals—and glancing about himself.

"Well, if it ain't somebody I knew once. Let me see, let me see if I can place you . . . nope, nope, been far too long, can't seem to recall who you are."

"Funny man," said Trace, climbing up into the left side of the wagon. "Everything all right here?"

"Sure is," said Chaw. "Unless you count an odd visit by a fella with a badge on his chest."

"Oh?" said Trace. "Happen to be the marshal, did he?"

Chaw described his visitor to Trace. "Man didn't say a thing to me, just stared me down and eyeballed the load. He was close enough that I could read that very word on that shiny star. Why, he must polish it two, three times a day, he's that proud of himself and what he's got up to in life!"

Trace nodded. "He is full to the brim of himself, that's for certain. We had quite a chat. Wish you had been there."

"Fill me in while we roll toward camp. I'm nursing a powerful hunger."

"Oh, I will," said Trace.

"Good. Say, I was looking forward to a night on the town. Seems to be a bustling place."

"Well, if it's any consolation, you'll not be missing much."

"Why's that?" said Chaw, working the lines and turning the big team in a wide arc.

"Because Richness is a dry town."

That alarming news caused Chaw to let the lines go slack in his hands. He looked at Trace with wide eyes and a slack mouth. "You don't say!"

Trace nodded. "I do. Learned as much from Hector."

"And you didn't think I ought to know this frightening slice of information?"

"Nope," said Trace, hiding a tired grin. "I was afraid you might balk and leave me to tend to things all by myself."

For the next few minutes, as they rolled slowly out of the bustling and sizable burg of Richness, Chaw mumbled and spat and growled and glanced at Trace now and again. Then, when it seemed he'd sputtered enough, he would mutter and growl a bit more as they wheeled on out of town in the direction the fellow had indicated would offer good camping alongside water.

As they traveled on up the road along what they both hoped would be their last quarter mile of the day, Trace related his revealing conversations with the marshal and with his son.

"Well," said Chaw. "I can't say any of that surprises me. You?"

"Nope," said Trace. "Too bad, but I understand."

"You understand? Don't tell me you're siding with that fool and his precious consortium!"

"No, just the part where he and his townsfolk have all been promised prosperity."

"Now, see, that's the trouble with the world! Everybody wants to be rich. But at what cost? Me, I don't need anything more than what I'm seeing here. Give me a few meals now and again to take the edge off, maybe some whiskey to tamp down the vittles, and a pipe of an evening around a crackling fire, and I'm bound to be pretty much the happiest fellow you have ever met. I guarantee it."

Trace had heard all this before, and he didn't doubt Chaw one bit. But he did know that the man was prone to being a mite cranky when he was low on funds. But only because then he couldn't indulge in his beloved aforementioned whiskey, plus women, and a few quick rounds at the blackjack table.

Trace settled back in his seat. All he wanted just then was to see a cleft boulder. That brought to mind a similar such rock, and jutting tree roots, from his childhood days back in the hills of Vermont.

He would wander off into the forest, away from the farm where there were always chores to do, it seemed. Maybe he'd take along a fishing rod, maybe not. It never really mattered. On the hottest days of summer, when it seemed the entire world was about to melt like candle wax, he would wander on into the nearby woods.

Then he would find a shady spot beneath towering, shade-giving maples or oaks and nestle in between big roots. Then he would just plain watch as the seemingly quiet forest would slowly come back alive after hushing on his arrival.

He was a quiet lad and did his best to imitate the Indians that were all but gone from that place but that used to live there in abundance many years before, or so he was told by his Gramps. But it seemed no matter how gingerly he placed his feet, Trace was never able to sneak on into the deep woods undetected.

He always ended up silencing everything about him, at least for a time. And then he could count on a red squirrel or two setting up an agitated sneezing, squeaking tirade high up in their branch kingdom.

Sometimes Trace would take along a sling and fire acorns at the rascals. He never hit them, not that he wasn't trying, but it was fun to annoy them. Mostly, though, he would settle into the comfortable, cradlelike gap between the tree's big roots and doze away an hour or so.

Life on the farm had been good, he knew in hindsight, but it had also been mighty hard work, rising well before the rooster each and every day of the week, month, and year. They'd feed the cows and pigs and sheep, chickens, geese, oxen, horses, on and on.

It seemed there were always more and more hungry critters about, and all had to be fed and watered before he and his Pap and Gramps would go back into the house, where a big feed always waited for them.

Mama and Gran would bustle about laying it all out there for them. The old Glenwood stove would fill the place with heat. And then there were the sounds and smells of thick slabs of bacon snapping and popping and frying in the pan, and the scent of fresh, hot biscuits.

And the taste of those biscuits, when the butter melted away, soaking into each and every bite, was about like he figured heaven should be. And there were fresh eggs the color of a bold sunset, fried up by Mama just the way he liked them, which was just the way his Pap liked them.

"Hey, pard."

Trace looked to his left.

"You keeping an eye on where we're supposed to camp?"

"Oh yeah, let's see." Trace reddened. He was so tired, and he knew that Chaw was, too, given that they had slept next to no time at all the night before.

It was all too easy to be lost in thought and memory. That was something old men did, not a man in his prime, which was how he still saw himself.

"It's not far, according to the landmarks that fellow at the depot mentioned. There!" He nodded. "See that boulder with the cleft? I reckon that's the one."

"Looks to be." Chaw halted the team. "You look all done in, pard. Just hold them here. I'll hop down and scout it so we don't paint ourselves into a corner with the horses and wagon."

"I admit I feel done in," said Trace, raising his voice so that Chaw might hear him as he snooped the camp spot about twenty feet from the wagon. "I need sleep tonight. If that cigar-gnawing bum pays us a visit, I've a good mind to let him take whatever it is he wants. As long as it isn't my life."

"Or," said Chaw, climbing back in the seat, "your clothes and your eyeball. Remember what he did to that poor fella back in the hills. Paco, wasn't it? And that last one they mentioned while we were there . . ."

"Pinky."

"Yeah, that's the one," said Chaw. "Hoo boy, what a way to go."

CHAPTER 16

It didn't take them long to settle into camp. The spot was just what the portly depot owner said it would be, a wide, even patch well off the roadway, but still visible to and from the lane. Water was there, too, as described, flowing in a clear, bubbling, happy-looking stream not but fifty feet from the campsite.

It hadn't rained in a spell and a previous tenant of the site had thoughtfully left a decent-sized pile of fodder for the horses. It wasn't musty-smelling and so would be most welcome to the men, who were going to have to purchase more food for the four hungry working horses of their team before they departed Richness on the morrow.

They would use that feed and gladly, and without worrying too much about it because it was bound to go to waste that very night, if the fat man's prediction came true regarding the coming rains.

That big old boulder marking the site did indeed look to have been cleft by either lightning or the hand of some mighty god at one time or another.

"Same thing," said Chaw, sporting his disdain for anything that told him how to think and live.

Religion or, more to the point Chaw's views on it, was yet another topic that Trace was most familiar with. It was one they had gnawed over with some frequency while on the trail. For some reason, and Trace had yet to fully figure out why, Chaw had always been troubled by talk of his faith, although Trace knew the gruff Rebel to be a deeply spiritual and thoughtful man.

Trace didn't much think about it himself, except that he knew there was something bigger than him in the world, and that was a mighty comfort. He suspected Chaw felt the same, but he knew that the buckskin-clad Southerner did not like anything smacking of hypocrisy.

Usually Trace just let him yammer on until Chaw drifted to silence and fell to musing. And that was about what happened while they each worked at their various chores about the camp, getting all the usual tasks taken care of. The first was to take care of the horses, who were tired and far beyond hungry and thirsty.

And then there was the preparation of their own food. Trace and Chaw were both wolfishly hungry. Next, they gathered fuel for the fire, and once they were able to light their fire, Trace set to cooking while Chaw erected a stout rain shelter, for them and for the horses, out of the ample supply of ropes and tarps they carried in the wagon.

"Suppose what that fat man said doesn't come about?"

"What part of what he said are you talking of?" said

Trace, taking care to ensure the harnesses were under cover.

"That rainstorm he predicted."

"Well, those low black things up in the sky, you know, the ones that have been dogging us all day? They don't look like they're here to keep us dry."

"All right, all right," said Chaw. "I just hate to put all manner of extra work in on a thing when it ain't necessary."

"But how do you know it's unnecessary?"

"Oh now, don't start twisting my words about, man. You know what I mean."

"Right or wrong, it's time well spent," said Trace; then, looking at Chaw, he said, "Just in case."

"Yah, yah, I guess so. . . ."

"Ho there in the camp!"

It was a friendly voice, but a strange one to them, and they bristled, each annoyed with himself that he hadn't heard anyone approaching.

"Who be you, then?" said Chaw, eyes narrowed and no hint of a smile on his face.

The man to whom he spoke looked hard right back at him, a thin smile playing on his mouth and nowhere else on his face.

He was a man of medium height, as near as Chaw could tell, given that the fellow was on horseback. He was clean-shaven, clear-eyed, either gray or blue, tough to tell given the distance of twenty feet or so separating them.

This made little difference to Chaw and Trace, not so much as the fact that there were ten or perhaps a dozen other mounted men behind the man, arrayed in a somewhat regular scatter just beyond him. As with the man who spoke, they were all well-armed, and all had their eyes on the two freighters.

None of them looked ready to draw, but given the shared bold look of them all, Trace guessed it wouldn't take much to tighten them up.

Finally, the man said, "You are a rather forthright character, aren't you?" As the stranger in the lead said this, he urged his mount forward. The other men following close behind.

Trace and Chaw stood, hands on hips, revolvers unthonged, loose-limbed and ready for whatever play this stranger and his gang might deliver into the midst of their quiet camp. Life on the trail had taught them to always be on their guard, always be ready.

Not that they always were, but so far, their way of dealing with situations had worked. If they woke up dead one day, Chaw had said more than once, then they'd know they should have taken more precautions.

"I reckon that's far enough," said Trace with a friendly but cool smile.

"Now, now, gents, there's no cause for concern. I will be blunt: I am merely here to inquire as to the name of your employer."

"What makes you think we have an employer?" said Trace.

The man snorted a quick laugh. "Look, I don't wish to insult you—"

"Then don't," said Chaw, staring the man down hard.

"But," continued the man, "often a freight wagon and

team such as this," the man nodded to indicate the wagon and burden beasts, "is owned by a freighting firm, and you two men look to be part of that rugged, noble breed of freelance freighters. Am I correct?"

Chaw and Trace said nothing but continued to eye them.

"I'll take that as a yes." The man continued to smile, but it was no smile connected with the man's eyes. Finally, he said, "Let me guess. You two are in the employ of that insufferable widow and that grubby little man named Hector. In other words, Sligo Star Freighting. Am I correct?"

Neither Trace nor Chaw spoke, but continued to stand and await the man's continued speech.

"I'll take that also as a yes. Now, tell me," said the man, rummaging in his vest pocket with a cautiously placed two fingers. "Not reaching for explosives or weapons, gents. Just this."

He pulled out a cigar and ran the length of it under his nose as he eyed them. He must have seen something there that intrigued him, for he paused and said, "Oh, oh, I see. The sight of a cigar has done something to you. Dare I say you have had an encounter with cigars lately that might diminish in you the urge to enjoy one for the rest of your days? Let me guess . . . Cigar Tim, as the locals call him?"

His smile had slumped, but not his gaze. "Am I correct? If so, I need to know where that . . . that man is."

Again, Trace and Chaw remained quiet. Finally, Trace said, "I sense that this Tim fellow you referred to is not one of your favorite people."

There was a quick flicker of something on the stranger's face; then his visage lost emotion once more.

"You've asked plenty of questions," said Trace. "My turn."

"Go ahead. Ask as many as you like," said the man, holding his cigar poised before his mouth.

"Just the one," said Trace. "For now." He regarded the stranger a moment, then said, "May I safely assume you are here representing the consortium?" He watched the man's face closely and was not disappointed in what he saw. There was a slight twitch there.

Although doubtful that he was surprised that Trace and Chaw were aware of the consortium, somehow it seemed that this man did not like to be bested, even in a light way such as this, in conversation.

"What of this . . . consortium?" said the man, trying, it was quite apparent, to regain some edge, however meager, in the conversation.

It was Trace's turn to smile, as if he knew far more than he did, which was true and likely quite evident.

"Cut the cute stuff, fella," said Chaw. "We set up camp and are fixing to eat grub and you are annoying me. If you want to know something that you think we might know, then get to it and ask. Otherwise, go away."

Trace winced inside. It was true that Chaw when hungry was prone to being bearlike. When hungry and already annoyed, he could be downright unbearable.

The stranger took the hint with a smile. "As you wish . . . fella. Perhaps we can chat when you are fed and rested, and hopefully in better humor."

"We're going to be busy," said Trace, hoping to get this foolishness over with.

"No matter," said the man. "I will find you. At some point, I am quite certain our paths will cross again."

Before Trace could reply, the man touched his hat brim. Half smiling, he turned his horse and rode away, not slowly but in no great hurry, either. His men parted their ranks for him, and then followed with no backward glances.

As soon as he was out of earshot, Trace said, "That man obviously doesn't like this Cigar Tim character."

"Who would?" said Chaw, turning his attention back to prodding the campfire.

They bantered back and forth while two large deer steaks sizzled in the pan. Chaw had purchased them from a fellow who was butchering the beast on their way into town. The fresh meat smelled mighty toothsome, and before long Trace found himself less and less sore with the odd situation bubbling up with that stranger and his well-armed gang.

Once they had eaten and tended the horses again, they settled back before the fire, their backs to the thicket beyond, and with the water slowly pushing and gurgling southeastward to their left.

With the town to their right, they felt relatively assured that they were not going to be sneaked up on in the night. At least not from the direction of the creek, or from the brambly mess behind them.

"I'll take first watch if you want," said Chaw. "Besides, I think you did it first last time, no?"

"Might be," said Trace. "I don't recall."

They sipped coffee lightly laced with whiskey and enjoyed tobacco in their pipes. Chaw's was a homely, knobby thing he'd carved from a maple burl some years back. Trace used his trusty corncob pipe.

They'd agreed many years ago on the trail that pipe smoking was something most men should do as it would calm them down and make them far less prone to making such mistakes as marrying and raising a large brood and taking on a mountain of debt by buying a farm from a bank.

Yes sir, they agreed, all that misery could be avoided by taking up smoking the pipe and, of course, roaming the trails of the world looking for just enough adventure to keep a single fellow from being lonely in all the ways a fellow might feel such.

It didn't take long after they had finished their meal and were enjoying a cup of hot coffee before another interruption drifted on in. It came in the form of rain. Cold, hard rain.

Both men had already settled down with their long guns by their sides and their revolvers unthonged. That was when the first drops began pelting down.

"Good thing I encouraged you to rig up the tarps," said Chaw. "Going to be a long ol' storm, I just bet."

Trace ignored the comment and made certain everything he could tuck under cover was done so. Moments later he settled back down and rejoined the calm Chaw in another quiet pipe session.

As the night drifted on and the rain gentled down into a steady but gentle, all-night soaker, they each mused, lost down his own trail of thought. The fire burned lower and the fire's glow weakened.

The horses were rested, well-fed, watered, and standing hipshot. They were also fairly dry and going to be of little concern for them this night. The men hoped that staying awake would be their most formidable task. But spelling each other to be on watch was one thing they would not skip out on. Especially given that representatives of the consortium were afoot.

CHAPTER 17

The next morning, they were up and fed and filled with coffee. And the lot of them were dressed and harnessed—Trace and Chaw and the horses—and making once more for the Richness depot, guiding the team through puddles of standing water in the roadway from the previous night's rain.

It took them a scant two hours in Richness to unload and then reload with what little they were contracted to haul back to Mankley.

As they rode on out of town, they spied the same cursed stranger from the night before riding in their direction. This time he was alone.

Chaw said, "Too good to last."

"Maybe so," said the Yank, "but as I said last night, if I'm right and he's no fan of Cigar Tim, that might somehow play to our benefit. Not much, mind you, but . . ."

"True," said Chaw. "But I reckon it'd be like having one enemy sidling up close to you than another. Ain't none of it makes me feel very good at all."

"Same here," said Trace. "But he's determined to talk with us, so I don't think we have much choice."

They rolled onward, came abreast of the mounted man, and instead of slowing and hailing them for a chat as he'd proposed the night before, the man merely smiled and touched his hat brim and rode on.

Trace turned his head and watched as the fellow rode on up to the lawman's office and dismounted. He turned back around. They rode on in silence, making for Mankley via the southerly road, as there was nothing much to say about the man and his odd visit of the night before.

Presently, Trace said, "I can't help it, but I keep thinking of that poor fool back in the hills with his snakes and such. I'm still feeling odd about it all."

"Aw, heck, pard, don't you go feeling guilty. You had no choice but to shoot the man, although I have to say that he was destined for that very fate sooner rather than later, I am as sure of that as I am sure my name is Chaw Dagworth. Might even be he forced our hand, if you know what I mean."

"Sure, I wondered that, too. And it's not like I've not had to shoot a man before. He or his slithering friends were destined to kill one of us, if not both. But it's a rum feeling, nonetheless." Trace sighed and clucked the horses, working the lines on their backs at the same time.

CHAPTER 18

It took Trace and Chaw three more days to make it back to Mankley. They encountered no other folks, save one mule-riding drummer of nostrums.

He wore a string tie and a bowler and appeared to have been sampling his own wares rather heavily from the fumes radiating off his breath when they spoke briefly in the roadway. After exchanging pleasantries and little else, the drummer bid them adieu and he and the mule wobbled off westward to Richness.

The next day they reached Mankley, and Hector and the widow were mighty pleased and surprised to see them and to hear of their experiences.

The widow made a proper feast that evening, and later, Hector broke the news to them that a second wagon was fully loaded and needed to get back in there. The relay messaging service he'd helped set up had let him know that much of their stockpile of goods had been savaged by raiders, the sacks and kegs scattered and slashed and smashed.

"Does that mean what I think it means?" Trace squinted at his boots.

"If leaving tomorrow morning is what you two think I mean, then yep. Can you handle it? Them folks are about starved out up there."

Trace looked at Chaw, then they both looked at Hector. "You think we'd decline to help starving folks after a meal like the one the widow just fed us? Count us in."

Chaw nodded. "I'll say. But I do wonder if maybe the widow might consider a nightcap of that tasty whiskey she brought out our first day . . . ."

"You mean this whiskey?" said a voice behind them.

The two pards spun to see that once again the wily widow had sneaked up on them. But they were fine with what they saw—her shapely form, her lovely smile, and the tray she held before her. Balanced atop it was a bottle and four glasses.

"You realize," said Trace, "if we're attacked, we're sitting ducks out here. No way can we see in every direction all at once."

"That's what I can count on with you, Trace."

"What's that?"

"Your amazing ability to point out the obvious in a situation."

"Why, thank you, pard," said Trace. "All I'm getting at is that if we are attacked—"

"Hold right there!" said Chaw. "You know as well as I do that it's not *if* but *when* we're attacked."

"Okay, then, and I can't disagree, when we're attacked, and if we're pinned down, I'm not so sure we'll be able to protect the horses, unless we turn them loose, but that's foolish."

"Darn right it is!" said Chaw, clucking the horses on and gentling the lines on their backs. "If we can somehow run off those phantom attackers and can then get back on our way, we'll be doing it afoot!"

"Naw," said Trace. "I'll just harness you. After all, you're always telling me how tough you are. That'd be your chance to prove it."

"Any more of that, you Yankee chicken, and I'll show you tough!" Chaw held up a thick, scar-knuckled fist and wagged it.

"Ha," said Trace, turning back to the problem at hand.

And so it went, with nothing much happening until they were well and truly into the mountains. By Chaw's rough guesswork, they were going to make Boarwallow Gap early the next morning if they rode the team hard until dark. And dark was about an hour off.

They decided to keep on. And ten minutes later, everything changed.

A bullet whiskered in from somewhere ahead, upslope on the road's south side.

Trace felt the hot sizzle and sting as it sliced the barest bit of the outer rim of his left ear, up high, boring a tiny crescent and forcing a quick, yipping cry from him. He reached up with his left gloved hand and clasped at the side of his head, drawing it back bloody.

"Pard!"

"I'm all right. Nicked in the ear."

Chaw grunted in sympathy and pinched off another shot. "Much blood?"

"Some. Stings something fierce, though."

"I know it, pard," said Chaw. And he did, too, as they both knew. He'd been through the same thing, although it was his right ear that had attracted a bullet from the gun of a drunken cattle thief on a trail drive, their first, four or five years before.

Chaw's wound had been preferable to the one sustained by a kid who'd been on the drive with them. Nice kid, all had agreed, that Billy Tompkins. And then he took a bullet in the back trying to save the herd.

That hard memory came back to Chaw and Trace both, at the same time, as a flash of fulsome memory tinged with the bitterness of regret at the poignant loss of a good and too-young friend.

It was that charge of remembrance that allowed each man, the once nicked and the newly nicked, to give quick thanks that they were still among the living and would not likely be laid low by paltry and random, ill-aimed gunshots. At least not at that moment. Who knew what the next minute or five would bring to them?

"Be thankful you wasn't moved the wrong way but a couple of inches."

"Yep. Doesn't help, though."

"I know that, too. Need a kerchief?"

"Nah, I'm good."

They hunkered low, and Chaw, working the lines, did his best to keep the team rolling hard and not getting the wheels too close to the roadside. It didn't work.

Shots rained down at them, plinking and thudding

into the wagon's thick planking and driving holes in the tight tarpaulin. The horses, spooked by the sounds of the fusillade, dug hard and churned gravel. Lathering and heaving, they ran as if they were on fire. It was all Chaw could do to keep the wagon on the roadway.

But as they suspected, their luck withered as the front off-side wheel dug hard into the softer scree and soil of the north side of the road. Chaw stood, wedged his legs between the front of the boot well and the seat, and bent forward, bellowed curses and yanked hard on the lines, trying to slow the team and get that wheel out of the rutted roadside.

But it was too late—the rear off-side wheel dug in hard, too, following its front-running brethren, and that, as they knew, could prove fatal. To the wagon, to the horses, and to them. At that speed, there was no coaxing the team to take a southerly course, especially when there was precious little roadway to spare.

The thing they feared happened with eyeblink speed; the left side of the wagon began to rise up as the right-side wheels churned ever deeper and farther off the roadway.

"She's going!" shouted Chaw, and he stood, leaning to his right and yanking with all his strength on those lines, trying despite the odds to slow the team and right the failing wagon. It didn't work.

The fully loaded wagon rose up, up, and Trace shouted, "Jump, Chaw! Jump!"

Even as he said it, he leapt as far and with as much muscle as he could offer the effort. He landed, rifle in hand, in decent shape, all things considered. He went down on his left knee, shoving the thing into a soft, grassy spot between two head-size rocks.

As soon as he righted himself, he spun, in time to see the wagon skid on its right side, sliding a good dozen feet before creaking and grinding to a halt, dust clouding and gravel spattering the roadside undergrowth.

Beyond the front of the wagon, he saw all four horses, lathered, sides heaving, heads working like pump handles. They were all upright and trembling, still trying to tug the twisted, impossible traces.

And then the wagon gave a lurch, jerked forward another foot, and the team kept right on going. Soon enough, Trace saw that the horses had broken free and were making slow, lurching progress up the westward road, dragging a few ragged bits of wood and snapped leather and chains.

"Chaw! Chaw! Where are you?" For long moments, Trace heard nothing save for the rubbery snorts of the disappearing horses. He shouted again. From the other side of the wagon, he heard, "Are all you Yanks so blamed loud? My word!"

He heard a clunking and then Chaw's big, hairy head appeared between the topside wheels. He looked down at Trace. "You land all right, pard?"

Trace blew out a pent-up breath. "Yep. You?"

"Sure thing," said Chaw. "When I finally saw there was no saving her, I gave up the ship. Seeing as how you did it first, I reckon we know that makes it official."

"Oh? What's that?"

"That Yanks are cowards and Rebs are true to the end."

Just then a pair of shots whipped down at them from the southern hillside beyond, up behind Chaw's exposed back. He yelped and dropped out of sight, then reappeared within seconds around the back side of the wagon, huddling by Trace.

"Who's the coward?" said Trace.

"Hush up, Yank."

"We been pinned down here behind this cursed wagon for far too long," said Chaw, doing that knee-shaking thing he always did whenever he was irked or had been inactive for more than three minutes.

"Your knee's bouncing like a rowboat in a hurricane."

Chaw stopped and looked at Trace. "That don't make half as much sense as you want it to, you know."

Trace ignored the comment. "I had hoped we could have made this run without hubbub."

"Yeah, well, I don't know about hope. Seems like it left these hills a long ol' time ago. And by the way, that's the second time you've used the word *hubbub* in the last couple of days."

"So?" Trace squinted as he pulled the kerchief away from his ear and looked at it.

"How's the ear?" said Chaw.

Trace glanced at him. "Causing me hubbub."

Chaw grinned and shook his head. "Least it's still

attached. Don't appear to be bleeding much. That's good."

"That's because the kerchief is red."

"Oh."

"But it's pretty much stopped oozing, so I can—" Trace looked up from the kerchief and said, "Chaw, one o'clock."

Chaw glanced to his right, repositioned his rifle, and touched the trigger. The rifle coughed once and they heard a quick yelp. "One less," said Chaw, then spat a stream of brown juice.

"Seems to me they didn't plan this out very well."

"Naw, they didn't! But if it had to happen, I for one am glad of their poor planning. Left us with a run-off team and a flipped wagon. But it was a wagon filled with goods. Got us enough victuals by the looks of these spilled sacks of cornmeal and coffee beans and flour and such that we could hold off an army for quite a spell, I expect."

Trace refolded the kerchief and held it to his ear once more. "Before you get to feeling like you've pulled one over on them, keep in mind that we can't do a cursed thing without water."

Chaw spat and chuckled.

It held a knowing edge that Trace recognized.

"I guess you getting your ear shot and all, you didn't catch sight of that little stream burbling away not but twenty feet behind us, now did you?"

"I did, and I knew you'd bring it up, but you're overlooking the simple fact that one of us would have to get down there and fill a canteen now and again."

"No, I ain't neither. Because if they could pick us off when we was fetching water, why then surely they could have at us when we're crouched here like we're doing right now!"

With that, both men glanced behind, each cautious to ensure they weren't inadvertently leaning too far to either side enough to risk another lucky pinched shot that the next time might well result in a more serious wound than a grazed ear.

So far, nobody had crept around either side of them. Each man had recognized that they were fortunate in a dumb-luck sort of way. They had been flipped and pinned down in such a manner and in such a spot that anyone trying to outflank them would be seen by them.

They also knew that such a scenario would only hold for so long; then the raiders would angle well off, cut wide, and then come at them from behind. It was just a matter of when that would happen.

"Well, it ain't an auspicious start to our new jobs, I can tell you that much."

"Chaw, did you just say *auspicious*?"

The buckskin-clad Southerner narrowed his eyes. "Yeah, what of it?"

"Nothing," said Trace. "It's just that I never heard you use that particular word before. Heck, I'm not sure I even know what it means. You?"

"Well, 'course I do!"

"And what does it mean, then? I ask only because I don't know, and as you know, I do like to keep my vocabulary sharp."

"Well, it . . . it's . . . oh, hang it, I don't have to explain every little thing to you, now do I?"

Trace hid a grin and resighted down his rifle's barrel.

A snapping sound pulled his gaze up from the rifle barrel and to the left. Nothing moved, but he knew he had heard something there.

"What was it?" whispered Chaw.

"Don't know yet." Trace continued to eyeball the land, keeping his breathing to a minimum, keeping his head down and holding his breath. It wouldn't do to get shot any time, but especially not now. That might well prove a death sentence for Chaw, and as much as Trace found it not a little sad, that surly Reb was as close as he was likely to get to family anymore. There was nobody left for him back in the hills of Vermont, after all.

"There," he said, offering Chaw a slight nod without taking his eyes from a slightly wagging pine branch. "Those rocks beneath that branch that's moving. I'll bet whoever it is is holed up behind that cluster of boulders."

"Hmm," said Chaw, squinting and eyeing the rocks. "I reckon you're right."

They both knew Trace's eyesight was the superior among the two men, and Chaw deferred to his pard whenever there was doubt.

"Looks like they're tiring of lobbing lead at us from in front. Now they're set to sneak around us."

As if in response to Chaw's statement of the obvious, another bullet whistled in and struck the thick planking of the wagon, thunking and embedding there.

"Hey," said Trace, looking over his shoulder at

Chaw. "What if we bring the fight to them instead of sitting here, waiting to get shot?"

"Hmm," said Chaw, nodding his head.

Trace knew that meant he had already sold his pard on the idea. "Full dark will be coming along in about an hour more or less. My guess is they're trying to get in position to close in on us then. We could do the same, but from outside of them."

Chaw nodded with more vigor. "You're thinking of the ol' Rebel double flank, I reckon."

"Nope. Thinking of the ol' Yank double flank."

"No sir! The boys in gray invented it and you blue-bellies mooched it."

It was a conversation they'd had countless times in the past, varying little from one to the next, but always the same theme—trickery, deceit—before ending in private chuckles as they silently formulated next moves.

They managed to stay hunkered and hold off any more advances, which turned out to be rather paltry attempts. This solidified their guess that the attackers were waiting them out, likely to strike in the dark.

"I dislike them having the upper hand."

"I know you do," said Chaw. "Me too. Nothing for it, though. Not until we can get on out there and parcel off a few shots of our own."

Trace nodded. "They know there are only two of us, but I can't get an accurate count of how many of them there are."

"At least four, that much I think I know."

Trace nodded. "So if we each take a flank . . ." He

didn't need to finish his thought. Both men knew what to do next.

"Me," said Chaw, "I'm going into my night fighting way of doing things."

Trace knew that meant Chaw would be lugging no rifle, just his revolver. But his most important tool would be his big, wide-blade hip dagger.

It was an effective way of traveling light and especially in the dark, despite all the looking they had been doing over the terrain between where they were and where they wanted to be.

Each man knew he'd likely bark a shin or topple off-balance colliding with some rock or tree or log that had moved from the very spot they'd placed it in their mind. Somehow it always ended up that way.

Finally, there was no more guessing and waiting. Dark had whispered in as it always did, cat-footing down in between and on top of them as if called in by a conjurer's hand. They'd agreed to kindle a small fire, hoping that their attackers would see this and think that the men didn't realize they were being surrounded.

They hoped that the attackers would think Trace and Chaw were trying to get away with the comfort of a small blaze to heat coffee or some such. With any luck, Trace thought, that would be the beginning of the attackers' downfall—*believe in the weakness*, Chaw and Trace were trying to show them. Meanwhile, the two freighters would have beelined outward, one northeastward, one northwestward.

And that's just what they did, leaving behind their

rifles, the relative safety of the side-flipped wagon, and the tiny fire.

The men long ago gave up wishing each other luck at the outset of risky forays. Although neither would admit to being particularly superstitious, each nonetheless secretly regarded verbal offers of luck as having the potential to somehow foul the outcomes of their efforts.

Instead, they nodded to each other and then melted into the near dark. As they had been pinned down close by the crotch of a draw, a deep fog had begun to seep in, smoky and thick and filling the spaces with its chilling self.

It was a gift, they knew, and one they did not take lightly. Nor did they assume that the attackers would not regard it the same.

Before he crept more than a few paces northeastward, Trace bent even lower and halted, buttoning up his coat to the throat. It hid the only part of his garments that might be visible in the dark: the whiteness of his shirt. Satisfied that he'd covered it up to the best of his abilities, he resumed his skulking, low, cat-footing route.

Trace knew from much experience in darkness such as this to keep low and step with boldness, yes, but mostly with caution. And to slow his pace, despite an urge to dart.

Twice he'd employed similar modes of flight when he'd been escaping from a wrathful man he'd heard thundering home to his woman. Each time it had been the very woman whose company Trace himself had been enjoying just moments before. The first time he'd almost not escaped with his life. He also had not escaped with his trousers. Luckily, he'd snagged his coat and boots on his way out of there, although he had lost a good hat.

On this night, however, he pushed from his mind all thoughts of past fun and daring and concentrated on not getting shot and not making any sounds. The second point would, without doubt, lead to the first.

He recalled from not long before, when eyeing the scene in daylight, that the more-or-less straight route he intended to make had had two impediments that might upset his plans. The first was roughly halfway between the wagon and the scatter of yet more boulders close by the tree line.

Trace made it to that first big rock, kept low, then hunkered even lower when he felt it before his knee. He had figured earlier he could edge around it, keeping his big hip knife gripped in his left hand while feeling his way around the rock with the fingertips of his right.

His grazed ear still throbbed as if the devil himself was gnawing on it, but he was grateful for the pain of it, for it kept him alert and focused, more attuned to presences on his periphery in the darkness.

So far, he'd heard nothing save the quick, light scuffing of his own boots. He wished he'd thought to change into his camp moccasins, for they always proved the quieter option. But he shoved that thought from his mind. Too late, and thus a waste of his concentration.

The fog was helping him, yet it might also be hurting him, too, for it was of a slightly lighter hue than the darkness into which it coiled and wafted. And as he disturbed it, it slid and eddied like swirling river water around rocks.

He was nearly ready to let go of the boulder and dash forward once more toward the next impediment he recalled in his intended path. It was the dry girth of the last of a length of log from a giant of a tree a long time ago. He had seen earlier that there were plenty of trees about, but none looked to have matched the bulk of this fallen brute.

Another dozen feet perhaps and he'd have it. Once he reached it, he also might have a fight on his hands, for it had looked a likely thing behind which to hide and fire, for himself and for the raiders.

That was when he heard the distinct sound of a boot scuffing gravel. And it hadn't been his own. It scraped once, as if a man, moving with the slowness that caution, inexperience, and fear, brought forth. He hoped so, anyway. He'd guessed at such things in the past and come away with the scars to prove his incorrect assumptions.

Trace held still, kept low, and let the coolness of the fog drift and eddy and settle about him once more. He would wait a few seconds for the man to resume movement after his blundering, gravelly misstep.

It didn't take long. Trace nearly grinned in the dark as whoever it was resumed his steps. Grit on grit, grinding. The man paused once more, still aware, no doubt, he was making far more noise than he should.

Trace also thought he heard, back behind him, a hurried stomping, as if someone were rushing to get from one point to another. *A whole lot of us are, apparently*, he thought.

He knew it would not likely have been Chaw. His pard, while a big, burly fellow, was as light on his feet as a dancing child. That said, there was no way Trace would pay him that compliment to his face. That man was already far too full of his Rebel self.

Trace thought that the nearby scraping, hesitant steps might be moving closer. He held, nearly ready to resume his own cautious trek. He held and was glad of it, for whoever it was apparently had no notion that Trace was poised, knife in hand, before him. *Come to me*, he thought.

As always in such instances, when he was ready to act in a violent manner, Fullcup Trace gritted his teeth hard as that familiar quiver of regret washed over him. It was regret for the thing he was likely about to do. He would take a life if need be.

It would be one more deep-carved, black gouge on his soul. The latest in a long tally of such marks that would never wear clean, no matter how many sleepless nights he gnawed his way through. *But it's him or me, us or them*, he thought, and set himself for what he hoped would be a quick struggle.

With luck, he would be able to get behind the fellow, clamp a big hand over the man's face to shut him up. He hoped it would keep him from yelping, first in surprise, then in anger and alarm, which would rouse the others and let them know that their prey was on the move.

Then Trace would slide his dagger between the man's ribs or jerk his head back hard and quick and to one side, with bold decision. Something like that would be ideal—quick for them both. But that wasn't what happened. Not at all.

Meanwhile, Chaw was having a bit of a time himself in sticking to the route he'd mapped out in his head. It had to be there and nowhere else because, even if it was not dark, the fog that had emerged proved to be a mighty impediment. It behaved like ground-hugging smoke, filling everywhere before, around, and behind him.

He reached the boulder he'd been aiming for, but only because he used the back of his left hand, which he'd held out before himself, as a bug with long feelers might to determine the best way forward. It was his knuckles that told him, with a grazing rap, that he was a bit off course.

He paused, crabwalked to his left, and laid his hand against the reassuring bulk of the round-topped rock. It proved a bit above knee height and wide enough to have hidden someone behind, at least from his view from earlier, back at the wagon.

Chaw cast a glance over his right shoulder toward their camp, such as it was, and was still able to see the low, irregular flicker of paltry flame from the minute fire they had made. It would die soon, and then the attackers would know for certain, if they were dumber than they seemed, that he and Trace were on the move.

Had their wee ruse fooled the attackers? He shrugged off the thought. He needed to concentrate on what he was doing and where he was headed, not the past, not even the immediate past. It was wasted effort.

Holding still with one hand on the rock and the other clutching his big, dagger-bladed knife in the other, Chaw did his best to hear everything, and in particular anything that might tell him if one of the enemy was close.

After that thought, almost without pause, his guts tightened as he heard a stifled cough. It was brief and could well have come from a horse some ways off into the brush, but that was not what he thought it to be.

The quick, sharp sound had come from a man; Chaw knew it, and what's more, that man was not a dozen feet from him, ahead and slightly to the right, smack in the direction he had been heading before he felt the big rock with his left hand.

That gave Chaw pause, and he held low in his crouch before the rock. Had the man heard him? Chaw knew he'd taken every precaution he could as he'd snailed his way forward.

He was not as fast a mover in the dark as was Trace. But he reckoned that haste might well prove his pard's undoing one day. Then again, it had served the Yank well all these years, much to Chaw's annoyance, and Chaw had to admit that Trace was either born into a gifted role in life or he was pretty darned good at making the most out of his haste.

Either way, Chaw reasoned, he didn't much care. And he had to make progress himself, because he knew it was but a matter of time—minutes, not an hour or even a half hour—before something was going to happen.

What did happen was not something Chaw was prepared for. Quick steps, echoing those he imagined Trace was taking across the way in the night, sounded, not far ahead. Perhaps it was the coughing man. The steps moved toward him, perhaps making for the boulder, too.

Chaw licked his lips and awaited whoever it was that kept drawing closer, taking mere seconds to close the gap between them. There was something odd about those sounds, those footsteps. Something Chaw could not figure out.

Then the sounds stopped; the man obviously had become aware that his footfalls were far too noisy. He was also about six, perhaps eight feet from Chaw. The big, buckskin-clad man ran a tongue tip over his teeth, hefted his knife for the hundredth time, as if weighing an important purchase.

Then the stranger resumed his quickstep journey and then there he was, fully revealed before Chaw, barely two feet away. And then there were two of them. One must have shadowed so close behind the first that his footfalls had deceived Chaw.

He realized all of this at the same instant that the first man before him perceived Chaw's presence. And then that first man dove at the big Rebel.

Before he knew what was happening, Chaw was down, pinned on his back, his shoulders held by one of the men. The other, he assumed, was an eyeblink of time away from slicing him deep and forever.

Chaw also knew that even if he yelled for Trace, who would for certain come running, there was no time.

Not that he would do that to his friend, for that would be leading him right into the mouth of the grizzly, so to speak.

Trace would bolt straight for the commotion, his unerring ability to track a sound, even in the dark and fog, leading him to his doom, if his pounding boot steps didn't give him away first.

No, thought Chaw, the notion whipping through his mind at lightning speed, he would do this on his own, fight or die. He'd been in worse situations. Or had he?

That was enough to let instinct take over. Chaw flailed his not demure bulk and, writhing and growling low like a bull grizz, he heaved his midsection upward and twisted his hips at the same time.

The effort paid off, but not as he expected. The man atop him did not appear to want to give up his seat, but neither did he lash down with a knife—not yet, anyway. What did happen was that the man pinning his shoulders released one of them—Chaw's right—and drove a fist hard and fast straight into the side of Chaw's head.

The blow dizzied the big Reb with immediate effect, and he barked a hard, guttural oath, more raw animal sound than any word he'd ever been taught. Even addled and at the same time as he bucked, Chaw freed up his left hand from beneath the knee of the straddler and wasted no time in snatching a big handful of the man's thick wool coat.

It was too much coat for the weather, and although that thought passed through his mind, Chaw's concern was for jerking the man from atop him. It half worked.

For that was the moment when the man pinning his

shoulders drove a second punch to his head. As dazed as Chaw was, he didn't let it slow up his grabbing efforts.

He felt the man straddling him jerk to Chaw's left, lifting the fellow's left knee off Chaw's pinned right arm. The arm that still held—or so he hoped—his knife, for he was beginning to feel numb along that arm.

He wasted no time in jerking up that arm, feeling that, yes, he still held that knife in it. He gripped tight with fingers he could barely feel and was rewarded with a strangled gargling, gurgling yip as his honed blade tasted meat and bone.

The stink and wetness of hot blood as it gushed from the man's sagging body was quick and startling. Chaw recoiled, bucking harder and writhing, but not hard enough to lose his grip on his knife. Mustn't lose it, he knew, for in the dark and with who knew how many of these vicious predators around, he might not lay his hands on another weapon.

Then he realized he was a fool, as now that the masking of sound was no longer a concern, at least to him and at least for the present, he reckoned he still had his sidearm. He referred to the hefty steel revolver jokingly as the Death Doctor, because it gobbled lead pills and doled them out like a demonic medicine man might to patients it despised and wished dead.

But there was no time in that riotous, bucking moment for fumbling for the weapon, no matter how effective it might be. He also knew, now that silence was no longer a useful method of masking the sounds this scuffle had unleashed on this too-quiet night scene, that the attackers would also not be hindered by using only knives or fists. They, too, would use guns.

With a last mighty heave, Chaw was able to free himself from the brute pinning his shoulders.

He jerked hard with his left paw, which still gripped the wool coat of the stabbed, sagging man atop him, and jerked the fool hard to his left. The man, now robbed of much of his living energy and rapidly becoming bereft of strength, collapsed to the earth.

The big, buckskin-clad man did not wait, but rolled to his right, keeping his grip on his knife, which had slipped free of the straddler's body.

Chaw reckoned that for a blow to rob a man of that much strength that quickly, his lucky lunge with the knife had sunk into something vital. Perhaps it had even nibbled at the outer edges of the man's very heart.

It was not something he dwelled on for long because in that flashing, slashing moment, Chaw knew he had to save his own skin. But it was something, he knew, that he would come back to later. As he always had, ever since he had been forced to take another man's life in the early days of the war.

He'd managed to avoid doing just that for so long, it had sometimes amazed him how he'd been able to do so. Unlike so many of the men he'd known and had grown up with, including uncles and brothers and cousins, Chaw had never felt that the killing of another man was something to be regarded as a rite of passage, as a way of proving himself a man.

Heck, he'd never felt particularly proud of killing for food and skins any of the beasts of the woods, air, and waters from where he'd grown up as anything to brag on, either.

But at least with them he could reassure himself that they had likely led wild and innocent lives up until the moment his bullet or knife or arrow—and, once, a spear—had put a stop to that free life.

He'd always regretted even more any of the killings he'd done that had not rendered the beast dead within moments of the blow, but rather had required a second or third effort, thus dragging out the pain and suffering.

The difference in the killing of men was that there was no consolation of food or skins backing up the final violent act.

That did not mean he would not do what was needed to defend himself or friends or family members. And although he did not need to say it to Trace, the man was as close or closer to Chaw as any family member he'd ever had.

He rolled, feeling another blow land on him from the man at his shoulders, but as he was on the move, the fist slammed into his retreating left shoulder.

It still hurt like the devil and skewed his retreat, but at least it wasn't another drubbing to the head. He didn't know how many more of those he could take. The man had to be a big brute for that club of a fist to deal such blows. And Chaw knew he was not a wilting flower himself, so that was saying something.

Chaw worked to spin and scramble to his knees at the same time, for he heard the man growling like a bear and sensed him lurching himself at Chaw across the four feet or so separating them.

Chaw shoved himself backward, using his left hand as a pivot on the gravel and earth before him and whipping his knife-wielding right arm around in a wide arch.

It struck something a couple of feet before him. It was something at once solid and yet yielding, too. And it was something that shrieked and squealed and recoiled. Instinct caused him to wince as he realized he'd caught one of the unseen devils.

That was when he heard boots on earth stepping hard and quick behind and to his left but moving toward him fast. He jerked his knife arm back and spun at the same time to set himself, still on his knees, for an attack.

It never came. Instead, he heard the boot steps drawing ever closer, then begin to surge right on by him. He realized that whoever it was—not anyone he would consider a friend in this game—they were unaware of him there in the darkness. That meant the fellow was likely rushing fast toward Trace, to help out whoever of the rascals were at work over that way.

Chaw knew that if he was alone, he'd let them go, for it would buy him time. But Chaw was not alone, and the fellow was in a mighty rush, and it rubbed Chaw's fur the wrong way to let that rogue make for Trace, and on a dead run, too.

This could serve him well, if only he had another knife to spare. For he was a pretty good aim with the thing, able to sink a blade's tip in a log, butt end or broad side, the visible part of the knife quivering from the force of the throw. But that was during the day and with an unmoving target. At night, and in full dark, and with a moving man as the target? Those bets were off.

Then again, he did not want to send any man toward Trace. If what Chaw suspected was true, his pard was having much the same difficulties he was—folks popping up out of nowhere in the darkness, all riled and all bent on killing anyone they even mildly thought might be an enemy.

He shrugged and drew back his arm, then whipped it forward with scarcely a moment's hesitation, trusting what his ol' Gran called "inner sight," and let loose.

There was a whisper of time when he heard nothing save for the slight gasping and moaning of the man he'd wounded earlier somewhere to his right, then a low grunt and gasp as the man who was his latest target slammed to the earth.

All this he heard but saw nearly none of. Then, as Chaw shoved to his feet, he realized he could actually see—not much, but enough to let him stumble forward toward the hunched form now a dozen or more feet back toward the way from which he had come.

As he darted low toward this figure, it came to him why he could see basic shapes about him now—the high-up clouds had lessened to reveal scant but useful moonglow that not so much shone down as lit just enough to reveal larger shadowed elements about him.

One of the shapes ahead of him was that hunched man. He had slumped farther by the time Chaw was nearly on the fellow. He had two reasons to scurry back toward this man—he needed to retrieve his knife and he needed to make certain the rogue was dead or out for the duration of the fight. It also came to him that now that he could see others, they could also see him. It was a big risk, but one he had to take.

Chaw kept low and reached the man's side. He dropped to his knees and glanced to his left, toward where the rascals were emerging from. He saw another man, also on his knees. It was the one he'd sunk his knife into the second time. The other, he presumed it was the first, was flat out to one side, unmoving, so far as Chaw could see.

That quick glance had to be enough to suffice him for the time being, he knew, because this man beside him, although he, too, was flat on his face, was still writhing.

Chaw bent low over him and raked a stiff forearm over his form, but an inch above the man's back, from rump to shoulders. His arm clunked against what he hoped to feel—his dagger sunk deep in the man's back.

He fingered it and felt that the blade had sunk into the man's back more than half of its ten-inch length. It had entered to the right of the man's spine, somewhat horizontally, and so the blade, rather than hitting bone, must have thrust its way between the backside curve of the ribs.

Chaw wasted no more time but danced his fingertips along the knife again quickly and wrapped his right hand's fingers tight about the handle. The man beneath him quivered as he jostled the blade. It had to be tickling something deep in the man's chest.

Yet again he felt a quick, hard knot of regret lodge in his throat, but what could he do? He reasoned that the fellow was bent on doling out death to him and Trace, so it was a game of whoever dealt the death blow first won the fight. This point went to Chaw.

It might not always be that way.

And within seconds, that proved to be true.

What little light had been offered to them diminished once more as the clouds seeped back into dominance, clotting out everything else, it seemed, and draping everything with that stifling, inky blackness.

Curse that weak-kneed moon, thought Chaw, feeling scorn for the way it was unable to overcome the power of the clouds. He knew his thinking was silly and unreasonable, but he didn't care. The night was becoming what he had hoped it would not, somehow. There was killing and wounding and there would be more, and now he was exposed.

He wiped his knife's blade with his right hand on the stabbed man's coat, then felt the man's waist for another knife. There he felt only a revolver, which he decided quickly that he didn't need.

He was about to give up the momentary distraction when he felt something along the fellow's left side, forward on the man's waist. It was a bump, nothing more, but unyielding, and so he determined that it was not a fold in the fellow's wool coat.

Chaw looked about him quickly once more, although the renewed cloud cover assured there was precious little to see. But he knew he had been seen, had to have been, as he'd reached the fallen man and had tugged free the knife.

He felt with his left hand, fumbling, silently urging himself to move faster, faster, and alternately cursing himself for trying to take the man's knife. But finally, after shoving aside the thick wool coat's hemmed bottom.

Then he found it. He fumbled and finally his fingertips felt the rawhide thong loosely tied about the top of the handle, below the butt, snugging it and keeping it from jostling out of the sheath.

The thick fingers picked at it once, twice, and the flimsy knot parted. Chaw's fingers closed about the handle, and he tugged the knife free of the sheath. Even as he did so, he sensed movement, a rushing more felt than seen, coming at him from his left, above where the other men had been.

He looked up, pulling backward, shoving up off his knees, a knife in each meaty hand now. But he was not quick enough, and the dim, low shape hurtled fast at him, then landed on him, bowling him over backward and knocking from his left hand the knife he had but moments before snatched from the waist of his latest victim.

Chaw's head smacked the ground hard, and he felt an immediate buzzing inside his much-battered pate. It was a good thing, he reckoned, that he couldn't see much because it might make him feel even more like throwing up.

The man who'd launched himself atop him flailed and struggled to scramble back at Chaw after overshooting the mark by a couple of feet. It gave Chaw just enough time to roll onto his right side. The scene that played out felt strangely familiar to him. With suddenness that marked so much of this evening's brief but rapid events, Chaw felt tired, as if somehow he had been drained of his vital life juices right there and then.

This would not do, he knew, for that feeling in a fight led to one thing, and that was defeat. He shook his head, making the buzzing and dizziness worse, but strangely enough, it also gave him something to cling to, something to distract himself back into a fighting mood.

Then the other man was on him, and Chaw felt the kiss of steel sink into his side. He'd been stabbed. He felt the wet warmth leaking from him. It only served to make him angrier—with himself, to be sure, but mostly with the demonic little brute frenzying himself all over Chaw.

The man felt to be about half the size of Chaw but was moving twice as fast. This would not do. While he still had his vital energy, the big man in the buckskins fought back, with as much vigor and rage as he could muster. He well knew that at any moment the wound he'd been dealt would begin to render him the lesser of the two fighting men.

Chaw snarled, his lips parted, but his teeth were set tight together in a sneer of defiance at the situation in general. His own right arm wielding that trusted blade lifted high and then drove down hard at his adversary. He had to be careful lest he end up stabbing himself, half laid out as he was.

On his second hard downward stab, Chaw felt the knife bite into something, but the man who wriggled and growled atop him didn't seem slowed by the blow. Chaw wasn't waiting around, however, and delivered another ramming stab even as he snatched upward at the man with his left arm. He grabbed the man's arm by the elbow and held it, stiff and as far from him as he could, not letting go for one moment.

The man's free arm clawed at Chaw's face, and he felt the rascal's long nails raking his cheek just below his right eye. He squinted and jerked his face away, and the snatching hand dragged with it, as if the fingers sought to bore their way into his flesh.

Chaw jerked his face hard to the right, and the man's hand followed with him, locked as it was, clawlike, into his cheek. But this put the man's bony wrist right across Chaw's mouth. So the big Reb parted his ample teeth and bit down hard on the little brute's arm, not letting go even when he tasted the man's life juice.

It did the trick, for the frenzied man howled in ragged pain, emitting one of the louder sounds thus far of the night. It also had the effect that Chaw wanted, which was to get that beast's freakish, talon-like grip off his face.

The man pulled back, but Chaw held the fellow's other wrist in a tight grip, his fingers almost encircling the skinny man's arm, despite the fact that he wore a coat.

Chaw took advantage of the man's moment of pain to roll hard and fast, bucking and upsetting the little man from his paltry half perch astride Chaw's gut. At the same time, Chaw pulled his right arm back once more and drove it where he knew the fellow to be—because he still held the man's knife arm.

All of this happened within two seconds of Chaw biting the fellow's wrist. But they would prove to be the most crucial two seconds of the night for Chaw Dagworth.

Meanwhile, Fullcup Trace, proud Yankee, felt something thick and solid slam into his left shoulder. It shoved him sprawling into a smear of grass, bare earth, and gravel.

The attack, for that was what his mind told him this was, had been delivered unto him without the warning of the sound of boot steps and breathing. Nor did he feel the movement of rushing air, or the faintest of warnings—the tickle of the smell of sweat and the clinging of woodsmoke and bad food from a befouled campfire.

None of this had he detected as he slammed to his side and then flopped facing downward, his chin smacking the earth. Even before he shook his head to dispel the blooming ringing and thudding of pain from his rattled teeth and jaws, Trace rolled with the blow.

He shoved himself with his knife-free right hand to right himself, to get up onto his knees and then to his feet once more. He cursed himself, thinking that he should have known it would begin in such a manner.

But that was a fool's thinking, he reasoned as he pivoted and stood, crouched, at the same time turning to face his attacker. He managed to do this before whoever had collided with him drew closer.

In the dim darkness, Trace could just discern the outline of a figure, a man gathering himself just as Trace was doing. Apparently, his attacker also had lost balance and had knocked his pins out from beneath himself in barreling into Trace.

As he scrambled to get to his feet before the man slammed into him once more, this time with a knife or gun leading the way, it came to Trace that perhaps that first attack was unintended. Perhaps the man had been rushing to get from one spot to another before being detected somehow by his enemy, Trace or Chaw. But now Trace was known to him.

As if in answer to his thought, the dim shape halted not two feet before him. "That you, Jared?"

It was a whisper, low, barely audible, and coarse, as from the throat of a man too worked up and unable to catch his breath. Also, perhaps the voice of someone who smoked too many cigarettes or cigars and who drank too much burning whiskey.

All of this slipped into Trace's mind with eyeblink speed and none of it mattered much to him. Fortunately, he was likely being mistaken for one of the enemy camp, thanks to the darkness.

He grunted a low response: "Yeah?"

That was when the man moved closer, a small, awkward movement because, as with Trace, his opponent was also crouched, all but kneeling in an effort to keep himself low and difficult to see.

"Where you at? Can't see."

Trace froze for a moment, not anxious to draw closer to the man, and in no hurry to reveal himself.

"Jared?"

Now Trace began to feel bad. He'd prefer the anonymity of a night fight with a stranger, barreling into each other, heated up with anger, and this fool had gone and made it all human and personal again. He despised that feeling because it made him not want to do what he needed to do to the man.

But there was a middle way. "Yeah?" said Trace, in what he hoped was another convincing whisper of a lie, transferring his big hip knife to his right hand.

At the same time, he unthonged his revolver and slipped it out of the holster and held the barrel and cylinder in his left hand, with the butt of the handle out, hammer-like. He rushed forward and let his inner sight guide him.

This was something Chaw was always yammering about that his ol' granny had preached to him. Trace pulled that arm back and delivered a hard knock right where he felt certain the side of the man's head would be.

The blow connected with something solid, because it sent a jarring wave up Trace's arm. At the same time, he heard a groan, higher-pitched than he expected to come from this hoarse-throated fellow.

The sound tailed off into a mewling noise and, although it was pitiful to hear, Trace shook it off and pivoted, poised to deliver another blow. He reached out with his knife hand, keeping his index finger and thumb gripping tight about the knife's handle, and the other three fingers outstretched, patting with his hand to feel for the man.

The fellow wasn't where Trace suspected he would be, so he crouched even lower and kept patting before him, ready to spin the knife and drive it into the man, or deliver another head-thunking blow with the gun's butt.

Then he felt a wad of cloth—the man's coat—and further quick pats revealed it to be the rascal's shoulder. The man was obviously not responding. He wasn't even groaning.

Maybe I hit him too hard, thought Trace. But he kept on feeling with his fingers the side of the man's neck on up to his head. If the man wore a hat, it was not decorating his pate now.

Another second passed, and then he felt warm wetness, a sticky feeling, and he knew it was blood. He shoved gently with the back of his fingers and the man's head jostled, but he didn't make a sound and didn't flinch. He was unconscious or worse.

That was all Trace needed to know. He shoved the revolver into its holster and transferred the knife back to his left hand as he cat-footed forward. He was now somewhat confused, at least for the moment, as to where the boulder he'd been crouched before now sat, at least in relation to where he was moving.

He didn't have long to wait for an answer. His left knee barked hard against something much harder, and a quick, slight blast of breath slipped through his hastily clamped lips.

A feel with his right hand told him that, yes, it was indeed the big rock. Or at least one big rock. He didn't recall seeing others anywhere near where he suspected he still was, despite the brief tussle, so it had to be the same one.

Doesn't much matter, Trace told himself. *It's not like I'm going to move the thing just because it's in my way.*

He scooted around it and, keeping low, continued on

the route he had been taking before he'd been tackled, wary now more than ever. That first attack might well have been an accident, but the odds of that happening again were slim to none. He'd be expected, especially since they hadn't been silent in their fracas.

Off to the right, a dozen feet or so away in the darkness, something moved. It sounded as if leather had been dragged over stone, a soft scuffing but not gravelly, not on the ground.

Trace seized in place, keeping low and holding his breath. The seconds passed, then he heard the soft scuffing, dragging sound once more. Although it was faint, this time it was much closer. He kept still, pleased that he had been crouched low to begin with. He could hold that way for a bit longer, but he had stopped while his feet were a pinch too close together, ready to take another step.

He could wobble there in place for a few moments more, but then he really had to move a foot to maintain balance. And then he would, for certain, make a sound. And then the man would be on him.

Trace had no interest in being slammed into again. He was also tired of mincing his way into the enemy camp. The plan had been for each of them, him and Chaw, to cut wide and dole out hard retaliation to the invaders. Even though they couldn't see them and had no definite idea of how many there were.

On the other hand, the attackers knew without much doubt that Trace and Chaw were the only men they needed to deal with.

Then none of this mental chatter, as he thought of it,

mattered because he felt the first creeping twinges of a cramp in his left calf, high, just below knee height, but in the meat of the muscle in the back.

He knew from painful experience that this was going to end up one way and one way only: He'd have a hard knot in there, growing tighter and denser by the second. It would feel as if someone had stuck a short, wide blade in a fire, got it glowing good and orange-hot, and then jammed it into his leg muscle.

Trace had to move. He forced his weight hard onto that cursed left leg, then, even with the knot of cramp tightening, he used it to shove off with. He aimed himself low and headfirst at the barely discernible dark mass to his right.

It was a good six or eight feet away and it took him two and a half strides before he collided with it. And that mass was a man for certain. But it was a man made of brick and rock and wood and iron. As if a man had been cobbled together somehow with a locomotive.

As soon as Trace slammed into the big brute, he sensed, despite the fact that he caught the fellow at least a little off guard, that his attack was barely enough to rattle the giant.

Trace was no tiny, tender violet himself, and his momentum and broad-shouldered impact succeeded in driving the man's legs—he guessed the first one he struck was the man's right leg—askew enough to spin him. That was his quick plan, anyway.

But the man did not go down. He sort of jigged in place and quickly regained his footing. At the same time, he brought down a big fist, like a sledge made of meat and bone, hard on Trace. Because of his low stance and the fact that he'd collided with the man's tree-trunk legs, the Yank was still working to spring up himself.

That fist hit Trace between the head and shoulder, right at the root of his neck, and drove him once more downward. This time his right leg buckled at the knee, and he gasped, letting out a bark of a cry that shamed him even as it slid out of his mouth.

He regained his senses fast and shoved himself to the left, away from that swinging club arm, or so he hoped. He reckoned he could go the rest of his hopefully long life without ever taking another such blow by another such fist.

Trace darted back a half pace and stood upright fully for the first time in long minutes. He wondered about the severe and permanent and mortal damage a fist like that could and would do to his skull, to his face, to his chest, to his guts. It bore no more thought, for he wouldn't be able to muster the strength to retaliate.

Instead, Trace bent to his right and, doing his best to ignore the throbbing pain at the base of his neck, he feinted forward, slashing with the knife held out like a snake's flicking tongue.

The steel tooth tasted nothing, but he heard a slight whistle as the keen tool sliced air. He swung it back, and he knew right away that the tip did some damage, for he heard a whisker of an interruption in the breathing of his sizable adversary. Just a hitch, but it was enough to hearten Trace and renew his flagging certainty.

That was when Trace realized he could now see, or

at least he could make out more than mere dim black shapes, most of which were shadows but a few feet from him. He knew them to be rocks, trees, and of course, one large man, who was now a bit bent over. But the beast was still not making much in the way of sounds.

Had his blade cut the big brute? There was no way for Trace to know this, but there was an opportunity for Trace to get good and gone from that spot. Then it came to him that perhaps the man was waiting him out, poised like a jungle cat ready to pounce.

It was enough of a thought to force him to reconsider his next move. It also occurred to him that with each second that passed, he could now see. And so could his large foe.

And that was all the quick rumination that Trace had time for, because more moonlight shafted in, and the brute looked on Trace at the same time that Trace looked at the big man. Each peered right in the eyes of the other man.

It was by chance that Trace looked up that high, and it was high up. The man he'd been fighting, in a foolhardy way he now saw, was much, much larger than he had thought moments before.

And although it was still dark enough to hide all the details of the big man's fleshy visage, the fellow looked down at Trace with increasing disgust quickly turning to rage.

And Trace saw why—his second slashing with the knife had resulted, as he'd sensed, in wounding the adversary. But it was not a mortal blow; it was a cut to the man's left thigh, halfway up from the knee. He knew this because the man was slightly crouched, holding that slashed leg with a big hand.

If any momentary thoughts of the big man being slow and lumbering came to Trace, they flitted out as quickly as the brute emitted a low, seething growl. Then he bent forward, launching himself at the stunned Yank.

Trace recovered in time to dart to his right, but the brute whipped a big arm out to his left and clawed at Trace, catching him on the shoulder and drawing him in. Trace went with it for a moment and lunged, driving his knife out and up. He felt for a flicker of an instant that he was going to be able to sink his blade in the man's gut, but he hadn't reckoned on the fellow's other arm, which snatched with a big, sloppy movement, at Trace's left side.

The fingers of the big man's hamlike hand flexed wide and grabbed Trace's coat and shirt, and kept clamping, pinching hard on the meat of Trace's side and pulling backward at the same time.

It felt to the haggard Yankee as if some vital organ deep in his innards was being pinched and squeezed and crushed all at once. At the same time, he realized that his one hope, the latest thrust of his driving knife point, was now angled far too wide and hadn't even managed to cut the fellow's coat.

Then the big man did something to Trace that he was not prepared for, if any part of a fight to the death could be said to be prepared for—the brute jerked him up off the ground.

This was amazing to Trace because he was a pinch over six feet himself, or had been before he began skulking around at night in the foothills of the mountains, bent over like a hunchback monkey.

Trace was also no skinny man, but trim about the waist, as he always had been, and wide at the shoulder, wider, he liked to think, than most men. But none of this seemed to matter to the giant he was battling.

The fellow hoisted him off his feet and, with speed that shocked Trace, he snatched at Trace's clothes and jerked him sideways so that he was parallel to the earth, then worked him into another half spin.

Trace found himself hanging upside down with his coat flapping below his head as if it were a cape. He fought, squirming and jerking, but the man held firm, with a leg in each hand. The man's left fist gripped the thick canvas trousers of Trace's right leg.

The worst part of this humiliating pose was that the fellow had spun him so that Trace was faced away from the large, grunting, growling man. If Trace hadn't seen him in the moonlight, he might almost be persuaded that he was fighting a bear and not a man.

Then the man began jouncing him up and down, jerking him as if he were a butter churn or some such. Trace hoped Chaw was not witnessing this. The Reb would never let him forget it.

Trace realized there would be no seeing, at least for the time being, as the scant moonglow they'd been given had once more been secreted away as if by a drowsy conjurer. The dense clouds closed together again, blocking that glow.

It didn't slow Trace from his efforts to free himself, and he flailed upright, bending at the waist and striking with renewed vigor at his big foe. With each jab and thrust, the big man seemed to sense it and jerked out of the way.

Trace remembered from what he'd seen that the man was dressed in woolen clothes, which only meant he would have to stab all the harder, which he did with each lunge upward.

The man pulled and pulled and, as his discomfort increased, Trace realized the savage was trying to pry him apart, as if he were a roasted turkey's wishbone. If the giant succeeded, there would be one big loser in that wishing game, and Trace didn't want to go down that way.

After two more attempts, Trace gave up trying to rise, bending from the waist and slashing at air. He turned his attention to the man's hands. He knew they were bare because he'd seen them moments before, when anything close-up might still be seen.

His first stab was a bad one because the man sensed what he was doing and, while he maintained his grip on Trace's leg, he jerked that arm to the side, while still holding the other firmly. Trace didn't think he'd ever be able to ride a horse again, such was the growing extent of the throbbing, hot pain he was feeling at his tortured groin.

It felt as if his very hip bones had begun to stretch and would soon pop apart, then snap, tearing flesh and muscle and clothes. And then he would be undone, tossed to the earth, a useless yet still living scatter of meat and bone lumps fit only for coyote fodder.

With tight-set teeth and spittle flecking through them, his breath coming in short, frenzied bursts, his cheeks and nostrils puffing in and out like a smithy's bellows, Trace whipped his knife where the big man's left hand gripped his trouser fabric.

He was wrong with the stab, because he felt the tip of his knife tickle his own skin at the lower meat of his left leg. Too late he pulled back, uttering a quick cry of pain, pain he caused himself.

He bit back a fruitless curse and instead used the moment to learn from, for he jerked that blade back and then upward, quick and as steady as he was able to muster. He drove the tip of the big hip knife at the man's hand.

It sunk in, although Trace was uncertain what part of the man's hand received the blow. He didn't much care, only that the blade finally tasted more than a whisker of blood.

The effect, as the blade punctured flesh, was immediate, and the man let go of him with that hand. The brute retained his grip with the other, an encircling claw hold about Trace's right calf.

For a long moment Trace dangled there, lunging and whipping that knife, striking at anything that looked or felt as if it might belong to a big, angry, growling beast of a man.

He gave it one more upward fight and rose and swung the knife overhand. The blade sunk true, cutting the man's right coat sleeve as if Trace were a butcher working to sever a joint of meat.

The knife once more tasted blood, and the man made the loudest sound he had uttered so far in the fracas. He emitted a howl, low and growling and feral. His tight-gripped right hand released and he dropped the Yankee with a suddenness that Trace had not expected.

He thudded to the earth, landing on his right shoulder. He heard a crunch and his head bent to the left. A hot flash zinged up from the top of his spine into his head, and Trace was unable to do much more than lay flat and quiver, so painful was the moment.

Meanwhile, the man had backed away from him, grunting and sucking in big draughts of air, as if he had been underwater and only then had managed to poke his head above the surface.

As Trace lay there slowly regaining his senses and working to rise to his knees and turn at the same time to face the retreated fellow, he heard the man's odd noises.

Could the beast even speak? Likely, thought Trace, but then again, maybe he had hired on with the foes to be just what he was, a large, formidable presence.

With all this scuffling, Trace wondered, as he righted himself and skittered around, surely there were others of the attackers not far away. Unless they were trusting that the big man was handily taking care of whichever opponent he was now wrangling with.

Trace hoped that was the case; he had no desire to tangle with more than one of them at a time, and especially not when one of them was a big brute of a man he had already slashed and angered.

Before Trace could shove himself up to a standing position once more, his knife still gripped firmly in his right hand, the big man made his play, bending low and ramming right at Trace.

He only sensed this was happening at the very last moment, given the darkness, but it offered him enough time to jerk to his left. The giant barreled past him, barely clipping Trace on the side.

As the big man stumbled past, clearly becoming fatigued and sloppier in his still surprisingly quick movements, Trace pulled his right arm back, the dagger gripped firmly, and drove it forward.

The blood-wet steel found purchase once more in the large man's body, this time in the man's right side, somewhere below the ribs and above the waist off to the side. The big brute's flapping wool coat, shirt, and thick undershirt slowed the keen tip's progress, but even with those impediments, the knife slid into the man's side a solid three inches.

It proved far enough—the man bellowed like a surprised bull and staggered to his left, nearly taking Trace's knife with him before jerking to a halt in his mad, rampaging run forward.

He spun and, still gasping and bawling hot, ragged breaths, he made another mad run forward, his bleeding right arm and hand now clamped to his side. It was a weak attempt to hold in his amply flowing life juices, and it would prove to be a futile effort.

By the time he reached Trace, he was losing his fight with life and had begun to wobble and stagger more than ever. With a final bellow and gasp, the big man quivered, upright and spasming, as if he'd been jerked from behind by the shoulders. His big, shaggy head whipped backward and he dropped, staring skyward as a thin ray of moonlight leaked through a fault in the clouds.

CHAPTER 19

Dawn arrived far sooner than either Trace or Chaw had thought it might. They were each hidden, crouched and exhausted, both in their bodies and in their minds. And those minds continued to play the caution game with them. Every shadow that emerged as light began to glow the scene about them from far away in the eastern sky revealed a new potential danger.

It didn't matter to their frazzled yet still intent minds that as light began to reveal what they were surrounded with and what they were facing, nothing was moving. Nothing seemed alive. Nothing but them.

Chaw was on the verge of shouting to his pard twice when something stilled his tongue. It was too cursed quiet. Or maybe he was feeling too nerved up. At the beginning of the day, the patch of forest such as this, he didn't care where it was, always began to hum and buzz and flit with the waking up of the critters who lived there.

But not this one. *Too quiet*, he whispered to himself as he kept low, shifting as little as possible from behind the boulder he'd secured some time before.

It felt like hours earlier, and it may well have been. He had no idea. Time, it seemed, had lost its ability to do most anything of use. The longer Chaw hunkered there, the more annoyed he became.

Laying low and letting things happen to him was not his way. And he was keenly worried about Trace. As far as taking care of oneself, his pard was the most capable fellow he'd ever met, not that he'd ever admit such to that uppity Yank.

But even the most accomplished fellow could still bump up hard against poor timing and bad luck, which meant good timing and good luck on the part of his foe. Chaw and Trace had both been the recipients of each, time and again. So what, Chaw wondered as he shifted his weight on his sore ankles, had Trace come up against in the small, dark hours?

And then Chaw began to make out shapes about himself—a low, log-like hump that became a man's leg, then torso. To be certain, he looked away and then let his eyes drift back to it, allowing them to adjust to the scant light offered.

The longer he hunkered, enduring that interminable thing called waiting, the more shapes he began to pick out. As the light increased, he was able to determine that there were three bodies within his sight, and their locations corresponded roughly in his mind with the seemingly haphazard, darting course of pursuit he'd undertaken in the dark.

He wanted to look back toward their camp, knowing it had to be in sight, but it was behind and around this rock and one other. He didn't dare shift his position.

At least not until he could be certain, as much as was possible, that there weren't others of the foe forces lurking nearby, doing the same thing he was—crouched behind boulders, waiting him out.

So Chaw waited, unhappy about it and annoyed and irritated and sick of listening to his belly growl. He'd already made water off to the side, and now he was thirsty and wanted a cup of water as much as he wanted a cup of steaming coffee.

And a fat-rimmed steak heaped with fried onions and garlic, and beside it a mound of barely mashed taters with a knuckle-deep dent holding a knob of fresh butter. And atop it all, hot, thick, dark gravy, nearly black and aswim with meaty bits.

It was no good; he couldn't quit such thoughts. They seemed to breed like bunnies in his mind, one plate full of heaven-sent aromas and lip-licking treats after another. His gut roiled and growled like a baby grizz was in there, doing its best to claw its way out.

But finally it was light enough that he had to risk movement. Either that or he'd seize up and fall over where he crouched.

He felt certain that his bones had already begun to fuse together, locking him in position right where he was. Nonetheless, he mustered the strength to pull himself down lower; then he turned his head and looked behind himself, toward a thicker patch of woods and away from the edges of what had emerged as a clearing of sorts. He'd come to think of it as a small battlefield.

Chaw saw about what he'd expected to see back behind him—a few trees, scrub brush, a scatter of boulders, most too small to hide a man, but big enough to conceal a dog or a child, neither of which did he think were threats to him just now.

Maybe the enemy had beat a retreat under cover of the dark. If so, he'd not heard them. Perhaps the ones left had already been far enough away when all this began that they departed without him hearing.

He pivoted on his left knee and shifted, groaning softly at the pain of movement and also the relief at doing so. A double-edged sword, he thought. And he'd take it, gladly, even if he didn't like how he felt at first.

He stretched and looked as far as he could toward their camp, their wagon, and their horses. Or where he remembered them to be. Of the beasts, he saw nothing. This did not surprise him, since they had run off, albeit at a slowed pace given the remnants of wreckage they were dragging. That didn't mean they weren't about somewhere nearby.

He needed to scoot over to that other big boulder blocking his view toward the camp and the hillside up above and beyond.

He pulled in a quick, deep breath, thought, *to heck with it*, and then whispered something that Trace had taught him, by way of utterance, over the years. Something his pard's own Gran used to say in such a situation: "In for a penny, in for a pound."

He kept low and shoved himself forward, intending to keep low and move fast to the boulder. As long as there weren't folks snugged down in the brush to his right, which looked to be porous enough that he could see no hunched shapes behind it, then he should be well hidden from most other directions.

What Chaw didn't count on was the fact that while his mind was ready to commandeer the situation, his body, particularly his legs, the knees and ankles and hips and feet, had grown used to not moving.

They hadn't moved much at all, in fact, for what surely had been hours. He took that first step, a groan escaped his tight-pressed lips, and the big man in buckskins slopped sideways, crashing to his left shoulder with a wheeze and a hard slam of his head to the gravelly earth.

As soon as his head bounced once, he rolled to his right, panic and fear seizing his innards. Even as he moved, he did his best to gain his feet and scuttle backward or forward, whichever direction he needed to.

The entire time he held his breath, certain that at any second he would hear the crack of a gunshot and at the same time, and far too late, he would feel a bullet gnawing its searing path into his back, front, chest, belly, arm, neck, head. . . .

It didn't quite happen that way, and as he dragged and shoved himself forward, tucking close beside the next big boulder, he kept his breath stoppered. Still, what if this was it? What if there was no more fuse left on his stick? What if the enemy was waiting him out?

Yes, he told himself as he scrambled, it would be just his luck to roll up out of this foolish mess with a twin-barrel gut-shredder pointed smack at his big bearded face.

CHAPTER 20

On waking, Fullcup Trace found himself in much the same situation as did Chaw, fighting doziness and exhaustion from a night's lack of solid sleep and from brawling in the dark with men intent on killing him.

In the emerging dawn's bruise-colored glow, he came around to wakefulness because of a mighty sore feeling all over his body. It began with his toe-tips and crept northward right through the ends of his frazzled hair. Every bit of him ached.

And then he recalled why, and he nearly groaned as visions of darkness and things in the darkness emerged and tried to kill him. And then there was that giant . . . He nearly groaned again as more of this flooded into his mind. But he didn't, because he also recalled where he was.

Pinned down at the edge of that clearing. Pinned down by the man they suspected was that annoying fellow and his team of ruffians who'd pestered him and Chaw at their camp outside of Richness.

Sure, he was feeling bad, but given that his flexing fingers and feet, knees, elbows, and neck all functioned, he was obviously still alive. *Could be a whole lot worse, Trace*, he told himself.

And then he felt a flash of shame because his pard, Chaw, popped to mind. He'd been thinking solely of himself and yet Chaw, too, was out there somewhere, feeling as he felt. With any luck. If not . . .

"No," Trace whispered to himself. "Can't think that way."

He had been stretching his legs alternately with his shoulders in an effort not to seize up. He knew as soon as light filtered on into the small clearing that as well as him being able to see, it would slowly and surely reveal him to the eyes of his enemy.

The new day began to emerge, and light grew without his being aware of it. Then, all of a sudden, or so it seemed to Trace, he could see things before him that, although they had been there moments before, had been hidden from his view.

He fought with the mounting urges of needing to visit a tree and needing food and, most of all, a good, long pull on a canteen. And then, dare he think of it, he could use a cup of coffee or three, as Chaw put it.

And Chaw, of course, was foremost on his mind. That Trace had made it through the brutal night—and he did not know how—was a blessing. But had his pard?

The big, gruff Southerner had, from the first day they had met, been a righteous pain in his backside for a good many minutes of each day's time. The rest of the minutes—most of them, if truth be told, he had to admit—were just fine.

And yet they had been chumming together for so

long, he could not imagine his life without the funny, wry, witty, ignorant, annoying, smelly, loud, ornery man who had become his closest friend.

Trace had always been a loner as a boy, an only child back in the hills of Vermont, and while he had certainly had friends, he could recall no close attachments to other boys. Instead, he had worked alongside his father and grandfather, tending to the various chores that a dairy farm in the hills of a rocky, wooded state required of a fellow all throughout the year.

They had done it all, from repairing fences and stone walls in pastures to tending to the sugar bush for maple sugaring season in the early spring. And then there was haying, milking cows and shearing sheep, tending the vegetable gardens and chicken coop. And of course there had been the never-ending task of cutting firewood, a job he was still convinced had no end. Literally.

And if back then somebody had told him that he'd end up anywhere other than those hills, which at times he still pined for, so in love with them had he been, and in many ways still was, he would call that person a loon.

And if someone had told him he would have a friend he felt at least as close to as a man might a brother, he would laugh at them. And yet here he was.

So where was that mad Rebel? Where was Chaw Dagworth? Had he made it through the previous long, rough night? Was he alive or dead?

Trace knew he was risking his neck foolishly because he poked his face up over the near ragged edge of the boulder behind which he'd crouched, however long before. He'd not intended to slip into a doze, but sleep had come knocking hard and he'd answered that cursed door.

But now he was awake and getting the blood back into his feet and hands and it was time to move. He saw nothing over the rim of rock, save for dim shapes emerging from a thick ground-hugging fog.

He had to find Chaw and . . . *and then what, Trace?* "Bah," he whispered, trying to suppress grunts as he struggled to his feet. He ignored as best as he was able the stiffness and dull aches of a body that had been slashed and pummeled.

His legs in particular were sore as heck. As if he'd spent a week astride a devil bronc who had no intention of ever being broken. But he knew that it was due to the rough treatment by that cursed giant of a man.

Trace checked his holster and belt—revolver and knife were still there. He palmed the gun, slid it out, and gave it a quick, close-up viewing. Chambers were still filled, nothing seemed broken. He walked forward, slow and low, gun in hand. He was far too close to the center of the small open patch, yet far too sore to pursue the prudent course and skirt the spot, flitting from boulder to boulder like a smart man ought to.

He had to make time, even if risking exposure in the open was the wrong thing to do. Every second he waited was another second of light growing and blooming, brightening the space.

He bent low, ignoring the aches and stabs of hot, lancing pains in his side, shoulder, and one knee; he'd check them all later. He wasn't bleeding too bad, as far as he could tell, so he could afford to ignore the pains.

Right now, he had to find Chaw. He'd low-walked a dozen feet and heard and soft clicking sound, from dead ahead. Not twenty before him sat a big ol' boulder.

"Hold it right there!"

Trace froze. And then something about that voice made him squint his eyes and begin a grin. "Reb?"

"Yank, that you?" With that, Chaw's big, hairy head rose up from behind that boulder. "Good to see you, Yank! Nearly cored that homely face of yours with a well-placed lead pill. Good thing for you my reflexes is slowed from lack of food and coffee."

Trace shook his head and made for the big rock as Chaw stood, stomping a leg and brushing dust from his buckskins. "You see any sign of living raiders?"

"Nope," said Trace. "It's quiet, but unless they're sizing us up for a dose of bullets right now, I'd say they vamoosed."

"Left behind a few, though." Chaw nodded toward the slumped forms along his side of the clearing, then looked toward where Trace had come from and noted other unmoving bodies as well.

Trace did the same, taking in the situation and looking around for sign of anything amiss. Then he looked back to his pard. "You look as if you've been rolling in the dirt, Chaw."

"Yeah, well, I've had a time of it, that's for certain."

"What say we make for the wagon, see what we can salvage or turn up? At least in the way of coffee?"

"Now that's a plan, pard."

They made their way over to the upturned freight wagon. It looked much the same as it had before dark descended the night before. Of the horses, there was no sign.

"Hope those beasts—our team, I mean—weren't killed by those raiders," said Chaw.

Trace nodded. "Hector would be heartbroken."

"Not to mention the horses."

As they busied themselves with rummaging for the makings for a meal, each kept an eye on the directions from which they still might be ambushed. Before long they had a blaze kindled, a pan hosting popping bacon, and a coffeepot heating.

"Why didn't those rascals set fire to this wagon?" said Chaw, prodding the sizzling meat with a twig. He could not bring himself to use his hip knife for that purpose. At least not until he could give it a proper streamside scrubbing.

Trace shrugged. "It's what I'd do if I were them."

Chaw nodded. "I reckon the survivors felt themselves far too abused by the likes of us!"

"Or they had to be somewhere by dawn. Easy enough to ride a horse along the roadway. Maybe lit a lantern once they were out of range of us."

"Where would they need to be?" said Chaw.

"Boarwallow Gap." Trace looked at his pard. They both knew what that meant. If they were going to be of any use to those poor miners, it was high time they got moving. After coffee.

After a quick meal, they rummaged in their goods and found jerky, dried fruit, and waterskins. They each filled a pocket with bullets for their revolvers and rifles. They also swapped out their socks and shirts and spelled each other at scrubbing off down at the nearby stream.

Cleaned up and loaded up, albeit lightly, they set off afoot, westward up the road.

"You recognize this place?" Chaw squinted and surveyed the scene as they walked out of sight of the wagon.

Trace looked around. "Well, given that we drove the team through here a week back, sure I do."

"Just that, yeah," said Chaw. He nodded westward. "We ain't but a couple hours on foot, I reckon, from the Gap. It's the closest settlement, for sure. Mankley's too far behind us. For now, anyway."

Trace nodded, sighed. "Yep, and we best get to it."

They walked on, doing their best to feel appreciative for what they did have—namely, their lives. A close second to that was the fact that, while the team had run off, at least the raiders had not set fire to the freighted goods.

They walked on, but toward what, they had no idea.

They endured three hours of hard slogging and little speaking. They'd stopped once roughly an hour and more into the arduous, uphill walk, at a small but clear stream. There they rested for ten minutes, drank their fill, and topped up their skins with fresh water. Then they pressed on.

An hour and a half later, they heard distant cracks and pops, intermittent and random. They knew what it was—gunfire—and heard this trouble long before they hiked into view of what passed as downtown Boarwallow Gap. What they heard, they knew, was not good.

They'd been paralleling the roadway to avoid being fully out in the open most of the time. Much of that time it didn't seem to matter because the tree growth was sparse and boulders were not densely packed. They were able to move from one to another enough to remain hidden.

As they walked on, it seemed to them that the remaining raiders had not taken the roadway toward Boarwallow Gap to escape. They had likely cut cross country to save time.

Had Trace and Chaw more time, they knew it would be prudent to track the brutes. They had to stop at some point, and then the boys could finish what they began. Each also knew that they were lucky to have escaped alive from what had obviously been a raid intended to result in the deaths of the freighters.

They noted an increase in gunfire, and it sounded as if it hailed from in front of them, but perhaps closer than the town.

They hurried, despite their tired, sore legs, and soon they came upon the big rock around which the roadway wound down into town. They climbed to its right, northward, and spread apart, leaving roughly fifty feet between them. Each man kept low and peeked up and over the ragged line of rock; then they surveyed the scene below.

At first it made little sense to either man. Then they realized that what they were seeing was yet another invasion, an attack on the little mining camp itself. This was not terribly surprising, but what did startle each man was the fact that the attackers were far below them, and arrayed, according to the puffs of smoke from their shots, all about the edge of the town, which sat below the invaders.

Chaw and Trace realized they were in a unique situation. They were looking down at the backs of the raiders, who were in turn looking down at the little cluster of buildings comprising Boarwallow Gap proper.

With a nod, they each shimmied back down the gravelly slope and met up once more, conferring and confirming what they saw.

"I make out six, maybe eight," said Trace.

Chaw nodded. "It's likely they are the same outfit who attacked us and left us for dead in the night," he said. "They're trying to do the same to Slattery and the others."

"Yep," said Trace. "We had best pick them off. Or at least as many as we can."

"Hate to do that, as they are settin' ducks." Chaw scratched his beard. "Don't much like the idea of popping at a setting beast, even if they are foul beasts."

"Neither do I," said Trace. "But we were sitting ducks when they attacked us. And so are the folks down there in the Gap."

"True as true can be. Count me in."

"Only good thing I can see is that most of the members of the Holdouts don't live right in town. They might be along soon. Or maybe they are already, who knows?"

"Hope they don't shoot us," said Chaw, checking his revolver and his rifle. Trace knew his pard was only half kidding.

A hasty plan was cobbled together. Each man would do much as they had earlier and would split up with the intention of coming at the raiders, who appeared to be arrayed along this eastern side only, and not also along the north, south, or west edges. Yet.

The town was at the bottom of a cusp in the hills, so surrounding it would not be a problem. But only if the raiders had enough men.

"You ready, pard?" said Chaw.

Trace nodded. "I'll make for the south; you take the northern end. We should each be able to reach the rascals in the center." He nodded toward just below them. "Sound good?"

"Yep."

Once more, the pards nodded to each other, and then with no more chatter, they kept low and made for their respective directions, keeping below the ragged ridge-line just above. Given the ripples of earth and jags of rock, they were soon lost to each other. No matter, as each knew the other would follow through, unless something dire prevented him from doing so.

Trace reached a spot he felt would give him decent sight lines to the partially revealed hidey-holes of the raiders. From the looks of things, the attackers weren't in any hurry to scramble any closer to town. It looked to the Yank as if they were content to lob lead on down at the Gap all day. Maybe they'd attack closer in the night.

He reached the relative safety of a pair of boulders that formed a decent little cornice where he might set up shop. He also knew that he shouldn't get too cozy there, because as soon as he opened up on them, the raiders would melt into the downslope rocks. Some might even try to scramble back upslope and rout him.

He'd have to fire fast and, even more importantly,

he'd have to fire with accuracy. He kept in mind all the folks these hired killers had laid low, no matter if that brute, Cigar Tim, was among them or no. They were all the same breed and all deserved to nibble a lead pill.

One last check of his rifle, then he laid it out, tipped back his hat, and waited for the next volley. He didn't have long to wonder.

A puff some ways downslope to his left, southerly, rose up, then a blink of a moment later he heard the crack. His squint in that direction showed what looked to be a patch of blue topped with black. A shirt and hat, perhaps? Then smoke rose from a shot northward of the shooter, somewhat straight downslope of Trace.

A bounty of possibilities, thought Trace, as he held his breath and delivered a shot to the blue-and-black speck to his left.

He was already in motion, working a new cartridge into the chamber and angling right of where he'd shot, when he heard a yip. He thought he saw a bit more blue rise up and then drop, as if a man had jerked upward a good half a foot, then dropped down.

He'd call that a hit, if he was a betting man.

Then his sight settled on the spot in the tumble of rocks where he'd seen the second shot's smoke drift upward. For a long moment he could not locate a thing that looked like anything but the gray and brown of rock and slope, weathered and ragged.

And then he saw the slightest of movements of something lighter-colored, a tan something, lighter than buckskin. It moved once more, to the right, and held there. Another shot from that precise spot cranked down toward the town, and Trace knew he had his second setting beast in sight.

He lined up, held his breath, and squeezed. The shot was, once more, true. Or at least he hoped so. For the light tan thing snapped at that moment to the left and out of sight. What gave him confirmation was the sudden appearance of an arm holding a rifle right where the tan thing had been.

The arm was not held up in any way like a man might hold a limb, as if he were pointing. Rather, this arm looked to be flailing. After the first jerk, the rifle dropped. Trace heard the clatter of steel on rock.

And then the arm jerked again and dropped from sight. He took that as a sign that all was not well in that man's camp.

That was two raiders accounted for. Two out of six or eight. It was then he realized he'd heard a shot around about the second time he'd fired. That shot had come from far to his right, upslope. Had to be Chaw. He hoped so, anyway. Otherwise, it was someone nested in there, about where Chaw was.

Trace waited for long minutes, wiping away single drops of sweat runneling down off his forehead and stinging his eyes. The day was hotting up, as Chaw was fond of saying.

It was vexing not seeing any other of the enemy, especially when he knew there were more of them arrayed downslope of him. He suspected they'd ceased their firing because it finally dawned on them that they, too, were being sniped.

At least he and Chaw were able—for a time,

anyway—to keep the raiders from raining lead down on the town. Trace didn't have time to think about how many of those folks in the Gap had been laid low since this fusillade began.

Minute after long minute crawled by. Trace suspected his pard was growing antsier with each breath he drew. The big Rebel hated waiting for anything. "Except death," Chaw had once said with a half grin.

Yep, thought Trace, *that's one thing most folks don't seem to be in a hurry for*.

If Chaw had been successful—and Trace didn't doubt it, as the man was a very good shot—then that would be three, perhaps four, of the enemy number nibbled away. But all it would take was one to deliver pain and death to him and to Chaw. Trace told himself to be patient and wait them out. At least for the present moment.

From the sudden bawling and ruckus far to his right, that was not what Chaw had chosen to do. Oh-oh. Trace peered that way and saw his pard's big, buckskin-clad form bounding down the slope, picking up speed—more than the Reb intended to, Trace bet.

But it looked to Trace as if Chaw was all in on that run, making for the town.

"The fool!" growled Trace, annoyed that just because a fellow was agitated with sitting still didn't mean he had to risk his neck unnecessarily. But that was Chaw's way.

The problem was that Chaw would now be a target for the raiders as well as the unknowing Gap residents. They would think that one of the raiders was making his way straight down at them.

Trace pulled back, cursing Chaw the entire way back

upslope, for he was now risking his own neck. But he had to provide cover fire for the fool Reb.

He made it back up to the top of the slope and over, in relative safety, all without drawing fire, for which he was surprised and grateful. At the same time, he heard shots from ahead and downslope toward the town, and guessed it was the raiders shooting at Chaw.

Trace loped northward, keeping low and cutting up-slope once more, choosing boulders he guessed, from the boot scuffs in the sandy soil, were also where Chaw had been.

All this took precious time, perhaps half a minute, and then he was ready to help his fool of a friend. Trace saw first Chaw's broad back, arms akimbo, rifle clutched in one hand and revolver in the other.

But the fool hadn't figured on risking losing his footing, and unless he kept up his breakneck pace, he would topple. There was no way he could deliver a few shots on his way down, let alone defend himself.

Trace showed up just in time, too, he reckoned, for below him, but above Chaw, he saw a tall drink of a man rise up and, cool as you please, level downslope on Chaw's retreating form.

The man was no doubt a raider, and he was also unaware of the fact that Trace was behind him. He wasted no time in letting the fool know he had shown up.

His bullet caught the man in the right shoulder; Trace knew that if the fellow was a man at all, he would survive the blow. But it should put him out of the action, at least for the time being.

What it did do was a surprise to Trace. Sure, it prevented the man's shot he had managed to squeeze out, for it ricocheted well wide of his mark, namely Chaw. But instead of yipping and dropping his gun and slopping to his knees in a bloody and confused rage, the tall raider retained his grip on that rifle.

He swung as if he'd expected to be shot from behind, and raised that rifle again, his face a drawn, red clot of pain, to be sure, and his shoulder spurted blood as if someone were inside of him working a tiny pump to get it on out of there. But he looked square at Trace, who was in the act of crouching once more, intending to scurry to his left to take on more raiders.

And as he looked, his eyes narrowed, and he shouted something Trace could not make out. The man raised that rifle, slower than he should have, but that wounded wing hampered him. At the same time, another man not but twenty feet to the slim man's right popped up, looking upslope.

His eyes also fixed on Trace, and then he, too, began to raise his own clutched rifle to bear on the Yank. Trace felt a slight flicker of confidence somewhere deep inside, knowing he had the upper hand in the situation. But only if he acted now.

He sucked in a breath and doled out a shot to the thin man's chest, where it punched in hard, as if it were a tiny gray fist. This time the fool reacted as if shot—his arms whipped high and wide and the rifle spun even higher, flying away, then clattering downslope. The man fell backward with a strangled cry, but Trace suspected it was a heart shot, and that the foolish fellow was dead when he hit, collapsing into the rocks he'd hidden behind to deliver cowardly bullets down on Boarwallow Gap's residents.

All this played out in a background sort of way in Trace's mind, for as soon as he had pinched that trigger, he ratcheted in another shell at the same time as he spun to his left. He leveled on the man just as the second fellow was doing the same to him.

Trace's bullet reached its home first, buzzing into the man's head in that divot at the top of the nose, smack between the brute's bushy eyebrows.

The man's own shot had pinched off nearly on top of Trace's, but it had gone astray. Still, as Trace jerked left and downward, he heard the bullet, intended for him, zip by and smack into gravel not far upslope.

He glanced downslope and saw the last of Chaw as the man neared the end of his crazy run, switchbacking now that he had more control of his speed. Chaw didn't appear to have been shot, which was a bitter relief to Trace. He'd have words with the fool Reb later.

Just now, he had to wait a bit to see if there might be more raiders. There was no way he could do what Chaw had done, as Trace had nobody upslope looking out for him.

And then behind him, Trace heard a sound that no man wanted to hear—the throaty, steel clicks of a hammer being thumbed back into the deadliest position of all.

A gruff man's voice said, "Hold on right there, mister. Don't you move. Don't even twitch."

CHAPTER 21

While he'd been back up on the slope, and barely settled into position, Chaw had managed to lay low a raider, a foolhardy fellow who left his shoulders and head exposed to the day. And to Chaw.

"Too easy," whispered Chaw, and then the man, who he'd already aimed on, tracked someone with his rifle, squeezed off a shot, and shouted, "Woo-hoo! Got me one of them Holdouts!"

That was all Chaw needed to hear to help him get over any slight fragment of remorse he might have about shooting a man in the back. He triggered the rifle, and the victorious raider shouted, "Waah!" and collapsed forward, a burst of crimson flowering over his upper back.

"Take that, you sad excuse for a man," growled Chaw to himself in a low tone.

As he expected, his shot drew the attention of a couple of the raider's fellows, who reacted first out of instinct, their searching faces poking up out of hiding. And then, on seeing Chaw, their eyes widened and they jerked back down. But Chaw had marked the spots and doled out a bullet toward each.

The second one resulted in a screech, but Chaw knew it was from the spray of rock chips his bullet had whipped up. It was likely the man was not shot but spattered and bleeding from a couple of dozen painful, tiny cuts. That might well put him out of the action for a bit. *Good enough*, thought Chaw.

He pulled back down and, in a lull, listened as various shots rang out from far below and off to his left but up high. He assumed that was Trace, giving the other raiders a hard time.

And then Chaw heard a woman scream, then scream again, something that sounded an awful lot to him like "Not my baby! No!" The screams came from downslope in the Gap.

A woman being terrorized was enough to fire up the Reb, but a woman whose child was being wronged somehow was all too much for him to bear.

Chaw glanced to his left, then right, and saw no sign of raiders, although he knew there was at least one who had ducked down out of sight and managed to escape his scant, quick efforts. But that was just too bad. Chaw would have to do his best to cover himself with a quick few shots as he cut downslope.

He had to get down there to the Gap before something awful happened to a woman and her child. He checked his two guns, pulled in a big breath, stood, and barreled downslope, cutting to his right, northward a bit, to give himself room between him and where he knew the raiders to be, off to his left.

It was tricky, trickier than he had thought—not, he realized, that he had put much thought into this decision—to see where he was going to set his churning feet and keep an eye on the terrain below and make certain he was sending bullets in a direction close to whoever might pop up to lay him low.

And then Chaw realized that the slope was steep—far steeper, in fact, than he had anticipated. "Oh no!" he gasped as his legs churned faster and faster, as if they were powered by a steam engine that had pistoned right out of control.

He managed to pop off two shots at the slope to his left, hoping that might deter whoever was no doubt sighting in on him at that very moment.

Trouble was, he could not stop. He could not even figure out how to make himself fall. So Chaw kept on slamming and swerving downslope. Even when shots began whipping at him.

He heard three, four, then he found he had stumbled to within twenty feet of the bottom of the slope, a heck of a lot closer to the backs of the scatter of shanties that made up the downtown of Boarwallow Gap.

Chaw saw an ideal spot to swerve to his right, in hopes of switchbacking his way down, and thus slowing his awful and reckless run. It worked. Almost.

CHAPTER 22

The man's hard, brittle voice had barely ceased its threat when Trace heard another voice. A woman's voice, that said, "Mr. Trace?"

He did not yet turn, for he had been given a sizable warning and he didn't dare to do anything just yet. But that voice. That woman's voice was familiar somehow. And did it have an Irish lilt to it?

"Yes?" he said, still not daring to turn. He was also trying to figure out how to spin, duck, maybe jerk to one side, and pinch off a shot, all at once.

And then another voice, the threatening man's voice, said, "My word, Widow! It is him!"

Trace turned to see none other than Hector and the Widow Roscommon, just upslope of him, both staring down at him with guns drawn and cocked.

As Chaw pivoted to his right to avoid a boulder, his left knee struck a projecting rock from yet another annoying boulder, and he folded like a bad hand of cards.

He collapsed in a heap, his rifle clattering on rocks beside him.

Biting back a yelp of pain, Chaw heard, closer now, a woman's voice shouting. Then her voice was overridden by a man's low-toned bark, "Shut up!" and then a thudding sound. The woman's voice went silent. But a new sound, that of a crying wee one, rose up.

A man's voice growled, "Oh, you kids . . . more trouble than you're worth!"

Chaw scrabbled to keep low and check out his rifle. It looked as if it hadn't sustained serious damage, but he had no more moments to give it a good looking-over. He still wasn't certain how he made it this far without at least one of the hill-nesting raiders shooting him in the back, but if that was a gift from on high, he'd take it.

Despite all the ruckus and commotion and noise and dust Chaw figured he'd stirred up, he heard no more shots whipping down at him, although he thought he might have heard three, four shots traded back up the slope.

Might be that Trace was keeping a watchful eye on him. He hoped so, for that meant his pard was also all right. And if that was the case, he knew he'd be getting an earful from the Yank about being reckless.

At the moment, none of that mattered a whit to the Reb, because he was already on the move, keeping low and making tracks down the last of the slope toward the sound of the child's voice.

"Shut it, I'm telling you for the last time!"

Chaw reached the bottom of the ravine in time to

hear a man shouting alongside the shack before him. The distance between where Chaw was—half tucked behind a jag of sagged gravel and earth banking—and where he needed to be—the back of the building—was but a dozen feet. But covering that distance would leave him exposed once more. Well, more than he was, anyway.

Nothing for it, he told himself, and bolted for the shack. He felt no bullets digging into his back, but he didn't breathe until he reached the safety of the far side of the plank-and-log-walled structure.

Chaw hotfooted it along the wall, hugging the shanty with his left side, and came to the end just in time to see a greasy-looking fellow raising his right arm, the ball of a scar-knuckled fist topping it. The man was red-faced and about to deliver a solid pounding punch to a whimpering child.

Chaw recognized the wee one as the little half-naked creature who'd been in the street when he and Trace drove on out of Boarwallow Gap those long days before, making their way to Richness.

The child was still half clothed and still holding its wastrel of a dolly. But the child was now crying, and so innocent, it did not know to cower or cringe under the coming assault.

"Hold right there, curse you!" growled Chaw, a sneer matching his riled tone.

The brute turned surprised eyes on Chaw.

"Don't you move," said the Reb, stepping forward, his rifle trained on the rascal's gut.

The child was not in the man's arms but was tied

about its waist with a hank of rope that looked to be looped about its mama's apron tie.

And the mama lay on the ground, flopped on her right side. The side of her head facing upward bore a nasty-looking welt, red and bubbled. There was no time in that moment for Chaw to see if the woman still breathed.

"What have you done, you filthy . . ." Chaw let it go and strode forward, gun barrel several feet from the brute.

The man, still with his fist raised, eyed Chaw now with narrowed slits and a hard set to his mouth. The fellow's other hand held a revolver, and Chaw saw that the man was inching that gun around his lean belly.

"You do that and I'll pop you right here and now, vermin." Chaw's voice was low and cold. He had shot his guns a number of times that day, and one more, as justified as this one felt, would not nibble at his sleep in the least.

The man must have been hard of hearing, for he kept on with his sneering, wolfish look and with that sneaking sliding of his revolver, all the while keeping that fist raised, as if to appease Chaw.

"I warned you," said Chaw as he touched the trigger.

The bullet at that close range made quite a show. It drove deep into the man's half-turned torso, and Chaw saw blood, meat, and bone cloud outward as the man spasmed.

The beast looked down at himself, his arm and fist still raised; then he dropped his revolver. As he began to topple, his eyes looked back to Chaw with a questioning glance, as if to say, *Well now, I never really thought this would happen to me*.

Then he fell.

By good fortune, he dropped to the dusty earth a foot from the crying child.

The gunshot and the subsequent spray of gore had unfortunately affected the child. The sound gave it a whole new reason to howl, and the blood and bits of the now flopping, gasping man had spattered over, and a bit on top of, the child's mama.

As he had earlier stuffed his own revolver back into its holster, Chaw set down his rifle and, now with both hands free, dropped to his knees and scooped one arm about the child, who was yowling something fierce.

He pulled the young one close, hugging it to him—and he saw now that it was a little boy. Kneeling by the mother's side, for he had assumed this was the child's mama, Chaw felt her neck for a heartbeat. It was there, near as he could tell.

He jostled her shoulder and said, "Ma'am! Ma'am, get on up now!"

The somewhat rough treatment worked, for she sucked in a harsh breath and coughed, and her eyes opened. She winced and said, "Aah, ohh," as Chaw knelt closer, shoving the all-but-dead man away, and raking the man's revolver out of his reach, too, just in case.

"Well, now, stranger, that's a mighty fine thing you've done there."

Chaw spun and looked up over his right shoulder, straight into the steel snout of a pistol. Beyond it, a thin man regarded him with an amused look. "But you up and shot my friend, Rex."

"He was abusing a woman and a child."

"Yes, I see that," said the man, not wavering one bit as he held that gun on Chaw's face. "To be truthful, he was not my friend. Nor did I like him in the least. We worked together, though. That counts for something."

"I see," said Chaw, working his arm up and down to shush the whimpering child. "That tells me you're one of these raiders hired by the consortium."

The man shrugged. "That isn't much of my business. I work for Dade Wilks. Talk to Dade if you want to whine about the consortium. Now," he wagged the pistol, "stand up and turn around. Nice and easy. And leave the child there."

"But what about the woman?"

"What about her? She's coming around. Leave the child to her and stand. And keep the hands high. Or I'll gladly do for you what you did for Rex, there."

As if replying to the man, Rex shuddered, and a long, wheezing groan leaked out of his mouth, and then he was still.

"Good riddance," said the man as Chaw stood. "Keep your back to me." The man reached over and shucked the Reb's revolver. "Now bring those hands around slow behind your back."

Chaw did as he was bidden, all the while trying to think of a way to overcome the man without getting himself, or the woman and child, shot. He could think of nothing. But he was steaming angry with himself. All this way and now he was getting caught with his trousers down?

"Look here," said Chaw, slowing his hand-moving progress.

"Shut it and keep those hands high and tight together behind yourself."

Chaw did as he was told and felt the man doing a one-handed tie of his wrists with a length of thick rawhide. The man must have looped it first because he quickly jerked it hard, and the rawhide cinched tight, causing Chaw to wince.

"Hurt?" said the man.

"Yep."

"Good."

Chaw felt him finish lashing it, then he tied it off somehow, and Chaw was good and sunk.

"Now, march over there to your left and on up the street."

They walked up the deserted little lane. Chaw saw no one about the raggedy doorways of the handful of shacks. They came abreast of the empty little stable where just the week before they'd unloaded the wagon and had a fine evening with the town's much-abused residents.

"Hold on, now. Boss will be along."

"Oh good. I was afraid I'd miss out meeting him."

"You already did, freighter. We saw you outside of Richness some days back. And we know you aren't working alone."

That's where Chaw had seen the man. He'd not engraved on his mind all the faces of the men who'd accompanied that brassy fellow who'd yammered at them at their campsite back along the creek near Richness.

"Coming back to you, is it?"

Chaw shrugged, said nothing.

"Well, the boss won't be happy to see you freighters again."

"No?" said Chaw.

"Nope. The boys were supposed to have stopped you back in the hills."

Chaw sensed an opportunity and dove for it. "He'll only be half as angry, then."

"How's that?"

"Your men killed my pard back on the road. Caused us to tip our wagon and lose the team. A right mess, it was."

"Hmm," said the man. "Small comfort, I guess."

They were silent a moment, then the man said, "You don't seem bothered by your pard's death."

Chaw shrugged again. "He was annoying. And a Yankee. Same thing, really."

The man chuckled.

"So, where's the rest of your gang?" said Chaw, looking about at the empty little mining camp.

"They'll be along. The ones you didn't shoot up on the hill, anyway. Rest have been busy gathering the miners hereabouts. The Holdouts, I think they call themselves."

"What makes you think you all can round them up like sheep?"

"Because that's what we do. We make a success of a

bad situation. Folks only call in Dade Wilks when the ones they already hired have failed."

"Oh," said Chaw. "You mean like Cigar Tim?"

"What do you know about him? Where is he?"

Chaw liked that he'd struck a nerve with the man. Could be something he could use in his favor. "Might be I do know something of his whereabouts, in fact."

The man shoved his pistol's barrel hard into Chaw's back. "Best let me know, then. Right now."

"Huh," said Chaw. "See, now, getting something jammed in my back doesn't seem to help my memory none."

"Neither will a bullet in the head."

"Ha. Funny man."

"Nothing funny about being dead. Now don't push that luck of yours anymore."

And then they had no more time for palaver, because the very man Chaw recalled from the campsite near Richness rode slowly into view at the far end of the street. Behind him walked four men, bound and staggering, their faces bruised. Behind them rode two men with guns.

Chaw recognized three of the men afoot, miners, despite their swollen, bloodied faces.

Dade Wilks came to a halt a dozen feet from Chaw and his captor and nodded at them.

"I see you've been busy, boss," said the man behind Chaw.

"Oh, we rounded up a few folks, you know," said Wilks, winking as if he were the star of a stage play.

"And I see you are a peacock!" shouted Chaw, jerking from the yank his captor gave him.

Dade Wilks chuckled. "Why, yes, I do believe I am at that. Just in moments when I am feeling as if I have gained the upper hand. And those moments, I am happy to say, are not infrequent. Isn't that right, Chauncey?"

The man holding Chaw said, "That is a fact, Dade. Sure enough is."

"There's a whole lot more Holdouts than that," said Chaw.

"No doubt, no doubt," said Wilks. "But they'll be along. And under their own power, too."

One of the bound, bruised men—Slattery, thought Chaw—said, "Don't count on it."

"Oh," said Wilks, "but I do. I do, in fact, count on it. And so should you."

"Why on earth would I do that?" said the beaten miner.

"Because if they do not, then you will surely die."

"Just how do you intend to get the rest of the Holdouts on down here, then?" said Chaw.

"Why, by the very simple matter of the process of elimination," said Dade Wilks. "You look confused. Let me explain. You see, in a big, bold, loud voice, I tell the Holdouts—for I am certain they are all listening from somewhere not too far off, somewhere we can't quite see them hiding—something along the lines of . . ."

Here Wilks leaned back in his saddle and pulled in a big, deep breath. Then he lifted his face skyward and, turning his head slightly as he did so, as if he was making certain that all the surrounding hills might hear him, he bellowed, "Now listen here! Listen closely! I have five men!" He looked at Chauncey, his eyebrows raised.

To Wilks, Chaw's captor said, "And a woman and child! Back yonder." Chauncey jerked his head to indicate the direction behind him.

Wilks smiled and nodded, then resumed shouting toward the hills: "And a woman and a child! And if you Holdouts don't all file on down here in the next forty minutes, I will kill one of them every . . . oh, six minutes!" He repeated the details in his loud shout, and his voice echoed and faded.

For a long moment nobody moved. All eyes were on the smiling Wilks.

"You . . . you wouldn't dare," said the bruised, battered miner Chaw recognized as Slattery.

With eyeblink speed, Dade Wilks shucked his revolver, palmed it, cocked it, and drove a lead pill straight into Slattery's head. The miner stood wavering a moment, then he slopped to the earth.

"Oh, wouldn't I?" said Wilks, smiling and shoving the gun back in its holster.

"Now . . . now look," said Chaw, half expecting to get shot for opening his big mouth. But he knew he had to try. "What if I told you where to find . . . Cigar Tim? Huh? That keep you from murdering these folks?"

Dade Wilks stared at him, then said, "I am nothing if not a man of my word. If you manage to tell me where I might find that old colleague of mine, I give you my word that I will turn all these folks loose once more.

Well," he looked down at Slattery's still form, "all save one. He needs more help than I can give."

"Well?" said Chauncey.

"Now don't rush me," said Chaw.

"I assure you," said Wilks. "You have no more bargaining power. If you do not tell me where I can find Cigar Tim, and then if I do not find him there, I will shoot you and them. And yes, the child and the woman, too."

"But that wasn't the deal!" growled Chaw.

"Deal, deal. I am Dade Wilks. I make the deals; you are simply here to fall into line. One way or another. Isn't that right, Chauncey?"

"You bet, Dade."

One of the other tied-up miners had been sobbing, and he was trying to stop, but it was difficult for him, and he kept making a hiccuping sort of sound.

Wilks sighed. "Do stop that, you fool. I am not in the mood. Say, Chauncey, where are the men? I expected more of them. And why is that man still alive, anyway?" He nodded toward Chaw. "He's one of those freighters, isn't he?"

"Yes, Dade. He escaped the men last night, it seems."

"Seems so," said Wilks. "Say, it must be time to kill another of these fools, no?" He looked at Chaw once more. "Unless you have something to tell me. Like Cigar Tim's whereabouts? Hmm?"

Chaw licked his lips and Wilks said, "As I feared. Too good to be true, Chauncey. Kill the freighter and we'll call it good for six minutes. Then, I think, the woman."

Just then, a sliding, scuffing sound from the broad hillside to the east, behind the little line of huts, drew their attention.

Striding downslope, switchback fashion, were five figures.

Chaw couldn't be certain, but he thought one of them sure looked like Trace. And another was a woman. That made little sense to Chaw, but then again, he knew there were a few women in and around Boarwallow Gap.

A few moments passed. Two of the figures were walking ahead of what Chaw saw now was clearly his pard. A smidgin of relief at seeing that cursed Yank made him smile.

And although it made no sense to him at all, he was beginning to think he'd bet a dollar or two that the woman and the other, smaller figure beside Trace were none other than the widow and Hector. Made no sense that it would be them, but something told Chaw otherwise. He had a twinge of the gut flutters, and that was always a sure sign.

He looked at Wilks, who was squinting up the slope. "Can't make them out, Chauncey, you? I do believe some of our men have managed to rustle up a few more miners. And a woman among them! Chauncey, we might just have ourselves a fun night after all."

Chaw bit back a bloom of hope. If Wilks and Chauncey didn't yet know the folks coming down the hill were who Chaw was strongly suspecting them to be, then somehow Trace might be able to get the drop on them. He knew his pard was playing it fine, but that Yank was wily.

Chaw bet Trace was getting as close as he dared before leveling down. Trouble was, he would be putting the widow in danger. And that was unacceptable to Chaw. And he knew that Trace felt the same way. So what was the play, pard?

The five switchbacking figures continued to advance. The two in the front walked awkwardly, and Chaw saw why—their hands were tied behind them.

Then, without warning, the two men in the lead seemed to look at each other; then they bolted, splitting apart, one dashing left, the other right.

Chaw also saw, now without any doubt, that the three folks behind them were Trace, Hector, and the widow. And each carried a gun. The widow and Hector with rifles and Trace with a revolver.

That was when all manner of things happened at once—Trace dropped to a knee and fired, first at the man fleeing to Trace's right. That one dropped hard, face-first into a rock. Trace did not see this as he wasted no time in thumbing back the hammer while he pivoted to his left, locating the other man and firing. As with the first, that man dropped, but before doing so, he jerked high and fast, his body resembling a crescent, as if he had been stung square in the back by a mighty bee.

At the same time, Hector whipped his rifle to his shoulder, snugged it to his cheek, and instead of laying low one of the departing men before him, he peeled off a shot downslope—right at the men who were guarding the straggling miners. Because those two mounted men had already raised their own rifles to their shoulders and were aiming upslope, but not yet firing.

Right next to Hector, the widow had spread her stance, and a smidgin of a second after Hector's shot cranked out, her gun fired. Hector's bullet caught the first mounted guard square in the chest, and the widow's shot caught the second guard smack in the middle of his forehead. Both men dropped fast from their saddles.

As soon as Trace opened the ball, Chaw sidestepped and pivoted to his left, exposing his captor, Chauncey. For the moment at least, the move kept that man's gun from the center of Chaw's back. In the same motion, the big freighter dropped low, bending at the waist and with no more thought than that, rammed the bewildered Chauncey hard in the midsection.

Chaw felt the hard steel of the man's gun against his forehead as he collided. He kept going and his captor folded in the middle and collapsed on his back in the street, his revolver going off right beside Chaw's temple. He didn't let up his attack, despite the fact that his entire head felt as if it had just been slammed with an exploding tree.

Without his hands to snatch and grab with, the Rebel had to rely on his head, shoulders, and knees. Sloppily straddling Chauncey, Chaw shoved himself upright enough to jam his right knee down hard on the now-bucking, shouting man's left arm, pinning it. But it was Chauncey's right that still held the revolver.

Try as he might, Chaw could not get him to release his grip on the killing tool. He jammed hard with his left knee and finally managed to pin the arm, within seconds after the man slicked back the hammer. Chaw jammed hard, forcing his weight on that limb.

That was when the man gasped from the pain of it and his fingers, more out of reflex than out of intention, convulsed and the revolver dropped to the ground.

Chaw kept hard, deliberate weight and pressure on each arm, because it wouldn't take Chauncey but a moment with that free right hand to snatch up that gun and end Chaw's days right there.

"No, you don't!" barked the freighter. In his still-thudding, ringing head, his shouts sounded huge and cavernous.

Still, the man struggled and clawed and kicked, trying to dislodge the big Reb from atop him.

"Simmer down!" bellowed Chaw, and then he did the only thing he could think of doing at the time—he whipped his head down hard and fast at Chauncey's face.

Too late, the raider saw what was set to happen. His eyes bloomed wide and he was about to shout when Chaw's big, shaggy head collided with his own. Their foreheads met and each man jerked away, dizzy. But only Chaw remained conscious.

"Ohhh," he moaned, forcing himself to sit upright. He'd figured that, as bad as his head already felt, one more wallop couldn't do him much more harm. Now he wasn't so certain. He sat atop the thin raider and blinked, shaking his head as if to dispel an irksome fly. It didn't work. At least not right away.

By then Dade Wilks was snapped from his moment of smug, blissful reverie and had clawed free a revolver.

He brought it to bear on the approaching folks from the hill.

At the same time, the three miners afoot behind him scattered, two of them ducking behind the now dancing and riderless horses of the guards. One of the miners had worked his bound hands free enough to help his fellow. Together they loosened their wrist ropes and snatched up the dropped rifles of the two fallen guards.

Wilks had snapped off two revolver shots, but the sudden commotion spooked his mount and the horse began to dance. He cursed it and tried, not successfully, to calm it, jerking the reins and growling.

The two armed miners each took one side of Wilks's horse and drew down on him.

He nearly shot one, but saw that he was in a losing situation, flanked by trigger-happy miners with just cause for rage. One of the men barked at him to drop his gun. The boss man of the hired brutes did just that and raised his hands high

The other miner grabbed Wilks by the left boot and jerked him hard. The boss man lost his balance and slopped from the saddle, landing in the dust face down, sputtering and spinning and churning his boots and howling his rage at the entire raw situation he found himself in.

Within a minute, Trace was by Chaw's side. He kicked away Chauncey's gun, then helped his pard to his feet and untied him, all the while keeping a boot on the raider's chest.

"You good, pard?" said Trace, eyeing Chaw. "Shot?"

"Naw, not shot. Just befuddled a bit. I'll come around."

"Good. Maybe you'll have knocked sense into that big bean of yours."

"Listen here, I could ram my head against boulders all day long and still have more sense than you were born with, Yank!"

As he bent to drag the moaning Chauncey to his feet, Trace smiled, knowing for certain that his surly pard was going to be all right.

And within a few minutes, Chaw's vision centered on one of a thing instead of three, albeit with fuzzy edges. The ringing in his ears tapered off to a dull whistling, and the bruise and cut on his forehead seemed to take kindly to the staunching efforts of the tut-tutting widow and her lace hanky.

"Thank ye, ma'am." The big man blushed.

"Foolishness, Mr. Dagworth! You could have gotten yourself killed and then where would we be?"

Before he could answer, she smiled at him and patted his shoulder, and he followed her over to what appeared to be a growing crowd of miners. And in the center, Dade Wilks and Chauncey stood, arms bound behind their backs, each scuffed and begrimed.

They were surrounded with haggard-looking but fired-up miners, all armed and not a one of them appearing to be in a mood to negotiate much of anything with the two raiders.

Just then, a cackling shriek rose up from the far end of town.

Chaw, Trace, Hector, the widow, and all the miners

directed their attention northward up the trail that led down out of the hills and ended up forming the main street of Boarwallow Gap.

At that far end, but walking in fast, strode a black-haired woman in a grimy, foul dress. Ahead of her staggered a stout, bound, hatless man. From his ambling, lurching gait, he appeared to be either supremely inebriated or much abused.

She shrieked something else that sounded to Chaw like part words, part scream, part maniacal laughter. Then she shoved the staggering man forward, ahead of her, and they all saw that she held a big revolver on the man. As they came abreast of the shacks, she stopped.

The man kept walking forward, and the woman shouted, "*Parar!* Stop!"

He did as she commanded, not turning around but weaving in place.

She kept the revolver trained on him but bent to the woman and child who had been beaten by the now-dead Rex, his body lying nearby. The woman was sitting up and comforting the child in her lap.

The dark-haired woman spoke to her and the woman seated on the ground slowly rose to her feet and, carrying the child, followed the grimy, dark-haired woman. She prodded the haggard man and the foursome advanced.

Then, within forty feet of the group, she halted the little group once more. She held out her left arm and muttered something to the woman and child. They walked forward toward the larger group, who all watched this situation with confusion.

Finally, as the woman and child reached them, the woman with one side of her face a bruised mess said, "It's Marietta! Got herself Cigar Tim. . . ."

That news brought the throng to life, although none reacted with more exuberance, tinged with rage, than Dade Wilks. He lunged forward, shouting, "He's mine! Let me at him! She's robbing me of my revenge! Nobody crosses Dade Wilks and lives to tell! Cigar Tim, you—"

But he shut up when two miners slammed fists into him, one in the face, knocking his head to one side, and one in his gut, doubling him over. He gasped and wheezed out the words, "Robbin' me . . . she's robbin' me!"

Meanwhile, the woman had jerked the bound man around so that the group of onlookers saw them each in profile. Then she reached in a big, sagging, grimy pocket of her dress and pulled out a handful of something. Or several somethings. They were dark and as long as a man's hand, thicker than sticks.

Her prisoner stood before her, weaving and shaking his head. She said something low to him and he shook his head harder. "No, no, no. . . ."

"You don't have a choice!" she shouted. Everyone heard her. Then she jammed those things into his face, stuffing them into his sagged mouth.

"Cigars!" someone in the group said.

"Eat them! You will eat them all, Cigar Tim!" Marietta shrieked the words as she stuffed them into his now jerking face. She was successful in getting more than a few cigars into his mouth, for he began gagging and jerking his torso, as if he were waking up.

"No! No!" came his muffled shouts, and as if someone doused him with a bucket of cold stream water, he lunged at her, mouth filled with mangled cigars, looking as if he intended to knock her down and stomp her.

Marietta stepped back once, and as he barreled at her, into her, she tugged the trigger and he stiffened, howled, and slopped forward on top of her, knocking her to the ground.

Trace and several of her miner friends rushed to her, but before they reached her, they heard another shot.

They dragged Cigar Tim from atop Marietta and saw that she had jammed the revolver's barrel into her chest. Her broken heart was now bleeding out its last. But there was a smile on her face.

CHAPTER 23

"Some time ago," said the widow, stretching and standing up straight, and looking at Dade Wilks.

Not a man there could take his eyes from the stunning visage that was the Widow Roscommon, wrapped as she was in a tight black mourning dress.

"I sent a wire back East," she continued. "To someone who owes a mighty debt of favor to my dead husband's father, himself a very wealthy and powerful man back in Ireland, don't you know. He also received a wire from me. And he's also a very angry man, because his son was taken from him. And from me."

"That so?" said Wilks. "Why should I care?"

"You should care because the man to whom I sent the wire, the man who owes my father-in-law so very much, is a man named Horace Dibley."

Beside her, Hector chimed in, "Say, Wilks, you might know him as His Right Honorable Justice Horace Dibley!"

The result on hearing the man's name was immediate and interesting. Dade Wilks's smile slid from his mouth and his face turned gray. "You. . . you . . . but . . . they call him—"

"Yep!" said Hector, smacking his thigh. "That'd be Justice Dibley, the Hangman!"

"Hmm, now that I think on it, rumor has it," said Trace, "that Dibley hates, with a passion, hired gun-hands. Why, he made quick work of the Jonesy gang. And then there was Peder Olsen up in Minnesota way, and then . . ."

Wilks swallowed and said, "Well, so? What of it? Why should I care?"

"Because, Mr. Wilks," said the Widow Roscommon, "he is on his way to Mankley and then on to Richness, personally. Well, with the various members of his legal retinue. He travels with an entire crew of lawmen at all times. His life has been threatened so often, you see. But as I said, he owes my father-in-law, Lord Roscommon, a favor."

"But . . . the law. There are marshals in Mankley and Richness! They both know me!"

"Yes." She smiled. "And they are known to Justice Dibley as well. In fact, I shouldn't be surprised if he is not terribly far away, in fact. That wire was sent some time ago."

"But . . ."

"But nothin', you rascal!" growled Hector. "Now shush up and get your hands behind your back. Higher!"

Hector and Chaw went through and lashed the arms of Wilks and Chauncey. As near as they could tell, that was all of them left alive. If there were others up on the hillside, it seemed they knew which way the wind blew and had made the most of the opportunity to escape. They might also be hunted by Holdouts.

"Going to be a long walk back to Mankley with this lot," said Chaw.

"Nah, not too bad," said Hector. "Me and the widow, we got a small buggy up yonder, east of town. And we managed to find the team you two sorry excuses for freighters lost on me!"

"You found the horses?" said Trace.

"Sure I did, no thanks to you two," growled Hector. "They come right up to me, they did. Trailed them behind us. But we stopped yonder, as I said, when we heard all the shooting. Figured you two goobers would be in it up to your necks. And you were! Good thing we come along when we did."

The widow shook her head. "I think, with your help, Mr. Trace and Mr. Dagworth, we should be able to right that wagon and bring it here. Then, when it's empty, we'll be able to ferry these men back to Mankley, perhaps just in time to meet up with Justice Dibley and his retinue."

Dade Wilks groaned and Hector giggled. "That's about the size of it, Wilks."

The rest of the Holdouts trickled down out of the hills. Trace and Chaw were surprised to see there were perhaps a dozen of them. And they all came armed and angry and herding four more of Wilks's men.

The Holdouts all surrounded Wilks and his men in the middle of town and vowed to keep an eye on them until Chaw and Trace and Hector and the widow returned.

On their way back up the hills out of town, toward

the buggy and team, Chaw cleared his throat and said, "Widow, ma'am . . . um." He glanced at Trace.

Trace nodded and picked up from there, knowing exactly what his pard was about to say because he felt the same way. "Widow Roscommon, ma'am—"

"It's Miranda, gentlemen. Call me Miranda."

"Yes, ma'am," they both said, their cheeks and ears reddening.

"What was it you wanted to say?" she said, looking at them with a drawn brow.

"Well, ma'am," said Trace. "Miranda, ma'am, the thing is, this has been quite a trip. Yes, it has." Trace looked at his pard for confirmation.

Chaw nodded with vigor.

"And well, as much fun as it has been to work for you . . . you see, we're just not freighters by nature. So, if you could . . . when we all get back to Mankley, why, we'll just—"

"Draw our pay and leave you to it!" said Chaw, nodding.

"Yes," said Trace. "After all, it sounds as if you have everything all taken care of. Yes sir, it sure looks like the Holdouts might be able to keep their claims."

For a long moment, nobody said a thing; then the widow turned to them. "It's a shame, what you say. Oh, I understand, but it's a shame, you see. As I, well, I am not in a position to pay you gentlemen. Not yet anyway. But soon, very soon, there will be more money and business than I can handle. Isn't that right, Hector?"

The old man nodded heartily, his head bouncing up and down as if it were a child's plaything. "Oh, you bet!

You bet. Why, as soon as Justice Dibley gets things all straightened around, you'll have to buy yourself a bigger safe! And I ain't fooling!"

Trace and Chaw didn't know what to say. All they wanted was to sample a nice quiet glass of whiskey and then be on their way. Finally, Chaw said, "So what you're tellin' us is you fibbed to us. Back in the diner. Over pie."

She nodded. "I did, gentlemen. I did, and I apologize for it. It was not something for which I am proud. But I was desperate."

By then, the foursome had reached the buggy and the unlikely sight of the four big freighting horses standing there hipshot to the side of the roadway, lightly lashed to the rear of the buggy.

"I suppose that's all right," said Trace. "Considering."

"After all," said Trace. "My ol' Granny used to say that crying once you've spilt the milk ain't no way to live your life."

"Thank you, gentlemen." For the first time in their acquaintance with her, it looked as if the widow was blushing in their presence, and not the other way around.

She reached into the buggy, pulled out a picnic basket, and flipped it open.

Chaw and Trace both ogled its contents. They had briefly forgotten what a mighty cook she was. And nested in the midst of the bread and cheese and meats and fruits and nuts was a bottle, brand-new and unopened, of fine whiskey.

"Be still, my thumpin' heart," muttered Chaw.

The widow laughed and said, "Hector, will you do the honors?"

"Sure thing, Widow." He set up four glasses, topped them up, and passed them around.

"Gentlemen," she said. "A toast."

"To what?" they both said.

"To an offer you can't to say no to."

The widow and Hector glanced at each other and, smiling, downed their whiskey. "What are you waiting for, gentlemen?"

"Um, what offer, ma'am?"

"Why, shares in Sligo Star Freighting, of course. Hector and I and the two of you will own the soon-to-be biggest, most powerful freighting firm on this or that side of these mountains. I will of course, own controlling interest. And Hector and I will set up our primary offices and depot in Richness, and you two will run your end from Mankley."

"Umm," said Chaw, staring at his whiskey, and then at Trace.

"Umm," said Trace, staring at his whiskey, and then at Chaw.

"What say you?" she said.

"You bet!" they both said together.

Several days later, in Mankley, Chaw and Trace found themselves at the bar, working on beers.

"You know she ain't ever going to set her cap on either of us, you know that, don't you?" said Chaw.

"Sure, sure. But that doesn't mean a man has to give up and stop trying, now does it?"

"So, does that mean I'm going to have to whup you

to within an inch of your mangy hide's existence every step of the way?"

"It means you're welcome to try," said Trace. "It's little more than a petty annoyance to me. But a minor challenge. And I do like my challenges."

"I'll say," said Chaw. "Just waking up each day must be trial enough for such a sap as yourself."

Trace sipped, set his beer down, and said, "It's the constant whining sound from you that I find the thing that requires the most endurance."

The barkeep flipped the towel over his shoulder and stood back with his hands on his hips, eyeing them both. "Now look, you two, I have heard about everything a man can hear in my job, and I know when two men are working themselves into a lather and spoiling for a fracas." He leaned forward, planted his big hands on the bar top. "You both knock it off or I'll knock your heads together and no mistake!"

"What do you reckon?" said Chaw, glancing at his pard.

Chaw looked the barkeep up and down, then nodded. "Yep, I think we can take him."

The barkeep pulled in a big draught of air through his flexed nostrils.

"Now, now, now." Trace held up a hand. "I didn't say it'd be any time soon, now did I, pard?"

Chaw sipped his beer. "I hope not. I have a whole lot of drinking to do, and the night is young . . . ish."

"Agreed." Trace finished his beer, setting down the mug with a gasp of delight. "Bartender, another round for me and my pard, here!"

"And he's paying," they both said, glaring and grinning at each other.

Arriving by cattle car with two of his beloved horses,
Jesse Derringer is not your typical railroad employee.
With the eyes of a scout, he looks for trouble
before it becomes a problem for the construction
crews—and sometimes starts trouble himself.
Usually, he handles hot-tempered troublemakers with
a cool head and steady hand. But then there are
problems like Felix Reardon. A wealthy rancher with
a sprawling cattle spread, Reardon refuses to give up
a piece of his land for a new US Army post.
He will not negotiate.
He will kill without conscience. . . .
It's Derringer's job to defuse the situation—
before it ignites a full-blown bloodbath.
Jesse Derringer is about to learn
the true definition of troubleshooting.

National Bestselling Authors
William W. Johnstone
and J.A. Johnstone

DERRINGER

First in a new Western series!

Live Free. Read Hard.

williamjohnstone.net
Visit us at kensingtonbooks.com

On sale now, wherever Pinnacle Books are sold.

CHAPTER 1

General Grenville M. Dodge sat beside a small fire on the bank of Lodgepole Creek drinking a cup of coffee. His column of one hundred and fifty cavalry had totally routed a party of about forty Arapaho warriors who had been raiding settlers between Crow Creek and Fort Laramie. They had been fortunate to attack the Arapaho camp while the warriors were still asleep in their blankets. The forced march to catch the Indians was the suggestion made by the general's personal scout, Sergeant Jesse Derringer. It was Derringer who found the Indians' camp at the base of a line of mountains after they raided a small settlement north of Crow Creek. The few Indians who had escaped the attack disappeared into the steep mountains of the Black Hills, so Dodge decided to have breakfast before starting the march back to Fort Laramie.

"You send for me, General?" Jesse Derringer asked when he approached Dodge.

"Yes, I did, Sergeant," Dodge replied. "Did you get something to eat?"

"Yes, sir, I ate," Derringer said. "What can I do for you?"

Dodge smiled in response to Derringer's submissive attitude. The general would be willing to wager that he was the only person on the planet who commanded much respect from the burly sergeant. "Now that the horses have had a chance to rest, I'm going to go on a little scout up into those mountains to see if those Indians kept running. You wanna go with me?"

"I reckon I'd better," Derringer said, thinking that wasn't the smartest idea the general had ever had. "You want me to mount up a detail of fifteen?"

"No, I was thinking about just the two of us," Dodge said. "I feel pretty sure they're not planning to attack us. You said you were sure they headed for home, didn't you?"

"Yes, sir, but I didn't know you were plannin' to go ridin' up into the mountains by yourself." He paused for a few moments before asking a question. "This have anything to do with the railroad?"

"As a matter of fact, it would be interesting to see if there's any place the railroad could go through this line of mountains. It would sure cut off a lot of miles of track if it could, and they're too damn high to climb."

"I expect it would," Derringer said. He knew how interested the general was in the construction of the cross-country railroad and that he had already been involved in planning the path of that track. The general had told him it would shorten the route a hundred and fifty miles if the tracks were brought this way from Council Bluffs, if they could go straight across this line of mountains. It was by coincidence that they followed the raiding party to the base of the very mountain range that was blocking Dodge's preferred path to the West for the Union Pacific Railroad. Since they were here by chance, it would seem a shame to leave without giving the general the opportunity to estimate the possibility of somehow getting past this mountain range.

"Jesse," Dodge said, "when we leave here, we're going straight back to Fort Laramie. I don't know when I might get a chance to get back to this place again."

"That is a fact, sir," Derringer responded. The general only addressed him by his first name when he was asking a favor, instead of giving a direct order. "I expect we oughta go up those mountains and take a little look around." He felt pretty sure they wouldn't find any of those Arapaho warriors waiting for them. "I'll get the horses."

They followed the path the fleeing Arapaho warriors had taken to ascend the mountain, since it was obviously the easiest way up. All the way to the top, Derringer kept a cautious eye on the trail left by the Indians. They had made no real effort to disguise their retreat, and once they reached the top of the ridge, they varied their direction only to the extent of picking the easiest way down the other side. Only then was Derringer willing to dismiss them from his concern.

Dodge wanted to scout the ridge to the north first, so they made their way along it for almost a mile before they stopped when they found the mountains grew higher the farther north they rode. "Too steep to climb and too far to tunnel through," the general conceded.

When he looked at Derringer for a response to his comment, he found the sergeant staring at a large outcropping of rock ahead of them. Staring back at them, a lone Indian warrior stood motionless, as fully surprised as they were. When Derringer pulled the Henry rifle out of his saddle scabbard, the Indian turned and fled, disappearing in the rocks.

Derringer was immediately after him. "Stay here!" he told the general. "I'll try to see if he's alone!" He gave his horse a kick and worked his way through the rocks where he found a trail on the other side, leading down the mountainside. He caught a glimpse of the Indian just before he disappeared again when the trail bent around a clump of trees. When he got to that clump, he reined his horse to a sliding halt because he saw the Indian he had been chasing pulling up before a camp beside a small stream. *A war party*, he thought, for they were wearing paint. He did a quick count of those he could see and figured there were about twenty of them. The one he had been following didn't dismount but was gesturing wildly and pointing back in the direction he had fled. "Damn," Derringer swore, and wheeled his horse around when he saw the warriors scrambling to get to their horses.

He started yelling to Dodge before he reached him. "War party! We've got to ride like hell!"

"Can we hold them off?" Dodge yelled back.

"Too many!" Derringer answered. "We've gotta ride like hell," he repeated. The general still waited until Derringer caught up to him before falling in behind him, preferring to have the rugged scout lead the way. They rode south along the ridge as fast as they safely could to the sound of war whoops from their pursuers. It began to look as if they might be trapped on top of this mountain ridge, so when they came to what looked like a narrow pass, Derringer didn't hesitate; he guided his horse down into the pass and followed it. To his surprise, it continued to gradually descend until it took them all the way to the prairie floor. "You all right, sir?" Derringer asked when he reined back to let the general catch up.

"That was a helluva ride," Dodge said. "They didn't even see us drop down in that pass, so I expect they're wondering where we went." He laughed in relief. "I'll tell you the truth, I thought you'd lost your mind when you dropped down in that gully. And I thought I was crazy to follow you. How did you know that narrow ravine was a pass that would take us down to the prairie?"

"It just looked like a narrow pass that would just naturally lead down to the prairie," Derringer lied. In fact, he had given up hope of outrunning the war party and was looking for some place where they might hold them off. But since it had turned out to be a safe way down to the bottom, he figured he might as well take credit for a smart move.

Dodge just shook his head, still amazed that they had escaped. "I'll tell you one thing, though. If we can save our scalps, I believe we've found a pass through which the Union Pacific can go."

"Well, then, I reckon the scout was worth it," Derringer responded. "I expect we oughta get along back to the column now before those boys up there on that mountain figure out we ain't up there no more." He paused before suggesting another option. "Unless you wanna wait for that war party to find out we're down here on the plains, so we can lead 'em back to our camp. It ain't but about a mile from here and then they wouldn't waste all that war paint they're wearin'.'"

"I don't know what that war party was doing up on the top of that mountain," Dodge remarked. "Where were they going? There's no settlement south of these mountains."

"That's a fact," Derringer said. "I suspect they mighta been thinkin' about settlements east, back along the South Platte, and there's a few of them. Hard to tell what they're thinkin' now. They might run into those Arapaho we chased up on top of that mountain. If they did, then they know there's a column of a hundred and fifty soldiers right behind them."

"I know we put a stop to that Arapaho raiding party, but we're two and a half days' march back to Fort Laramie," Dodge said. "I swear, damn it, I can't leave now when we know there's a war party of twenty or more savages probably on their way to attack some settlement east of here."

"I reckon I could go back up there and ask 'em what they're plannin' to do, so we'd know what we oughta do," Derringer japed. "Since it ain't but about a mile back to camp, how 'bout we take you back to your command? Then I can come back here and keep an eye on this war party. There ain't no sense in makin' a hundred and fifty men worry about their commandin' officer when they could just have to worry about one sergeant."

The general couldn't help chuckling in response. "I'm

sure Colonel Walsh is standing ready and willing to take command of the column in the event of my absence."

Derringer started to laugh but stopped short. "He might get his chance," he said when he saw the warrior suddenly appear in the mouth of the narrow pass. "It's time to go!" He gave the general's horse a smack on the behind just as they heard the war cries coming from the base of the mountain. They were off at a gallop with what appeared to be twenty-two screaming Cheyenne warriors in hot pursuit. "Head for the gap in that line of trees!" he shouted to the general. "I'm gonna slow 'em down some!" Dodge did as he was instructed and continued to gallop toward the gap in the trees that outlined the creek where his men were camped.

Derringer pulled his horse to a stop and wheeled around to face the war party chasing them. One particular brave was out in front of the rest of the war party and he was gaining on them. So Derringer drew his Henry rifle from his saddle scabbard. He waited for the horse to be still while he cranked a cartridge into the cylinder, guessing the warrior was at a distance of about one hundred and twenty yards and closing fast. Then he took dead aim and knocked the racing warrior off his horse. Thinking also to put the detachment of soldiers on alert, he fired twice more at the war party. It caused them to spread out and those with rifles answered fire. "That oughta do it," he said, then wheeled his horse again and raced after General Dodge. *Now it's up to you, Colonel Walsh,* he thought. The colonel was already up to the surprise. He stepped out of the trees and signaled the general to come to him. Seeing him,

General Dodge headed straight for him, and Derringer was not far behind.

As he rode into the cover of the trees, Derringer passed through a long line of soldiers lying in ambush and waiting for the command to fire at the charging party of unsuspecting Cheyenne warriors. Derringer's first thought upon riding into the safety of the trees was, *That answers the question. They didn't run into the fleeing Arapaho on the mountain.* He and the general quickly dismounted and took cover while Colonel Walsh commanded the men to hold their fire. When the war party was about thirty-five yards away, he gave the order to fire, and the trees erupted in a long line of rifle fire that decimated the hapless Indian war party. It was reduced to half a dozen in a few minutes' time and half of them were wounded. They promptly retreated as best they could. Walsh reported to General Dodge and asked if he wanted to mount a patrol to go after the survivors. Dodge gave him a *well done*, but said no. He thought the war party had been sufficiently discouraged from any raids they had sought to perform on any settlement. "We'll start back to Fort Laramie after the noon meal."

With six other soldiers, Derringer walked out among the bodies left on the prairie. Their purpose was to make sure all the bodies were dead, so as not to prolong suffering. Those who survived the ambush would most likely come back to take care of the dead after the soldiers left. Derringer's purpose, however, was to identify the dead, and he found that he was right in thinking they were Cheyenne. He reported the fact to General Dodge and Colonel Walsh. Walsh, known for his sense of humor, made a suggestion when planning future campaigns. "Instead of mounting patrols of fifteen or more men, why not just send you and Sergeant Derringer out as bait? And you can just lead them back to an ambush like you did today." Overheard by some of the soldiers close by, it became a running joke among the regiment.

The ambush of the Cheyenne war party happened in September of 1865. It turned out to be the last campaign of that nature for the general and the sergeant. During the following months, the general was called back to Washington to plan the building of the railroad while the sergeant was assigned to a cavalry regiment. In May of 1866, General Dodge resigned from the army and later that same year was appointed chief engineer of the Union Pacific Railroad. When news of the general's appointment finally got around to Sergeant Jesse Derringer, he was not surprised at all, and he was happy for his old boss. He realized how much he missed the days when he was the general's personal scout and how little he liked serving in a regular cavalry company. So he decided to resign from the army, fully convinced he had no desire to retire from it. He preferred to find out what else was out there to see before he became too old to see it. It had been some time before the war since he had been back to the family farm near Omaha, so he decided to visit the old homeplace. His younger brother, Dan, and his wife, Shirley, had taken over the farm after his parents were gone. They had passed away while Jesse was serving in Dakota Territory.

Jesse's visit with his brother was a brief one, lasting only a couple of days. Although Dan and Shirley made a show of welcoming him home, Jesse was aware of a sense of concern from both of them that he was planning to claim his inheritance and move in with them and their two boys. He assured them that he had no desire to settle down on the farm, so he would be on his way again the next day. His statement relieved the tension immediately and they persuaded him to stay over an extra day. When he left, Dan asked where he was heading and Jesse simply answered, "West."

CHAPTER 2

William C. Cartwright, assistant construction supervisor, sat at his desk in the Council Bluffs office of the Union Pacific Railroad. He was studying a large map spread out across the desk when one of his clerks stuck his head in the door and announced that there was a gentleman who wanted to see him. Cartwright was not inclined to waste his time granting interviews to newspaper reporters, so he asked, "Newspaper reporter?"

"I don't know," the clerk responded. "He doesn't look like one. He was a rather direct gentleman, however, when he said it was important."

"Oh, he did, did he?" Cartwright replied. "Did he give his name?"

"Yes, sir. He said his name is Derringer."

"Derringer?" Cartwright responded. "The only Derringer I know about is no gentleman. Send him in here, Lewis. Hell, I sent word for him to come see me." He got up from the desk to receive him when Lewis withdrew his head from the door and opened it for Derringer to come in. "Sergeant Derringer!" Cartwright announced, grinning from ear to ear. He stepped forward to extend his hand to the tall, serious-looking man.

"Sergeant?" Jesse Derringer responded with a genuine look of surprise. "It's been a while since anybody's called me sergeant. I mustered out of the army when there wasn't nobody left to fight. How did you know I was in the army?"

"I know that you served as a scout for my boss at Union Pacific, General Grenville M. Dodge, and I know he's looking for you."

"I heard that General Dodge was workin' for the railroad," Derringer said. "I didn't know he was lookin' for me, though. How did you know I was in Council Bluffs?"

"I didn't," Cartwright responded, "but the general remembered you had a home in Omaha before the war and he thought you might be passing through here sometime on your way there. So I gave your name to the bartender at the Whistlestop Saloon. And I told him if Jesse Derringer ever stops in, tell him I want to see him and it's important."

"Yes, sir, it sure surprised me when he told me that," Jesse said. "Mickey Deal's his name, ain't it? The last I heard about General Dodge was that he won an election for congressman, but he's workin' for the Union Pacific Railroad now." He looked around him and nodded, smiling. "I see they fixed him up in a nice office."

"Yes, but he doesn't spend much time in it," Cartwright was quick to reply. "My job is assistant superintendent of construction for the railroad across the country to connect with Central Pacific Railroad to form a transcontinental railroad. The general is in the field with the surveyors, mapping out the right of way for the tracks, so I'm glad you got here when you did. General Dodge wants me to offer you a job with the Union Pacific."

"That's mighty thoughtful of the general, but I don't know anything about workin' on the railroad," Derringer responded as he pictured himself swinging a pickax or driving a spike, and it wasn't the kind of work that suited him.

"Mr. Derringer, the general says you're the best damn scout he's ever had the pleasure of working with," Cartwright informed him. "He said that maybe you're the only man he trusts to fill the job he's got in mind. The railroad has given him the task of planning the route of the railroad from Council Bluffs into Dakota Territory. Right now, General Dodge is at Crow Creek Crossing where they're building a bridge across Crow Creek. After Crow Creek, they're faced with a rougher route to follow up across what the general's calling Sherman Hill. The general said that back in 1865, in the Black Hills campaign, your outfit had to escape from an Indian war party, and it was you who found a pass out of that mess. He said he thought at the time that it would serve as a pass skirting the Black Hills for the railroad, west of the Platte River."

"Yes, sir," Derringer remarked with a chuckle, "I remember that time."

"So how about it? Are you ready to go back to work as the general's scout? You'll go on the Union Pacific payroll starting today if you are. I can authorize some advance expense money so you can get what supplies you need right away."

"Well, I could say I'd have to think about it, since I had other plans," Derringer said, "but that would be a lie. So I reckon I'm your man." He didn't say as much to Cartwright, but when he mentioned the money in advance, it was a done deal. His financial state was down to pocket change. When he rode into town the day before, the thought that he would ever see General Dodge again never entered his mind as a possibility. And with winter coming on, he was expecting to be riding the grub line, hoping to sign on as a cowhand with some rancher.

"Excellent!" Cartwright responded. "That's going to make the general very happy. He's told me some tales about your time in the army."

"Is that right?" Derringer responded. "Well, I hope you didn't believe all of them."

"When did you get in town?" Cartwright asked.

"Yesterday mornin'," Derringer answered.

"Did you take a room in the hotel?"

"No, sir, I spent last night in the jailhouse," Jesse told him.

"Oh? Did you drink a little too much of the demon whiskey?" Cartwright asked.

"No, sir, I only had a couple of drinks, but the fellow at the end of the bar had way too much to drink. And I reckon it affected his eyesight, because he said he didn't like the way I was lookin' at him. He invited me to settle it with our guns, and when I told him I druther not, he said he was gonna shoot me down, anyway. When he drew his gun, I grabbed his arm and he shot himself in the leg. The bartender sent for the sheriff, and I reckon we musta caught him at a bad time, because he took me to jail, even though Mickey and I both tried to tell him I didn't shoot that fellow. I didn't put up too much fuss about it, though, since I'm a little short of money and I couldn't afford a hotel room. I figured I'd at least have a place to sleep and maybe a meal or two, and they put my horses in the stable, too. So I figure I came out ahead on that deal."

Cartwright shook his head, not sure if Derringer was serious or not. "If you're broke what were you thinking about doing next?"

"I was thinkin' about maybe robbing the bank, but I hadn't made a final decision on that yet, so I'm glad you have a job for me."

"I'll get you a room in the hotel tonight," Cartwright said, thinking Derringer was joking, but not willing to bet on it. "So you'll have tomorrow to take care of your horses and any needs you might have in personal supplies or ammunition." He looked at the clock on the wall. "It's about dinnertime," he announced. "Let's go to the hotel to get something to eat. Then I'll get a room for you for tonight and tomorrow night. Then you can hitch a ride on a train that's leaving at ten o'clock Wednesday mornin', heading for the end of the track."

"How far will that take me?" Derringer asked, since he was going to have to buy supplies for the trip. Cartwright said the general was at Crow Creek Crossing and that had to be about five hundred miles from Council Bluffs.

Cartwright took another look at his map. "Here's where they were when he wired me two days ago.

Based on the rate they've been laying track, about three miles a day, that ought to put them close to Crow Creek."

"Well, I'll be . . ." Derringer started. "How many days will I be on the train?"

Cartwright shrugged. "Depending on how many hours they travel a day, I'd say about two and a half days."

Derringer shook his head and grinned. "I expect it would take me the better part of two weeks to ride my horse that far. I reckon I won't need as many supplies as I thought."

As Cartwright suggested, they walked down to the hotel dining room for dinner. Jesse left his two horses tied at the hotel hitching rail. After dinner, they went to the front desk in the hotel to get Jesse a room. When that was taken care of, Cartwright took a roll of money out of his pocket and peeled off fifty dollars and gave it to him as an advance. "That oughta be enough to get you set to travel," he said. "Are your horses in good shape?"

"Yes, sir," Jesse replied. "I always take care of them, so they'll take care of me. I'll take 'em back to the stable. I just picked 'em up before I came to your office."

"Tell John Walker to put the fee on my bill," Cartwright said. "He seems to take pretty good care of my horses. I've got to meet with some people this afternoon, so I'm going back to the office. I may not see you tonight, so check in with me sometime tomorrow. All right?" Jesse said that he would, so Cartwright started back to his office with the air of a man who had accomplished an important item on his list of things to do. "Don't spend all that advance in the Whistlestop," he called back.

"Right," Jesse responded as he took his rifle and his saddlebags off the gray gelding. "I'll spread it around in the other saloons." Then he took his things up to his room before taking his horses back to the stable.

"Howdy," John Walker greeted him when he rode up to the stable again. "I didn't expect to see you back so soon."

"I got a job when I got outta jail," Jesse replied. "So I'm gonna need to leave my horses with you until Wednesday mornin'. But instead of the sheriff paying for 'em, this time you can charge General Grenville Dodge's account, or the Union Pacific's, whichever."

"Is that so?" Walker responded. "You goin' to work for the railroad?"

"I reckon so," Jesse shrugged.

"Doin' what?"

"Whatever he says," Jesse replied. "I worked for General Dodge for quite a while as a scout durin' the war and after that in the Indian Wars. Looks like I'm gonna start out doin' that right away, scoutin' for the railroad this time."

"So you'll be leadin' the Union Pacific Railroad across the country to join up with the Central Pacific Railroad?" Walker asked.

"I wouldn't put it that way," Jesse said. "General Dodge is the one who says which way to go. My job is just to take a look to see if there's anything he might stub his toe on ahead of him."

"That still sounds important, so you better be careful you don't run into nobody else like Stony Packer before you leave town," Walker said.

"Who's Stony Packer?"

"He's the fellow you shot in the leg yesterday that landed you in jail," Walker said with a chuckle.

"I didn't shoot that fellow," Jesse immediately replied. "He shot himself. I tried to tell that sheriff that I was just tryin' to keep him from shootin' me. Hell, he pulled the trigger, the damn fool."

"Tell you the truth, Warner Black ain't really the sheriff. He's just takin' on the job until we get another one," Walker said. "He's the blacksmith and I expect the situation was a little bit unusual for him and he wasn't sure what to do."

"To be honest with you," Jesse confessed, "I didn't give him any argument that amounted to much because I figured I could use a bed for the night. He was pretty reasonable about it this mornin', though. Even got me a breakfast before he let me go."

"I expect there's a lotta folks that woulda liked it better if you had turned Stony's gun up at his head, instead of down toward his leg," Walker said. "Him and those two saddle tramps he hangs out with think they own the town, now that Luke Collins left to take the marshal's job in Omaha. It wouldn't be a bad idea to stay clear of those two friends of his while you're at it."

"It'd help if somebody would hang a sign around

their necks with their names on it," Jesse said. "I really didn't pay much attention to who was with him yesterday."

"Travis Stacy and Rob Gentry," Walker announced. "Each one of 'em is worse than the other one."

"Well, now, right off, that don't sound too good," Jesse remarked. "I was hopin' to enjoy some of the town's hospitality before startin' out on a trip that's liable to take almost two and a half days on a train. And when we get there, there won't be a saloon to celebrate the journey."

Walker chuckled again. "Yeah, but you'll be part of history."

"That's right," Jesse replied, "the part they throw out of the chamber pot when they empty it. What time will you open up in the mornin'?" Jesse asked, changing the subject.

"Usually around five thirty or six," Walker answered. "So I reckon that's when I'll see you that mornin'."

"I reckon," Jesse replied. "It's gonna be just like bein' back in the army again."

He left the gray gelding he called Clem and the sorrel he called various names with John Walker in the stable while he spent some of the money Cartwright had given him to replenish his stock of ammunition. Cartwright didn't say anything about food during the train trip, so he figured he'd better buy something he could gnaw on during the trip. He found a message Cartwright had left for him when he came back to his room. It was an invitation for him to join his party for supper in the hotel that night.

Jesse was surprised to discover it was a bigger group of men than he had imagined. There were surveyors, which he had expected, but in addition, there were land agents and speculators, as well as military officers and personal friends of the general. He was left with little doubt that the Union Pacific intended to build a solid town at Crow Creek Crossing. Jesse enjoyed the supper and a couple of drinks afterward, but he felt like a square peg in a round hole in a social setting with officers, politicians, and executives of the Union Pacific Railroad. So he retired to his room at the hotel after a polite good night to Cartwright. "Use tomorrow to get everything you think you'll need for a couple of days' ride to Crow Creek Crossing," Cartwright told him.

"Yes, sir," Jesse responded. "That gives me plenty of time to do the little bit I need to do." He took his leave then and Cartwright fully understood he was more comfortable elsewhere.

As he had told Cartwright the night before, he had very little to do to be ready. Much of his day was spent with his horses to make sure they were fit and ready to go on a long ride. As a consequence, he spent a great deal of time talking to John Walker at the stable and found the man one he would count as a friend. They agreed to meet after supper at the Whistlestop for a drink or two after John closed the stable and went home for his supper. "You sure the little woman will think it's a good idea to let you out for a drink?" Jesse asked. "Better not let her know I was in jail night before last."

"Ain't no problem," John replied. "I'm the one who does the thinkin' in my house. 'Course she tells me what to think."

"I reckon I'll just have to wait to see if you show up," Jesse japed. "And if you don't, I'll take a drink for all the poor men who took that rocky trail called matrimony."

Visit our website at
KensingtonBooks.com
to sign up for our newsletters, read
more from your favorite authors, see
books by series, view reading group
guides, and more!

BOOK | **CLUB**

BETWEEN THE CHAPTERS

Become a Part of Our
Between the Chapters Book Club
Community and Join the Conversation

Betweenthechapters.net

Submit your book review for a chance to win exclusive
Between the Chapters swag you can't get anywhere else!
https://www.kensingtonbooks.com/pages/review/